Prais

"The prolific Modesitt kic
boasts an early modern
without the pollution. . . . h
surprises from stock ideas remains undiminished."
—*Kirkus Reviews*

"Excelling in his characterizations and the verisimilitude of his world-building, the author of the long-standing Recluce novels and the Spellsong Cycle crafts an intriguing series opener about the magic of creation and perception."
—*Library Journal*

"Readers will look to future installments for the derring-do promised by Rhenn's martial studies and frequent mentions of stormy international politics."
—*Publishers Weekly*

"There are strong female characters, as is the norm for Modesitt's novels. The women he develops don't need to be masculine to be strong. . . . Fans of David Farland should find this work enjoyable. . . . It is odd to call something realistic fantasy, but in this case it works. There are definite laws that are followed and a realistic economic system. The government that is developed is a reaction to the world built upon the actions of others in the past. There is a little bit of a mystery to be solved in this story as well. . . . I look forward to the next volume, and I am sure many of you will, too."
—*SFRevu*

TOR BOOKS BY L. E. MODESITT, JR.

*forthcoming

Imager

The First Book of the Imager Portfolio

L. E. MODESITT, JR.

TOR®
fantasy

A TOM DOHERTY ASSOCIATES BOOK
NEW YORK

NOTE: If you purchased this book without a cover, you should be aware that this book is stolen property. It was reported as "unsold and destroyed" to the publisher, and neither the author nor the publisher has received any payment for this "stripped book."

This is a work of fiction. All of the characters, organizations, and events portrayed in this novel are either products of the author's imagination or are used fictitiously.

IMAGER: THE FIRST BOOK OF THE IMAGER PORTFOLIO

Copyright © 2009 by L. E. Modesitt, Jr.

All rights reserved.

A Tor Book
Published by Tom Doherty Associates, LLC
175 Fifth Avenue
New York, NY 10010

www.tor-forge.com

Tor® is a registered trademark of Tom Doherty Associates, LLC.

ISBN 978-0-7653-6007-6

First Edition: March 2009
First Mass Market Edition: February 2010

Printed in the United States of America

0 9 8 7 6 5

For Steve and Marge Bennion,
in recognition of quiet courage

ACKNOWLEDGMENTS

After working with David Hartwell and Tom Doherty for more than twenty-five years, during which time Tor has published all of my books, now totaling more than fifty, it's long past time to acknowledge in print the debt I owe to them both for believing in what I write and in supporting it by publishing the books with care and consideration.

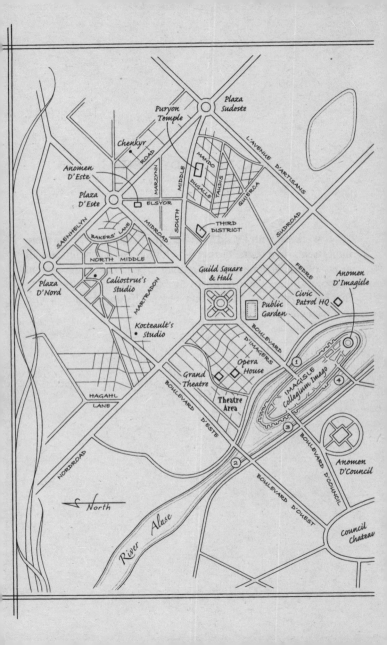

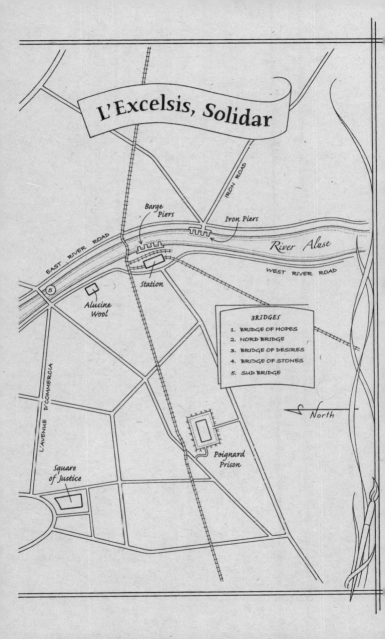

Apprentice
and
Journeyman

1

743 A.L.

*Commerce weighs value, yet such weight is but an image,
and, as such, is an illusion.*

The bell announcing dinner rang twice, just twice, and no more, for it never did. Rousel leapt up from his table desk in the sitting room that adjoined our bedchambers, disarraying the stack of papers that represented a composition doubtless due in the morning. "I'm starved."

"You're not. You're merely hungry," I pointed out, carefully placing a paperweight over the work on my table desk. "'Starved' means great physical deprivation and lack of nourishment. We don't suffer either."

"I feel starved. Stop being such a pedant, Rhenn." The heels of his shoes clattered on the back stairs leading down to the pantry off the dining chamber.

Two weeks ago, Rousel couldn't even have pronounced "pedant," but he'd heard Master Sesiphus use it, and now he applied it to me as often as he could. Younger brothers were worse than vermin, because one could squash vermin and then bathe, something one could not do with younger brothers. With some fortune, since Father would really have preferred that I follow him as a factor but had acknowledged that I had little interest, I'd be out of the house before Culthyn was old enough to leave the nursery and eat with us. As for Khethila, she was almost old enough, but she was quiet and thoughtful. She liked it when I read to her, even things like my history assignments about people like Rex Regis or Rex

Defou. Rousel had never liked my reading to him, but then, he'd never much cared for anything I did.

By the time I reached the dining chamber, Father was walking through the archway from the parlor where he always had a single goblet of red wine—usually Dhuensa—before dinner. Mother was standing behind the chair at the other end of the oval table. I slipped behind my chair, on Father's right. Rousel grinned at me, then cleared his face.

"Promptness! That's what I like. A time and a place for everything, and everything in its time and place." Father cleared his throat, then set his near-empty goblet on the table and placed his hands on the back of the armed chair that was his.

"For the grace and warmth from above, for the bounty of the earth below, for all the grace of the world and beyond, for your justice, and for your manifold and great mercies, we offer our thanks and gratitude, both now and evermore, in the spirit of that which cannot be named or imaged."

"In peace and harmony," we all chorused, although I had my doubts about the presence and viability of either, even in L'Excelsis, crown city and capital of Solidar.

Father settled into his chair at the end of the table with a contented sigh, and a glance at Mother. "Thank you, dear. Roast lamb, one of my favorites, and you had Riesela fix it just the way I prefer it."

If Mother had told the cook to fix lamb any other way, we all would have been treated to a long lecture on the glories of crisped roast lamb and the inadequacies of other preparations.

After pouring a heavier red wine into his goblet and then into Mother's, Father placed the carafe before me. I took about a third of a goblet, because that was what he'd declared as appropriate for me, and poured a quarter for Rousel.

When Father finished carving and serving, Mother passed the rice casserole and the pickled beets. I took as little as I could of the beets.

"How was your day, dear?" asked Mother.

"Oh . . . the same as any other, I suppose. The Phlanysh

wool is softer than last year, and that means that Wurys will complain. Last year he said it was too stringy and tough, and that he'd have to interweave with the Norinygan . . . and the finished Extelan gray is too light . . . But then he's half Pharsi, and they quibble about everything."

Mother nodded. "They're different. They work hard. You can't complain about that, but they're not our type."

"No, they're not, but he does pay in gold, and that means I have to listen."

I managed to choke down the beets while Father offered another discourse on wool and the patterned weaving looms, and the shortcomings of those from a Pharsi background. I wasn't about to mention that the prettiest and brightest girl at the grammaire was Remaya and she was Pharsi.

Abruptly, he looked at me. "You don't seem terribly interested in what feeds you, Rhennthyl."

"Sir . . . I was listening closely. You were pointing out that, while the pattern blocks used by the new weaving machinery produced a tighter thread weave, the women loom tenders have gotten more careless and that means that spoilage is up, which increases costs—"

"Enough. I know you listen, but I have great doubts that you care, or even appreciate what brings in the golds for this household. At times, I wonder if you don't listen to the secret whispers of the Namer."

"Chenkyr . . ." cautioned Mother.

Father sighed as only he could sigh. "Enough of that. What did you learn of interest at grammaire today?"

It wasn't so much what I'd learned as what I'd been thinking about. "Father . . . lead is heavier than copper or silver. It's even heavier than gold, but it's cheaper. I thought you said that we used copper, silver, and gold for coins because they were heavier and harder for evil imagers to counterfeit."

"That's what I mean, Rhennthyl." He sighed even more loudly. "You ask a question like that, but when I ask you to help in the counting house, you can't be bothered to work out the cost of an extra tariff of a copper . . . or work out the costs for guards on a summer consignment of bolts of Acoman prime wool to Nacliano. It isn't as though you had no head for figures, but you do not care to be accurate if something doesn't interest you. What metals the Council uses for coins matters little if one has no coins to count. No matter how much a man likes his work, there will be parts of it that are less pleasing—or even displeasing. You seem to think that everything should be pleasing or interesting. Life doesn't oblige us in that fashion."

"Don't be that hard on the boy, Chenkyr." Mother's voice was patient. "Not everyone is meant to be a factor."

"His willfulness makes an ob look flexible, Maelyna."

"Even the obdurates have their place."

I couldn't help thinking I'd rather be an obdurate than a mal. Most people were malleables of one sort or another, changing their views or opinions whenever someone roared at them, like Father.

"Exactly!" exclaimed Father. "As servants to imagers and little else. I don't want one of my sons a lackey because he won't think about anything except what interests or pleases him. The world isn't a kind place for inflexible stubbornness and unthinking questioning."

"How can a question be unthinking?" I wanted to know. "You have to think even to ask one."

My father's sigh was more like a roar. Then he glared at me. "When you ask a question to which you would already know the answer if you stopped to think, or when you ask a question to which no one knows the answer. In both cases, you're wasting your time and someone else's."

"But how do I know when no one knows the answer if I don't ask the question?"

"Rhennthyl! There you go again. Do you want to eat cold rice in the kitchen?"

"No, sir."

"Rousel," said Father, pointedly avoiding looking in my direction, "how are you coming with your calculations and figures?"

"Master Sesiphus says that I have a good head for figures. My last two examinations have been perfect."

Of course they had been. What was so hard about adding up columns of numbers that never changed? Or dividing them, or multiplying them? Rousel was more than a little careless about numbers and anything else when no one was looking or checking on him.

I cut several more thin morsels of the lamb. It was good, especially the edge of the meat where the fat and seasonings were all crisped together. The wine wasn't bad, either, but it was hard to sit there and listen to Father draw out Rousel.

2

745 A.L.

Authority always trumps reason, unless reason is the authority.

The Council of Solidar opened the Chateau of the Council to the public exactly twice a year, at the last day of summer, the thirty-fifth of Juyn, and at the depth of winter, the thirty-fifth of Ianus. Father insisted that I come with him because I'd just turned fourteen and finished the grammaire. In another month I'd begin my apprenticeship with Master Caliostrus, one of the more successful portraiturists in L'Excelsis.

"Since you cannot and will not be a factor, Rhenn, you need to see what great art really is." My father must have said that at least three times while we rode in the carriage along the Boulevard D'Este and across Pont D'Nord and then another mille along the Boulevard D'Ouest. Once we reached the base of Council Hill, we had to leave the carriage and wait in a long queue under a white sun that blistered down through the pale blue summer sky. The gatehouse ahead of us was built of alabaster, as was the Chateau above, but the surface of the stones of both had been strengthened by imagers centuries and centuries before, supposedly by those of Rex Regis after he had taken L'Excelsis from the Bovarians and made it the capital of the land he had unified and renamed Solidar. The walls shimmered white and inviolate, as pristine as the day they were laid, sort of like an eternal virgin, I thought, trying not to snigger at the thought.

"Rhenn, you are not to exhibit amusement at the misfortunes of others." Father's eyes darted toward a crafter who was looking down at a spreading dark brown stain across his trousers. He still held the handle of the clay jug that he had swung up to drink. Fragments of pottery and a dark splotch on the wall suggested he'd been less than careful in lifting his jug.

"Sir, I was thinking of a terrible joke that Jacquyl told yesterday. Seeing the gatehouse reminded me of it."

"Likely story." The good-natured gruffness of his response suggested that he believed me, or at least that he knew I was not laughing at the poor crafter, a mason's apprentice or junior journeyman, I would have judged by the stone dust on his sleeves.

A good glass passed before we reached the head of the queue short of the burnished bronze gates and the gatehouse. The Council guard there stood in the shadow of the tiny portico, but sweat had dampened the pale blue linen of his uniform tunic into a darker shade.

"The next ten of you," the guard announced.

Father strode ahead. He always walked quickly, as if he might miss something if he weren't the first one. The paved walks were white granite, flanked by boxwood hedges in stone beds. "See those hedges, Rhenn. That's what a hedge should look like, not with twigs and leaves sticking out haphazardly."

"Yes, sir." Rousel was supposed to have trimmed the little branches on our hedge, after I cut the larger ones, but he'd gone off to play. There'd been little point in saying so, because Father would just have said that it was my responsibility. But if I'd dragged Rousel back, he would have complained, and then Father would have punished me for being too strict.

After we walked up the wide white stone steps, Father cleared his throat. "There are three arches—a main arch flanked by two smaller arches. All three lead into the Grand Foyer."

I didn't say anything. We'd studied the Chateau in grammaire, and I knew that.

Father took the center archway and hurried inside, out of the blazing sun. It wasn't that much cooler, but being out of the sun was a relief. I glanced up at the faux dome of the foyer.

Father followed my eyes and gestured upward. "You see the stonework there?"

"It looks well done." It wasn't stonework at all, but flat painting designed to trick the eye into believing it was stonework.

"You think you could do better?"

"No, sir." Father was always doing that—comparing me to an experienced artisan or factor or crafter. Of course I wasn't that good. That didn't mean I couldn't be in time.

Just in front of us was an older and all too bulbous man in a threadbare and once-white linen overshirt. He had planted himself before the first portrait on the wall on the right-hand outer wall of the foyer, cocking his head one way and then another. I started to move around him, but Father reached out and grasped my arm.

"Take your time. Study each one carefully, especially the portraits. You're the one who's going to be a portraiturist. You won't have another chance to see these for a time."

After the older man finally moved, Father pointed to the image of a trim black-haired man with sweeping mustaches in a black dress uniform with silver-banded cuffs. "That's a portrait of Seleandyr. He was the one who led the Council in the trade war against Caenen and Stakanar . . ."

I'd seen Factor Councilor Seleandyr before, if only from the balcony when Father had hosted the cloth factors' fall reception, and he'd never been that slender. His mustaches had drooped, as had his belly, and his thin hair had kept falling down over a low forehead.

". . . managed to keep matters from getting out of hand and made sure that the taxes to support the war were only temporary. His death last Fevier was a great loss . . ."

I'd heard the rumors that his death hadn't been from age, but from sweetmeats transformed into pitricine, after he'd eaten them, by an imager whose niece he'd procured for his son. Seleus had sworn it was true.

The next artistic object was a bust, and again we had to wait for the gyrations of the bulbous fellow before Father led me forward. "Charyn. He was the last rex of Solidar, and the one who founded the first Council . . ."

I knew all too well those details of history, but all I could do was listen.

We made half a circuit of the foyer and reached the point where it opened, through three arches that mirrored those of the outer entry, onto the landing at the base of the grand alabaster staircase leading up to the Council chambers. Father marched right up to where the guards were posted. On the pedestals that formed the base of the rose marble balustrade of each side were a pair of sculpted statues—a winged man and a winged woman.

"Angelias—they're the work of the great Pierryl, Pierryl the Younger, that is. What do you think of them?" Father turned to me.

"The workmanship is excellent, sir."

"They're great art, Rhenn," murmured my father. "Can't you see that?"

"Father . . . the carving is outstanding, but they're ridiculous. Those tiny wings wouldn't lift a buzzard, let alone a child, and certainly not a man or woman." I didn't mention that each wing feather had been sculpted to a length of nine digits, not quite the ten of a full foot, and that wings that small would not have had individual feathers that large.

Father began to get red in the face. "We will have a talk later, young man."

"A sea eagle has wings almost that broad, and the largest weigh but half a stone."

"An angelia is not an eagle," snapped my father.

"No, sir. They're much larger, and they would need far larger wings to support themselves if they were truly to fly."

"Rhenn! Enough."

I'd said too much, but Father's opinions on art were limited by his own shortcomings and lack of understanding. I managed to placate him with pleasant inanities and agreements for the rest of our visit, consoling myself that, by the next time the Chateau was open to the people of L'Excelsis, I would be apprenticed and studying under Master Caliostrus.

3

In art and in life, what is not portrayed can be as a vital as what is.

750 A.L.

At breakfast that first Mardi in Juyn I sat near the end of the long table—as usual, because the only one junior to me was Stanus, who'd just become an apprentice. He sat on the other side and one place farther toward the end. Shienna was to my right, and Marcyl was across from me, with Olavya to his left and Ostrius on his father's right.

"I'll need some golds from the strongbox after breakfast," Caliostrus said to his wife Almaya, seated to his left. "I can get some imagers' green from Rhenius."

"I'm certain it's less dear than from Apalant." Her voice cut like a knife.

"You're the one who insists on the strongbox and keeping all the golds here."

"After what happened to my father when the Banque D'Rivages failed, and the Pharsi lenders came to collect . . ."

"I know. I know." Caliostrus looked down the long table. "Tomorrow, Craftmaster Weidyn will be here at the eighth glass of the morning. He will be here for two glasses."

What Caliostrus was also saying was that he didn't want the sitting disturbed, but why would he ask that for a craftmaster, rather than a High Holder or a factorius? I'd heard Weidyn's name at my parents' table, but couldn't recall his guild.

"Why is he a craftmaster, Father?" Marcyl's big black eyes fixed on Caliostrus.

"Because he's one of the best cabinetmakers in all of L'Excelsis. That's why."

"It might be nice to have something of his," suggested Almaya.

"It would indeed, but it's less than likely," replied Master Caliostrus. "A single sideboard of his, and that'd be one of the plainer ones, would fetch at least a hundred golds. That's if it ever came up for sale, but his work never does. People commission him a year in advance."

"They commission you in advance, dear," offered Almaya.

Despite her words, Master Caliostrus was fortunate, I knew, if a patron commissioned a portrait a season in advance— and paid upon completion and delivery of the framed work. That was one reason why I was the only journeyman in the household, besides Ostrius, who would soon doubtless become a junior master, and who would in time inherit his father's studio.

"But not so far in advance. People feel that cabinets and sideboards last longer than portraits. They do not. One only has to look at the artwork in the Chateau of the Council to see that. The chests and sideboards commissioned when Riodeux painted Rex Charyn have long since been turned to kindling and burned, but people still marvel at the portrait."

"And the bust," I added.

"The bust is by Pierryl the Elder and is far inferior to the portrait," declared Caliostrus. "Pierryl and his son—Pierryl the Younger—were diligent hacks compared to Riodeux. Sculptors have but to remove stone from stone. It is tedious, but it is more a craft than an art."

I'd heard Master Caliostrus declaim on that before. To create the impression of life and light on the flat surface of a canvas did take not only craftsmanship but an artistic sense. No one ever expected a bust or a statue to look alive, but merely to present an accurate representation, but everyone expected the best portraits to be good enough that the subject looked as though he could step out of the canvas and resume what he had been doing.

"Why do they get more golds than you, Father?" Marcyl persisted.

"Because what people will pay for often has no relation to its true value." Caliostrus lifted a large mug of tea, slurping slightly as he drank, not that he didn't slurp whenever he drank. Then he turned to me. "As for you, Rhennthyl, you also have a commission, far more modest, but one must begin somewhere."

"Sir?" I inclined my head, as much to conceal my surprise as anything. At last, after all the studies, all the criticism from Master Caliostrus, and all the glasses spent grinding and stirring and watching simmering pots of oils and waxes and solvents and pigments, I would have a chance to show what I had learned and could do on a canvas for a real patron. I thought Ostrius might also have been surprised, since most junior commissions went to him.

"Craftmaster Weidyn's youngest daughter has never had a portrait. She's but eight, and I suggested you could do credible work."

"When will I start, sir?"

"Tomorrow as well." Caliostrus smiled. "You will have to work in her favorite doll and her cat."

The doll certainly wouldn't be a problem, but, for some reason, few cats cared for me, and that could pose a problem. "The cat . . . ?"

"I suggested that the cat be added later, after you had designed the composition, but I wanted you to know that you would have to work in the creature."

"Yes, sir."

"I want several possible rough designs ready for me by the end of the day. Oh . . . she is a redhead, I'm told."

That made everything worse. A redhead? Their color and complexion were difficult to capture on canvas without making them appear wan and pale. Once more, Caliostrus had presented me with something in a light that seemed far more charitable than it was in fact. A redhead—that was just the sort of portrait where an excellent effort would look merely adequate, and a good effort would come across as poor. That was another reason why I'd gotten the commission, instead of Ostrius. "I will most certainly have my work cut out for me, sir."

"Nonsense, Rhennthyl. A portrait is a portrait, and each commission is an opportunity."

"Yes, sir." I would just have to deal with another one of Master Caliostrus's near-insurmountable opportunities, that and Ostrius's concealed smirk from across the table. Stanus just looked bewildered.

Even as a recent apprentice, Stanus should have known the problems of portraying redheads. I'd heard that those were even less than the difficulties involved in living with them, but I'd been unfortunate enough in dealing with young women that I had no experience by which to judge such a statement.

"The designs before dinner, Rhennthyl, remember!"

"Yes, sir." How could I possibly forget?

4

750 A.L.

The most critical are not the successful, nor the complete failures, but those who might have achieved something of worth, save for small but crucial faults within themselves, for they can seldom bear the thought of how close they came to greatness.

Mistress Aeylana D'Weidyn twitched, then shifted her weight in the high-backed chair. After Aeylana's first sitting, I'd accompanied Aeylana and her aunt back to their home—if a small chateau three times the size of my parents' dwelling and grounds could be termed "home." While at the Chateau Weidyn, I had not only made a sketch of the actual chair that would be in the portrait, but also made the acquaintance of Charbon—a rather oversized feline with sleepy yellow eyes and a deep black coat—and done several quick sketches of him as well, one with Aeylana holding him.

Aeylana D'Weidyn was anything but an ideal subject. Even at age eight, she was lanky, with big bones and hands, freckles and a fair skin, and fine orange-red hair that, despite the dark green hair band, had a tendency to fly in all directions. Her eyes were a warm brown that somehow clashed with everything, and her eyebrows were so light and fine that she looked to have none at all.

"If you would please look in the direction of the easel, Mistress Aeylana?"

"Oh, I'm sorry. I was thinking about Charbon. He will be in the portrait, will he not?"

"Yes, he will." In fact, I actually had painted much of

Charbon, as if he had been sitting erect and regal upon the edge of the seat of the chair beside Aeylana. "He is most handsome."

"He's my cat."

I had some doubts about any cat being a possession, but did not have time to say anything because, at that very moment, Ostrius opened the studio door and marched over to my easel.

He did not even look in the direction of Aeylana D'Weidyn— or her aunt, who was accompanying her to the sittings. "Rhenn . . . did you finish compounding the deep brown?"

"No. There wasn't time before the sitting."

"When will you learn to finish things?" he snapped.

"I worked on it all morning," I said quietly.

"You didn't finish, and we don't have enough of the deep brown."

He didn't. That was what he meant. "Your father expects me to do a sitting when the patron is here. I'll get back to it once she leaves."

"You'd better." Without another word, he stalked off.

The aunt said nothing, but her eyes expressed more than any words she might have spoken as she watched Ostrius close the studio door with a firmness just short of slamming it.

"I don't—" began Aeylana.

"That will be all, Aeylana," the aunt said firmly.

"If you would please look at the easel, mistress," I repeated.

"I can do that."

She could. She just couldn't keep doing it for long.

I looked at the left side of her head, just forward and above the ear. Her hair had been a problem, because it was too bright to be captured fairly by any of the earthen reds, and the madder red would fade, while vermilion would darken at the edges where it touched the skin tones. Calizarin red didn't blend well with the naranje orange, unless mixed with at least a little of one of the ochres, but I'd worked in a tiny mixture of yellow and dull red ochre as a binder between the calizarin and the naranje. Even Master Caliostrus had nodded approval at that.

Had Ostrius been angry not just because I didn't have the deep brown formulated when he wanted it, but because he realized I could do something with the pigments that he couldn't?

I pushed that thought away. If I didn't do well on the one portrait assignment I had, I wouldn't get another any time soon. I concentrated on seeing Aeylana as she was, and on working on the hairline around her right ear.

By the time the glass chimed out from the nearest anomen tower, I thought I had that section right, and I smiled, both at Aeylana and her chaperone. "Two more sittings at most."

"Good. It's hard to sit still that long."

"Aeylana . . ."

"I apologize, sir."

"I can remember when I was your age," I said with a smile. That got me a giggle in return.

In moments, the two had gathered themselves together and departed for the carriage waiting below. In scarcely longer than that, Master Caliostrus had entered the studio, his brow knit in a frown.

"Ostrius said that you had not finished the deep brown formulation and that you were less than deferential . . ."

"Sir, I was most deferential. I started directly after breakfast, Master Caliostrus, and I took no breaks, until just before Mistress Aeylana D'Weidyn was due to arrive. You told me never to be late in dealing with a patron, and I could not have begun the compounding yesterday, sir, because the raw earth did not arrive until just before dinner last night."

"Ah . . . yes . . ." Caliostrus paused. "You will get to it right away?"

"As soon as I clean up brushes and trays, sir."

"Good." Almost as an afterthought, he glanced at the partial portrait, his eyes going to what I had painted of the cat. "You definitely have a talent for the cat. In time, if you work on that, along with other skills, it might prove . . . remunerative. Some of the wealthier older women in L'Excelsis do dote on . . . such companions."

He stopped at the door and looked back. "Don't be too long. Ostrius does need the brown."

"Yes, sir."

If Ostrius needed the brown so much, why wasn't he down in the shed working on the formulation? Or, if he didn't want to get dirty, he could have taught Stanus how to do it. But then, that was still dirty work and required patience, both of which Ostrius avoided whenever possible.

5

753 A.L.

Mistaking a name for its substance is one of the roots of evil; holding to substance over names is a source of joy.

I never understood why so many people made a fuss about weddings. I certainly wondered that once again as I stood there in the garden courtyard of Remaya's parents' dwelling beside Rousel as we waited for Remaya to appear.

Weddings are merely an affirmation of what has already happened. They're necessary for most people, as are the rings that symbolize them, because public affirmations strengthen private commitments, but by the time of the ceremony they're usually foregone conclusions. If they're not, there shouldn't be a ceremony. After eight years of courting and unblemished affection, for Rousel and Remaya both the ceremony and the rings were more for everyone else than for them, but that is certainly the case for all too many ceremonies.

Ceremonies can also provide a different kind of closure. I hoped this one would, because I had been the one to find Remaya, and from me she had found Rousel. Likewise, after all the years of distrust of those of a Pharsi background, my parents had been forced to accept Remaya. How could they have not? She was beautiful and intelligent and loved Rousel, and her parents, while only tradespeople, were far from impoverished. It didn't hurt that Rousel was following in Father's footsteps as a wool factor, either.

"You have the ring?" Like all bridegrooms, Rousel wore a formal green waistcoat, trimmed in deep brown, with a matching green neck scarf.

"Right here." I kept my voice low.

We stood in front of the left side of the arched canopy of flowers. Behind it, wearing green vestments, was Chorister Osyrahm. Behind us stood our family, Father and Mother on the right, then Culthyn and Khethila. Even with them, but to the right, were Remaya's parents, and her older sister and two younger brothers.

A pair of viols began to play, indicating that Remaya had left the house and was approaching, but neither Rousel nor I looked back because we were not supposed to see her until she stood beside him. I did hear a few whispered comments from the small group of family and friends behind us, and all were about how beautiful she looked, but I knew that without looking. I'd known it far longer than Rousel, and with far less effect.

Before long, Remaya stepped up beside Rousel, and they exchanged glances and smiles. She wore a white gown, along with the bride's sleeveless green vest, also trimmed in the same rich brown as Rousel's.

Chorister Osyrahm smiled beatifically at both of them, then began to speak. "We are gathered here today in celebration of the decision of a man and a woman to join their lives as one. The name of a union between a man and a woman is not important, nor should anyone claim such, for the name should never overshadow the union itself. Rousel and Remaya have chosen each other as partners in life and in love, and we are here to witness the affirmation of that choice."

He nodded for them to step forward under the canopy, then waited until they stood under the arch of flowers.

"In so much as the only true and meaningful commitments in life are made without deception and without reservation, and without a reliance on empty names and forms, do you, Rousel, affirm in full honesty that you commit your body, your spirit, and your free will to this woman, and that you will put no other before her, so long as you both shall live?"

"I do."

Chorister Osyrahm then turned to Remaya and repeated the same charge and vows.

"I do." Her voice was warm and husky.

"The rings, if you will."

I handed the ring to Rousel.

After taking the simple gold bands, one from Rousel and one from Remaya, Osyrahm held them up so that all could see them before lowering them and addressing the couple. "These rings are a symbol of love, for gold cannot be changed, nor imaged into what it is not. In exchanging and accepting these rings, you have pledged that your love will be as unchanging as the gold of which they are made, that no tyranny of names substituting for substance shall ever cleave you apart, and that your love for each other will endure in times good and evil, through sickness and health, and in darkness and in light, so long as your spirits endure." Then he returned the rings to them.

Remaya, in the Pharsi tradition, was the first to place her ring, easing it onto Rousel's finger. Then he slipped his ring upon hers.

"From two have come one, and yet that unity shall enable each of you to live more joyfully, more fully, and more in harmony with that which was, is, and ever shall be."

The chorister stepped back, and Rousel and Remaya kissed under the canopy of late-spring flowers.

Then they turned and faced family and friends. Remaya's sister Semahla stepped forward and handed the small green wicker basket of flower petals to Rousel. He held it while she scooped out a handful and cast them forward and skyward. Then she took the basket, and he scattered his handful.

After that, they walked back toward the roofed section of the courtyard, and Semahla and I followed.

We had barely stepped into the shadows when Remaya turned back to me.

"Thank you so much, Rhenn." Remaya's smile was dazzling, but it always had been, even when I'd first seen her at the girls' grammaire when she'd been twelve. "Without you, I would never have met Rousel, and never known this happiness, foretold as it was."

Foretold. She'd said that when she had first laid eyes on Rousel. Those with the Pharsi blood have always been said to be able to see what will be before it comes to their eyes. "I'm so glad everything worked out for you two." What else could I say? I managed a wide grin as I looked at Rousel. "You heard that, brother."

He grinned back. "How could I forget?"

I loosened my own neck scarf, because the late-spring afternoon was warm, even in the shade, especially in the formal waistcoat and matching trousers. They were the finest I'd ever owned, and a gift from Rousel.

He'd been kind, and very matter-of-fact about it. When he'd given it to me, made-to-measure, he'd said, "I'm the one who wants you beside me. You're an artist, and I can't ask you to purchase a wedding suit. Besides, you can keep it for good occasions."

I'd just leave it stored with my parents. I certainly wouldn't need anything that fine for anything involving Master Caliostrus.

At that moment, everyone surged around Rousel and Remaya, and Semahla and I stepped back. I'd only met Semahla a handful of times, and she was certainly bright and pleasant, if more angular than her younger sister.

"The past few days must have been crowded," I observed.

She laughed. "Hectic, but fun. Everyone likes Remaya. She's always been the kind one."

"I'm sure you are, as well."

"It comes naturally to her. I have to try."

I supposed I could have said the same about Rousel, except it would have been about charm. He could charm anyone, just by looking at them.

Serving girls appeared, carrying trays with goblets of sparkling grisio. I picked two goblets off a tray and offered one to Semahla.

"Thank you." She inclined her head, then took a sip.

So did I. The coolness helped a dry throat.

"Rousel said you are a fine artist."

"I am an artist. Some days I think I might someday become a master with a studio."

"The portrait you did of Remaya is lovely. Everyone says so. Mother looks at it and wishes that Remaya would leave it with her."

"Thank you." I'd done the best I could. It had been my wedding gift to them. What else could I have given?

"Oh . . . Remaya needs me." With that, Semahla slipped away.

That was for the best. I'd about run out of pleasantries, not that Remaya's family weren't good people. Her father was a spice broker, which placed him between a factor and a shopkeeper, but meant he was still a tradesperson of sorts. Still, from the house, they certainly weren't poor.

Rousel eased over to me. "How are you doing?"

"Fine. How about you?"

He grinned sheepishly. "I just wish the dinner and the toasts were all over."

I could understand that. "You only have to do this once."

"Twice. Once for me, and once for you. Maybe three times. Culthyn might want us."

"You're an optimist."

"Now that you've made journeyman, you need to look around for someone," Rousel said.

"I'm not ready for that. I only get my own commissions now and again." I didn't point out that I wasn't a successful factor's assistant, because both Father and Rousel would have noted that it had been my choice not to go into trade. But then, I would have made a botch of trade. "Besides, it will be almost another five years before I can even be considered as a master portraiturist. It might be years beyond that. The masters don't easily approve other masters."

"You can still look."

I had looked, and she'd married Rousel. I just smiled. "We'll see."

"Rousel!" That was Remaya.

"You better go."

"Don't be too hard on me when you give your toast."

"I won't." And I wouldn't. We don't choose where our hearts lead us.

6

An artist must appeal to perception, not accuracy.

Contrary to poetry and populisms, Avryl is far from the cruelest month of the ten. Rather Feuillyt is, for it is in the month after harvest when everyone comes to understand that the bounty of nature and man could have been far greater than it was, no matter how much better the gathering of grain and golds happened to be than in previous years. So it was no surprise to me when Master Caliostrus appeared on the twentieth of that Feuillyt, to stand behind my shoulder and peer at the uncompleted likeness upon my easel. The twentieth of every month is a Vendrei, of course, whether the year is 754, as it was, or any other year.

"That's not an acceptable portrait, Rhennthyl."

Without Factor Masgayl being present, I'd been working on the detailing of his crimson and gold brocade vest, a vest that, for all its richness, had seen better days, not that the portrait would show that. "Sir?"

"You can't do that with the eyes."

"But that's the way the factorius looks, exactly the way he appears." Incautious as that statement was, coming as it did from a journeyman portraiture artist to his master, we both knew that the portrait was far more flattering than the reality of Masgayl Factorius, one of the more junior, yet least self-effacing, factors in the city.

"It is not the way he looks," replied Master Caliostrus, "not to himself and not to those who patronize his establishment, and not to his family."

The problem was not with my eyes, but with those of Master Caliostrus, for his had become a slave to his desires for influential patrons, rather than lenses of artistic impartiality.

"You do not paint a man with deep-set beady eyes, even if his eyes are as hard and as tiny as those of a shrewt," Caliostrus went on. "That is, if you wish to remain a portraiture artist in L'Excelsis. Without satisfied patrons, even if you become a master, you will not remain long an artist. You will not become a master, because I certainly cannot support or lend my name to a portraiturist who is insensible to the self-images of his potential patrons."

"Then, Master Caliostrus," I replied, gently setting my brush on the edge of the oils tray, "how am I to comply with the dictates of the guild? What of the goal of artistic precision?"

"*Artistic* precision, my dear Rennthyl, is the goal of obtaining the precise image that will please the patron. You most certainly did so in pleasing Craftmaster Weidyn and young Mistress Weidyn. So far, you also seem to be pleasing Mistress Thelya D'Scheorzyl and her parents."

I had been able to please Master Weidyn because the true visage of his daughter had been pleasant enough and because he could not have cared less how true the portrait had been so long as his wife and daughter were content. The same looked possible with Thelya, although I had barely begun that portrait. I certainly had no problem with Caliostrus's logic, nor with his desires to increase the girth of his wallet. My difficulty lay elsewhere. "As artists, do we not have a duty, in some fashion, to present an accurate and precise view of what lies before us?"

Caliostrus laughed, as I knew he would. "The only people in all of Solidar who reckon the need for a precision that grates upon all sensibilities are the Imagers of L'Excelsis. In fact, they might be the only ones in all of Terahnar. That is because power allows impartiality."

"So you're saying, master, that if I want to be impartial, I should not be a portraiturist, but an imager?"

"You don't even want to try to be an imager, Rhennthyl. Renegade imagers, if they do more than minor imaging, risk their lives, even if the imagers do not catch them. In the out-lying districts, imagers are considered disciples of the Na-mer, and people believe they create hidden names of ruin and despair with each image that they make real. Most of those who try to become true imagers die young, entering Imagisle by the Bridge of Hopes and departing in a cart over the Bridge of Stones. Most who do survive spend the rest of their lives slaving for their masters, trying to create images and devices that never were and never could be—or dying slowly as they fabricate parts of machines for the armagers of the Council."

How was that so different from what I did, handling the portraits for those of lesser affluence for Master Caliostrus, mixing pigments, and combining oils, powdering charcoal, and a thousand other mundane and mind-numbing tasks?

"All you young artists think that you, too, could be great. . . ." Caliostrus let his words die away into silence be-fore punctuating the silence with a snort. "Greatness isn't what you think it is, Rhennthyl. Be content to be a portraitu-rist. And fix those eyes." He turned away without another utterance.

My corner of the large studio was the one in the southwest—where the light was harshest and brightest and washed out everything. But it did have a single window, one that was open because the fall air was cool, but not cold, and, while I'd always loved the use of oils to create, I'd never much cared for the odors of the paint. Most artists didn't seem to mind, I supposed, because they only created a visual image, not one that embodied touch and taste and scent, although the very best paintings could evoke a sense of that.

From the far corner, Ostrius said, "He's right, you know, Rhenn. In the end, all that matters is reputation and golds." Standing by his easel, he held a palette knife he had just wiped clean. "The test of a reputation is whether the artist's golds last as long as he lives."

That was easy enough for him to say, since, as his father's eldest, he'd inherit the studio and the reputation, not that the stocky Ostrius was not a capable portraiturist, for he was, and he'd just made master, if tacitly under the understanding that he would remain within his father's studio for the near future. He was also anything but artistically adventurous.

"That observation is discouraging, true as it may be," I pointed out.

"It doesn't make it less accurate."

Thinking about what Master Caliostrus and his son had said, before I lifted the brush to get back to detailing the vest of Masgayl Factorius, I glanced out the second-level window. As with most artists, Master Caliostrus had placed his workrooms and studios on the second level, with the gallery and storerooms below, and the family quarters above. From the heights of Martradon, one could see Imagisle a good three milles to the west, a granite ship pointed upstream in the River Aluse, its masts the twin towers of the Collegium Imago. From that distance the three bridges looked as slender as hawsers mooring that ship to the city that surrounded it.

7

*The world and its parts are as they are; accuracy is a
term man applies to his small creations.*

At precisely one glass before noon on Lundi, Masgayl
Factorius arrived at the second-floor door to Master Caliostrus's
studio. I had barely gotten there myself, after washing up,
because I'd been working on grinding pigment stock in the
shed in the rear courtyard, and the Belishan purple had been
more than difficult to get off my fingers and from under my
nails. I had to grind and mix the pigments—or those requiring greater care—not only for myself and Master Caliostrus,
but also for Ostrius, who certainly couldn't be bothered with
such, and Stanus, who seemed unwilling to learn anything of
any great difficulty.

My fingers were numb, of course, because Master Caliostrus didn't believe in spending coppers on coal for heating
wash water for apprentices or journeymen, at least not until
the turn of winter. Yet a thorough washing was necessary,
because the purple could pervade anything else I touched,
and I didn't want to spoil the portrait or one of the smaller
studies I was working on to enter in the annual journeyman's
festival in Ianus, barely more than a month away.

"Good morning, honored factorius." I held the studio door
for him as he eased his bulk past me.

"Good day, such as it is." He forced a smile. "Before we
start, let me see what you have there, young Rhenn."

I closed the heavy oak door and followed the heavyset
factorius to the easel in my corner of the studio. He stood

before the easel, then brushed back his thick and oily gray hair and nodded. I had widened the eye spacing just a touch, as well as lightened the skin beneath the eyes a shade or so. That would reduce their apparent beadiness.

"Not so flattering as one might wish, but accurate, and adequate. You do have an excellent touch on the vest, as well as the fabric of the chair—even if I did bring you a sample." He turned and moved toward the far plainer chair in which he sat for me, taking off his silver-trimmed traveling cloak to reveal the vest and jacket matching those in the portrait. "But my daughter insisted that I be depicted in a chair identifiable as mine. Daughters are a man's joy and trouble. Sons are merely trouble."

"We do our best to be more than adequate, sir."

Masgayl laughed, a sound comprised of a certain emptiness as well as amusement and rue. "You're more than adequate, young Rhenn, and adequate is more than sufficient. Now that I am a factorius, it will not do that my foyer is without a portrait, but one by a proclaimed master would only declare my arrogance. No . . . modesty suits me far better, and I will get a good work from you at a lower cost than from your master, and you will gain in reputation as others see your work." He settled into the chair.

I adjusted the easel. "You do not fear that they will say you have no interest in great art, sir?"

"What they say and how they will act are not the same. They will act on the prices of my goods, not upon my appreciation of art. Besides, art is no more than a craft, one that takes talent, there is little point in denying that, but a craft nonetheless . . ."

As I worked to get the squint in his eyes better, and catch the little crease that ran above the main one than extended from his left eye upward for just a fraction of a span, I found myself thinking about the factorius's point that art was but a craft. Could everything be reduced to little more than a craft, a set of skills that those with talent and determination could master? My brush almost wavered, and I pushed away the thoughts. For the moment, the portrait came first.

I had but worked less than half a glass when the studio door opened and Master Caliostrus entered, carefully carrying a canvas. A chill breeze swept into the studio, and with the wind came Stanus, lugging the master's traveling case with its paints, oils, solvents, and brushes. Caliostrus let Stanus pass, then set the canvas on the nearest empty easel before closing the door. He turned and inclined his head to the rope factor. "Greetings, factorius. I had heard that you now have a new device for twisting and braiding cable for deep-sea vessels."

"I've had it for two years. The demand is so great I have just completed installing a second."

"That must have been what I heard. People are talking."

Masgayl snorted. "They always talk. Only imagers never talk. They don't need to. And artists and portraiturists shouldn't say much, but let their work speak for them."

"We do try, honored factorius. When you are finished with today's sitting, would you like to see the work I am doing for the daughter of Imager Heisbyl?"

"I am certain it shows an excellently attractive woman. Whether or not it resembles the lady might well be another question."

I almost missed a brush stroke at those words.

"All my work resembles those whom I portray, most honored Masgayl."

"Oh . . . I'm quite assured that it does, perhaps on their best days in the best possible light." The factorius offered an ironic laugh. "Your journeyman does you credit, Caliostrus."

After what Masgayl had just said, I wasn't certain that I wanted that credit, but I said nothing and switched my concentration to the drape and the play of the light on the right lower sleeve of the factor's bastognan-brown jacket. There was something there. I could see it . . .

Then, it was there on the canvas, just as I had visualized it, but I wasn't aware that I'd actually painted it. Still, the brush-strokes were there, if a touch more precise than usual, more the way I wished they were than they sometimes were.

"He has talent and promise, honored factorius, and, if he

continues to listen," Caliostrus added with a touch of asperity, "he might even have more commissions such as yours."

That was a not-so-veiled reference to Masgayl's beady eyes, and I attempted to work on the smaller left section of the sleeve, trying to get the fall of the light and the creases just right.

"He might indeed," agreed the factorius politely. "Is that the portrait you mentioned, the one you put on the easel?"

"It is indeed. It is as of the moment most incomplete," Caliostrus said before lifting the canvas and carrying to where Masgayl could see it.

"Ah, yes," nodded the rope factor, "a most flattering image, but one certainly recognizable as the younger Mistress Heisbyl."

"I'm glad that you find it so." Caliostrus's words were strained.

"Don't mind me, master portraiturist. I'm cynical about far too much in life. I'd rather make cables for ships, but I also provide rope for the gaolers at the Poignard Prison. We all have aspects of what we do that we could do without."

Master Caliostrus retreated with the portrait. Once he had placed it on his working easel, he motioned for Stanus to leave and then followed, inclining his head to the factor just before he opened the studio door. "Until later, honored factorius."

"Until later."

Once the door closed, I went back to working on the area around the factor's eyes. Caliostrus had been right about one thing—the eyes were central to showing a true likeness.

When Masgayl finally rose at the end of the glass, he stretched, then began to don his cloak, which even he might need against a wind that was more indicative of the winter gusts of Ianus than reminiscent of the pleasant harvest breezes of Erntyn.

"Young Rhenn, you are most unusual for a portraiturist, even for a journeyman." Masgayl smiled courteously, but for the first time, I could sense a ferocity behind the smile. "The advantage of commerce is that one can be accurate and prosper. Doing so is far more . . . difficult . . . when one's craft depends on pleasing the perceptions of those who pay. Before long, you will doubtless have to choose between accuracy and perception . . . if you have not already done so."

"Sir." I just inclined my head politely. There was little I could or should have said, not given my position.

He smiled again, as if he had made a jest, then turned and left the studio. For a moment, I just stood with the chill wind of the coming winter gusting past me.

8

755 A.L.

Those who would judge a work of art reveal more of themselves than of the artist under their scrutiny or of his work.

For some reason, Samedi mornings in Ianus seemed colder than other winter mornings. The ceramic stove in the center of the studio did radiate warmth, but the windowpanes sucked that heat out of the room. The corner windows and those at the other end of the studio were covered with thick hangings, but not the others, because I needed as much light as I could get in order to paint the girl seated on the chair.

"Mistress Thelya . . . if you would please keep looking toward the vase on that table . . . that's it."

Her governess refrained from uttering a word.

"Yes, Master Rhennthyl."

I didn't correct her this time. There wasn't any point to it. Mistress Thelya D'Scheorzyl was all of nine years old. She was sweet and had the manners of a much older girl, thankfully, and the attention span of a gnat, not-so-thankfully. She stroked the cat in her arms gently. The cat had yellow-green eyes and a long silky white coat with tortoiseshell accents. Given that Thelya's mother had insisted that her daughter be painted in a silver-gray dress, I'd had to find a blue-gray-shaded pillow on which the cat could rest in order to get enough contrast between the cat's coat, Thelya's pale complexion, and the dress. Even so, I'd had to change the shade of the pillow in the portrait to get those colors and contrasts so that they enhanced her prettiness rather than clashed with it. I still worried about the eyes . . . there was something there I didn't have quite the way it should be.

"You'll make Remsi look good, won't you?"

"You and Remsi will look good together," I replied, working on Thelya's jawline.

In some ways, depicting her cat, the rather languorous Remsi, was the easiest part of the commission, because Remsi was almost totally white with the exception of tortoiseshell paws, tail, and ears.

The jawline still wasn't quite the way I wanted it. I looked to Thelya, fixing the side of her face in my mind, then at the canvas, and the brushstrokes. The oils on the canvas shimmered, then shifted, ever so slightly. The brushstrokes were still mine, but the jawline was cleaner—and right. I'd only been able to do that recently, but I knew what I was doing bordered on imaging. Yet it was only with oils, and it was cleaner and faster than scraping and repainting and certainly better than overpainting. For all that, I wasn't about to try it often, only when I had a very clear image in my mind—and definitely not when Master Caliostrus was around.

I worked to get the rest of the left side of her face finished before the ten bells of noon chimed—and managed to do so as well as finish the cat's face as well, setting down the brush just as the first bell rang.

"Can I see?" asked Thelya, scampering off the chair, but still holding the cat.

"We still need two more sittings," I said to the governess.

"Then . . . next Mardi afternoon, at the third glass of the afternoon, and next Samedi, at the ninth glass of morning." She nodded brusquely.

Thelya scurried past me to look at the canvas. "That's Remsi! It looks just like her."

I forbore to mention that was the point of a portrait and just smiled.

Once I saw them off, I put in another glass of work on details for the portrait that did not require their presence. I used what little of the oils I had left on a small work, a still life, which I could not do for hire or sale, but only for open exhibit at the annual festival—the only venue where an artist could exhibit or sell out of his discipline—although it would be next year's festival, since the final judging on this year's submissions would be later in the evening.

Not more than a quarter of a glass had passed, just after I'd finished cleaning the fine-tipped brush that was my own, when Master Caliostrus entered the studio. "Don't forget to bank the stove before you leave. I'll not be using the studio this afternoon. Nor will Ostrius."

Of course, the most honored heir and junior master wouldn't be working on a Samedi afternoon. "I'll take care of it, sir."

"When will you finish the Mistress Scheorzyl portrait, Rhennthyl?"

"Two more sittings and then a few days of fine work after that, Master Caliostrus. She'll be here on Mardi and next Samedi."

"I suppose the delay can't be helped."

"Her parents have limited the sittings, and no more than a glass a time."

He extended a thin cloth bag. "Factor Masgayl finally paid for the portrait, and here's your share, Rhennthyl. Go out and celebrate."

I eased the coins from the bag—eight silvers. I just looked at Caliostrus.

"Half of the fee goes to the master outright. You know that. Then there are the costs for the framing and canvas, not to mention the pigments and oils. There was that one brush you forgot to clean, and replacing it was two silvers."

"Yes, sir. Thank you, sir." All I could do was nod and agree. Masgayl Factorius had paid five golds for the portrait

I'd done, and out of that I'd gotten eight silvers. Not only that, but I knew he'd paid Caliostrus on Lundi, and Caliostrus had waited almost a week to pay me. Charging me for the brush was mostly fair. Mostly. I'd mislaid it when Caliostrus had dragged me away from cleaning for some chore he'd thought important and I couldn't even recall. And it had been an old brush. It seemed to me that after painting portraits for close to three years, while still doing almost all the chores for the studio, I ought to be receiving more than one part in five of the commission, especially since I received nothing else except room, board, and training.

Both Factor Masgayl and Factor Scheorzyl had come seeking my work, not that of Master Caliostrus. Yet . . . even though I did my best to save my coins, I certainly did not have enough to open my own studio—and that did not include the ten golds necessary for the bond to be posted with the Artists' Guild, not to mention Master Caliostrus's recommendation and the concurrence of the Portraiture Guild.

"Don't forget the stove, Rhennthyl," Caliostrus added before he left, climbing the steps up to the family quarters.

After finishing my cleanup and washing up, later on Samedi afternoon I made my way down toward the Festival Hall, walking out Brayer Lane to North Middle and then southwest on the Midroad.

I stopped at Lapinina. I did deserve a bit of a treat. It was little more than a tiny bistro, tucked between a coppersmith's on one side and a cooper's on the other, on the southeast side of Guild Square, between Midroad and Sudroad, just a little place with three windows and a half score of tiny tables. But they knew me.

A trace of rime ice clung to the outer doorframe, but when I opened the door and stepped inside, careful to close it quickly, the warmth and smells of cooking—garlic, baked bread, roasted fowl—enfolded me. All the tables were taken. They usually were.

"Rhenn! Over here!" At the smallest of the tables, squeezed in beside the brick casement separating two windows, sat Rogaris. No one else had such an elegant black spade beard, especially not another journeyman artist, but I supposed that came from working in the studio of Jacquerl, one of the most esteemed of portraiturists in L'Excelsis.

The table where Rogaris sat was so small that on the side across from him was only a stool. It was empty, and I eased onto it. "Thank you."

"You've done the same for me more than a few times." He grinned, then raised his mug. I could see the faint steam of the hot spiced wine.

"What will you have, Rhenn?" asked Staela, the wife of Ruscol, who owned Lapinina.

"The special fried ham croissant and the better spiced hot wine."

"That'll be half a silver."

I extracted the five coppers from my wallet and handed them over—and she was gone.

"What are you doing here?" I asked.

"Getting warm. I was over at the exhibit. I saw your study. You didn't enter a portrait?"

I shook my head. "I wanted to try something else." I saw no point in painting a portrait for which I would likely not get paid. It was better to try something else and stretch my abilities.

Staela reappeared and set the hot wine on the table in passing. I cupped my hands around the mug, letting the heat warm chill fingers, before I took a first sip. Then I held it at chin level and let the warmth coming from the mug caress my face.

"Cold out there, even for mid-Ianus," observed Rogaris.

"Cold enough," I admitted. "Are you going back over to the Festival Hall?"

Rogaris shook his head. "Master Jacquerl said there wasn't much point in my entering any studies this year." He smiled. "Besides, Aemalye has the night off, and the governess's quarters to herself." He stood a last swallow from his mug, then set it on the table.

"That sounds promising."

"Most promising. We're saving for the bond to open my

own studio, and we'll wed once I make master, a year from this coming Agostos." Rogaris stood. "Until later, Rhenn, and best of fortune this evening."

"Thank you." I slipped around the table and took the narrow chair, just before Staela returned with the chipped brown crockery platter on which was my croissant, along with three fat rice-fries drizzled with balsamic vinegar.

"Eat hearty," offered Staela as she hurried away.

I took a small bite. I wasn't in any hurry. The judging results wouldn't be announced until the sixth glass, and the bells of the fifth glass hadn't yet rung. I couldn't help but think about Rogaris. He was less than three years older than I was. I couldn't conceive of being married soon, not after growing up with Rousel, and then Khethila and Culthyn.

I savored the golden-brown fried ham croissant, alternating with bites from the crunchy fried sticky rice. Then I sat at the tiny table and sipped the warm winter wine, enjoying the melded taste of wine and spices—cinnamon, cloves, and shaeric.

Eventually, I finally finished the last of the winter wine, as much because Staela kept glaring at me as because I was in any haste, and rose, leaving a copper for her and making my way back out into the cold and across the tightly set paving stones of the avenue to the square itself. Festival Hall dominated the Guild Square. Properly speaking, they were the Artisans' Festival Hall and the Artisans' Guild Square. Each of the four main artisans' guilds had a wing of the building, and in the center was the Festival Hall proper. The north wing was the province of the masons', stonemasons', and sculptors' guilds; the west wing was that of the cabinetmakers' and woodcrafters' guilds; the south wing belonged to the various representative artists' guilds, including the portraiturists' guild; and the east wing was that of the glassblowers' and various metalcrafters' guilds.

The guild wings were closed and locked, and I entered the hall through the door between the east and the south wing, nodding at the guard in gray just inside. The four huge ceramic stoves—one for each wing, so to speak—kept my breath from steaming, but the cavernous space was cold enough that I wasn't about to loosen my jacket.

The display works were hung by guild, and I walked to where mine had been placed, on the far left end of those submitted, one of three—out of nineteen—that didn't have a portrait component. My painting—a study, really—depicted a chessboard seen from an angle. In addition to the pieces still in play, one could see two goblets of wine, one on each end of the board. The goblet at the end with the fewest pieces taken off the board was more than half full and held a dark red wine, a claret almost as black as the pieces beside it. On the white end of the board, the goblet held but a trace of white wine, a grisio, in my mind. The white imager had been laid on its side, signifying resignation, because in three moves, black would have won by checkmate.

As I stepped back, someone coughed, politely, and I turned.

A tall figure, wearing a solid dark green woolen coat and scuffed but sturdy brown boots, looked at me. His face was thin, accentuated by a wispy white goatee and high cheekbones. His eyes looked to be watery gray in the fading light that sifted through the high clerestory windows. Only half the brass wall lanterns had been lit, but the lamplighter was making his way around the outer walls of the hall. "Ah . . . you'd be Rhennthyl, young Caliostrus's journeyman."

"I'm Rhenn." Young Caliostrus? He was older than my own father, if not by much.

"Good work there. It won't win, though."

"Why do you say that?" I had my own ideas, but I wanted to hear what the old artisan might offer—if he was an artisan at all.

"It's understated. Symbolic, too, and the symbol is the one that no one wants to face."

"Defeat? A setback? The favor of the Namer?" Like it or not, we all faced setbacks, sooner or later.

"No . . . being forced to resign in the face of superior ability. Don't you know that's the greatest fear of any artist? It's not the fear of death, but the fear of being forced to admit someone else is better. The mark of the Namer is nothing compared to that." The old artisan laughed. "You'll see, young fellow. That you will." Then he turned and walked away.

I couldn't say that I disagreed with his words, but why had he even bothered to speak to me? And who was he?

A rotund man walked toward me, and it took a moment to recognize Master Estafen. I'd been introduced to him once before, and I'd seen him from a distance upon several occasions. I didn't know any of his journeymen or apprentices, but he had several of each, and perhaps the most successful portrait studio in L'Excelsis, with the possible exception of Jacquerl. Although the judges were never revealed, I wondered if he might be one of them.

I inclined my head in respect. "Master Estafen."

"Journeyman Rhennthyl. I saw old Grisarius talking to you."

"Was that who it was?"

"Oh . . . Grisarius is just the name everyone calls him. Once, he was Emanus D'Arte, and considered one of the best portraiturists in L'Excelsis. But he did a seascape of a beach near Erlescue. Nothing wrong with that, so long as he didn't sell it. He not only sold it, but he sold it to one of the master imagers, a Maitre D'Esprit, no less, and then told everyone." Master Estafen shrugged. "After that, the guild had no choice. He was expelled. He had enough put by, I guess, to keep some rooms off the Boulevard D'Imagers. He comes every year to look at the works entered by the journeymen."

"I thought he might be an artisan of some sort, but . . ."

"He was one of the greatest, but, like many who are great or close to greatness, he thought he was above the rules that govern a guild. Or a city." He paused, then added, "Or a land."

"Rules are necessary," I admitted.

"I saw your work, Rhennthyl. It is good. You could be an outstanding portraiturist. Do not make life harder for yourself than it has to be. A good artist has enough difficulty becoming both great and secure in his position."

"Yes, sir." I nodded most politely.

With a warm smile whose depth was more than a little suspect to me, Master Estafen nodded and moved away.

In turn, I nodded to some of the other journeymen walking around. Belius was a landscape artist, but his studies were too gray. Morgad had a piece that wasn't bad, but it was a portrait of an older man that suggested both corpulence and greed, and accurate as it was, I doubted it would be considered for an award. Aurelean, as always, strutted around and avoided mingling with anyone who toiled for one of the "lesser" masters, such as Caliostrus, even though his master, Kocteault, wasn't always considered among the "greater."

On the other hand, Elphens, who was by far the best-dressed and most stylish of all the journeymen, smiled broadly and insincerely and even spoke. "It's good to see you, Rhenn. I enjoyed your study piece. It was most thought-provoking."

"Thank you. Your gardens were most intriguing." That was the best I could do.

Before long, Arasmes, the scrivener for the Portraiture Guild, stepped up before the middle of the displayed works. He didn't shout or yell. He just waited until the handful of journeymen standing around stopped talking and looked in his direction. I remained well in the back, in the shadows, doubting my work would be considered, but hoping nonetheless.

"The judges have decided on the prizes for this year's journeyman competition." Arasmes took a long pause, then announced, "Second recognition—and the prize of two golds—goes to Aurelean D'Kocteault for his portrait of Mistress Karlana D'Kocteault. The judges would note that this study is a fine example of a traditional portrait."

I had to agree. It was indeed an example of tradition. There wasn't a single item of originality or true artistry anywhere, and I hadn't seen an original brushstroke in the entire painting. It didn't hurt that Master Kocteault was the previous guildmaster of the Portraiture Guild and that the portrait had been a flattering image of Kocteault's elder daughter, who did not look anywhere near so fair as Aurelean had depicted her.

"First recognition goes to Elphens D'Rhenius, along with the prize of five golds. The judges would like to commend journeyman Elphens for his creative use of light in his study of the lower gardens on Council Hill."

I managed not to snort. Creative use of light was appropriate—since the indirect light he'd depicted in his view of the gardens through a fall mist would have required the sun to be in three places—or that there be three suns in the sky. But Elphens was the journeyman for Master Rhenius D'Arte, considered by some as an equal of Estafen or Jacquerl.

For all that I had expected something like that, the walk back to Master Caliostrus's in the chill and the dark was less than pleasant. The wind had picked up, and tiny flakes of ice pelted my exposed face, head, and neck. Many of the lanterns outside doors had blown out, and with the storm above, the rays of neither moon penetrated the clouds to offer light.

When I finally reached my small room, my feet were close to numb, and I could not feel the tip of my nose. Even as a journeyman, my quarters were on the street level, between the storerooms and the gallery, where the noises, the odors, and the cold were always the greatest. It took me two tries to slide the door bolt into place. My fingers were so cold that I had to fumble with the striker for several moments before I finally lit the small lamp on the chest.

I pulled off shoes that were both cold and damp, undressed down to my drawers quickly, hung my shirt and trousers on the pegs beside the tall and narrow chest, then wicked down the lamp and blew out the last flicker of flame before clambering into bed. Fortunately, when I'd left home to apprentice to Master Caliostrus, Father had sent me off with heavy blankets and even an old but serviceable comforter. Occasionally, when I visited, Mother slipped me silvers, reminding me that they came from Father, but that he was too proud to hand them to me personally. I had the feeling she was telling the truth about that.

As I lay there in the cold in my narrow bed, slowly warming up, I tried not to think too hard about the patent unfairness of the Festival Hall judging. I'd known it wouldn't be any different from what had happened, because it had been that way for the previous years, ever since I'd first been an apprentice. Even in the chill of my chamber, before long I was more than warm enough, even in the depths of a cold Ianus, and eventually, I drifted off to sleep.

I woke somewhere in the darkness, so black that I could see nothing. Had the freezing flakes of the night before piled up so high that they had covered and blocked all light from my single narrow window? I felt around, but my blankets and comforter were gone, not that I felt cold, and I sat up, only to discover that I'd been lying on a bench of some sort.

How could that have been? Where was I? Why was it so dark? I knew I'd gone to sleep in my own bed. I needed light. I needed a lamp, one that was lit!

Suddenly, there was light, and I was back under my blankets, peering at the bright glow of the lamp on the chest across from the bed. I just looked at it for a long moment, then to the door, but the bolt was still in place. The window hangings were also shut.

I *knew* I'd blown out the lamp. I'd even checked it, and I'd never turned the wick up that high because it burned oil too quickly. Was I dreaming?

Gingerly, I eased out from under the now-warm blankets and comforter. The chill, especially from the ancient cold tiles on my bare feet, assured me that I was awake as I crossed the short distance to the chest. The topmost part of the lamp mantle was not that warm, but the lamp had been wicked up.

Had I lit it in my sleep?

The chill of the floor tiles certainly would have awakened me. I'd been dreaming about needing light, needing a lamp, but just dreaming about light didn't light lamps. I made sure I wicked down the lamp before blowing it out and hurrying back under my blankets. Then I watched the lamp, but it did not light itself.

Again, I slept.

9

*Reality is an illusion based on the understanding
of the perceiver.*

The walk to my parents' dwelling felt even farther than to the Guild Square, although the distance was about the same, except I had to walk east, rather than south, but that might have been because Solayi was even colder than Samedi had been, with a wind that howled and sucked every bit of heat out the paving stones and buildings along the Midroad. The angled pale white light of the sun, even in midafternoon, seemed to radiate chill rather than warmth. I finally thumped the bronze knocker on the door, and Nellica, the new servant, opened the door. As I handed her my coat and scarf, I was more than happy to be out of the cold.

Mother scurried into the foyer. "You're looking well, Rhenn, if a bit chilled." She wrapped her arms around me for a moment. "Come in and warm yourself by the parlor stove."

I didn't need a second invitation and followed her through the left archway and into the family parlor, not the formal parlor.

Khethila was curled up on the corner of the settee closest to the large ceramic stove, a thin book in her hand. She looked up and smiled. "Rhenn!"

"Khethila." I eased around to put my back to the stove. "What are you reading?"

"Madame D'Shendael's *Poetic Discourse*."

I'd heard of her. She had gathered a group of High Holders' wives and even some assistants to the Council to her evening salon, where all manner of topics were discussed, many of which reputedly suggested a certain lack of prudence in dealing with the Council. "She's rather controversial, isn't she?"

"She does ask questions. Lots of them."

"Such as?"

Khethila bounded to her feet, the book still in hand. "Listen to this." She cleared her throat and began to read in a husky voice that reminded me that she was no longer a child.

> *"At hearth, in bed, with feet near bare,*
> *agree with smile demure and fair,*
> *our position's home; is that where*
> *our spirits, our role, and place declare?"*

Just at that point, Father stepped into the parlor through the doorway from the lower study. "You're not reading that trash again, are you, Khethila?" His eyes flashed, and I could sense he was even more angry than he'd been when I'd told him I'd never be a factor.

"She's only telling Rhenn what's in the book, dear." Mother shot a warning glance to Khethila, before stepping forward and taking Father's hands. "Besides, we don't get Rhenn here that often anymore, and we'd all like a pleasant dinner."

Father glared at Khethila, and she lowered her eyes, but her jaw was firm.

"Let me have Nellica bring you your wine." Mother continued. "Would you like some of the Dhuensa, Rhenn? Or hot spiced winter wine?"

"The spiced, please. It was a cold walk here."

"Rousel always hires a carriage when he and Remaya visit." That was from Culthyn, who had slipped down the front main staircase from the upstairs sitting room.

"He's a factor," I pointed out. "I'm an artist."

"Master Caliostrus has a carriage," Culthyn pointed out. "Why don't you?"

Culthyn clearly took after Rousel, but I only said, "Because

I'm not a master yet, and don't have my own studio. It takes longer when you're an artist."

"Father could help with the studio."

"He can't," I pointed out. "You can't open a studio unless you're a junior master artist, and that takes at least five years as a journeyman, and you have to be approved by your master and by the guild board." That approval required either great talent, or a certain amount of quiet "gifting," but the five-year requirement was absolute.

"That's awful when you're as good as you are," Culthyn declared.

"That's the way it is, and I can't change it."

Nellica reappeared with a tray holding a goblet and two mugs, offering the tray to Father first. He took the goblet. I took one of the mugs, and Mother the other.

"We're having stuffed and sauced fowl," she said. "With all the wind and chill, it seemed a good hearty meal."

"It sounds wonderful." Especially since my board at Master Caliostrus's didn't include dinner on either Samedi or Solayi night, although I could have bread and cheese from the kitchen. I took a sip of the spiced wine, far better than that at Lapinina, not surprisingly, since Father always had a good cellar and Mother could make the best use of it.

"I even have a hot winter pudding for dessert," Mother added.

"Which all of us have had to keep Culthyn out of," said Khethila.

"There was more than enough," muttered my youngest brother.

"There wouldn't have been," noted Khethila.

Before long we had gathered in the dining chamber, where Father did allow me the grace of sitting at his right and motioning me to offer the blessing.

"For the grace and warmth from above, for the bounty of the earth below, for all beauty and artistry in the world, for your justice, and for your manifold and great mercies, we offer our thanks and gratitude, both now and evermore, in the spirit of that which cannot be named or imaged . . ."

"In peace and harmony."

"That's the artists' blessing, isn't it?" said Khethila. "I like it."

"A blessing's a blessing," Father said dryly, gesturing for everyone to sit down. "So long as we respect the Nameless, the words can change a bit."

Personally, I preferred the artists' version, but then, I hadn't heard the crafters' version, or that of the imagers, assuming that they had a version.

After carving and serving the fowl, then settling into his chair, Father politely asked me, "How is the portraiture business coming?" He always referred to portraiture as "business."

"I've had three commissions in the last month or so, that is, commissions where the patron asked for me to do the work. The one I just finished was of Masgayl Factorius."

"Ah, yes, the rope factor. Does cables and hawsers as well. Turns a shiny silver or two on the heavy cabling."

"You and he see many things in the same way." That was fair enough, although I had the sense that Masgayl Factorius was far more ruthless than Father.

"Did he pay well?"

"After costs, my share was a gold." I didn't have to mention the charge for the ruined brush. "Master Caliostrus gets half the fee, before costs."

"You'd . . ." He stopped at a glance from Mother. "Do you have other commissions?"

"I'm doing a portrait of Mistress Thelya D'Scheorzyl. That one will be done in about two weeks, because she can only sit for one glass, usually only once a week."

"Scheorzyl . . . Scheorzyl . . . Oh . . . he's the principal advocate-advisor to the Council."

I hadn't known that, only that young Thelya's parents were well connected and well off, since she had a governess and a special feline.

"Her mother was a beauty," added Mother. "I suppose she still is, but she usually stays at their estate in Tiens. Something about the air in L'Excelsis. What about the daughter?"

"She's but nine, and very polite. She's pretty enough now

and looks to be the kind who will turn heads in a few years. She might be too sweet, though."

"That's always a problem," suggested Khethila.

"And exactly why might that be a difficulty, daughter?" asked Father.

Khethila ignored the glare and smiled politely. "You wouldn't be half so well off or half so happy, Father, if Mother didn't occasionally suggest that matters might be better handled in another fashion. Girls who are too sweet often merely agree."

"I doubt that will ever be a difficulty for you." Father did manage a rueful smile before turning to me. "What do you think about the threats that the Caenenan envoy made last week?"

"I hadn't heard about them," I had to admit after swallowing a mouthful of the juicy fowl. "What did he say?"

"You hadn't heard?" asked Culthyn. "How could you not have heard?"

"I was working, unlike some young people," I replied.

"He uttered some nonsense about our belief in the Nameless being blasphemy and then went on to say that, if any of our people in Caenen tried to blaspheme against their Duodeus god/goddess, they'd be burned alive."

"What did the Council do?" In spite of myself, I was a bit interested.

"As usual, they dithered. We ship hundreds of tonnes of the fine woods from there—mahogany, ebony, rosewood, not to mention cotton and . . ."

"And elveweed," added Khethila.

"That's not a subject for dinner," Father said firmly.

"Why not?" she demanded. "When the carriage takes me to grammaire, I can see some of the sansespoirs smoking or chewing it. Some of them just lie there—"

"Where?" asked Mother.

"On the stoops of the taudis below South Middle. The wall's low enough to see over it."

"I'll have Charlsyn take you a longer way from now on," Mother announced in a hard tone that brooked no argument.

"They'll still be smoking it, and it comes from Caenen. The civic patrollers don't do anything, either. They just ignore it."

"Khethila . . . I cannot do anything about the degenerates of L'Excelsis, but I can do something about what you see. You are not being raised like a taudischild . . . or a . . ."

"A Pharsi?" Khethila suggested.

Father cleared his throat, loudly.

"Why does the Council let them sell elveweed here?" asked Culthyn, abruptly.

"They don't," replied Father. "It's prohibited."

"Then why do the sansespoirs have it to smoke?"

"That's because sailors and smugglers sneak it in. They can get golds for small amounts," I pointed out.

"Have you ever smoked any, Rhenn?" asked Culthyn.

"No. I wouldn't want to." Why spend golds on pleasure that was gone before you even knew it? Besides, I'd seen what the addicts looked like, and I never wanted to end up like that.

"Don't some artists?"

"Some of the abstractionists do, but they're not part of the guilds, and no one buys their works." No one respectable, anyway.

"I think we've discussed this . . . filthy . . . subject enough," Mother interjected.

After a moment of silence, I turned to Father. "How is the wool business?"

"We're doing well. You know Rousel is doing well with the branch factorage in Kherseilles. That makes it easier to ship the heavier woolens to the north of Jariola and to the Abierto Isles. He's already increased our shipments by a third."

That sounded like Rousel. He could talk anyone into anything—anyone but me, at least. "He's doing well, then."

"Enough that our profits are up by a quarter."

"And he and Remaya are expecting," Mother interjected, "in early Juyn, they think."

"I'm happy for them," I replied, "and it's good that Rousel is doing so well." For now, I thought, hoping that Rousel was not sprinting to the edge of the precipice. I was spared having to say more because Nellica cleared away the dinner platters, and then returned to set the winter pudding and dessert plates before Mother.

The pudding was as good as she had promised, and I did take seconds, but then, so did Culthyn. After he finished his second helping, he stared at the remaining pudding.

"Seconds are acceptable at times, Culthyn," Mother stated. "Thirds are merely greed. Don't act like a Pharsi."

Culthyn counterfeited a disconsolate expression, then said. "Remaya's not greedy."

Khethila hid a smile.

"She's different," Mother said, turning to me. "Did you know that Armynd D'Sholdchild has offered a proposal to Khethila? For when she's older, of course." She smiled broadly.

"Mother!" exclaimed Khethila.

"Armynd has?" We'd been at the grammaire together, but he'd gone on to the university. His father held thousands of hectares of grainlands and vineyards out in the westlands. "He's even older than I am."

"An older husband is always better. He's more established. And you're not getting any younger, Rhenn. It wouldn't hurt for you to keep an eye out for a likely wife."

"As an artist?" murmured Father.

"Wealthy women have been known to prefer artists, dear. Look at Madame D'Shendael. She's a High Holder in her own right."

"But she had to marry another to keep her rights," Khethila interjected.

"Do I have to hear her name all the time?" asked Father.

"You asked."

"Her husband is a landscape architect, not an artist, and he designs grand gardens."

"He's still an artist," Mother affirmed, "and Rhenn is going to be a great artist."

"He'd better hurry, then," Father replied with a laugh, pushing back his chair.

As Father rose, Mother looked to me. "Will you go to services with us?" Her voice was not quite pleading.

Solayi night was when most families in L'Excelsis went to

services, those who respected the Nameless, that is. I supposed I did, in my own way. I had nothing better to do, and Mother had never asked that much unreasonable of me, unlike Father. "Yes, but I'll have to leave right afterward. Master Caliostrus . . ." I shrugged without completing the explanation.

"We understand." Mother beamed.

Once everyone was bundled into their coats, we stepped out the side door where Charlsyn had pulled up, and I squeezed into the coach on the rear-facing seat with Khethila and Culthyn. At least, once the service was over, and it was never that long, I'd be much closer to Master Caliostrus's dwelling.

"Isn't this almost like old times? Now, if Rousel were just here," Mother said.

"If Rousel were here, none of us would be able to move," Culthyn observed.

Even Father smiled at Culthyn's wry tone.

We arrived at the anomen early enough, a good quarter before the sixth glass, so that we didn't have to hurry, but that also meant we had to stand in the cold until the service began with the small choir singing the choral invocation—"Paean to the Nameless," I thought.

Chorister Aknotyn had been at the Anomen D'Este since I could remember. His high tenor pierced the gloom as it always had in the wordless ululating invocation. Then he spoke.

"We are gathered here together this evening in the spirit of the Nameless and in affirmation of the quest for goodness and mercy in all that we do."

The opening hymn was "Pride Leadeth to a Fall." I merely mouthed the words, mainly because I was in fact proud and unwilling to have others hear just how badly I did sing.

After that was the Confession.

"We do not name You, for naming is a presumption, and we would not presume upon the creator of all that was, is, and will be. We do not pray to You, nor ask favors or recognition from You, for requesting such asks You to favor us over others who are also Your creations. Rather we confess that we always risk the sins of pride and presumption and that the very names we bear symbolize those sins, for we too often strive to arrogate our names and ourselves above others, to insist that our petty plans and arid achievements have meaning beyond those whom we love or over whom we have influence and power. Let us never forget that we are less than nothing against Your nameless magnificence and that all that we are is a gift to be cherished and treasured, and that we must also respect and cherish the gifts of others, in celebration of You who cannot be named or known, only respected and worshipped."

"In peace and harmony," we all chorused.

Then came the offertory baskets, followed by Chorister Aknotyn's ascension to the pulpit for the homily. "Good evening."

"Good evening," came the reply.

"And it is a good evening, for under the Nameless all evenings are good, even those that seem less than marvelous . . . and we all know that there are many of those . . ."

Aknotyn's dry aside brought low murmurs of laughter to the congregation.

"The other day a youngster asked me why we do not name the Nameless, and I almost repeated the Confession to him, but I realized that he was asking what really was behind the Confession. While our meeting place, the anomen, means place of no name, in fact we name everything, and so often when we name it, we assume that we know it. The name becomes the identity, and it is always a limited identity. Look at it in this fashion. You have a friend. Let's call him Fieryn, and we'll say that he has red hair and a certain lack of patience. Each time that you encounter Fieryn or talk to him or watch him, you build a more complete picture in your mind, and when Fieryn is not around, in effect, to you, that picture *is* Fieryn. But is the picture really Fieryn? Does it include the time he spends with his crippled cousin, whom you do not know? Does it include the glasses he has spent telling stories to his failing aunt who cannot leave her bed? Or the time he drank too much and kicked a poor simpleton? Yet, by calling up his name, we think we know Fieryn. But do we?

"Using names to excess and thinking that the name is the individual is often called the mark of the Namer, because one of the great sins in life is to accept that a name is all that there is of reality . . .

"Now, if there is so much we do not know about those we call family or friends, how much more is there about the Nameless, who created all that there is, that we cannot know and will never know? . . ."

Chorister Aknotyn went on to describe the magnificence of the Nameless and the unmitigated presumption of mere mortals to offer a name and think that they might know even a fraction of what the Nameless might know or understand. I'd heard similar homilies before, and I couldn't say that I disagreed. The only thing I might have added, if only in my mind, was the question of whether the Nameless, with all that magnificence, would even have cared what I thought or did.

While the walk from the Anomen D'Este to Brayer Lane and Master Caliostrus's establishment, even by the winding Bakers' Lane, was only half the distance I'd walked to get to Father's, I didn't even have to do that. Mother had Charlsyn go that way—and she slipped me two silvers as well, when Father wasn't looking, just before I got out of the coach. So I wasn't all that chilled by the time I reached my room.

10

755 A.L.

A good portrait reveals what is seen; a great one also reveals what is not.

I was halfway into the last sitting with Thelya on a far warmer and more pleasant Samedi morning—and the second one in Fevier—when I found myself looking at her eyes again. I'd been worried about them—not the shape or the shadows, but the color of the irises—for the last several sittings. The problem was simple. Her eyes were green, but I was limited to zinc blue-green and verdigris, and the zinc green wasn't intense enough, and the verdigris was far too fugitive to be used for Thelya's eyes, even if I used a touch of a clear varnish-glaze.

What I really needed was imagers' green, but only Master Caliostrus had that, along with the lapis blue, and they were so costly that I'd never see them, not as a journeyman, and certainly not so long as I worked in his studio. The most I'd ever seen were tiny dollops here and there. Still . . . I wouldn't need all that much. I glanced toward the converted ancient armoire that held his pigments, then shook my head.

If I could just have used the tiniest bit of that brilliant green, and then shaded the eyes from yellow-flecked zinc green to the brighter imagers' green on the sides of the pupils—right there . . .

I swallowed. I'd done it again. What I'd visualized, seen so clearly in my mind, had appeared on the canvas before me. That was a form of imaging. There was no doubt about it, but exactly what use was imaging that could only make small changes in oil paints on a canvas?

I couldn't help smiling as I studied the face on the canvas. That little change had made all the difference, bringing her eyes alive, and creating a subtle but clear linkage between all the elements of the portrait.

I finished just before noon, after refining just the hint of an errant curl above her left ear. Then I set down the fine-tipped brush and stepped away from the easel.

"Thank you, Thelya. We're finished for now, and today was the last sitting. The portrait should be ready in a few days."

"It isn't done now?" She bounced off the chair, holding Remsi so tightly that the cat gave a meow of protest.

The governess raised an eyebrow. She never spoke when a gesture would do.

"Some of the background isn't finished, but I don't need you to sit for that."

"Can I see?"

"You can . . . if you really want to."

She stopped well short of the easel. "You're saying that I shouldn't."

That stopped me. For a pampered nine-year-old to catch that suggested more perception than I'd thought she had. After a moment, I said, "You certainly can, Mistress Thelya, but I'd rather that you be surprised when you see the fully completed portrait."

"Like presents at Year-Turn?"

"Something like that."

She nodded. "I can wait." Her words were more about her than about the portrait, and, for some reason, I thought about Chorister Aknotyn's homily the week before, about thinking we understood people because we knew their names and had seen them often enough to believe that what we had seen was all that they were.

"I'm sure you can." I smiled. "It won't be long. Thank you for being so good at the sittings." I turned to the governess. "Thank you."

"The quiet was most restful." Her lips did not quite smile.

Once Thelya, her governess, and Remsi left, I spent a bit

more time just looking at the canvas. I had a few things to finish along the edges, but it was a fine portrait, probably the best I had done.

At that moment, Ostrius stepped into the studio, bringing with him a gust of cold air that suggested the past several days of comparatively mild weather were about to end. Almost as if to say that he didn't have to follow his father's rules about keeping the door closed in winter, he stood just inside the studio, holding the door open. "We need a little fresher air in here."

"Suit yourself," I replied. "My sitting's over."

He closed the door and walked toward my easel, where he stopped and glanced at the portrait. After a moment, he said, "Not bad. You almost got the skin perfect."

Much that he knew. I had gotten Thelya's pale skin perfect. He would have added the faintest touch of earth brown and yellow to flatter her, but that would have left anyone with any discrimination who saw the portrait vaguely unsatisfied without knowing why. "That's the way I saw it."

"You need to see them the way they see themselves, Rhenn. That's what makes a portraiturist a master."

After all the years with Master Caliostrus, I was getting to hate the way Ostrius tried to sound like his father. Master Caliostrus might be demanding or picky, but most of the time he was looking to improve what I did—or at least make it more attractive to a patron. Ostrius was just using his father's mannerisms to assert himself, and that trait had worsened since he'd been confirmed as a master, if a junior master. "It's certainly what brings many of them golds."

"Golds last, Rhenn, if you have enough of them. Reputation is fickle, and skills vanish with age."

He was doubtless right, but the way he said the words was annoying. I forced a laugh. "You're suggesting that we need to use our skills to amass golds before those skills fade."

"What else?" He walked to his pigment chest, unlocking it and putting several new brushes inside. Then he locked the chest again. "Don't forget to bank the coals in the stove."

"I'll take care of it."

"I'm sure you will." Ostrius flashed an insincere smile as he left the studio.

It wasn't that long before Master Caliostrus appeared, while I was finishing the last touches on the rust-brown hangings at the left edge of the portrait.

"Where did you get that green?" Master Caliostrus pointed to Thelya's eyes.

I knew I shouldn't have left the eyes that way, but they were perfect. "Sir?"

"That's imagers' green. Were you in my paints, Rhennthyl?"

"No, sir. I thought about it, but that would have been wrong." I gave him an embarrassed smile. What else could I say? "When I was cleaning the studio last Meredi . . . there was a little dollop of it on the edge of the side table, and it was hard, but I worked at it with oils over the past few days, and I managed to work in just a little bit . . . I thought . . . well, for her eyes, it seemed perfect."

"Hmmmph." Caliostrus walked to the old converted armoire that held his pigments.

That didn't bother me—if he were honest—because I hadn't touched his pigments. I wouldn't have dared. I could hear him mumbling. "Not here . . . there . . . hmmmm."

After a time, he returned and scanned the portrait of Thelya D'Scheorzyl minutely, then nodded. "It is quite good. I would have softened her skin a touch, but you chose to render what you saw. That might be best for a child." He smiled. "That way, if you do one later, you can soften it." He paused. "You'll pardon my concern about the eyes, but imagers' green is almost as valuable as liquid silver. You must have worked very hard to stretch that small dollop."

"I did, sir. It would have been better if I could have used a touch in the corner of the cat's pupils, but . . ." I shrugged helplessly. "I wouldn't have tried so hard, but I kept looking at her eyes, and they needed to be more intense, and the zinc green, even with a glaze . . ."

"You did what you could, Rhennthyl, and I'm certain

Madame Scheorzyl will be pleased with the portrait." Calio-strus paused. "I'm glad that you didn't try to use verdigris. The effect would have faded in a few years, even with a glaze."

"I'd thought so, sir."

"Even without that little bit of imagers' green, you could have heightened the effect with a little yellow ochre there . . . and there." His stubby forefinger pointed.

"I still could . . . and should, then, sir."

He nodded.

"Thank you."

"I still have a few skills you haven't picked up yet, Rhennthyl."

"More than a few, sir."

"You'll be finished by Meredi, ready for framing?"

"Yes, sir."

His eyes did linger on the portrait for a time before he turned. "You'll bank the coals?"

"Once I'm done, yes, sir."

"Good."

I did take his suggestions about the ochre yellow, and it took almost a glass to get it right. By then I was ready to leave. I did have enough coppers to go to Lapinina, and who knew, there might even be a pretty face there.

11

755 A.L.

Happiness cannot be pursued through art, nor art through happiness.

The younger unmarried crafters and artisans got together in the Guild Hall the next to the last Samedi of every month, the twenty-eighth of the month. It wasn't anything organized by the guilds, exactly, but they did let us use a corner of the hall without a charge, even for the two guards. There were musicians, and we'd pass a hat for them, and everyone usually had a good time—or at least a time away from the worries of the week.

That Fevier Samedi, I was standing by the outer wall of the hall, talking with Rogaris and Dolemis, while we shared a bottle of Fystian, a white vintage perhaps a half step above plonk. Rogaris held the bottle, as always, no matter who had bought it—me, in this case.

". . . you think this Caenenan thing will lead to war?" Dolemis kept looking past us at Yvette, as she swirled past in the arms of someone I didn't know. Yvette had been his girl for years—until she'd suggested formalizing the arrangement.

"What Caenenan thing?" asked Rogaris, taking a swig of the Fystian.

"The Caenenan envoy threatened that they'd kill any of our people who blasphemed their god or goddess or duality or whatever," I said. "That was weeks ago."

"No . . . they did," Dolemis explained. "It was in the news-sheets this afternoon. Some clerk in the embassy in Caena burst out laughing at one of their religious processions, and their armites lopped off his head on the spot. The Council is debating the matter."

"Cut off his head for laughing?" asked Rogaris. "You can't be serious."

"What do you expect from people who are arrogant enough to name their god?" I had more than a little scorn for people who thought a god cared whether they ate certain foods on certain days or who believed that people would be blessed or cursed or live forever or be tortured for eternity if they didn't follow a set of rules laid down by some dead prophet or another. If there happened to be an all-powerful and almighty deity—and I had my doubts—he or she or it or whatever wasn't about to care about who followed what dogma.

"Everyone's not like us," Rogaris said. "Most of them are stupider, and that's not giving us Solidarans much credit."

"You think the Council will send imagers?" asked Dolemis.

How would I know that? I didn't even know what an imager could really do in a war, except I knew no one much wanted a strong one against them—but there hadn't ever been that many war imagers, not from what I'd read in the histories, not since Rex Regis, when his unknown imager had done strange things with walls. I had no idea if there were any at the Collegium Imago now. I supposed that wasn't something anyone would want to reveal.

"Rhenn! Come dance with me!" called Seliora. She had jet-black hair and eyes to match, and she wore a black jacket with crimson trim above a crimson skirt and black dancing boots. I'd heard that she worked as an upholsterer and embroiderer for one of the furniture crafters in the artisans' area off Nordroad north of the Boulevard D'Este, but she'd never said, and I hadn't asked. "You've talked long enough."

"If you would excuse me," I said, "I'm being summoned by a pretty woman, and that doesn't happen that often."

"It would if you'd let it," quipped Rogaris.

"You never said what you thought would happen in Caenen," protested Dolemis.

"We'll send ships and troops, and people will fight and die, and they'll still lop off heads, and then we'll either kill enough of them that they'll stop doing it, or they won't, and then we'll lose more troops until we quit and declare victory." I called the last words over my shoulder as I hurried toward Seliora.

"Declare victory about what?" Seliora asked as I slipped my arm around her waist and began to dance with her, ignoring the fact that the waltz seemed a bit fast to me.

"The Caenenans . . . politics, again." I really didn't want to talk about it. I supposed I could be conscripted if the Council declared war, but they usually didn't conscript journeymen artisans or crafters. Apprentices were often conscripted, as were journeymen without masters.

"Dolemis always talks politics. Yvette said he even mumbled about it in his sleep."

"She actually listened?"

"I think that was the trouble."

"Well, he can't do anything about it, not unless he works and becomes a craftmaster, because the Council is elected from the guilds, the factors' associations, and the High Holders, and you have to be a craftmaster to be eligible, and he never will be because he spends too much time talking about politics rather than crafting cabinets for Sasol," I added with a laugh.

For a time, I did not speak, just enjoyed dancing and holding Seliora. She wasn't slender, but certainly not heavy, rather muscular. I enjoyed seeing her smile. Over the past year, we had talked and danced occasionally, and I knew she was interested in me . . . at least a little bit.

When the musicians stopped, so did we, but she didn't move away, and neither did I.

She looked up at me. "Everyone says you think you're too good to have a girl who might have actually lived within a few streets of the taudis or the Pharsis."

I had to laugh. "The first girl that I fell in love with was a Pharsi."

"How old were you? Five?" Seliora quipped back.

"More like thirteen."

"And I suppose you threw her over for some factor's twit?"

"No. She threw me over for some factor's twit, rather quickly. She married my younger brother almost two years ago. She said that when she saw him, it had to be."

Seliora looked hard at me. "Is that a joke?"

"No. They're expecting their first child this summer. They live in Kherseilles now."

The musicians began again, this time a fast variana, and Seliora took my hand. "Another dance." Her words weren't a request, but I was happy to comply, and she said nothing more as we moved to the beat of the music.

When the musicians stopped, I was breathing a little faster than usual.

"You shouldn't let that spoil things," she said. "You're good-looking. Rogaris says your work is good enough that before all that long you'll be a master artist with your own studio."

"At least three more years, and he's being kind."

"Rogaris?" Seliora laughed.

She had a point, but I shook my head. "It's not just that. I'm just beginning to get commissions, and they're still not all that frequent. How could I support a wife or a family?"

"Some women do make more than a few coins in honest work." She smiled warmly.

"I'm most certain you do."

"And being married doesn't mean you have to have a family right away."

"That's true." I grinned at her. "Are you asking me to propose to you?"

Seliora actually lowered her eyes, if only for a moment. "I am part Pharsi, if that helps. My grandmother was one. She came to L'Excelsis as a servant."

"If you take after her, I doubt she stayed one very long."

"No, she didn't. She was the one who started the business."

"You . . . your family . . . ?" I hadn't realized that.

"Papa and Aunt Aegina are the master crafters. They make

the chairs and the settees. Mama and I choose the fabrics and do the additional embroidery designs."

I had wondered about the fact that Seliora was usually better dressed than the other young women, but I'd learned that some women spent every last copper on clothes.

I inclined my head. "I'm—"

"Please don't tell anyone, especially Dolemis. He's a terrible gossip."

The music resumed, another waltz, a slower one, and I turned to her. "I still would have asked for another dance."

She smiled. "I know. I do foretell more than I say."

We spent most of the evening dancing, and I did walk her and two of her friends home, even if it meant an even longer and colder walk back out the Boulevard D'Este to Master Caliostrus's establishment. The entire way, I wondered what she had foretold that she hadn't said.

12

755 A.L.

Flattery is almost always perceived as either accurate or justified.

On Jeudi afternoon, I was in the work shed powdering red ochre, using the ancient mortar and pestle that looked as though they had been in Master Caliostrus's family for generations. Despite the sunlight outside, a chill breeze seeped through the bare plank walls. Powdering hard red ochre was sweaty work. The chill made it even less pleasant, especially if I crushed it and twisted the pestle too hard, because then some of the powder seeped into the air and then stuck to my sweat. Later, it got cold and itchy, and scratching just made it worse.

I consoled myself that the situation was only temporary because Stanus had finally run off, after throwing a bucket of hot ivory-black scraps at Ostrius. The scraps had burned holes in Ostrius's shirt and given him several welts on his neck, but it would have been worse had not Ostrius been wearing a leather working vest. If the civic patrollers caught poor Stanus, he'd spend at least a year in the mines, but, in the interim, assuming that Master Caliostrus could find and accept another apprentice, everyone expected me to do all the apprentice chores as well as my own, not to mention painting whatever commissions might come my way, not that I had any at the moment.

Still . . . the Scheorzyl portrait had turned out well, and I'd even gotten a half-gold bonus. I had to wonder how much extra the Scheorzyls had paid Caliostrus. But my name was getting around—at least to families with daughters who liked cats.

Everyone in the household was edgy that morning. As I'd left the table after breakfast, Madame Caliostrus had murmured something to her husband that had sounded like "your worthless brother skulking around here again." I'd known Caliostrus had a brother, and I'd even seen him a few times over the years—and smelled him, reeking of plonk so cheap that not even the poorest apprentice would have drunk it. That morning, Caliostrus had snapped back, but I hadn't heard what he'd said. I'd just wanted to get away before Ostrius made another comment about my lack of foresight, especially since it was really his shortsightedness, not that he'd ever admit it.

I checked the powder. Still too coarse, but getting closer to what was necessary to mix with the oil and wax that were melting over the small iron mixing stove in the corner. I went back to grinding, wishing that Stanus were still around, or that Caliostrus would get another apprentice so that I didn't have to do everything.

The shed door opened, and a gust of wind swirled ochre powder up around me, and I began to sneeze.

Ostrius stood there, glowering at me. "How long will it be before you can mix up the pigment?"

After I could stop sneezing, I just looked at him, noticing that he'd replaced the dressing covering the burn on his neck.

"Answer me. When will we have red ochre pigment?"

"Not until tomorrow. I won't have enough powder until later today, and then it will have to be blended and cooled . . ."

"You should have gotten to this earlier." He glared at me. "We're both waiting for the pigment."

"No one told me until this morning." I didn't point out that talking to him slowed me down—or that he'd been the one to use all the red ochre pigment for his portrait of High Chorister Thalyt and that he hadn't bothered to tell anyone that there hadn't been more than a palette knife's worth of it remaining.

"You should have known."

What could I say that wouldn't make him even angrier? Especially since Ostrius had never been the type to listen to reason or consider himself the cause of anything. He'd been the cause of the problem with his attitude and his mistreatment of Stanus, not that he'd ever been pleasant to me, either, but I had the advantage of having parents who had some position, unlike poor Stanus, whose father was dead and whose mother was a seamstress.

With a last glare at me, he stalked off, leaving the work shed door open. Of course, the wind gusted again and blew some of the finer powder I'd just ground right out of the pestle and up around me. I began to sneeze more, and by the time I got the door closed, I'd probably lost half a cup's worth of ground ochre powder. At that moment, I would have liked to strap Ostrius to a worktable and then slowly pour fine ochre powder down his throat and nostrils until he choked to death.

I recovered some of the powder from the bench top beside the mortar, and then went back to work. But I kept having to stop and sneeze. There was no help for it. I needed to brush the fine grit and powder off me and wash my hands and face, or I'd never get much done.

After carefully and quickly opening and closing the shed door behind me, I walked toward the service pump house in the corner, past the low wall that separated the garden from the more mundane and less attractive working areas of Master Caliostrus's establishment.

Despite the chill and the wind, Shienna was pruning the bare-branched grape vines—even the leaves were used, mainly for the dolmades her mother made and which one enjoyed the first several times they were served, but which became less than entrancing by the onset of spring. Some of the less perfect leaves were used with copper plates for making verdigris, but that green pigment was used only for quick treatments, because it was so fugitive if exposed for long to bright light.

Shienna was a sweet girl, unlike her elder brother, but to say that she was plain would have been an exaggeration that not even an imager could have transformed into truth.

Still, she was sweet, and I did smile. "Mistress Shienna, how lovely your cheeks are today, like the paleness of a fresh white peach . . ."

"They're wind-chapped and red, but you're always so dear, Rhenn. I don't believe a word, but the kindness is appreciated."

"And your hair shimmers with a lustre beyond that of the greater moon in the fullness of harvest." I have never held myself to be bound by the dictates of foolish consistency, particularly when dealing with young women—except, strangely, for Seliora—since most so often professed what they esteemed in a man, and then bedded his exact opposite, while refusing the man who embodied what they said they preferred.

Inconsistency I did not condemn, nor even foolishness, but the hypocrisy of professing an ideal, whatever it might be, and defending it verbally and vociferously, while secretly betraying it by behavior, I generally found disgusting. Unless such betrayal was accomplished with such wit and grace that it might be termed admirable, and then it was what one might call polished evil.

"Rhenn!" Ostrius called from one of the studio windows overlooking the rear courtyard. "You are not grinding or powdering when you are jawing!"

I looked up and smiled politely. "I can't powder when I'm sneezing because someone opened the door and blew powder all over me."

Caliostrus appeared in the window beside his son. "No excuses, now, Rhennthyl!"

"Yes, sir." I managed not to grimace or grit my teeth, but I would have liked to submerge both of them in powdered ochre.

"Don't mind Father," Shienna murmured. "He likes to shout because it proves he can."

"He is the master portraiturist," I replied.

"Well, just don't stand there!" Caliostrus shouted down.

I kept my lips together and resumed my progress toward the service pump house, imagining both Caliostrus and his worthless elder son being consumed by an explosion of paraffin from a container heated too hot on the studio stove because Ostrius was too lazy to check it . . . flaming wax everywhere, and fire washing over them . . .

Whhoosshh!

I turned to see flames exploding through the open window where Caliostrus had been a moment before.

For a moment, I just stood there, frozen.

Crumpp! Some sort of explosion, a small one, shook the upper level. As fragments of glass and some tile fragments pattered on the pavement, my mouth dropped open. The entire second floor of the building—the studio level—had become a mass of flame, and the flames were rising higher.

"Mother! Marcyl!" screamed Shienna.

I ran toward the outside steps and sprinted up them, trying to ignore the heat radiating past me as I scrambled upward past the second level up to the family quarters.

Olavya stumbled out of the upper doorway. "Father!"

"Where's your mother?" I demanded.

"Inside . . . Marcyl's sick."

I only took two steps into the kitchen area before I almost ran into Almaya, who was half-pulling, half-dragging Marcyl. I just grabbed him from her and staggered back outside and down the steps. I could feel and smell my hair being crisped as I hurried down past the second level. I could also smell another sickeningly sweet smell, and I could barely keep from retching as I carried Marcyl into the far corner of the courtyard, where I set him down.

Somewhere in the distance I could hear the fire bells ringing. I knew that nothing would stop the conflagration already raging through the building. Then . . . I did retch.

13

755 A.L.

Images create their own memories.

The fire brigade arrived, but all that they and we could do was to pump water over the rest of the courtyard to keep the fire from spreading. The fire consumed everything so quickly that, well before sunset, only the blackened stone walls stood, the bare remnants of what had once been Master Caliostrus's studio, dwelling, gallery, and apprentice and journeyman quarters. Madame Caliostrus had lost her husband and eldest son, all the paintings, and possibly all the coins in the strongbox. Compared to them, I'd lost nearly nothing—my clothing, what brushes and paints were mine, and close to two golds in coin.

I'd thought about paraffin exploding all over Ostrius and consuming him in fire . . . but . . . how could I have imaged that? All I'd ever done in the way of imaging were tiny things like changing the position of a few brushstrokes of oil on a canvas. It didn't seem possible that I'd done that. How could I have done it? Paraffin and wax could explode into fire if not watched closely—and Ostrius was seldom as careful as he should have been. Yet . . . there had been the lamp I'd found burning on the dressing chest. But what about that second explosion? What had been up in the studio that could have exploded so quickly?

In the twilight, colder than usual for early Maris, the water on the courtyard stones was beginning to freeze in corners that had been shaded, and I had to step carefully as I approached Madame Caliostrus. Her face was more lined than I recalled, and her eyes were focused somewhere else.

"I'm so sorry."

She shook herself. "You did what you could. I don't know if I could have gotten Marcyl out without your help." She paused. "What will you do? There's nothing . . . nothing here."

"I can live with my parents for a little while. Perhaps I can find another portraiture master. Or . . ." I didn't know what else I might do, because I'd have to start over as a journeyman with someone else—if they'd even have me. But I didn't really want to go into the wool trade. I'd end up working for Rousel, because he was better at it. That just would have been too much. "What about you?" I had to ask.

"My sister . . . she can help. They have space." Tears began to well in the corners of her eyes. "Caliostrus . . . Ostrius . . . how could it have happened? Caliostrus was so careful."

I didn't want to point out that Ostrius wasn't, not because her son had been careful, because he seldom was, but because . . . had it really been his doing? I had a hard time believing that a wishful, if hateful, mental image of mine had created a fire and then an explosion, but I also had an equally difficult time thinking paraffin could explode so violently and quickly without Master Caliostrus noticing something before it happened.

"I don't know. I was down in the shed grinding ochre, and I had been almost all day."

In the end, I said good-bye and slipped away, walking

through the cold twilight, shivering as I did, because my warm coat had also gone up in smoke. Spots on the back of my neck offered hot and painful twinges.

My ears and fingers and nose were numb by the time I used the knocker at my parents' house. Even the burns on my neck were numb.

Nellica opened the door. "Young sir." She looked askance at me. "Ah . . . were you . . . there is a dinner."

"Just tell my parents that I'm here because of unexpected circumstances . . . very unexpected." I didn't ask to come in. I was too cold to ask. I just stepped into the front foyer.

"Yes, sir." She eased back toward the dining chamber, where I could hear laughter.

Almost immediately, Father bustled out, and I could sense his glare even before I could see it. Mother trailed him, her brows knit in worry.

"Rhennthyl! What are you doing here?" demanded Father. "Did Master Caliostrus throw you out? I told you—"

"Chenkyr . . . let him speak. He's shivering, and he's not even wearing a jacket. And his clothes are covered in soot."

I hadn't even really noticed that. "There was a fire. I was in the courtyard grinding and powdering pigments. There was an explosion and the entire second level—that was the studio level—exploded in flames. Master Caliostrus and Ostrius died in the fire or the explosion. The whole building was destroyed, the studio, the quarters, the family spaces. I helped the family escape the flames, and tried to assist the fire brigade." I shrugged. "I have what you see."

Father, for once, was taken aback enough that he was silent for a moment. "I see."

"If you would not mind my sleeping somewhere here . . ."

"Culthyn has your old room. You know that," Mother said quickly, "but the chambers where Rousel and Remaya stay are available. They're a bit musty . . . because we weren't expecting them until the first week in Avryl. Rousel doesn't want to leave her alone while she is expecting, and he has to come back to work out the rest of the year's shipments."

"Musty is fine," I said. Anything was fine at the moment.

She turned to Father. "You take care of the guests. I'll be with you shortly."

"Ah . . . yes." He nodded to me. "I'm glad to see you're all right. We'll talk later."

Mother waited a moment, until Father had closed the door off the hallway into the dining chamber. "Are you all right?" She looked intently at me.

"As right as I can be." Considering that I might have imaged the explosion that killed my master and his son, considering I'd lost everything I had personally—except for the clothes on my back and a wedding suit—and considering that I had no idea whether I could find a place with another master artist . . . or what I might do, given the fact that, if I had imaged the explosion, what I had done was effectively murder, as well as an offense against the Collegium Imago.

"You're freezing. I'll have Nellica get you a plate and some hot food, and some spiced wine. You can eat in the family parlor, right in front of the stove. It's still warm, and I'll have her find you some dry and warm clothes. We'll see you after our guests leave. They're most important for your father. He's interested in a large contract for the Navy."

"You'd better see to them."

"After I make sure you get fed and warm."

Before long I was wrapped in a heavy wool robe in front of the parlor stove with a platter of chicken naranje and basamatic rice with orange sauce. I ate slowly, trying to think matters through.

Even if I had imaged the fire into being, I had not really meant to kill Master Caliostrus, but I could not say that of Ostrius. Yet intended or not, the deed had been done, and I needed to discover what else I might image, for I was not about to travel the Bridge of Hopes and make my case to the imagers that I should be considered for their Collegium on the basis of an image that had killed two men.

"Here is some more of the hot spiced wine, sir . . ." offered Nellica, pouring some into the mug on the side table.

"Oh . . . thank you."

"Was it a terrible fire, sir?"

"I'm afraid it was, Nellica. Master Caliostrus and his son Ostrius died. I was working down in the grinding shed when it happened, or I might have been burned or injured."

"Sir . . . there's a burn or two, little ones, it looks like, on the back of your neck. After I serve the dessert, I çan get some ointment . . . and some warm water."

"Thank you. That would be good."

When she left, I took another sip of the hot spiced wine.

My parents would house me for a few weeks, but certainly not longer, not unless I had something firm in mind, and not without more than a few questions, and more than a little pressure to return to the fold, so to speak.

I tried to wait for them, but their dinner went on and on. So I decided to go back to the main-floor guest chamber. Nellica had set out water and towels, and the water was still warm. I washed up and then sat down in the one armchair. I thought I might try to see if I could image something, but I was so tired that my eyes kept closing, and I finally just stumbled over to the bed and climbed under the covers and went to sleep.

Before I knew it, Nellica was knocking on the chamber door on Vendrei morning.

"Your parents would like to know if you would care to join them for breakfast."

That was as close to a summons as possible, and I struggled awake, finally mumbling, "If you'd tell them that I'll be there in just a few moments."

"That I will, sir."

I just pulled on the heavy robe and some slippers that had been left and padded down the back hallway. They were both in the breakfast room.

Mother set down her tea. "Are you feeling better this morning, dear?"

"I'm still tired and sleepy," I admitted, settling into the chair at the side of the oval table.

Nellica immediately set a large mug of steaming tea in front of me, too hot even to sip.

"I can certainly understand, dear, seeing a fire like that

and helping fight it, and then walking all the way here in the cold." Mother sniffed, but sympathetically.

Father finished chewing a mouthful of what looked suspiciously like trout and egg soufflé, took a swallow of tea, and cleared his throat.

I put my hands, still cold, around the mug of tea and waited for the onslaught.

"It's clear the portraiture business wasn't for you," Father said briskly. "These sorts of things, tragic as they may be, aren't to be ignored as portents. I also heard you had the best painting in the journeyman's competition, but that it wasn't picked because it was too . . . unconventional."

The reference to my painting of the chessboard surprised me. I hadn't mentioned it to him or to Mother or Rousel. "Who told you that?"

"I do have my sources, Rhenn. Merely being good at figures and trade isn't sufficient to succeed, especially not in L'Excelsis."

"I take it that your dinner was successful last night?"

"That's likely, but only time will tell." He fixed both of his slightly bulbous eyes on me. "Let us not change the subject. What do you plan to do?"

"I could say that I hadn't thought about it," I admitted, "but that wouldn't be true. I have thought about it, but I haven't come to a decision."

"What's to decide?" He snorted. "You don't have two silvers to rub together, let alone the five golds necessary to pay for another journeyman's position with a master, and that's if you could find one willing to take you on."

"I'm a good portraiturist," I pointed out.

"No, son . . . you're better than good. I saw the one you did of Masgayl Factorius. He boasted of what a great portrait it was and how little it cost him. Your ability is your problem. You're better than many who are masters. Why would they want to raise up someone who could compete against them for patrons as soon as you became a master? You're good enough that the guild couldn't possibly turn you down, even now. That means that no one will take you as a journeyman.

Those who might will fear retaliation from the others, and I couldn't afford the gifts required to get you accepted. It was costly enough when you were just a talented student coming out of grammaire. Now . . ." He shook his head.

"I wasn't asking."

"I know you weren't. That wasn't my point. What I was trying to get across was that if I can't afford that . . . you couldn't, either." He took a deep breath. "But you'll likely not listen to me, not yet. I'd suggest that you make the rounds of some of the other masters and see what reaction you get. Then, we'll talk." He pushed back his chair. "Take your time. You'll need to be sure, and I need you to understand how matters stand." Then he stood and smiled, and it wasn't a cruel smile, but one that was almost sad.

How matters stood? Even with his sources, he hadn't half the idea of where matters truly stood. Yet . . . what if he were wrong? I was a good artist. What if someone would take me on? How would I know if I didn't at least ask?

"All of us, all of us, Rhenn, we do what we can. You'll find that's true for you as well."

I just watched as he turned and left.

"He's just trying to be helpful, Rhenn."

"I know." And I did, but I wasn't finding his attitude as helpful as he thought it was. What was I supposed to do? Come crawling back to the factoring business and work for my younger brother at something for which I had little talent and even less inclination? Or throw myself on the mercy of the imagers of Imagisle? Who knew if they even had mercy?

After finishing breakfast, silently, I washed up, and changed into some older clothes that had been someone else's, possibly my father's or my late uncle's. I'd have to get another razor, and more than a few other items, assuming I could beg or borrow the coins from my parents.

Then I sat down in the chair and tried to image a small box. Nothing happened.

I walked over to the dressing table and picked up a polished bone hair comb—probably one of a pair of Remaya's that she'd left on one of their visits because she'd broken or lost the mate. I set it down and studied it, then concentrated, trying to image its mate, lying on the polished wood of the dressing table beside the first. I didn't see anything happen, but then, as if it had been there all along, a pair of combs rested on the wood.

I'd leave them, of course, if only to confound Rousel and Remaya, except that they'd probably just assume that someone had found or repaired the broken comb.

That proved to me that I could image something beyond oils on canvas. It also reinforced the likelihood that I'd been guilty of killing two men, even if it had been unintentional.

If I wanted to keep painting, I still needed to talk to some of the other portraiturist masters.

14

755 A.L.

In truth lies falsity, in falsity truth.

Chasys's studio was the closest of any of the portraiturist masters' studios to my parents, but it was still a long walk to Daravin Way. Thankfully, the morning was sunny, and the blustery wind of the day before had died down. Even so, my feet were cold by the time I stopped outside the small two-story dwelling that held quarters and studio.

I used the bronze knocker on the outside studio door, expecting Sagaryn to be the one to greet me, but Chasys himself appeared. He was a thin figure, slightly taller than I was, but no one would have thought so, because he was always stooped over. His graying brown hair was frizzy all over, but trimmed short. He wore a leather apron.

"Rhennthyl, is it?" He stepped back and held the door open. "Might as well come in and get warmed up."

"Thank you."

Chasys closed the door. Beyond him was the studio, a space less than a quarter the size I had worked in with Master Caliostrus. On the easel was a portrait, scarcely begun, but I could tell that it was of a young matron, not that I would have recognized many with the golds to commission such a work.

"After I heard what happened to old Caliostrus . . ." He shook his head. "Always knew he was spoiling that boy . . . man, I guess he was." Then he looked squarely at me. "Sagaryn thought you might be asking around. I liked that study you entered in the competition, that I did."

I had the feeling I knew what was coming, but I just said, "Thank you, Master Chasys."

"It's not that I couldn't use another journeyman, especially one with your skills, but . . . we've barely got enough work these days for Sagaryn and me. I haven't seen so little work in maybe ten-twelve years, and it's not just me. Jacquerl and Teibyn were saying the same."

That didn't surprise me, because Sagaryn had mentioned that times were sometimes tight, but I had to start somewhere. "Is there a master you might suggest?"

Chasys cocked his head, then frowned. "I don't know about Estafen or Kocteault."

"I've seen Kocteault's place, but not Master Estafen's . . ."

"Estafen . . . you walked within fifty yards of his place coming here. He's on Beidalt—the short place just beyond the end of Bakers' Lane."

Since Estafen was nearer, that was where I went next, a far shorter walk.

An apprentice opened the side door to the studio, painted white and trimmed with the thinnest line of green—zinc green, but green, nonetheless. Most doors in L'Excelsis were either stained and oiled or painted one color. "Might I say who's seeking the master?"

"Rhennthyl, from Master Caliostrus."

"If you would wait in the foyer . . . sir."

"Thank you." I stepped inside and looked around while the apprentice scurried through another door. Estafen's studio had a foyer, bare, except for a single portrait hung there on the wall facing the door. It was a most flattering image of a redheaded young woman, a subtle but direct indication that he could indeed portray redheads with skill. Still, I didn't think it was that much better than the ones I'd done.

"Yes, Rhennthyl, you do portray redheads well. It's one of your many talents." Master Estafen had slipped into the foyer so silently that I had not even noticed him, far more quietly than I would have expected from such a rotund figure.

"If I might ask, sir, how did you know?"

"I was privileged to see the one you did last year of Mistress D'Whaelyn. High Factor Whelatyn, the brother of the girl's father, asked my opinion. I told him that he could not have done better, except if he had commissioned one from a master."

I smiled politely. The portrait had been better than some of the masters' works with redheads, although I had to admit that the one Estafen had hung was quite good. "Thank you, sir. I imagine you know why I'm here."

"I could pretend to be dense and quite solicitous . . . but I won't." Estafen's smile was pleasant and cool. "I understand Master Caliostrus perished in a fire. Why no one suspects you of any part in it is, first, you were nowhere near where the fire started for half a day and, second, you have so much to lose, and nothing to gain. You, of course, could be my gain, but, alas, I already have two journeymen and two apprentices. None of them are quite so good as you, but they're most competent, and even I do not have enough work for them . . . and you as well." His smile turned apologetic. "Times are difficult, and with a possible war looming and trade and commerce profits being threatened, fewer of those with coins are likely to spend them on portraits." He shrugged. "I wish I could offer you more encouragement, Rhennthyl, but that is how it must be. I trust you understand."

"I understand your situation, sir, and I respect and appreciate your kind directness. You must understand that I must attempt to find a position. Do you have any suggestions, sir?"

"Would that I could suggest a master, Rhennthyl, but I cannot, and I fear that what you seek may prove most difficult. Because of your talent and aspirations, I would hope otherwise."

"As would I, sir." I inclined my head. "I thank you for your time, sir."

"The best of fortune to you, and I would be the first to hope that you find the proper master for your abilities."

I bowed again and took my leave.

As I walked back along the Boulevard D'Este, toward Jacquerl's studio, I thought over Master Estafen's words. They bore an ominous similarity to what my father had said. Estafen had as much as said that he wasn't about to have someone as good as I was as a journeyman.

It was early afternoon, and my feet were getting sore, when I reached Jacquerl's establishment on Sloedyr Way. I wished I'd had the coins for a hack, or the wealth for my own carriage, but if I'd had that, I wouldn't have been trudging from master portraiturist to master portraiturist.

Rogaris met me outside, even before I could knock at the door. "You can talk to him if you want to . . ." He raised his eyebrows.

"But he'll say no."

Rogaris nodded.

"I'll talk to him. I'd like to hear how he turns me down."

"I thought so." Rogaris shook his head, then opened the door—painted a dark brown—and stepped inside, waiting for me and closing it behind me. The wooden floors could have graced the foyer of many dwellings, far finer they were than most studios in which I had been.

Jacquerl stepped away from the easel, setting down a brush, and walked toward me. He was short and dapper, and even his leather apron was almost spotless. "Rhennthyl." He smiled politely. "Rogaris said you would wish to speak to me. I was so sorry to hear about poor Caliostrus. He was a good man, and we'll all miss him." He paused. "I assume you are here to see if there is any possibility of becoming one of my journeymen."

"That was my thought, sir."

"Directly said, as might your father have put it, a direct man, as factors must often be."

"He can be very direct, sir, more so than I."

"That well may be, Rhennthyl, but you never did strike me as a young man amenable to the subtle. That can be both a strength and a weakness in Solidar. That's particularly true here in L'Excelsis, where, at times, one must be subtle and perceptive enough to see what is and why no one will mention it, and yet strong enough to pursue what is necessary without seeming to do so." Jacquerl paused. "Then, there are other times, such as these. Much as I would like to support an artist of your ability, I cannot. The commissions would not be there, and we would all suffer. You will pardon me, I trust, if after all the years I have been a master, I would prefer not to suffer."

"I can appreciate that, sir."

The dapper portraiturist smiled, if sadly. "I wish it were otherwise, but we artists do not make the times. We only live in them and portray others who do." After a pause, he added, "My best to you."

Rogaris followed me out onto the front stoop. "I told you . . ."

"Who told them not to take me on?"

"What?"

"I'm not stupid, Rogaris. I may not be subtle, and I'm certainly not very good at being indirect, but your master as much as said he was told he'd never get another commission, or not many, if he took me on as a journeyman."

Rogaris shrugged. "I don't know. He didn't even say as much to me as he just said to you. I think it's a measure of respect to you that he said as much as he did."

That kind of respect I could do without, especially if it kept me from being a portraiturist. "I know you didn't have anything to do with it."

"You're still going to try others?"

"There aren't that many more left, but I will."

Rogaris nodded. "I thought you might. Best of fortune."

He watched as I walked off down toward the corner and the winding lane that would take me back out to the boulevard. I thought about stopping at the confectioner's on the corner, until I realized I had but a single silver and three coppers in my wallet—and no way to get more, except through the charity of my parents. That grated on my sensibilities, and I could feel more than a little anger churning inside me. Could it be that I was going to be forced to choose between being an ineffective wool factor or chancing the unknown world of Imagisle?

A half glass later, I stepped up to Master Kocteault's studio door.

Aurelean opened it. "Ah . . . dear Rhennthyl. After I heard the news about Master Caliostrus, I'd thought you might make an appearance at Master Kocteault's studio door. Alas, he simply has no position for a journeyman and is unlikely to have one for at least two years."

"Oh? Two years? That's rather precise, isn't it, Aurelean?"

"His very words were that one journeyman was more than enough difficulty and obligation, and since you—he was referring to me, of course—have two years before I'll recommend you for master, there's no point in talking to the poor fellow."

"Is he in?"

"Alas, he is not. He is doing a sitting at High Factor Zatoryn's—his wife. She is striking, quite beautiful, you know?"

"When will he be back?"

"I couldn't say, dear Rhennthyl, and I doubt that he would be able to tell you any more than I have. He might say it more diplomatically, but the message would be the same." His smile was oily, supercilious, and simpering. "We all wish you the very best."

He closed the door as I stood there.

There were still some of the lesser masters I could talk to, but I was getting a very strong feeling that my father had been all too accurate in his assessment of my prospects.

Still . . . there was no point in leaving any stone unturned.

I took a deep breath and began to walk the three blocks to the Boulevard D'Este. I had several milles to go along the Nordroad and then the Sudroad toward the Avenue of Artisans in order to reach the other cluster of master portrai-turists.

Collegium Imago

15

~

*The longest journeys are the ones where one
fears the destination.*

By noon on Samedi, I had visited every portraiturist master
in L'Excelsis, and not a single one had an opening for a journeyman, or at least not for me. Then I did some inquiries
about the possibilities in the Representationalists' Guild, and
the indications there were even less encouraging, because the
guild rules required a full apprenticeship under one of their
masters.

On Solayi, I kept mostly to myself, except for a short time
when Khethila slipped into the guest chamber. She was concerned, but I had the feeling her concerns were not totally
about me, and I wondered if she were having second thoughts
about the proposal from Armynd, but she didn't say, and, the
way I felt, I didn't ask.

After she left, I tried imaging more small things, such as
the comb, and encountered more than a few difficulties. Anything metal was difficult, if small, and impossible, for me, if
large. Familiar items were the easiest, but only those not too
familiar, perhaps because really familiar objects I had taken
too much for granted and not really studied. I did convince
myself that I had some small imaging talent, but I still wasn't
certain how I could have imaged a fire and explosion when I
had such trouble in imaging small household objects.

But then . . . whether I had or not wasn't the question. The
question was what I would do.

On Lundi morning, well before breakfast, I gathered together the few belongings I had and slipped out the side door
of the house when no one was looking. I couldn't pretend that

I wanted to be a wool factor, or any other kind of factor, and at twenty-four, I was already too old to enter the Military Institute or Marine Academy, even if I had wanted to be an Army or Navy officer—which I most certainly didn't. The craft at which I was best was painting, and that didn't seem to offer much future, at least in L'Excelsis. While I *might* be able to find a position in another city, I didn't have the coins to travel anywhere, and I doubted I could get the references I needed, not after what had just happened. Even if I could, I was looking at another five years as a journeyman, assuming I could find someone willing to take me on in cities I didn't even know, and most other cities couldn't support nearly so many portraiturists from what I'd heard. On top of that, I'd doubtless need Father's support, again, and I didn't want to ask more. I also doubted that he'd give it, not the way he'd been talking over the end of the week.

Yet . . . did I really want to go to Imagisle? Did I have a choice, really?

The air was chill, but the sun rose and warmed my back before I'd gone more than half a mille. Thankfully, the air was so still that it felt warmer than it really was. The stretch from the house to the Plaza D'Este wasn't bad, nor was the walk down the Midroad to the Guild Hall, but my feet and legs were getting sore by the time I was on the Boulevard D'Imagers heading toward the Bridge of Hopes, and I sat down on a stone bench a half mille short of the bridge and looked at the gray granite towers of the Collegium Imago rising above the bare limbs of the oaks that lined the riverside park on the east side of the River Aluse. In another month, they might be showing traces of green.

I'd always wondered why the Collegium had used gray granite for buildings, while the buildings on the Council Hill were hardened white alabaster. The imagers had been responsible for building both. As I sat at the edge of the parkway that bordered the boulevard, the wind began to rise, and the marginal warmth provided by the white light of the winter sun disappeared.

I stood, stretched, and resumed my progress toward the

Bridge of Hopes along the wide stone walkway paralleling the Boulevard D'Imagers. Just before the boulevard reached the river and the bridge, it intersected East River Road, and all the wagons and carriages and the handful of riders took East River Road north or south.

I darted across the road and stood on the causeway approaching the Bridge of Hopes, a granite span over the eastern channel of the River Aluse only slightly wider than necessary to accommodate a large wagon or a stately carriage. There were no stone markers announcing its name, nor any guardhouses. The roadbed, paved with smooth granite stones, arched slightly upward, so that the middle of the bridge, some fifteen yards out, was about a yard higher than the causeway at each end. At each side of the span was a wall a good yard high. There were no sidewalks, and the roadbed ran flat from wall to wall.

No one crossed any of the three narrow bridges to Imagisle unless they wanted to go to the Collegium, and not that many did. Both the Nord Bridge and the Sud Bridge, so called because one was north of Imagisle and one south, were the main city thoroughfares for those who wished to cross the Aluse.

I stopped once more, just short of the bridge proper. Did I really want to try to become an imager? I swallowed, forcing myself to think about how little I wanted to hear about what great work Rousel was doing in Kherseilles.

I took a deep breath and began to walk slowly and steadily across the bridge. Once I had crossed, I was faced with a choice. The causeway debouched into three stone lanes. One went north, one south, and one directly toward a single-storied granite building with a gray slate tile roof. I followed the lane to the building.

Outside the building I paused before a stone archway of the style called Glacian, supposedly because it was so spare and cold, just like the Monts D'Glace that separated the fertile and prosperous southlands of Solidar from the northern wastelands. Under the arch was a single door of gray-stained oak bound in shimmering brass. I took a deep breath and stepped forward, pressing the door lever down, then opening the door.

Inside was a foyer, square and five yards by five. The walls were smooth sheets of bare gray granite, without a seam in the stone. The floor was of the same seamless granite, and there was no sign of a join or of any mortaring of any sort where the floor and walls met. The ceiling was of featureless white plaster. Two square arches led from the foyer into short hallways—one to the right and one to the left. Directly opposite the entry was a table, also entirely of granite, except the top surface was polished so smooth that it shimmered. Behind the table sat a young man, wearing a light gray collared shirt, with a waistcoat of a darker gray that seemed to match his trousers, from what I could see. His boots were black. His brown hair was cut short, like that of a soldier or sailor. I walked to the table and stopped.

"Might I help you?" he asked.

"I think I need to see if I'm suited to be an imager."

"What makes you think you might be an imager? You're . . . rather older . . . than most who come across the bridge." He looked younger than I did.

I managed a shrug. "Because I can image small things."

"Oh? Would you mind showing me?"

I thought for a moment, then decided that a replica of the comb I had done the first time wouldn't be too difficult. I concentrated, creating the mental image of Remaya's comb. It appeared on the flat surface, just short of his hand.

For some reason, he seemed surprised, especially after he picked it up. "That's a rather good comb." He paused. "If you wouldn't mind waiting here for just a moment, I think Gherard Secundus might wish to speak with you."

Taking the comb, he stood and slipped away from the table, walking quickly across the foyer and through the archway to my left. After a short time, he returned. "If you would come this way . . ."

I followed him less than ten yards along the corridor—walled and floored in the same seamless granite—before we came to an open door. He stood back and gestured for me to enter.

I did.

Gherard Secundus stood beside the end of a long conference table in a chamber that held nothing besides the table and the ten chairs that flanked it, four on each side and one at each end. He stood beside the chair at one end, and he was attired in the same gray garb as the first imager, insofar as I could tell, but he did look somewhat older, perhaps almost as old as I was, and his short-cut hair was limp and blond.

He gestured to the chair closest to the one behind which he stood. "If you would like to sit down . . ."

I was more than happy to seat myself. My feet were sore.

"Petryn showed me the comb you imaged. It's fine work. What have you been doing?"

"Doing, sir?"

"You're too old to still be in the grammaire, and you don't look like an Institute or university student."

"Oh . . . I've been a journeyman portraiturist, with Master Caliostrus."

He stiffened, just slightly. "Rhennthyl D'Caliostrus? Is that you?"

"Not anymore. I'm just Rhennthyl." I certainly was too old to claim myself as Rhennthyl D'Chenkyr. "Master Caliostrus died in a fire last Jeudi."

He nodded. "Actually, you need to see Master Dichartyn. I'll be right back." He rose and left me sitting there.

A cold shiver went down my spine. Gherard hadn't known me, but he had known my name, and he had been given some instructions. Yet . . . I hadn't told anyone of my intentions to seek out the imagers.

Gherard did not return. Instead another man came. He was, not unsurprisingly, attired in exactly the same fashion as the other two imagers. Unlike them, however, he was older, graying, and radiated a certain sense of power. He also did not sit down. "I'm Master Dichartyn. You're Rhennthyl, formerly Rhennthyl D'Caliostrus?"

"Yes, sir." I stood quickly.

"Gherard said that you imaged a comb. I'd appreciate it if you would attempt to image this." He set a small topless box on the flat table, almost small enough to rest on my palm.

"Might I examine it, sir?"

"Please do."

I picked it up. It was cast or formed from some sort of metal, but none that I knew, for although it was silvery in color, it was far lighter than either iron or silver or even tin, I thought. All I could do was hold it, try to feel it, before setting it on the table and then concentrating on its shape and size and the feeling of lightness. Visualizing the box was somehow both easy . . . and difficult. Even so, another box appeared on the table beside the first. To me, they looked the same, but I was so light-headed that I had to put out a hand to the back of the nearest chair and steady myself. I'd never felt weak before when I'd imaged things.

Master Dichartyn looked at both boxes, then picked up the one I had imaged, then the other, weighing them in his hands. After a moment, he shook his head.

I wondered what I'd done wrong.

"You're an imager, and you could be a very good one. Given your background, Rhennthyl, I can't say that you'll like it, but you don't have much choice."

I already knew that.

16

*Accepting what is not is the hardest aspect of imaging,
indeed, of any profession requiring great skill.*

For the next few glasses, I felt like all I did was walk from
one gray building to another, or from one part of a building
to another, guided by Gherard, rather than Petryn or Master
Dichartyn. In the process, I gathered three sets of gray garments, five sets of paler gray undergarments, black boots,
imaged to fit my feet by a graying imager, as well as a stack
of five bound books. I also got a heavy gray wool cloak for
cold weather and a pair of gloves. One set of garments I
donned immediately, and the other sets and the books were
deposited in the narrow armoire in the stark gray room on
the second floor of the building that housed imagers of the
primus and secundus levels.

"For now," Gherard told me, as he guided me back toward
the first building, which I'd learned was the administrative
building, "you're a primus, but once you know the basics
about the Collegium, they'll probably make you a secundus."

"You don't have to serve a mandatory apprenticeship?"

He shook his head. "It's all by ability. There are some imagers primus who are over sixty. It's all they'll ever be." He
frowned. "There are some masters in their late twenties, but
no one's ever attained a rank above Maitre D'Structure before around forty, and there are only two Maitres D'Esprit."

I must have looked blank.

"There are three levels of regular imagers—primus, sec-
undus, and tertius—and four master levels: Maitre D'Aspect,
Maitre D'Structure, Maitre D'Esprit, and Maitre D'Image.
Most imagers in the Collegium are either imagers secundus

or tertius. Right now, I think there are perhaps fifteen Maitres D'Aspect, but there might be more."

The number didn't surprise me. There were only about that many master portraiturists in L'Excelsis. But with so few, I had to wonder why he didn't know the exact number.

"I hope you read well and quickly, because you're starting late, and you have a lot to learn. You'll have to learn basic chemistry, something about metals, and how living things— trees and people, mostly—work, and all sorts of things about combustion, but that's mostly for self-protection. Master Dichartyn will explain everything in more detail, including your duties."

He didn't say much more after that, but just escorted me back to the same room where I'd begun and left me there, where I sat for a time before Master Dicharytn appeared.

I immediately rose. "Sir."

He waved me back to the seat I had taken. "You have garments, quarters, and books now, I take it?"

"Yes, sir."

"Do you have anything personal that you would like to bring? You can have personal items like quilts, pillows, bedclothing, paintings or wall hangings, small rugs. No clothing, except nightwear, and no personal jewelry."

"No, sir. Most of my personal things were destroyed." And I certainly wasn't about to ask my parents for anything.

Master Dichartyn nodded. "Now . . . let me go over some very basic rules. First, until you are told otherwise, and only by a master, you are not to leave Imagisle. Usually, this restriction lasts anywhere from one to three months, depending on how fast you learn a number of things. Second, after we finish today, you are to take the map I will give you, and you will spend the rest of the day learning where every chamber and building on the isle is. Do not enter any room where the door is closed. . . .

"The dining hall serves breakfast from the sixth glass of the morning, a midday meal between noon and the first glass of the afternoon, and dinner at the sixth glass of the afternoon. Seating is roughly by position. There is a table for imagers primus, one for imagers secundus and tertius, and a third for maitres . . ."

I listened as intently as I could while he outlined the regimen of Imagisle. It certainly didn't seem any worse than being an apprentice.

"As for your duties . . . they're very simple. For now, you're to do what I tell you to do. I've given you your instructions for today. Tomorrow, at the seventh glass of the morning you are to appear and wait outside my study—it's two doors down on the left—until I summon you. I suggest you bring the volume on the structure of the Collegium and the responsibilities of an imager and read it, in case you have to wait. For the next several weeks, your duties will center on learning everything in the books you were given." Master Dichartyn smiled wryly. "I do have a simple question for you. Did you tell anyone you were coming here?"

"Why, sir?" The question made me wary.

"Because about half of the would-be imagers don't tell anyone, and then the civic patrollers contact us to see if you're here. It's much simpler if you just write a note or two to those who might worry, one way or another. In your case, I'd presume, to your parents, since you no longer serve a master portraiturist. There should be some blank stationery in the armoire in your chamber, as well as a pen and ink. If you'll bring the notes back to me this afternoon, I'll have them dispatched immediately, and your parents won't have to worry too long. Oh . . . and you do get a stipend. It's not much, only a silver a week, but we do feed and clothe you. Once you learn the basics of the Collegium and pass a proficiency test, or the equivalent, most of which you've already demonstrated the ability to do, you'll become a beginning imager secundus, and that's worth two silvers a week. Stipends go up in accordance with your position and how long you've been with the Collegium. So does the amount of space allocated to you."

A silver a week wasn't grand, but it wasn't absolute poverty, either, and the position already sounded better than attempting to be a wool factor under my father and Rousel.

"There are several other basics. First, we expect daily bathing and frequent laundering of your garments. This is for both safety and sanitary reasons, the rationale for which will become clear before long, I trust. The bathing is your responsibility; the laundering we have arranged, so long as you place your dirty garments in the proper place. There are two barbers in the building with the dining hall, and we expect short hair, as you may have noticed . . ."

When he finally finished what seemed a thorough overview of what was expected of me, he stopped. The smile vanished.

I waited, worried about what might come next.

"A word of caution, Rhennthyl. Imaging goes far beyond merely creating objects, and it can be dangerous," Master Dichartyn said. "That is why I must ask you not to attempt any more imaging except under supervision of a master or at his or her direction. Most people have no concept of what we do, and we try not to let them know. That is one reason why some imagers primus leave by the Bridge of Stones."

All guilds had secrets, or at least their practitioners did. Master Caliostrus had ways of combining waxes, oils, and pigments that he had sworn others did not know, and revealing such secrets could cost an apprentice or a journeyman his position, not to mention a stiff flogging. But . . . death? I tried not to swallow. I failed.

Master Dichartyn offered a crooked smile. "One advantage of dealing with someone older is that you understand fully the implications of what I'm telling you. Let me explain. We are not cruel, and contrary to what people may say, we do not arbitrarily or otherwise kill young imagers. Very few imagers face disciplinary hearings. Most who leave by the Bridge of Stones do so because they made a mistake in imaging. You have been a journeyman portraiturist. What will happen if you mix paraffin, oils, and waxes over a very hot flame—without care?"

"You'll get a fire." I wasn't about to mention possible explosions.

"Or worse." He nodded. "Now . . . what would happen if

an imager attempted to image all three right on a stove or in a fire?"

I winced.

"Exactly." He paused. "Now, that's really not a good example, but it should give you an idea of what can happen. There are many substances that should not be combined in imaging, and that is why you need to study the books you received and follow instructions most carefully—especially as you become more experienced."

I couldn't help but frown in puzzlement at his last words.

"In imaging," he explained, "the more you learn to do, the closer you are to great danger, from many sources. You may not understand this now, but for your own safety, please believe me until you understand why it is so."

There was no mistaking the earnestness or the direct concern in his words, but I did wish that he had not used the paraffin example, because it suggested that he had at least a suspicion that my imaging had led to Master Caliostrus's death. Yet . . . if he believed that, why would they accept me even as a beginning imager?

Abruptly, he stood. "That is all for now." He extended a folded paper, the map, I presumed. "Before you explore, please write those notes and bring them back. Knock on my door, once, then wait."

"Yes, sir."

He nodded, then turned and left me holding the map.

I walked slowly back to my new quarters, and I managed it without looking at the map. There I settled down at the table desk.

Writing the letter to my parents was hard, but better than having to tell them in person what I planned before I knew whether the Collegium would accept me. If I'd been rejected, what could I have said? Besides, then Father would have come up with another of his sermons on what was foreordained and how it was clear I was not meant to be a painter or an imager and how I shouldn't have tried to escape my calling as a wool factor. Still I spent so much time trying to get the words just right that there was less than a half glass left before noon by the time I handed the letter to Master Dichartyn.

"You spent some time on it. Good. I'll have it delivered this afternoon. Oh . . . you also have a letter box in the rear corridor outside the dining hall, next to the boxes that hold the newssheets. You don't have to pay for them, but you are expected to read them—regularly. By this evening, your letter box should have your initials on it—IP-RH. That's your position followed by the first two initials of your name. If someone else has those initials, you might have three or four letters following your position."

"Thank you, sir."

Master Dichartyn just nodded. "Tomorrow morning. Here." Then he turned and closed the door to his study.

With the map in hand, I began to navigate my way to the dining hall. I had gotten up early and eaten nothing except some bread I'd pilfered from the kitchen on the way out. The dining hall was within a larger building at the west side of the quadrangle behind the administration building where I'd first entered the Collegium. It was not nearly so large as I had imagined, and it held but three tables, a small table set cross-wise across the hall, and two longer tables parallel to each other and perpendicular to the smaller table. There was no one at the short table when I entered the hall just before the bells struck noon, but a number of younger imagers stood around the table on the right.

I eased toward a redheaded young man. "Is this the table for the imagers primus?"

"For us lowly primes, it is. You're new, aren't you?"

"About as new as one can be," I admitted. "I crossed the bridge this morning."

"I'm Etyen."

"Rhenn, or formally, Rhennthyl." As I stood there, I realized that several of the figures were young women. I also saw two older women coming through the arched doorway, one of them gray-haired, and walking toward the adjoining table, and a third, also gray, moving toward the masters' table with a white-haired man. I must have stared because Etyen spoke again.

"There aren't that many women imagers, but Maitre Dyana is a Maitre D'Structure. She's old, though."

"How old?"

"She must be forty-some . . . or even older."

Somehow, I didn't think of someone my mother's age as old, but Etyen couldn't have been much more that fifteen, and he must have come to Imagisle right out of a grammaire.

"Where did you come from?" I asked.

"From Asseroiles."

Asseroiles was more than three hundred milles to the northwest. "Are all the imagers in Solidar here at the Collegium?"

"Oh, no, but most of them are. There are three other Collegia. There's Mont D'Image to the north . . . well, it's actually northwest of Asseroiles, somewhere off the Nord Pass through the Glaces, and Westisle outside the harbor of Liantiago, and Estisle near Nacliano."

That did not seem like many imagers, not for a land the size of Solidar, stretching close to three thousand milles from coast to coast. How had the Council kept it all together before the steam engines of the ironway had made land transportation faster than horse and wagons?

"Rhenn here is new," Etyen announced.

Several of the primes looked at me. Most didn't, and people sat down as they came in without any blessing. I thought that odd.

"What room are you in?" asked Etyen.

"Fourteen, second level, south wing."

Someone nodded.

". . . Corsarius's room . . ."

Several primes looked hard at the fresh-faced youth who had murmured the words.

"What happened to him?" I asked.

"Bridge of Stones," replied Etyen in a low voice, adding even more quietly, "We don't talk about it."

Not talk about it? When someone died?

"You didn't come here straight from the grammaire?" asked the prime across the table from me. "Oh, I'm Lieryns."

"No. I've been an apprentice and a journeyman portraiturist. I didn't realize I could image until a little while ago."

"Sometimes, it's like that." Etyen nodded. "But I always knew."

"You always know everything," murmured someone.

There were low laughs from more than a few primes, and as I looked down the table, I was relieved to see that there were a few who looked as old as I was, if not older.

"You were a journeyman. You actually painted real portraits, then," observed Lieryns.

"Some," I replied, looking at the large bowl of rice being passed down the table. Behind it followed some sort of dish in sauce. "Mostly of girls and cats."

"Cats?"

"My master said I had a talent for painting cats, and I don't think he liked dealing with girls and cats. I did do one portrait of a factorius."

At that point, the rice arrived, and I served myself a solid helping, as well as of the tomato-sauced fowl chunks that followed. If the lunch fare was any indication, I was going to be better fed than I had been by Madame Caliostrus.

Sometime later, after several mouthfuls of food, and some swallows of a fair red plonk, I took another look around the table before speaking. "I haven't had a chance to read anything. What do we do, besides study?"

"Whatever we can," replied Lieryns. "I'm helping Master Schorzat in the chemistry laboratory, but mostly I image little things out of glass for his experiments."

"I thought there was a counselor-advocate to the Council named something like that."

"That's his brother," someone said. "Scheorzyl. Master Schorzat said his father wanted everyone to know the two were brothers."

My eyes went to Etyen. "And you?"

"I'm still working on making shapes with metals. They're harder."

I couldn't say that I learned all that much at lunch, but everyone was certainly friendly. Afterward, I left the dining hall and, map once more in hand, began to explore and try to memorize where everything was. No one seemed in the slightest interested as I wandered all over Imagisle and the buildings of the Collegium that Lundi afternoon. I still worried about why no one talked about it when someone died.

17

Imaging is based on what is, but, without great care, what an imager feels can change what is.

As Master Dichartyn had intimated, I had to wait to see him on Mardi morning. I sat on a bench outside his study reading the thin volume on the Collegium. I'd made it through fifteen boring pages when he opened the study door and an older imager walked out, somewhat stiffly.

"You may come in, Rhenn."

His study was small, not more than three yards by four, with a long narrow window, open just slightly. The space held two enormous bookcases, a small writing desk, two filing boxes stacked on top of each other, and two chairs, one with a cushion and arms and one straight-backed and not too comfortable. I sat in the straight-backed chair.

"Before we start, I'd like you to know that one of our messengers delivered your letter to your parents yesterday, late in the afternoon. They were relieved to know that you were safe."

"Thank you, sir." Mother was relieved at my safety; Father was more likely relieved I hadn't embarrassed him or gotten into some difficulty that might have cost him in some fashion.

"Now . . . when was the first time you realized you might have imaging abilities?"

"Not until around the first of the year." It was actually just a bit earlier, but not much. "I was working on a portrait, and I couldn't get the area around the eyes right. I could almost see how it should be—and then it was right, even with my brushstrokes, as if I'd painted it just as I'd visualized it. I still wasn't sure that it was imaging. I thought maybe I'd painted it and then imagined that I'd imaged it."

"And . . . ?"

"Maybe a month later, I was working on another portrait, and it happened again."

"And you didn't come to us then?"

"No, sir. I'd heard about how imagers had turned the alabaster walls of the Council Chateau into stone harder than granite, and how they could image parts of machines into being. All I could do was image just the slightest bit of oil paint."

"All?" Dichartyn laughed. "There are some seconds that can't do that and never will."

"I didn't know that, sir. It seemed very insignificant to me, and I was beginning to get commissions—the kind where patrons asked for me personally."

He nodded. "What did your master say?"

"I never told him about the imaging. When he talked about the imagers, he was quite clear that I should never want to be one, that most died young, and most of the rest never amounted to anything."

"He said that?"

"Yes, sir."

"I can see where that might give you pause, Rhenn." He leaned back in his chair and fingered his clean-shaven chin.

All the imagers were clean-shaven, I realized, unlike artists, most of whom had beards or mustaches, if not both. In that way, at least, I did fit in. I'd never liked beards.

"So why did you finally seek us out?"

"Master Caliostrus died in the fire. No one else would take me on. My father wanted me to become a wool factor. I thought that my small talents for imaging might gain me a place here."

"At least you have no grandiose delusions about your ability." Master Dichartyn laughed again, not totally unkindly, I thought. "It's very good that you did. Before long, you would find yourself imaging in ways that could be most destructive. Perhaps you already have and do not even know it. Sooner or later, that imaging would have been noticed by others."

"Not know it, sir?" I had an idea of what he meant, but I wasn't about to say so.

He smiled, knowingly. "You know more than you reveal, Rhenn, but I will explain, because you don't know as much as you think."

I accepted the rebuke silently.

"All people have daydreams, or dreams or nightmares, or wishes. We wish that things would appear or disappear, but what happens if the person who wishes that is an imager?"

The lit lamp! I swallowed.

"Did that recall something, Rhenn?"

"Ah, yes, sir. Sometime after the first time I imaged the oils, I had a dream, and I dreamed that it was so dark that I could see nothing, and I wanted light. The lamp on the chest woke me, because it was lit, and I thought I'd wicked it off. I never believed that I'd imaged the light. I'd just thought I'd been so tired . . ."

"You are *very* fortunate you came here before any of the imaging you did came to light." Master Dichartyn's voice was stern. "You have quarters to yourself. Do you know why?"

"No, sir."

"Every set of quarters in the Collegium is not only stone-walled but has a layer of very thin lead plate between the two courses of stone and under the floor tiles. The windows are all glazed with leaded glass, and those windows which open are designed with louvers so that there is no direct passage of air—or thought—in and out. Do you think that the Collegium went to that expense merely for your comfort?"

"No, sir." I had a very uncomfortable feeling about where his words were leading.

"No imager ever sleeps with another person, even his wife, and I mean sleep, not lovemaking. The Collegium is here not only to educate and improve imagers, but to protect others from those very same imagers. Yes, we have privileges, and those who become masters can live quite comfortably, and those who do marry can live in pleasant dwellings on the north end of the isle, but never think that we do not pay a high price for those abilities and services that we provide. Imagers who must travel are accompanied by obdurates, and, if they cannot sleep within iron or lead, must take strong drugs of the type that do not permit dreaming when they sleep. Those who serve in the Navy have lead-lined cabins, very small cabins, because lead is heavy, and weight is critical on many vessels. Those who marry and live here have special separate sleeping chambers in their dwellings, and must indeed live here unless they have the wealth to build similar quarters elsewhere in L'Excelsis. You can never spend an entire night with a woman you love, or any lover, for that matter, not unless you remain totally awake, and when you are tired, even that could present a danger to her, especially if she has malleable tendencies."

Master Dichartyn paused, letting me take in his words.

"One of the reasons for the initial restriction to Imagisle is so that you come to understand what damage even the least able of imagers can inflict upon others. A second reason is that you need to understand that we are so few that we could be wiped out to the last person. Yes, some of us do have the ability to kill or change others, and you are one of those who already possess that ability, whether you know it or not. But while we are individually powerful, for the most part, no one of us could face even a moderately large group of armed men and survive. We therefore do our best to show the Council our goodwill, our self-discipline, and our indispensability to Solidar. No imager can be allowed to jeopardize the others. Is that clear?"

"Yes, sir." It was more than clear; it was frightening. I wanted to ask about the imager who had lived in my quarters before me, but decided it would be best to wait on that.

"Good." The smile returned. "I'm going over to the laboratories this morning. I'd like you to accompany me. Then, this afternoon, I will give you a short talk on the introductory aspects of chemistry, and you will begin to read that volume. Tonight, after dinner, you are to read the first section of the book on the government and history of Solidar. You will find it is not like any history book you have read before, and I will be asking you questions about what you have read in both volumes when we meet tomorrow morning." He bounded out of his chair. "Now . . . let us go to the laboratories. . . ."

Already, I was beginning to wonder about the two sides to Master Dichartyn's being—the stern and the cheerful. He seemed to switch from one to the other both quickly and comfortably, but the change was more than a little disconcerting to me.

18

Learning requires unlearning.

On Meredi morning, right after breakfast, I picked up a newssheet and checked my letter box, not expecting to see anything, and found an envelope there. I recognized my mother's handwriting. I opened it quickly and began to read.

Dear Rhennthyl,
Your father and I were most relieved to know that you are safe at Imagisle. While your father had hoped that you would see your way to following his example in the wool trade, he accepts the fact that you must follow your own destiny. We both wish you the best in becoming an

*accomplished imager. In the note that Master Dichartyn
sent accompanying your letter, he said that you had great
promise. He also said it could be several months before
your initial training would allow you to leave Imagisle,
but that, beginning in Avryl, you could have visitors on
Solayi. I look forward to that.*

I swallowed as I finished the note. The way I read it,
Mother was relieved for me, and, since I wouldn't be a wool
factor, Father was glad to get me out of his hair.

At the thought that Master Dichartyn had sent his own
note, I gathered the three books—*Natural Science, History
and Politics of Solidar,* and *Imagers' Manual*—under my
arm and hurried down the walk of the quadrangle toward
Master Dichartyn's study through a blustery wind, barely arriving before the seventh glass began to ring out from the
tower of the Anomen D'Imagisle, located at the south end of
Imagisle.

As on Mardi morning, I had to wait, but I immediately
began to read more in the *Manual,* the part dealing with the
responsibilities of an individual imager. I'd only read another
page when Master Dichartyn opened the door and motioned
me into his study and into the chair across from his writing
desk. He remained standing.

"You've read the second section of the *Manual,* haven't
you?"

"I haven't quite finished it, sir."

That got a slight nod, but whether it was of acknowledgment or disapproval I couldn't tell. "What is the first responsibility of an imager?"

"To follow the Imagers' Code under all circumstances."

"What does it mean by 'all,' Rhennthyl?"

The manual hadn't gotten into definitions. "At all times
and places, sir?"

"What if you can't?"

"It's a responsibility, sir."

"You aren't answering the question." His voice remained
patient.

"I'm only guessing, sir, because the *Manual* doesn't say, but I would think that it means whenever and wherever it is physically and mentally possible."

"A definition such as yours stands at the edge of a very steep precipice."

"Yes, sir. People like to say that they can't do something because they're too tired or that they can't think clearly. I don't think the Code accepts those kinds of excuses. I was thinking more about broken bones or mortal injuries."

"You think correctly on that. The Code is not for convenience. It is designed for the survival of both the individual imager and the Collegium. What is meant by the prohibition on creating any form of duress on any individual who is not an imager?"

That had seemed obvious to me, especially after what he'd said the day before. "One doesn't threaten anyone, or say anything to give them cause for fear, and one doesn't take actions which create fear of either the imager or the Collegium."

"Very good. Why?" His questions from the *Manual* went on for a good half glass. Then, abruptly, he switched subjects. "That box I gave you to image? Do you know what it was made of?"

"No, sir. It was metal, but not a metal I've ever seen."

"You didn't think to look in your science book and see what it might be?"

"No, sir." I knew what was coming next.

"Tomorrow, I want you to tell me what it is, and why we use it for imaging tests. Now . . ." He extended two objects and placed them on the edge of his writing desk. One was a simple carved hollow cylinder, no more than a thumb's length in diameter and about the same in length. The second was also a cylinder, but solid and less than a quarter the size of the first. Both looked to be made out of bone or ivory, and neither had any markings on them. "I have an exercise for you." He turned the larger cylinder sideways, then placed a ruler on one side and a book on the other so that it wouldn't roll. He handed me the smaller cylinder. "Try to image a cylinder just like this exactly in the middle of the larger cylinder."

"Won't it fall?"

"It should, unless you know a way to stop gravity." He smiled. "That's not the point. You've already shown that you can image small things on a flat surface. One of the next steps is to image something into a place that's not so easy."

I took the cylinder and held it, letting my fingers run over it. Then I concentrated on imaging one just like it in the air in the middle of the larger cylinder. Nothing happened.

Master Dichartyn didn't seem surprised. "Take both cylinders with you and keep trying. It may take a while, but you should be able to figure it out."

I slipped both into the larger inside pocket of my gray waistcoat.

"This morning, you can accompany me on one of the small riverboats. Some of the primes are going to try imaging on the river. You might as well see if you can do it."

"Yes, sir." I didn't ask why imaging was harder on a boat, not after failing at the exercise he'd just given me. I just followed him out of the building.

Master Dichartyn walked briskly along the east side of the quadrangle, right into the fangs of the wind, a wind that had gotten even stronger and colder. We crossed the open space at the northeast corner of the quadrangle and took the stone lane another half mille north past the walled herb and vegetable gardens, now mostly fallow, until we came to a set of three piers.

Five primes stood on the southernmost pier, clearly waiting for Master Dichartyn. The riverboat didn't seem all that small to me—not at almost fifteen yards long. It had only one deck and the steam engine was in the rear, just forward of the paddlewheel, in a raised and covered enginehouse. The wheelhouse was roughly in the middle of the boat.

I looked out at the river, running as rough as I'd seen it, with whitecaps on the waves.

Master Dichartyn gestured for us to cross the narrow

plank to the boat, then followed after me, because I trailed the other five. A bearded sailor vaulted off the bow and untied the line fastened around an iron cleat, then jumped back aboard before the boat swung downstream with the current. The paddlewheel began to churn as the boat headed out into the river. Once it cleared the calmer water around the pier, it began to roll, then pitch as the pilot turned upstream into the current. Spray sleeted over the bow, and some splattered down like fat raindrops where I stood with the others, just forward of the wheelhouse.

One of the primes, a chubby fellow who looked barely out of grammaire, was turning pale before the boat was even ten yards away from the pier, and another just stood frozen, his right hand clutching the railing so tightly that his fingers looked like a claw. I had to spread my feet a bit to keep my balance as the boat continued both to roll and pitch.

"The first exercise is to image a cube like this," began Master Dichartyn, holding up a black wooden cube perhaps three digits on a side, "and to image it on the center of the third deck plank inboard. This one." He pointed with the tip of his boot. "You first, Geoffryn."

"Yes, sir." The chubby prime closed his eyes and seemed to tense all over.

A misty shape appeared on the plank, then solidified into a muddy black oblong box.

"A cube, Geoffryn." Dichartyn's voice was louder, rising over the wind and the engine, but he did not sound angry. "Do you recall the shape of a cube?"

"Yes, sir."

"Jakhob, you try."

"Yes, sir." The thin prime who had been clutching the rail just looked at the deck plank. His imaged creation was almost a cube, if slightly angled and muddy black, and it appeared above the next plank inboard, possibly because the riverboat was rolling.

The next three primes managed to image cubes, generally close to the center of the designated plank.

"Rhenn?"

I didn't like doing imaging in public, but those watching couldn't have been any more critical than Master Caliostrus had been when I'd begun as an apprentice. First, I visualized the cube, shimmering and black, and then I added the positioning.

The cube appeared, almost mirror-like, right at the middle of the plank. As it did, I realized that it was a shade too large. Abruptly, it shimmered, then reappeared as the correct size. I did feel a trace light-headed, and had to put my hand out, steadying myself on the railing.

"You used too much effort," observed Master Dichartyn. "You should have paid more attention to the size the first time."

"Yes, sir." Still, I was pleased, even if he didn't happen to be. My cube looked better, and had been imaged in exactly the right position—even the first time.

"Now . . . you're going to try the same thing—except I want you to balance your cube on the railing on the far side of the boat."

Three of the other primes couldn't image anything that far away, and one could only create a blob. The last one managed a decent cube on the railing, as did I, but they both slid off into the river when the boat rolled as the steersman made a turn.

"Take us back!" Master Dichartyn finally ordered.

That afternoon, Gherard took me on a quick tour of the various shops and laboratories, as well as showing me workshops in the large gray building north of the quadrangle. Then I went back to my quarters and began reading.

Already it was clear that Master Dichartyn's assignments varied widely.

I had to stay up later than I should have on Meredi night, but I did discover that the box was made out of a metal called aluminum. The science book described it as a light whitish blue ductile and malleable metallic element almost never found in pure form in nature, but common in natural chemical compounds. It was extremely difficult to refine, requiring special techniques involving potassium, and the price was something like a hundred and fifty gold crowns a pound. The little box I'd imaged, if I'd done it correctly, might have been worth ten crowns or so. No wonder Master Dichartyn had pocketed it—except I knew that he wouldn't have made off with it, even if the Collegium rules hadn't prohibited using imaging for personal gain.

The science book was different, almost strange, because it mixed things I'd learned years before with things I'd never heard or thought about. One section had a detailed set of plans for a steam engine of the type used on the ironway, but the next diagram was of a mining water pump, and beyond that was the axle assembly for a carriage or coach. But there were also anatomical drawings of human beings, very detailed, and clearly taken from dissections of cadavers.

The book on history and governing was the thickest of all, and to me, the hardest reading, even just leafing through it. The book led off with the Five Rights of Citizens:

> All citizens, whether they be men or women, are of equal stature before the law and as such may hold and dispose of property; unless an authority has reason and evidence to the contrary that is sufficient for indictment in a court of justice, they are presumed innocent.
>
> The laws of the Council take precedence over any and all local or administrative regional laws, ordinances, or restrictions, but no law enacted at any level may identify as a criminal offense any action already taken, nor encumber persons or seize their property without just compensation, save taxes levied on all and approved by the Council.
>
> No individual, whether a citizen or an alien, may be imprisoned without formal charges being posted and without being informed of those charges.
>
> All citizens, unless under indictment for a crime or imprisoned for such, have the right to travel unfettered throughout all regions and territories.
>
> All citizens have the right to petition the Council for redress of any harmful action taken by any level of govern-

ment, including the Council itself, and all such petitions will be made public.

After that, there were sections on everything, but as I riffled through the pages, just trying to get a sense of what was there, some paragraphs stood out.

A minimum of three Council members must be from areas within fifty milles of either east or west coast . . . and no more than three Council members can be from within 200 milles of L'Excelsis, with the exception of the sole representative of the Collegium . . . misrepresentation of domicile mandates immediate removal from the Council, loss of a master's position, and a fine of 1,000 golds. In the case of a High Holder, such a violation will also include forfeiture of one-fifth of all lands and assets . . .

With fifteen Council members in all, those non-imagers from L'Excelsis could never comprise more than twenty percent of the Council—something that I remembered vaguely—but the penalties I didn't recall ever seeing.

No refuse or waste, including any liquids, from a factorage or manufacturing facility, nor from any agricultural or commercial activity, nor from any watercraft, shall be allowed to flow or be placed into any waterway, nor shall any human refuse be so allowed . . . whether it be from an individual, a town, or a city . . .

According to that, if I read it right, even a cow couldn't piss in a stream, not without bringing a fine down upon the owner.

Rates for freight on any ironway must be levied on the basis of weight and cubic displacement. Those rates must be approved by the transportation subcouncil and by the Council before taking effect and must be posted for one month before being imposed. Changes may not be submitted

more than once a year . . . Freight or cargo accompanied
by a Council representative or a representative of the Collegium Imago has priority over all other freight . . .

That was suggestive in more ways than one, but of what I
wasn't sure.

19

*Imaging is as much an art in arranging perception
as in changing reality.*

I woke early on the following Mardi morning, and after I bathed
in the communal shower room—with water that I had the feeling was never less than chill—and shaved and dressed, I sat
at the writing table in my room, looking at the two cylinders.

More than a week had gone by quickly, each day following
a similar pattern. Breakfast, examination and instruction by
Master Dichartyn, which could be over in half a glass or drag
on for as many as two, followed by some sort of imaging exercises, lunch, some other activity involving observation or
instruction, ranging from watching experiments in the chemistry laboratories to watching or learning how to handle machinery in either the woodworking shop, the metalworking
shop, or the model shop. Then, when I was worn out, I had to
read and study.

On Lundi, the day before, I'd had to admit to Master Dichartyn that I still hadn't figured out the skill of placing a
small cylinder in the empty space in the middle of the larger
cylinder. It shouldn't have been that hard, because some of
the younger primes had been doing something like it, if un-
intentionally, during the imaging exercises on the boat.

Master Dichartyn had just looked at me as if I were truly stupid and then gone on to ask questions about what I'd read, and what I hadn't, in the *Natural Science* book. He'd started by asking me how much air weighed. I'd never thought about air weighing something, but since a barometer worked by measuring the change in the weight of the air, I suppose I should have.

Air weighing something . . . had his question been as random as it had seemed? But if air weighed something, then I really wasn't trying to image something into what I'd thought of as an empty space. Why was it easy to image something on a table? Because the air could be more easily moved? Or because I didn't have to work to hold it up as it was being imaged?

I kept thinking about it, all the way to breakfast, where we had oat porridge, along with raisins and bread, and two thin strips of bacon.

I concentrated on the idea of imaging a raisin into the middle of a spoonful of the oat porridge. A small gout of porridge spouted up.

"Don't let the masters catch you playing with your food," murmured Thenard.

Someone else snickered.

I forced myself to eat the mouthful of porridge. The raisin tasted fine, but should I have swallowed it? I looked at the handful of raisins sprinkled on top of the porridge. Why couldn't I image one of them into my spoon? Wouldn't it be easier than trying to create a raisin?

Carefully, I took another spoonful, one without raisins, and then concentrated on the raisin on the top of the porridge farthest from me, visualizing it disappearing and then reappearing on top of the porridge in my spoon. The one raisin vanished, then reappeared on the spoon's porridge. I could feel my forehead beginning to sweat, but . . . I'd done it.

That raised another question. I could feel the energy it took to do imaging, but why hadn't I when I'd first begun to image? Or was it that what I'd done was so slight that it just hadn't taken that much imaging? But then, there was the fire . . . Or hadn't I noticed the effort then because I'd been so angry and then so involved in trying to help the children out of the house?

Later, as I walked across the quadrangle through the misting rain toward Master Dichartyn's study, I couldn't help thinking about what I'd done . . . and what it suggested. By using imaging to move something, I'd also proved that it was possible to remove things, at least to some degree. If one removed the cartridge from a pistol aimed at one, or if one removed . . . I winced. I wasn't certain I wanted to explore those possibilities, not immediately. But I was beginning to understand exactly why the Collegium insisted on such strict rules and such secrecy.

As was usual, Master Dichartyn's door was closed, and I sat down on the wooden bench and began to read the sixth section of the *Natural Science* book, which dealt with metals and various alloys. I couldn't help but wonder how effective imaging might be in creating some of them, at least in small quantities.

Before long, the study door opened, and one of the older imagers, a secundus or even a tertius, departed.

"Rhennthyl?"

I immediately closed the book, stood, and hurried into his study and took my place on the still-warm seat used by the previous imager.

Master Dichartyn came right to the point, as usual. "Only a few of you will ever work in the laboratories. So why does the Collegium insist that you study science and work and practice in the laboratories?"

I gave the best answer I could come up with. "So that we'll be better imagers?"

"That's true as far as it goes."

I didn't know what to say to that.

"Your brain knows more than you recall at any one point," he went on. "If you have a friend, when you meet him, you don't think about everything you know about him at that moment, do you?"

"No, sir."

"But all your actions and all your words take into account everything you know, even if you don't try to remember it all. What all this study about metals and science is designed to do is to provide the same kind of knowledge in order to improve your imaging skills."

That made sense. I could see that I was already doing that.

"Do you have the two cylinders?"

"Yes, sir."

"Let's see what you can do."

I had the two cylinders, but I hadn't even thought about them. Still, was air any different from porridge, except thinner? I took out the larger cylinder and propped it in place sideways on Master Dichartyn's writing desk with two books that had been on the far corner, then held the smaller cylinder. Could I just move it? I decided to try.

The small cylinder vanished from my hand and appeared in the middle of the larger one, hanging there for just an instant before clunking down onto the bottom side of the larger cylinder.

Master Dichartyn's eyes flicked from my hand to the cylinder and then back to my hand. He nodded slowly. "I wondered when you'd make that connection. Some never do. They're the ones who remain seconds."

"Seconds?" I blurted.

"Right now, you have the raw talent of a tertius, but you don't have the understanding necessary for a secundus of your ability. We're going to have to work on that."

"Yes, sir." While I didn't mind the work, I didn't much care for the way in which he'd expressed the words.

"Why is there an absolute prohibition on an imager using his ability for any significant financial advantage for himself personally or for any other individual?"

I'd read that section. So I answered quickly. "That would give him or her an unfair advantage over others, and that would create anger against the Collegium."

"That's very true, Rhenn. It's also very incomplete. Can you think of other reasons?"

"It might create conflict within the Collegium."

"That's also true. I'd like you to think about that for a while. Let's look at it from another perspective. You mentioned that you'd used imaging in painting your own work, but what if you used your talent to copy an entire painting of a master?"

"It wouldn't work, sir. There's too much detail."

Dichartyn sighed and gave a weary smile. "That's a bad example, then. Let's take something simpler, a gold crown. You could probably image one now. Doing so would leave you weak and dizzy, if not in far worse shape, and, even if I said you could, you shouldn't try it, but in time you would be able to image a handful or so of them, at least in the right place. They'd be real gold, not counterfeit, and no one would be the wiser. Why would that be wrong?"

"Besides the fact that the rules of the Collegium forbid it?" I had to think about that. "I don't know that I can answer that, because that sort of imaging is work, and if I imaged real gold pieces, what's the difference between painting a portrait and receiving golds and creating the golds. I mean . . . someone mines the ore, and someone smelts it, and someone coins it, and they all get paid. So where is that any different from my imaging a gold crown?"

This time I got a cold look. I just waited. I really did want to know.

"Did you get a number of extra assignments in the grammaire, Rhennthyl?"

"Yes, sir."

"I can see why. Let me see if I can make this clear with a different example." He frowned. "You've heard of the Cyella Ruby, haven't you?"

"The one that sits on the scepter of the Priest-Autarch of Caenen? Yes, sir."

"He's the High Priest. What about the Storaci Emerald?"

"Yes, sir."

"What if you imaged an exact, an absolutely perfect duplicate?"

"Sir? How would I ever get close enough to see the originals?"

He gave me an even colder look.

"There'd be two," I said slowly, trying to think what he wanted.

"Yes, there would be." He paused, then asked, "What makes them so valuable? What would happen if you imaged two . . . or three?"

"Oh! They wouldn't be so valuable because they wouldn't be so rare."

"That's one thing. How would the owners feel about being robbed of that value? And if the valuable object has some religious context or value . . . does the duplicate? Who could tell which one happened to be the one with that value? What might the Caenenans do?"

"They could do . . . anything." Of that, I knew enough to be sure.

"You need to think about what the imagers of the Collegium image—you've seen some of what we do—and why we're so careful about what we allow to be imaged. Also, not all things imaged turn out to be true duplicates. I trust you can see what difficulty that might create."

"Yes, sir." I paused. "What laws would punish someone who could image who got caught by making a bad copy?"

"If that person happened to be an adult, older than eighteen, and the crime was a major offense, he or she would be executed. Committing any major crime through the means of imaging is a capital offense. Younger than that and they'd be sent to us for training. Some of them don't survive training, but imagers are rare enough that it's worth the effort. Some of the young ones don't know it's a crime, and some don't see that they have any choice."

I felt cold inside. I was older than eighteen, and I had been when the fire and explosion had killed Master Caliostrus.

"That should give you enough to think about for now. Today, I'm going to take you over to the machine shop for some instruction. Then you can help with cleaning duties."

That sounded like an assignment I'd rather do without, not that I had any choice, especially after what I'd just learned.

20

⁓

*Death always creates either guilt or fear, whether
either is acknowledged or accepted.*

I'd been at the Collegium three weeks and three days, and on
that Meredi morning, Maris eighteenth, I was shivering, even
under my covers. I forced myself from bed and peered
through the window. Outside, fat flakes of snow were drifting down from a dark gray sky, although not more than two
or three digits' worth of snow had piled up on the quadrangle. Spring was supposed to arrive in a week or so, but it felt
like winter. I pulled on the robe that had come with the room
and trudged out and down to the showers and bathing rooms.
I did like being clean and clean-shaven. I just didn't care
much for the process, and not in winter-cold weather.

On the way back from the shower, as I climbed the steps
from the lower level, I heard heavy footsteps. When I stepped
away from the landing, I saw two obdurate guards in their
black uniforms carrying a stretcher. They headed down the
hallway to an open door two doors before mine. Before I
reached that doorway they had entered and then come out,
carrying a figure covered with a blanket. One of them closed
the door one-handed, bracing the stretcher on his knee for a
moment, and then they strode toward me. I flattened myself
against the stone wall of the corridor, not that I really needed
to. Neither looked at me, but most obdurates ignored those of
us who were still learning.

Standing in the corridor between the now-closed door and
mine were two imagers. Although they looked to be several
years younger than I was, they were both seconds, and had
said little to me. From what I could see, they were both upset

and trying not to show it. The taller one's cheeks were damp, as if he'd wiped away tears.

"Who was that? What happened?" I asked.

The two seconds looked at each other, then at me, before one replied, "Mhykal. On his way to the Bridge of Stones."

All I knew about Mhykal was that he was an imager secundus, that he was of average height, a few digits shorter than me, and that he hadn't bothered to speak to me when we passed in the corridor or on paths of the quadrangle. People that young just didn't die in their beds. When they didn't answer, I asked again, "What happened?"

"Who knows? It happens. Not often. We're not allowed to say. Ask your preceptor."

Ask my preceptor? Before I could say more, one had retreated to his room, and the other was headed for the stairs.

I returned to my room and dressed deliberately, trying to make sense out of what I had seen. An imager second was dead, and his body was carted off. No one acted as if it were strange. Sad, but not strange. I'd heard that more than a few would-be imagers died, but hearing that, and seeing it the way I just had—that was another thing.

After finishing dressing, I stuffed my books in the canvas bag I'd been issued and then made my way downstairs and through the snow to the dining hall. I managed to find Etyen and sat across from him.

"There were obs in the quarters this morning, and—"

"I heard that. Mhykal, they said. I could have guessed he'd be one. He was always talking about what he could do."

"Like you?" quipped Lieryns.

"No. More like you."

"Me?" Lieryns's voice almost squeaked. "I wouldn't be that stupid."

"Why would Mhykal be one?" I pressed.

"You can get in real trouble imaging by yourself . . . least until you're a third or a master. There are lots of things that can happen. Be best if you asked Master Dichartyn to explain."

Lieryns and another prime nodded.

I ate slowly, but good as the fried ham, hot biscuits, and white gravy were, I had trouble finishing what I'd served myself. After breakfast, I had to wait almost a full glass for Master Dichartyn. I read the newssheet I'd picked up, glancing over the top story that mentioned the recall of the Solidaran ambassador to Caenen, and then took out the history text and started rereading the pages I'd already read three times.

"You look worried, Rhennthyl. Trouble with the assignment?"

"No, sir." I straightened. "Sir . . . before we start . . . might I ask a question?"

"Briefly."

"Sir . . . I was coming back to my room after my shower, and two obdurate guards had a stretcher coming out of a room . . . and there was a body under the blanket. The two seconds there wouldn't tell me what happened. They said that they couldn't and that I should ask you."

"That's something you'll probably see again . . . unfortunately." Master Dichartyn looked across the desk at me. "About a third of the imagers who arrive here as primes die before they complete their secundus training. Close to forty percent of the more talented ones die."

Forty percent, and he'd already told me I was talented?

"Would you like to guess why?"

That was the last thing I wanted to do.

"There's a saying about imagers. There are bold imagers, and there are old imagers. There are no old bold imagers. While it's not totally true, it's close enough. Tell me why."

When he put it that way, I did have an idea. "Imagers who are bold try things that are different, or in different ways, and too many things can go wrong?"

"We all occasionally have to try to accomplish different things. It's a matter of approach. The Collegium believes a graduated and cautious approach is the best one. We try to build on what you already know or have been taught. Some young imagers think they know better. Sometimes they do, but most of the time they don't. If they keep trying things without enough knowledge and supervision, sooner or later something will go wrong, often very badly, in one of two ways. They either kill themselves doing what they've been told not to do, or they get killed when they go out in L'Excelsis and start boasting or carrying on."

"Can't you do something?"

"What else would you suggest? We caution you. We try to show you how to do things in the proper ways. Are you saying we should have a tertius or a master spend every moment of every day with those of you who are talented? Or accompany you every time you leave Imagisle? We don't have enough masters or thirds for that. Besides, anyone who really wants to do something boldly stupid will find a way, and, frankly, we can't afford to have imagers who are stupid or publicly arrogant. There's too much at stake."

Master Dichartyn felt that way about the Collegium, but that wasn't much help to me personally.

"Now . . . tell me how the founding of the Collegium changed the history of Solidar."

I pushed away my anger at his near-indifference and tried to think. According to the history book, because imagers could create certain chemical compounds and metals, the Collegium gained greater and greater power by supporting the emerging merchant class, until the last absolute ruler and rex of Solidar, Charyn, ceded power to the Council once he realized that the imagers no longer supported him and were prepared to back a violent change in government, if necessary. So, being wiser than most rulers, Charyn requested a position as head of the Council for life, as a "transition," and everyone heaved a sigh of relief. Now, the book didn't put it quite like that, and I had the feeling it had been nowhere near that neat and sanitary. "The Collegium allowed a growth of collective power of the imagers . . ."

I just hoped that Master Dichartyn wouldn't be too critical, but I was still worried about what happened to Mhykal. I'd lit a lamp through imaging in my sleep and killed two men while not really trying to do so. Could I do something stupid enough to kill myself . . . and not even know it?

21

Love is both a name and an act; too often
the name triumphs.

On Solayi, the twenty-ninth, I struggled to get out of bed
in time for breakfast. There was no requirement to go to
breakfast—or any other meal, for that matter. But for me,
there weren't any alternatives. Even if I had been permitted
to leave Imagisle, I'd earned something like four silvers since
I'd been at the Collegium. That might have paid for two
cheap meals off the isle—and neither would have been as
good as what I was getting fed. At the noon and evening
meals, we even had wine, a grade that was a good plonk.

At breakfast and dinner, even during the week, I seldom
saw more than a few masters, and they were those who had
various duties on that particular day, nor were there that many
of the older thirds or seconds. On weekends there were even
fewer, but that made sense, because even the junior imagers
could leave Imagisle—except for primes in my position.

I was one of the older imagers there, except for Maitre
Dichartyn. He was seated at the masters' table with Maitre
Chassendri, and she was the maitre of the day. I sat down at
the primes' table, less than half full, and a rather sleepy-eyed
and groggy Lieryns staggered in and sat across from me.

"Too early," he mumbled.

"But it's a long time to lunch on an empty stomach."

"Wouldn't be here otherwise."

I glanced around the dining hall. There were only twenty
or so at the seconds and thirds' table, and perhaps fifteen at
the primes' table. "You don't go anywhere on weekends?"

"Nowhere to go. My people live out near Rivages. Ironway

only goes partway, and it's nearly a day trip each way. Besides, they're all foresters."

"You don't have much to talk to them about?" I asked, before pouring tea into my mug.

"Never did. Less now, and everyone else in town, they all look the other way if they see me coming. Oh, they'll talk if you greet 'em, and they're nicer to me than they ever were when I was just Leam's youngest, but they all look so uncomfortable."

"They respect you, then."

"More like fear. You'll see." Lieryns looked down into his mug of tea, inhaling slightly and letting the warm vapor caress his face.

"How did you discover you were an imager?"

"My da had too many pitchers of plonk one night, and he came storming in, tried to beat up Callia, and he ran into a door that wasn't there. Our cot never had doors, just curtains. Didn't take him long to figure it out, seeing as only Callia and I were there. Ma and the others were at Aunt Nuela's—she'd just had her third. Anyway, drunk as he was, that stopped him."

"It did?"

"Oh, he wanted to flog me into ribbons, but the masters don't like it, and there's a finders' fee for letting the Collegium know about imagers. It's a gold most places, maybe more if we're not beaten. Master Ghaend said that it was cheaper than holding hearings or trials for people who killed young imagers. My da was more than happy to claim it, and I usually bring them a silver or two when I visit." Lieryns shrugged. "It's easier that way. Besides, I've got a feeling that Llysira just might have the talent. She's nine now." He took a mouthful of the rubber-like omelet and chewed slowly. "Anyone else in your family show up as an imager?"

I shook my head. "Not that I know, and the way my mother's family keeps track of the bloodlines, I think they'd know."

"Maybe they do know. Maybe they don't say. Some folks don't want it known. They say it's a mark of the Namer."

Was Lieryns right? How could I know if people never

talked and I'd never known enough to ask? "You're cheerful this morning."

He yawned, then shook his head. "You ever have a girl-friend?"

"Once or twice. The first married . . . someone. The other . . . I don't know." That wasn't totally true. I'd enjoyed the company of a few over the years, and, for some reason, the only two I'd thought of in response to his question were Remaya and, sur-prisingly, Seliora, yet I'd only danced with Seliora on two or three of the Samedi get-togethers. "What about you?"

Lieryns shook his head. "The first time I went home, her mother met me at the door and said that she was . . . indis-posed. She's been indisposed ever since. For me, anyway. You'll be fortunate if your former girlfriend will even look at you."

That hadn't been one of my greater concerns. Even so, I had to wonder if I'd have that problem . . . or if I'd even have another woman friend. That was something else I'd find out.

After breakfast, I donned the heavy gray cloak and began to walk along the west side of the isle, on the gray stone walk just above the gray stone river walls. Council Hill was two and a half milles away, but the day was gray and hazy enough that I could barely make out the white walls of the Council Chateau, and they looked to be a lighter shade of gray in the distance. The gray everywhere was getting to me. I wondered how different it had looked in the days before Charyn, when L'Excelsis and Solidar had been ruled by a rex. Had any of the early rulers been imagers? None of the history books I'd read had said, only that the early imagers, especially those serving Rex Regis, had been a necessary adjunct to the power of the rex. But then, none of the books mentioned the Namer, either, or Rholan the Unnamer, or even the mark of the Namer.

I ambled north past the workrooms, the armory, and an area of dwellings, both large and small, seemingly placed with care in a park-like setting. North of the houses was a small park that covered the northern tip of the isle. Although it had benches and a small hedge maze, I saw only three people—a young woman with two small children, barely more than toddlers. I kept following the stone walk back down the east side of the isle. Just before I reached the Bridge of Hopes, I saw an imager, with broad shoulders and light brown hair, walking across the bridge. On the far side, waiting for him, was a magnificent black coach, trimmed in silver, with a matched pair of blacks. Standing beside the open door of the coach was a young woman, with long white-blond hair flowing out from a silver and black scarf. Even at that distance, I could tell that she was young and beautiful. I just stood and watched as the imager neared.

She leaned forward and kissed him on the cheek, but briefly, and with a certain stiffness. Then he helped her into the coach and followed. I couldn't help but wonder not only who the imager was, but how he'd managed to have a lady friend so clearly wealthy. Perhaps there was more appeal to being an imager than I'd realized.

22

Those who do not understand imaging assume that any rule of the world can be circumvented or changed with enough skill; that is so erroneous that it cannot even be termed wrong.

On Jeudi, the thirty-third of Maris, at the end of breakfast, when I'd been at the Collegium for over three weeks, Master Poincaryt stood and announced, "All members of the Collegium, except those with specific exceptions from me, will assemble in the gallery of the hearing room of the Justice Building at the eighth glass this morning." Then he sat down.

"That's trouble for someone," murmured Etyen.

"More than trouble," added Thenard.

According to the *Manual*, hearings were mandated only for serious offenses against the Council or the Collegium, but there was nothing written that indicated that the hearings were public and that all imagers were required to attend.

"Do you know who it is or what they did?" I asked.

"No," said someone down the table. "We only find out at the hearing."

If you did something against the Collegium, could someone just appear with guards or whatever and whisk you off to a cell and a hearing? Could they do that to me, for imaging the explosion that killed Master Caliostrus and Ostrius? I tried not to shiver, and instead looked down at the remnants of the egg-fried toast on my platter.

I slowly finished them, as well as my tea, then made my way to Master Dichartyn's study, where I sat on the bench in the hall and began to leaf through the manual.

"Rhennthyl?" Gherard stood in the middle of the corridor. "Master Dichartyn is preparing for the hearing. He asked me to tell you to read the eighth section of *Natural Science* and the first section of *Practical Philosophy*. He will see you tomorrow morning."

I went back to my room and struggled through five pages of the philosophy book before making my way out into the misty fog that covered the quadrangle and then to the Justice Building. The gallery consisted of wooden high-backed benches set on tiers that rose behind a low wall that separated the hearing area from the gallery. The benches flanked a central set of steps, coming down from the upper entry on the second level of the building. The lower level was very simple. At the east end was a dais a yard high, and from the middle rose a solid black desk with a high-backed chair behind it. The floor was of seamless stone, but a walkway of black stone, seemingly with no joins separating it from the gray stone around it, ran from the archway at the west end of the chamber to the foot of the dais. At the end of the dais, above where the black stone ended, was a black railing two yards long, supported at each end by black posts.

By the time all the imagers had filed in, the gallery was close to filled. From my best count, there were close to two hundred imagers there, ranging from primes just out of grammaire to graying masters.

"Is this most of the Collegium?" I looked toward Thenard, seated on my right.

He shrugged. "This is only the third hearing I've been to. That's in two years. There have been about the same number at each hearing."

Outside, the bells began to ring the glass.

"All rise." The words came from a dark-haired master standing by the west-end archway facing the dais.

As we stood, the justice—or hearing officer—walked in and then settled himself behind the desk on the high dais. He wore a long gray robe, like the Council justices, except his was trimmed in both black and red, instead of just black.

"You may be seated," announced the bailiff. "Floryn, Imager Tertius, step forward to the bar."

Floryn didn't have much choice about stepping forward. His hands were manacled behind him, and a thick black blindfold covered his eyes. Two large obdurates in black escorted him forward until he stood before the black railing. I wondered about the blindfold, but only for a moment. It would be hard to image anything if you couldn't see, and the position of the manacles prevented him from lifting his hands to remove the blindfold.

"Who stands to defend the accused?" asked the justice.

"I do." Master Dichartyn stepped forward and stood beside the small table on the right, facing the dais.

"Who presents the case for the Collegium against the accused?"

"I do." The thin blond man who stepped up to the table on the left was a man I'd seen at meals, seated at the masters' table, but whom I did not know.

"State the charges against the accused."

"The accused faces three charges. The first charge is that of counterfeiting the coin of Solidar, to wit, by imaging a gold crown that was not pure gold and by attempting to use such to purchase goods. The second charge is that of employing imaging to obstruct a civic patroller in the course of his duties. The third charge is that of attempted murder in the use of imaging against a master of the Collegium."

After the reading of the third charge, I could hear several indrawn breaths, particularly from a row of thirds seated below us.

"How does the accused plead? Guilty, Not Guilty, No Plea, or For Mercy?"

"For Mercy, Your Honor," offered Master Dichartyn.

The justice looked directly at Floryn. "Floryn, your defender has offered a plea of For Mercy. Do you accept that plea?"

"Yes, sir."

Even I could sense the defeat and resignation behind those two words.

"Seat the accused."

The two guards led Floryn to the table on the right of the chamber, behind which were two chairs. After they seated him in the one away from the black stone walkway, they took position behind him, while Master Dichartyn seated himself in the other chair.

"Proceed, Advocate for the Collegium," stated the justice.

The blond master nodded to the bailiff, who announced, "Sandyal, Imager Tertius, to the bar."

A lanky and sandy-haired imager who looked to be close to my age walked from the west archway forward to the bar.

"Sandyal," began the justice, "do you understand that you are required to tell the whole truth, and that your words must not deceive, either by elaboration or omission?"

"Yes, sir."

"Proceed."

"Sandyal," began the Collegium advocate, "you had a conversation with Floryn on Solayi, the twenty-ninth of Maris. Would you please recount what Floryn said he was going to do?"

"Yes, sir. We had the afternoon off. We had to be back for chapel, but the afternoon was ours, and Floryn said that he wanted to have some spiced wine and pastries at Naranje. I told him that I didn't have enough coin, and he said that he'd take care of whatever we bought. . . ."

Sandyal must have recounted every detail of the afternoon, and it took more than half a glass, but the gist was that Floryn didn't have any coin and that he imaged a gold. The serving girl thought it felt wrong and put it in a water-tester. It came up false. She told the owner of the patisserie, and he summoned the patrollers. Because she had also said that it came from a young imager, they summoned the duty master. The summons didn't reach the master before a patroller arrived. Floryn realized something was wrong and ran out of the patisserie. The patroller followed, and Floryn imaged something that tripped the patroller.

"Did you see what happened after that?"

"No, sir, except that Floryn ran across the boulevard—the Boulevard D'Imagers, sir—and down an alleyway. I just waited there in the patisserie. I didn't have any coins, and . . . I thought Floryn was going to pay. He said he would."

"I have no further questions." The advocate looked to Master Dichartyn.

"I have no questions."

"You may leave the chamber for the anteroom, Imager Sandyal."

Sandyal inclined his head, then turned.

"What will happen to Sandyal?" I whispered as he walked back down the black stone.

"He's restricted to Imagisle for the next year, and then they'll review it."

I didn't hear who said that, but it wasn't Thenard.

"Master Ferlyn to the bar."

The angular master who strode down the central black stoneway didn't look all that much older than I was. He had dark mahogany hair and a sharp nose.

"Master Ferlyn," asked the justice, "do you understand that you are required to tell the whole truth, and that your words must not deceive, either by elaboration or omission?"

"Yes, Your Honor."

Ferlyn's answers to the advocate's questions paralleled what Sandyal had said.

"Did you see what happened to the civic patroller?"

"Yes, sir. Floryn imaged a timber right before his knees. The patroller wasn't threatening Floryn. He was trying to keep him in sight until I arrived . . ."

That also made sense to me.

". . . when I caught sight of him in Milliners' Lane, Floryn tried to use imagery to block my vision of what was happening as well as making a personal attack on me. The details are in the documentation presented to the court. I request that those details not be stated in open court."

The justice looked to Master Dichartyn, but Master Dichartyn did not object to that request. For an instant, I wondered why, but then realized that there was a greater disadvantage to Floryn in having the details made public.

After Master Ferlyn's testimony, statements were read from the serving girl and from the patroller, and the patisserie owner.

Then the bailiff called out, "Vanjhant, Imager Secundus."

In moments, the chubby and blond young imager was standing before the bar, having been exhorted to tell the truth.

"Vanjhant, you listened to something that Floryn said several weeks ago. I would like you to recount what you heard."

"Yes, sir." Vanjhant licked his lips. Then he swallowed. "We were leaving the dining hall, and it wasn't that good that day. Least we didn't think so. Morryset was wishing that he could have a real pastry, and Floryn said that was no problem, that all you had to do was image a few silvers or a gold, whenever you wanted to, and go out across the bridge and buy one. . . . Chastyn said it wasn't that easy. Floryn said that so long as the gold was on the outside and it was heavy enough, anyone would take it . . ."

The advocate asked several more questions, then dismissed Vanjhant. After that, three more junior imagers were called, and all confirmed that Floryn had made similar statements.

"Are there any additional witnesses?" asked the justice.

"No, Your Honor." The words from both masters were nearly simultaneous.

"Your statement, master defender."

Master Dichartyn stood. "I cannot contest the facts in this case. Floryn did in fact image a gold that did not contain the proper gold content. Had the coin been of the proper weight, at most he would face a disciplinary hearing, assuming that his duplication of a coin would ever have been noticed. His life is at stake because his abilities were not equal to his self-confidence. As with many young people who realize that they have made a terrible mistake, he panicked. He attempted to stop a patroller from following him, but he did not use imaging in a fashion intended to do any permanent harm to the patroller. The same is true of his use of imaging against Master Ferlyn. Because his actions were based on poor judgment, and because his actions showed clearly his desire not to create permanent harm or injury to anyone, I request that he receive mercy, and that he be sentenced to five years in the duplication section of the machine works, and that he be restricted to Imagisle for ten years, and that any violation of either condition result in immediate execution of the sentence that would otherwise be imposed."

The way Master Dichartyn put it, the request for mercy seemed fair enough. Certainly Floryn would not be getting off lightly, but it was clear that the alternative was his death.

"Your statement, Advocate for the Collegium."

The blond master stood. "My colleague has presented an eloquent argument, and one that, in other circumstances, I would in fact endorse and support. Were Floryn an Imager Primus or Secundus, with perhaps a year or so at the Collegium, I would not hesitate to do so. Had he been here even two, or perhaps three years, I would probably support a plea of For Mercy. But Floryn has been at the Collegium for over five years, and his actions, as shown by the statements he made to all levels of young imagers, embody a thoughtlessness and a recklessness that, in time, could threaten the very Collegium itself. This was not the impetuous and isolated act of a young imager, excited over new abilities and unaware of the consequences. These acts were those of an arrogant and self-centered man who could only consider his own pleasure, and who created disruption and brought discredit upon the Collegium—all for a few mugs of spiced wine and two pastries. For those reasons, I must ask that the plea of For Mercy be rejected, that Floryn be found guilty of the charges levied against him, and that the appropriate sentence be carried out." The Collegium advocate inclined his head, first to Master Dichartyn, then to the justice.

"Floryn, Imager Tertius, to the bar."

The two guards half-urged, half-lifted Floryn from his chair and escorted him back to the bar, facing the justice. Then they retreated several paces and waited.

The justice stood.

"All rise!" ordered the bailiff.

I stood, feeling queasy as I did so.

"Floryn, Imager Tertius, this court finds as follows. First, the facts and testimony confirm that you did in fact commit the offenses with which you have been charged. Second, given your length of study at the Collegium, acceptance of a plea of For Mercy is not warranted. Third, the penalty for conviction on each of the three charges is death."

Floryn winced, as if struck.

Silence filled the space, from the court area all the way up through the gallery.

Floryn shuddered, then collapsed on the black stone floor before the dais. He twitched several times. Then he was still. The two burly guards stepped forward and picked up the body, lifting it easily up and onto their shoulders, and then carried it out.

The robed master looked down from the dais. "The sentence of the Collegium has been enforced. Justice has been done. So be it." After a moment, he turned and walked out through the smaller archway at the rear of the dais. Then, all of those below turned and departed.

I just stood there for a long moment, even as the imagers around me began to leave.

23

*Guilt provides far more effective motivation than greed,
for greed can at times be satiated.*

On Jeudi night, after too many glasses studying and worrying, I was particularly glad for my private quarters, because
I did not sleep well, not with dreams of facing a hearing for
the death of Master Caliostrus running through my nightmares. Not with the vision of the Collegium advocate recit-
ing how I had imaged my portraiturist master to death
because I hated his son. I also had visions of some master
imaging poison or something like it into my body, and being
unable to do anything at all against such an attack.

When I woke on Vendrei, far earlier than normal, with the
early-spring light barely seeping from cloud-covered skies
through leaded-glass windows, more questions rushed through
my brain. Had in fact the justice imaged poison into Floryn
as he had stood before the bar? Was that technique another
reason for all the anatomy drawings in the *Natural Science*
volume?

I shook my head. That technique could be applied to everything, if an imager happened to become strong and talented enough. But then, if that were so, of what use were
obdurates?

Breakfast at the prime table was as quietly boisterous as
usual. That bothered me as well, but I said nothing and did
my best to enjoy the ham rashers that went with the omelet
casserole. There were no letters in my box, not that I expected any, and I trudged through the misting drizzle that
sifted down on the quadrangle as I made my way to Master
Dichartyn's study.

The door was open, and he was waiting for me. "Did Gherard deliver your assignments?"

That was a pleasant way of asking whether I'd read them.

"Yes, sir. The philosophy is hard."

"If it weren't hard, it wouldn't be philosophy." He closed the study door behind me. "You look tired. Are you all right?"

Rather than answer that, because I wasn't certain how I was and didn't want to say, I said, "Might I ask you about the hearing, sir?"

"You may ask. I may choose not to reply."

"Why did Floryn not speak for himself? Is that forbidden?"

Master Dichartyn shook his head. "It is not, and most accused do speak for themselves. Floryn had a greater chance for mercy if he did not speak. It was not a great chance, but it was the only hope that he had."

"Might I ask why?"

"I would deny that to most junior imagers, Rhennthyl, but I will answer you on two conditions. First, you are never to repeat my answer to anyone, and after this meeting, not even to me. Second, you will make an honest attempt to explain to me why I am allowing you this liberty." He looked at me. "Do you accept those conditions?"

There was more there than I knew, but I also needed to know. "Yes, sir."

"Floryn's life was at stake, but what he did not understand is that his and every imager's life is at stake every moment of every day. Now . . . it is not arrogant to believe in one's true capabilities, but it is arrogant for an imager to declare those capabilities publicly, and it is unacceptably arrogant to overstate one's capabilities, particularly when we exist on the sufferance of the people. Floryn was incapable of speaking without revealing his arrogance, and arrogance from junior imagers does not set well with masters, particularly not with Master Jhulian, who was serving as justice. I tried to coach Floryn as to how he should speak, but his anger was so great that anything he said would have ensured his death."

"Was he a talented imager, sir?"

"Almost as talented as you may become, if you work hard at it." He paused. "Why have I let you ask this?"

The answer was obvious. It was also painful. "Because I could become arrogant, as Floryn was."

"Not quite. You would never be as blatantly, flagrantly stupid, and you are not the type to boast. You could be the type to boast to yourself and to act in anger, but in subtle and cool arrogance, when you feel yourself wronged or disregarded. How did you feel when you did not win the journeyman's competition last Ianus?"

"Wronged," I admitted, even as I wondered how he knew that, because I'd never mentioned it to anyone at the Collegium. "My work was better than those that won, and several masters admitted as much indirectly."

"Then why did you not win?"

I wanted to blurt out that they had played favorites, but there was more behind it, and Master Dichartyn would not have asked the question if there had not been. "I would guess that part of the competition was to determine who would follow the traditions and the unspoken rules of their guild."

"If that were so, then did you deserve to win?"

"I deserved to win on artistic merit, sir, but not if the prizes were to be given on blind compliance with unspoken rules."

Master Dichartyn nodded. "You don't like to admit that, do you?"

"No, sir."

"What happened to you there is the same everywhere else. All groups, whether the guilds, the Council, the High Holders, or the Collegium, have both formal rules—and these can be spoken or written or both—and unspoken rules. The unspoken rules must be observed and deduced by each member of the group, and in large part, acceptance and success depend on recognition of and mastery of those unspoken rules. Young people usually understand that such rules exist within their own groups, but many have a harder time accepting that other groups have such rules and that at least some of those rules may differ greatly from the rules they have already learned. Often they get most angry when the rules of those older and more powerful do not follow their preconceptions."

"Floryn didn't like it?"

"He came from a part-taudis background where one has to boast and overstate to be respected. He could never overcome that early training."

"What early training do I need to overcome?"

Master Dichartyn laughed, somewhat sadly. "I cannot say with certainty. I would judge that you need more to overcome your rebellion against early training. You may have become an artist because you disliked the constant counting and use of coins as a measure of success. Yet that is the measure of success in commerce, and you must accept the fact that such is the case with most people. Taxes and tariffs on commerce support all of Solidar, as well as the Collegium. Most people can reckon only with numbers, and they measure their worth by comparing their possessions and coins against those of others."

I would have to think about that.

"Rhennthyl . . . I have another question. All techniques and questions about imaging, beyond the very basic exercises that you've already had, are handled in private discussions and exercises with a master. Why do you think this is so?"

"You want to see what we can do when no one else is around. That would keep others from getting hurt if I did something really wrong."

"You could hurt me."

"No, sir. I don't think so. You wouldn't give us the instruction and tools if you didn't have some way of protecting yourself." I paused. "I don't know if I understand about obdurates, not after . . . yesterday. I mean . . . how can they . . . protect against . . ."

He just smiled. "There are two kinds of imaging. The process is the same, but the effects are not. If you try to change the way someone looks or their physical being through imaging, it will not affect an obdurate, and if you're strong enough, the slightest suggestion will change a malleable. Most people won't be affected, and the effect usually won't last unless the imager is a master, generally a higher-level master. That is not the same as if one uses imaging as a weapon, if you will, but to do that, one must be able to see . . ."

I understood. The obdurate guards might have been close enough to be affected by personal shaping imaging, if they were not obdurates, and the blindfold provided the rest of the protection. "Are imagers obdurates to some degree?"

"Almost always, but there are a few who are not. You are definitely not one of those." He cleared his throat. "Now . . . if we might return to my question. Are there any other reasons why we instruct you alone without others present?"

"You want to keep control of the situation?"

"What do you mean?"

"It could be that with more imagers around . . ."

This time, he shook his head. "No, one of the reasons for the isolation is for your protection. I can protect myself. You can't yet. What if another junior imager made a mistake?"

"Oh . . . I should have thought of that, sir."

"After you thought of my being hurt, you should have. One of the problems that young men have is that while they can think of what may happen to others, they don't think how their actions or those of their peers may result in great injury to themselves. Think of it this way. After the hearing, didn't you worry that someday some master might charge you with some offense?"

"Ah . . . yes, sir."

"Did you think about the fact that if you avoided doing unwise or prohibited acts you wouldn't have that worry?"

I hadn't, not really.

"You see?" He raised both eyebrows.

"But, sir . . . most of us have done things we regret or worry about, sometimes before we knew better . . ." I wasn't quite sure what I was suggesting was wise, but I *had* to know.

He nodded slowly. "That is true for many of you, generally for the most gifted, such as you. You are referring to the unfortunate death of your previous master, are you not?"

I just sat there, stone-cold. I shouldn't have said anything, and yet . . .

"You're surprised? I receive copies of all the patroller reports in L'Excelsis. We look at them carefully where deaths and strange occurrences are involved, particularly when a younger person is involved. It is often suggestive. Very few of the most talented imagers do not have a death or an injury to another that has come from their discovery or development of their ability. The only question is whether they worry about it or suffer for it. Those who do not suffer, or understand that they should, are useful only for the Army or the Navy, or for the machine works, for they have no restraints. I'm glad you brought the matter up, and even gladder that you did indirectly, at least indirectly for one who is not experienced in indirection."

"You knew and let me become an imager?"

"Had you not come to us, Rhenn," Master Dichartyn said quietly, "within the month, you would have been found dead on the street. You had the wisdom to understand what you had become, and the strength, even with the worry you carried, to cross the Bridge of Hopes. Why do you think it is called that?" His smile was wry. "Hope is always an expectation beyond anticipated reality, is it not?"

Put in that light, I had to agree with him. I nodded.

"You have learned what some never do. What you have not learned, but will, is that you will always bear the costs of what led you to become an imager, one way or another."

I had the feeling that he might be right.

"Next Vendrei, at the noon meal, Master Poincaryt will include your name among those imagers being promoted from primus to secundus." He smiled, but the smile vanished almost immediately. "Now that we have taken care of those issues . . . define a philosophical proposition for me, by its structure."

I had to think about what I had read, but some of the dread I had carried for weeks had lifted. Some of it.

24

~~~

Those who believe consider themselves blessed;
that is their consolation and their burden.

The first Solayi in Avryl, the first of the month and the last day I was actually restricted to Imagisle, Mother came to visit me. The afternoon was partly cloudy, but the morning had been sunny, and the air was pleasant. Her coach crossed the Bridge of Hopes right at the first bell of the second glass of the afternoon. I was waiting just off the bridge on the isle side, because that was where the *Manual* stated visitors should be met.

Charlsyn eased the coach into the waiting area, but he avoided looking directly at me as I stepped forward and opened the door.

Mother stepped out, and I offered her a hand, because there was no mounting block, although the gray granite curbing was somewhat raised above the paving stones. She wore a long black skirt and boots, with a short maroon jacket over a cream blouse, with a pale green scarf and maroon beret-style hat. In her own way, she made it all look good together.

"You're looking well, Rhenn." Her smile was practiced as she inspected me, and wider after she saw no obvious faults in my dress and deportment. "The gray does suit you, although it is a bit severe. The cloth of the waistcoat and trousers looks to be choice wool."

"I hadn't noticed, not exactly."

"Well . . . your father will be pleased to know that. It's a good grade for imagers, very fine, but not ostentatious."

"Master Dichartyn will be pleased to hear that." As soon as I spoke, I wished I hadn't said it that way, and I quickly added, "He feels imagers should never be arrogant or ostentatious."

"You should listen to him. No one should be." She smiled, and a twinkle appeared in her eyes. "I've even suggested that to your father once or twice, but don't tell him that I told you so."

"I wouldn't think of it." I couldn't help but enjoy the thought of her suggesting that he was arrogant.

We strolled down the walkway to one of the stone benches. Mother produced a small towel from somewhere and dusted it off. "It never hurts to be prepared."

"You're prepared for everything," I said with a smile.

"One can never prepare for everything, but when one prepares for what one can, it's much easier to deal with the unexpected."

"There's some truth in that," I conceded.

"So nice of you to admit that, dear."

I winced. "I'm sorry."

She straightened herself on the bench. "Rousel and Remaya will be arriving on Jeudi. Will you be able to come for dinner on Samedi, or will they need to come to see you here?"

"I'll be able to come on Samedi. This is my last weekend to be restricted to Imagisle."

"Good. I'll send Charlsyn with the coach. What time would be good?"

I didn't want to spend too long with Rousel and Remaya—or Father—but I didn't want to seem ungrateful. "I've always been free by the third glass of the afternoon."

"Should he meet you here?"

"I could meet him on the other side of the bridge. That way he wouldn't have to cross and turn the coach."

"That's settled, then. It will be so good to have everyone home. You know that Remaya's expecting in late Juyn?"

"I knew it was sometime this summer."

"She is a lovely person."

That meant that Remaya was far superior to her Pharsi background. "I knew that from the beginning."

"That may be, dear, but she's far better suited to Rousel. She enjoys talking about trade and wool, and she likes it as much as he does."

Mother did have a point there.

"Oh . . . I forgot to tell you. I should have written you. We have your painting—the one you entered in the art competition. Master Reayalt had it sent to us. Would you like it?"

The guildmaster of the Portraiture Guild had sent my study of the chess game? But who else would have? "If you don't mind . . . could you keep it until I'm a bit more . . . settled."

"We'd love to. I know just where I'll hang it until you're ready for it."

"I'd appreciate that."

"Tell me about being an imager . . . what you can, that is. I know that there must be matters you cannot discuss. What do you do?"

"Study and practice, mostly. I suspect I'm getting close to a university education in science, chemistry, and philosophy."

"Don't mention the philosophy to your father. He'll like the rest. What else do you do?"

"There are exercises in imaging, and I'm examined almost every day, except Solayi, by my preceptor. That's Master Dichartyn. In the afternoon, I might practice something in the laboratories or workrooms, or study. I've just been advanced to imager secundus, and starting tomorrow, I'll have to learn more of what imagers do, but I haven't been assigned yet."

"What does being an imager secundus mean?"

"I get a little larger stipend, and I can cross the bridges to the city whenever I have the time, so long as I don't miss any instruction or duties."

She nodded. "That's good. Are you getting enough sleep? What are your quarters like? Do you have to sleep in a bunkroom like the soldiers?"

I shook my head. "We each have our own rooms. They're not large, but they're comfortable, and the food is good. Not so good as at home, but far better than at Master Caliostrus's." Was my parents' dwelling really home anymore? Had it ever been, really, after I'd left the grammaire?

"I'm glad to hear that." There was a long pause. "Dear . . . this may be presumptuous, but can imagers marry?"

I couldn't help smiling. "They can, but generally they have quarters on Imagisle or among other imagers, unless they're very wealthy."

"I don't see why . . ."

"It's compulsory, but I'm told that the quarters for those who are married are quite comfortable. Those who are older and have families live in houses on the north end of the isle." I didn't feel right about explaining the reasons beyond what I'd said.

"Oh . . . I've seen them. They're well kept, and stylish, but a trace small, I would think."

All I could do in response was shrug and say, "Since I'm not married, I wouldn't know."

"Do imagers usually marry other imagers?" After a moment, she added, "That can't be. There aren't any women imagers, or not very many, are there?"

"There are some. I've seen three masters who are women, and perhaps ten or fifteen who are primes, seconds, or thirds."

"Then when you can, you should get out and meet some eligible women, some of the proper background." She paused. "You realize that Rousel was extraordinarily fortunate, don't you?"

What she meant was that most Pharsi girls would not meet her standards or fit in her world, but I only said, "I'm very aware of that. I can only hope to be that fortunate."

"A good background makes it far easier, as I'm certain you know."

I nodded, and after that, we talked of friends, and family and how my aunt Ilena—Mother's sister—refused to travel to L'Excelsis, even on the ironway.

Then, abruptly, she stood, and I followed her example.

"I must be going, dear. It has been lovely to see you, and to know that you are doing so well. I had my doubts, but I do think this imager business is for the best. Your father will be happy to know that." She leaned forward and kissed my cheek. "We will see you next Samedi."

I walked her back to the coach and watched as Charlsyn eased the team and coach around the narrow roundabout and back over the bridge. Then I walked back to my room and read—or tried to read—another section of *Practical Philosophy*. Many of the arguments there seemed anything but practical, such as the section that read:

> The ultimate philosophical principle is the advance from disjunction to conjunction, creating an entirely new entity other than the entities previously existing in disjunction . . .

After struggling through that, I closed the book and made my way to the dining hall, where I did appreciate the comparative relief of the evening meal on Solayi. Then, I and all of the imagers at the Collegium went to what the masters called chapel, but it meant the services held at Anomen D'Imagisle. They were a glass later than those at Anomen D'Este, to fit the Collegium schedule, I supposed. As at all services, we stood throughout—except for a handful of graying imagers emeritus, who had two special benches on the left below and forward of the pulpit. A small choir of imagers offered the choral invocation, and they sang well.

Chorister Isola was the only woman chorister of the Nameless that I'd ever seen, although I'd heard that there were others, because one could not know or presume whether the Nameless was male or female, or indeed both at once. Her voice did carry, and her soprano invocation following the choral one, wordless as it was, was far more pleasant than that of any other chorister I had ever heard. Then she opened the main part of the service.

"We are gathered here together this evening in the spirit of the Nameless and in affirmation of the quest for goodness and mercy in all that we do."

The opening hymn was unfamiliar—"Save Us from Naming"—but that didn't matter because I barely sang, with just enough sound so that I was not merely mouthing the words.

After the confession and offertory, Chorister Isola stepped to the pulpit for the homily. "Good evening."

"Good evening," came the reply.

"And it is a good evening, for under the Nameless, all evenings are good." She paused for just a moment before going on. "We all know, and you all have been taught since childhood, the sin of pride that can accompany naming, and we have all heard the stories about achievements and the purity of Rholan the Unnamer. Who among us has not shied away from the possible disgrace of bearing the mark of the Namer, but how many of you have thought deeply about the greatness and majesty of those aspects of life that are without a name? We come into the world, born of woman and man through the agony of a woman, often so painful that no words can describe that birthing. Likewise, there are no words to describe death, for those who pass through it cannot speak of it to us. For each of us, these are the beginning and the end, as we know them here on Terahnar, and there are no words that will do justice to either.

"Words cannot describe the most magnificent of sunrises or sunsets, or even the greatest painting of the greatest representationalist or the most beautiful of statues, or the most stirring and harmonious of melodies. Words are all that we have to convey to each other what we see and what we feel, but never should we accept a belief that words truly or fully describe the world created by the Nameless. Even less so than words do names describe what is . . ."

Chorister Isola went on from there. I thought it was one of her better homilies, and one that made me think.

On the way back from chapel, I matched steps with Sannifyr, another second, not necessarily because I'd disliked the younger primes, but as soon as I'd made secundus, they shied away from me. Sannifyr didn't say anything, and I didn't really know what to say to him, either. The walk back to quarters was fairly long, because the anomen was at the point on the southern end of Imagisle, but the night wasn't that cold, especially compared to those when I'd first come to the Collegium.

25

Deduction is limited by knowledge, and knowledge is limited by preconceptions.

On Lundi morning, when I made my way to Master Dichartyn's study, the door was open.

"You can come in, Rhenn."

I eased inside and closed the door, taking my seat opposite him.

He leaned back and fingered his chin. "How many people are there in Solidar?"

There had to be millions, but I didn't recall the exact figure. "Forty million?"

"The last enumeration showed around fifty million. How many are in L'Excelsis?"

"There were over two million in 750 A.L."

"How many imagers do you think there are here at the Collegium and in L'Excelsis?"

"If I've counted correctly, there are somewhere over two hundred and forty, sir."

"Add another fifty or so, and that's close enough. It doesn't include those who can image just a tiny bit and haven't been discovered, or those who have never discovered their talent, but most people with the ability get found out sooner or later. Later is seldom better, and very few survive. Let us just say that there are five hundred imagers in all of Solidar. What is that ratio?"

"One hundred thousand to one, sir."

"Now . . . does that tell you why caution is necessary in every imager action?"

"Yes, sir." It also told me that Floryn's greatest failing was telling anyone anything.

"What else should it tell you?"

What else could there be? "There can't be very many in the rest of the world, either."

"Why not?"

I'd had a moment to think. "If there were, we'd know about it. The Collegium seeks out imagers. If you can only find five hundred in Solidar, and we have more people than other countries . . ."

"You're making several assumptions. What are they, and are they correct?"

"It would be hard to hide imagers in other lands, but if you could find out so much about me, how could they hide imagers from you?"

"That assumes we would be allowed to look. While places like the Abierto Isles are open enough, and so is Stakanar, Ferrum and Jariola don't like snoopy outsiders and have rather unpleasant habits of making them disappear. The Tiemprans ban imaging and imagers, and the same is true of Caenen. You're also making assumptions about people. What are they?"

"Oh . . . that people are the same everywhere."

"Are they? If they are, what makes them that way?"

"Sir . . . I know I haven't traveled far, but I have seen people who have come from many places, and they all seem to love or hate, or want to be better . . . and I think we're all born with similar general abilities and wants."

"Is imaging something people are born with, or something learned?"

I was definitely unsure what Master Dichartyn sought . . . or why. "I don't *know,* sir, but I would say it's something people are either born with or not, but that they have to learn whether they have it and how to use that ability." I paused. "Does it have anything to do with . . . I mean there seem to be more men who are imagers."

"That's true, and women imagers almost always come from families where an older brother has the talent. Why that's so, we don't know, but there are traits that work that way. Very few women are bald, compared to men. But . . . back to the question at hand. If the imaging skill can arise in any people, why are there more practicing imagers in Solidar than in the rest of the world? If you can tell me that, it will provide the rest of the answer to the first question I asked and that you did not answer completely."

I had to think for several moments. Exactly what had I failed to answer?

"I'll give you a hint. Why are most bulls gelded and why is the Cyella Ruby valuable?"

After a moment, I answered. "Imagers are scarce but more plentiful in Solidar because we provide valuable and rare services and people are more willing to have imagers around so long as there aren't too many of us?"

Master Dichartyn nodded. "We have created an institution that not only fulfills needs, but also has established a reputation for being trustworthy in carrying out those duties for Solidar and for the Council. Without unique services, we have no value, and without trust, our value cannot be relied upon. And if there were too many of us, then no one would trust us. Because the Oligarch of Jariola can trust no one, what we do is either not done there, or done in a more costly fashion, and any imager is either executed or exiled. In Ferrum, they use machines and exile imagers because they cannot quantify how to value trust."

Abruptly, he looked up. "We have not gone over your philosophy readings, but I need to meet with the other masters." He paused. "The Puryon believers of Tiempre have faith in an omnipotent, beneficent, and just god. Write me a logical proof of why this is either so or why it cannot be so. Have it ready for me in the morning. That should provide some practical application of what you've been studying."

"Yes, sir." How was I going to prove that logically? And why was a philosophical proof a practical application?

"We'll meet outside the dining hall after lunch today, and I'll take you to your work assignment from there." He stood.

So did I, scooping up the unopened books and hurrying out of his study before him.

I had almost two and a half glasses before lunch, but, as I crossed the quadrangle under the first truly warm sunlight in days, I had no idea how I was going to prove or disprove the statement Master Dichartyn had given me.

"Where are you going so early?" called Johanyr from the stone walk intersecting the one where I walked. He was also a secundus, about my age, I thought, with short-cut curly brown hair and massively broad shoulders, as if he were better suited to be a stonemason or the like. We'd talked briefly over meals, and I had the feeling I'd seen him somewhere before, but I couldn't recall where.

"Master Dichartyn had a meeting with the other masters, but he gave me a logical proof to figure out, and I have to have it all written out by tomorrow."

"Some of the seconds are asking if you're trying to make third before summer and master in a year." He laughed, but the sound was hard. "You don't spend much time with the others, except at meals."

What he was saying was a warning . . . of some sort. "I'm sorry. I don't mean to be standoffish." I gestured toward a bench some five yards away. "Do you have a moment?"

"More than that. I didn't even get to see Master Ghaend this morning. They're all upset about something." He tilted his head, looking at me speculatively. "Master Dichartyn is the only other Maitre D'Esprit besides Master Poincaryt. Did he say anything to you . . . anything at all?"

"He never does," I answered as we walked slowly toward the gray granite bench. "He just asks question after question. This morning, he stopped in the middle of a question and said he had a meeting with the other masters, then told me my assignment and just about threw me out." That wasn't quite true, but I doubted anyone could have mistaken his abruptness.

"So he was worried?"

"I think so. He's never been quite that abrupt before." I stopped by the bench, gesturing. "We might as well sit down."

"Might as well. You were saying . . . ?"

"I don't talk about it much, but I was a journeyman portraiturist. I was even getting my own commissions, and I was thinking it wouldn't be too long before I could become a master, a junior master, and open my own studio. Then I imaged a little part of a portrait, just a little part, except it was green, and one thing led to another . . . and the girl I was interested in married my brother, and, all of a sudden, I can't be anything but an imager."

"Green? Why green?"

"Green pigment, true green, is almost as expensive as liquid silver. They don't let journeymen use it often, and only when a master is watching, and I wasn't a master yet."

"You were close to being a master portraiturist?" Johanyr's face softened slightly, but still bore a trace of incredulity.

"Several masters said I was good enough. I'd spent five years as an apprentice, and three as a journeyman." I shrugged. "I don't mean to be standoffish, but the change has taken some getting used to. When I started as a prime, I was five or six years older than most of the others. We didn't talk about the same things."

"I can see that." He nodded.

"I'm just trying as hard as I can just to catch up. There's so much I still don't know."

"Sarcovyt says that you're good at imaging things."

I managed a laugh. "How would I know? I know I'm good enough to be a second, but since I made second, I've never seen anyone else image anything. Before that, I never saw anyone but a prime even try. Master Dichartyn says that's for my own protection."

"It sounds like he's trying to get you caught up with where the rest of us are."

What Johanyr said made sense. "That's what I'm guessing. I really don't mean to be unfriendly . . . it's just been hard." That much was certainly true.

"None of us knew," he pointed out.

I tried to look embarrassed. "It's not something . . ." I shrugged. "It's my fault, but . . ."

That got a sympathetic nod . . . of sorts. "We usually get together for a while in the evening, a half glass before the eighth glass, down in the common room. You might try it."

"I didn't even know . . . I mean, I've seen the common room, but only in the day . . ."

His laugh at my confusion was genuine, and when we parted, I felt that I'd managed to avoid, for the moment, another pitfall. But I was going to have to be very careful until I could figure out how to develop protections of the sort that Master Dichartyn had mentioned.

I still also had to figure out and then write up the proof for Master Dichartyn.

When I got back to my room, it took me more than a glass, and several drafts to write what I did. At lunch I made a point of sitting across from Johanyr and Diazt and making a special effort to be friendly. I felt that they were warmer, but I didn't know, not for certain.

After I left the table, Master Dichartyn was already in the hallway outside the dining hall.

"We're headed to the materials section of the workshops. You've already figured out some aspects of substitution. Now you'll get a chance to learn another and put it to work." He turned and strode quickly down the corridor and out through the doors, moving as quickly as I'd ever seen him.

As we walked, he said, "The materials for the workshops come over the Bridge of Stones. That's where the name comes from. All the workshops have outside and inside entrances, and each workroom is lead-lined. That is so that no imager can affect the work of another. That is particularly important for some . . . efforts."

I was beginning to sweat by the time we reached the large gray structure a hundred yards north of the quadrangle. The building held the various workshops, not that I'd been in more than a handful of them. The door where we entered was on the main level on the west side of the building, beside a raised loading dock, behind which was a set of sliding warehouse doors. They were closed.

As we stepped into the workshop, a space not much larger than ten yards by fifteen, I could see that the length of the room was filled with barrels, four lines of them, stacked on top of each other three deep. Four small topless wooden crates were set on a workbench a yard or so from the nearest line of barrels. That was it—except for the older imager in somewhat dingy gray who hurried through the door at the other side of the workshop.

"Grandisyn, this is Rhennthyl. He's the new imager second I told you about." Master Dichartyn turned to me. "This is Grandisyn. He's a senior imager tertius. He knows more about imaging materials than most masters. I will leave you in his hands." With that, he hurried away.

"You're fortunate to have him as a preceptor," Grandisyn said. "Fortunate, but he'll make you work and think and then some."

"I have noticed that, sir."

"Just Grandisyn, Rhennthyl."

"Rhenn, please. When people use my full name, I always wonder just what I did wrong."

He laughed. "I can see that. My papa did the same." After a moment, he began to explain. "Your task will not be easy at first, but it is simple. All you have to do is image some of these aluminum bars." Grandisyn lifted a bar of a silvery metal out of the wooden crate on the right end, which had three of the small ingots in it, the only crate that did, then pointed to the barrels lined up along the wall. "It should be easier if you concentrate on imaging from the barrels. They're filled with high-grade bauxite. Master Dichartyn said you might have to work at figuring it out, but that you could do it. Take your time." He gave me a smile, then hastened off.

I was still holding the small aluminum bar, possibly worth several hundred gold crowns, and I was supposed to image more of them? In a way, from what I'd read, it made sense. Refining it was costly, and that made it very valuable, but why weren't we refining gold? Or platinum?

I wasn't quite sure what I was doing, but I concentrated on the image of the bar, the shining light metal, right on the workbench, and tried to visualize a vague link between the barrels and the bar I was attempting to image into existence.

A series of dull clanks followed.

Not only did I have a bar, somewhat larger than the one I'd been shown, but there was a line of aluminum fragments on the stone floor running spiderweb-fashion toward the barrels.

Obviously, my vague link needed to be far less direct.

I kept trying, and by the end of the fourth glass, I was exhausted, and my head was pounding. But there was a wooden box filled with the metal ingots, some of which had been refashioned from all the loose fragments I'd created before I'd figured out how to image without creating patterns of aluminum running from the barrels. Yet, in the end, refashioning from the fragments had been far easier.

I finally just sat down on the stool that had been tucked away under the bench. I was just too tired to do more. When I'd first imaged that small part of the Factorius Masgayl's portrait, I had had no idea how exhausting imaging would turn out to be.

Before long, Grandisyn walked in and crossed the floor to the wooden crate. He looked at the crate, and then at me. "Hmmmm. We may have to find other things for you. I'll be talking to Master Dichartyn. You look done in. Go get some rest."

I didn't need any more encouragement.

Back in my room, I slept for more than a glass and then had to hurry to the dining hall for dinner, where I ended up at the bottom of the table among several thirds I didn't know, but I did my best to be cheerful.

After dinner I went back to my room and read some more, but I was careful to make my way down to the common room about a half glass before eight. The common room was in the lower level on the north end of the building, little more than a narrow space some fifteen yards long and seven wide with tables and benches spaced irregularly. The wall lamps were infrequent and wicked down to minimal light, so that the impression was of gloom. I found Johanyr and several others in a corner, with chairs pulled around a newish-looking table of a design centuries old. It should have been battered, but wasn't. It took me several moments to realize why.

"Rhenn . . . pull up a chair." That was Diazt. "We were talking about what's got the masters all stirred up."

I lifted a chair and set it between Johanyr and Shannyr, then sat down. My feet hurt, and I still had a trace of a headache.

"Only half the masters were at dinner, and neither Master Dichartyn nor Master Poincaryt was there," said a short muscular secundus.

"They usually aren't," Shannyr said. No one looked in his direction.

"The newssheets said a Caenenan shore battery fired on one of our merchanters."

"Why would they do that?" asked Shannyr. "Merchanters don't carry cannon."

"What would that have to do with the Collegium?" I inquired.

Diazt laughed. "The Collegium has something to do with everything in Solidar."

"Master Dichartyn's your preceptor, isn't he?" asked Johanyr.

"Yes, but he didn't say anything, except he cut my session short this morning, and then let Grandisyn tell me what to do in the workrooms. He left in a hurry."

"They were all like that today."

"Did he let anything slip, even indirectly?" pressed Johanyr.

"The only thing he said was that both Ferrum and Jariola had nasty habits of making snoopy strangers disappear."

"I told you it couldn't be just Caenen!" declared Shannyr.

"Does the Council have any problems with the Oligarch there?" I asked.

"There's not a country in the world that doesn't have problems with the Oligarch," someone else said. I couldn't tell who with the quietness of the words and the dimness.

"There's not a country in all of Terahnar that doesn't have problems with Solidar," replied Johanyr.

"Because of imaging?" I suggested. "We don't have that many imagers."

"No one else has anywhere near as many."

"You can't have many imagers if you kill most of them as children," added Shannyr.

Diazt cleared his throat. "We still don't really know what has them worried. It has to be something important to have all the masters meeting twice in one day."

"It can't be just firing on a merchanter," said Diazt.

In the end, no one added anything, and I had to wonder who knew what, if anything. Still, I'd been there, and I had the feeling that I'd better drop in at least a few times a week.

26

To every man, his cause is the one most just.

On Mardi morning, I spent a glass outside Master Dichartyn's study reading *Practical Philosophy* because it was so boring that it seemed better to read it when I couldn't do much else. At those times when my eyes threatened to cross, I spent a few moments with the newssheet—*Tableta*—but there was nothing of great interest, except for the massive avalanche near Mont D'Image and the speculation that somehow the imager Collegium there had been involved. Also, according to the captain of the *Aegis,* a Caenenan gunboat had fired on his ship, but missed.

When another imager left—I recognized the tertius as Engmyr, whom I'd met at the dining table—Master Dichartyn beckoned me to enter. He looked less tense than he had the day before, and he was smiling as I closed the door and took my seat.

"Grandisyn tells me that you imaged a week's worth of aluminum ingots in two glasses. How do you feel?"

"I ended up with a terrible headache, and I almost fell asleep in the common room."

"Take time in between imaging this afternoon, and see if you can find a better way. Try several ways. Even if you can't, taking time between each effort will leave you less exhausted."

"Sir . . . besides testing imagers, what is aluminum used for?"

"Its rarity, except that it's not rare, except in pure form. It's just that, except for imaging, it's so difficult to refine and process that it is valuable. So the Collegium provides a certain amount to the Council, and they sell it discreetly to enhance revenues."

"But . . . aluminum?"

"It's unique, Rhennthyl. If you ever try to image gold, you'll understand. Imaging actually requires energy from you and from everything around you. It's a process of combining energy and material. A powerful imager has the ability to drain the life from everything nearby, including you, unless you have shields."

I tried to conceal the chill I felt. "Sir . . . I wanted to ask about that."

"In a moment, I'll tell you how to begin thinking along those lines, and why you are never to mention it to anyone but a master. Anyone. But first, about gold and platinum. To begin with, they're rare. Second, they're very heavy. The heavier anything is, the harder it is to image, particularly a metal. It takes great skill and energy, and the fewer gold fragments or ore that there is nearby, the harder it is. Some would-be imagers have killed themselves trying to image the impossible."

"Like trying to image gold in their chambers?"

"Exactly, but imaging certain metals—even in the midst of raw ore—can lead to death, and that death is lingering and excruciatingly painful. It takes several weeks, and the imager's hair falls out, and he becomes like a leper all over."

"Sir . . . if I might ask, why didn't you tell me this earlier?"

"You were told what to image and where. You were given quiet cautions. If a young imager won't listen, we keep him here on Imagisle and sooner or later, he'll destroy himself."

I couldn't help swallowing.

"Now . . . about shields . . . it's simply another form of imaging. You image an invisible shield . . . but one that only stops imaging."

"If . . . if . . . someone pointed a pistol at me . . ."

"You could—and should—image a harder invisible shield between you. Holding the shield might force you several steps backward when the bullet hit it, but that's better than getting wounded. By the same token, that sort of shield won't do much against a cannon shell."

I could understand that.

"Don't hold a hard shield long, not now. It will exhaust you. An imaging shield . . . with a little practice, you'll be able to hold that in your sleep."

"How will I know whether I have it right?"

"I'll start testing you. Beginning tomorrow."

Before he could ask more, I said, "Sir? Does the Collegium have special enemies?"

He snorted. "Do you need to ask?"

"I thought that we must, but I've never seen anything in the newssheets, and no one I know has ever talked about it, and you haven't, either."

He sighed softly. "You deduce too much without knowing enough to understand the implications. Think about this. While at Imagisle or the few other imager enclaves across Solidar and while in L'Excelsis, we all wear the uniform of the Collegium. Without those uniforms, what would distinguish us from anyone else? We don't look different; we don't have a way of speaking that would distinguish us from others of Solidar."

"So . . . some of us are spies? For the Collegium or the Council?"

He stiffened. "Where did you come up with that?"

"I've been thinking, sir. A master can kill someone in a way that doesn't look to be tied to anyone. If Floryn had been walking down the street who would have known how he died? You said that I would have been found dead on the street had I not come here. You said I could develop shields against a bullet, but not against cannon. Those suggest that an imager can do things others can't, but not things that would help much in any sort of battle. You also said that imagers provided value to the Council, and it has to be more than aluminum ingots."

A wry smile appeared on his face. "I knew you were going to be difficult."

I could feel a chill, and I was the one to freeze.

"Oh . . . you don't have to worry, not yet. That will come later, after you finish your training, and that will take a while."

That I would finish my training was a relief . . . in a way.

"I do think that you need to work on your shields, starting now. Try imaging something like an invisible fog between you and me."

I tried, and I felt an unseen pressure on my chest.

"That's not working. Try a curtain, a black curtain that stops all light, except that the curtain is one that you can't see . . ."

We had to work up to an actual visual wall, and then work back down to an invisible muslin screen before I managed to figure it out. By that time, almost a glass later, I was sweating all over. Master Dichartyn could have pointed out that imaging was sometimes far more work than anyone thought. He didn't have to. The effort spoke more eloquently than he could have.

He did raise his eyebrows. "Now . . . let's see your logical proof, Rhennthyl. I assume you did the assignment."

I handed him the single sheet with the few carefully written lines on it.

"Not very long for a proof." His voice was noncommittal.

What I had written was simple, but I hadn't been able to think of anything better.

> If there is an all-powerful god, nothing is beyond that god's power. If that god is beneficent, then there will be no evil in the world. If that god is just, the god will not allow injustice to befall the good and the innocent. Yet there is great evil in the world, and much of it falls upon the just and the innocent. A just god would prohibit or limit injustice, at least against the innocent, but injustice continues, so that if such a god is omnipotent, that god cannot be just. Therefore, if there is a god, that god cannot be omnipotent, beneficent, and just.

Master Dichartyn looked up from the paper. "This could be worded better."

"Yes, sir."

"Do you believe what you wrote?"

I hadn't liked writing the proof, and I'd liked the conclusion less, but I had to believe that there was some truth in the matter. "Mostly . . . sir."

"Mostly?"

"Well . . . if people aren't marionettes, pulled by strings held by the Nameless, they have to be able to make some decisions. That includes bad decisions. Bad decisions can cause evil."

"Then you're arguing that your proof is incorrect because a good and beneficent god has to allow free will."

I didn't like that any better. "I don't like the idea that so many people can be hurt by those bad decisions and that sometimes bad people are rewarded for their cruelty and evil."

"What do your feelings tell you about your logical proof?"

"It isn't logical? That I made a mistake?"

He laughed. "No. Your reaction was that you weren't logical or that you made a mistake in logic. Behind your reaction is a feeling that whatever is 'true' must be able to be expressed logically. Men, in particular, have a tendency to confuse correct logic with an accurate assessment of a situation. Be careful of any situation that you have to reason through logically, because if you have to work to reason it out, you're probably missing something."

Again . . . I had to think about that for a moment.

"Another problem is that we want the world to be logical and understandable, and we want people to act in a way that feels right and makes sense to us. That's true of most people in most countries. There are difficulties in that, though. Can you tell me what they are?"

"What makes sense to us doesn't make sense to them?"

"Precisely. We have different beliefs about what we feel is right and makes sense. We take for granted certain beliefs or truths. Other cultures take for granted other truths. According to our truths, their behavior is not right, and according to their truths, our behavior is not right."

That certainly made sense.

"So which is right?" he asked. "In the absolute sense, that is?"

"I can't say, sir. I don't know their truths."

"That's the logical answer, Rhennthyl. It's also an answer you will need to keep to yourself. Why?"

"Because everyone around me believes our truths are right?"

He nodded. "People do not like their beliefs challenged. They want certainty, and they want everyone to follow their way, because they are convinced that their way is the only right way. Oh, there are a few open-minded people about, but far fewer than claim they are."

I could see that as well, perhaps because I could recall all too well my father's belief in the superiority of a life spent as a factor.

"Let me ask you another question. We are always cautioned not to attach too much weight or significance to a name. But isn't calling the one who cannot be named 'the Nameless' just a convenient way of saying we're following the rule of not emphasizing names while doing just that?"

"Sir?"

"Isn't 'the Nameless' as much a name as 'Dichartyn' or 'Rhennthyl'?"

Once again, I had to think about that. He was certainly right and yet . . .

"Rhenn?"

"Sir . . . how can we talk about anything without names? We name metals, the colors of the rainbow, the objects in everyday life."

"Why are those different from the one who cannot be named? Or from you . . . or me?"

I finally grasped at an answer. "They're not alive."

"What about animals? We often name them. They're alive. What does being alive have to do with names?"

I could feel that there was a difference, but I couldn't find any words to express what I felt, and I finally shrugged, helplessly.

"Metals, objects, minerals . . . they cannot change what they are. All fundamental substances can only exist in three forms, like water, which we can see as steam, a vapor or gas, or as a liquid, or as a solid, as ice. The nature of most objects is limited, whereas we exist as solids, except we breathe air, which is a combination of gases, and blood and other liquids run through us. We are less fixed than the hard physical world in which we live, and yet naming suggests a fixity which is not true . . ."

But was it untrue? I doubted some people could ever change.

". . . Names are a necessary convenience, but they represent only a small proportion of what anyone is, and the more alive, the more powerful, the more talented anyone may be, regardless of whether they are good or evil the less their name tells of them."

I understood everything Master Dichartyn had said, but the more questions he asked, the more I wondered why he continued to press me on so many matters.

"Tomorrow, we'll go over the next section in the science book and sections nine and ten in the *History and Politics of Solidar.*"

I nodded politely.

"We're almost done here, but there's one last thing." Master Dichartyn stood.

"Yes, sir?" I also rose, wondering what else he could say.

"You can tell the other seconds that there was a strange fire at the Collegium at Westisle. That's the Collegium outside the harbor of Liantiago. That was what we were meeting about. We've decided on a course of action, but that is all you are to know or should know at this point." He smiled. "Good day, Rhenn, and pace yourself at the workshop."

"Good day, sir. Yes, sir."

I had thought about sitting outside and reading some of the history and politics, but it was misty and cold, not that it was actually raining, and so I took everything back to my room and started in on section nine—the one dealing with the administrative districts of Solidar.

That reading was dull, so dull that I was one of the first at the dining hall for lunch, but Johanyr, Shannyr, and Diazt were right behind me, and we sat together at the long second table.

"Did Master Dichartyn say anything to you?" asked Johanyr.

"He said that I could tell you the masters were meeting over a strange fire at the Collegium at Westisle, and that they've decided what to do, and that was all I needed to know."

"He said *that*?" asked Diazt.

"Close to word for word."

"What did you ask him?" inquired Johanyr.

I shook my head. "I never had a chance to say anything. He wasn't happy with my work in the workrooms, and he wasn't happy with my logical proofs, and he didn't like the way I handled some of the imaging exercises. I wasn't about to ask him anything."

Diazt and Johanyr exchanged glances.

"Not good," said Diazt.

"That he knew what we were talking about?" I asked.

There was a pause, enough to show that my concern wasn't all of what bothered them.

"They must have listening tubes in the common room, or someone told him," Diazt said.

"Or both," added Shannyr.

"He was delivering a message," I suggested blandly, trying to get more of a reaction. "But why would he care what we talk about? We can't have been the only ones who noticed that the masters were worried and meeting."

"It's not that," said Johanyr in a lower voice.

"What, then? Warning us to keep our speculations to ourselves."

The other three all nodded.

I didn't think that was all, but I only said, "There aren't enough of them to listen all the time."

Johanyr shook his head sadly, as if to suggest I didn't know what I was talking about.

I shrugged helplessly.

Diazt did grin, but only briefly.

27

Preparation is always an act of faith.

On Meredi and Jeudi, in addition to my studies and half-improving my ability to image the aluminum bars without exhausting myself, I worked on trying to develop stronger but invisible shields against imaging. I didn't meet with Master Dichartyn at all, but Gherard gave me reading assignments. All he said was that Master Dichartyn was away. The common room was deserted both nights, and I didn't see Johanyr and the others anywhere. Even though everyone was pleasant and cheerful at meals, that worried me, because it suggested that they thought I'd been the one to report what they'd said. At the very least, it didn't show much trust.

On Vendrei, I waited half a glass before Master Dichartyn summoned me into his study.

"What is the difference between aqua fortis and aqua regia?"

"Aqua regia is the stronger, and it can dissolve even gold. Aqua fortis will dissolve silver, but not gold . . ." From there I managed to recall most of what was in the science text.

After that, he had question after question, all about aspects of science.

Abruptly, he stopped. "You know what's in the books. After we finish here, go over to the laboratories and find Maitre Chassendri or one of her assistants. Tell her or them that you need to be shown and to learn the preparation of both aqua regia and aqua fortis."

"Yes, sir."

"Why is there but one imager on the Council?" asked Master Dichartyn.

"Isn't it part of the reason why no more than three councilors can be from L'Excelsis?"

"Yes and no. He represents all the imagers in Solidar. Also, for administrative purposes, Imagisle is not part of L'Excelsis. It's in the book, but even if you didn't catch that, you should have known better, Rhennthyl."

Reprimanded twice in one sentence. I hated feeling stupid. "Oh . . . because there are no patrollers on the isle, and because the Collegium has its own justicing system?"

Master Dichartyn nodded and asked again, "Why only one imager?"

"I don't know, sir. I don't recall anything in the book about that."

"There isn't anything in the book. I'm asking you to think about it. Is that so very hard, Rhennthyl?"

I was definitely not impressing Master Dichartyn. So I gambled and said what I thought.

"That's all that is necessary. No one can make the Collegium do what it will not."

"You give us too much credit." But he smiled. "It's more accurate to say that the Council has great respect for the Collegium and would prefer to work with the Collegium. If the Council's imager opposes something, the Council reconsiders the matter."

"Who is the imager on the Council now, sir?"

"Master Rholyn. He's very good with words and thinks well on his feet."

After a moment I recalled Rholyn had been the advocate for the Collegium at Floryn's hearing.

"I'd like to test your shields. Are you maintaining imaging shields?"

"I think so."

Abruptly I could feel myself pressed back in the chair.

Master Dichartyn shook his head. "You can detect someone, but you need a second level behind them."

"How do I do that?" I wasn't certain what he meant.

"You need to train your mind, just as you trained your hands and fingers as an artist, to react to situations. The moment your shields feel any imaging pressure, those second-level shields need to spring forward."

I didn't even have the faintest idea of where to begin.

"I'll press at your shields gently, and you erect a stronger set . . ."

Once more, I was sweating and exhausted when he finally said, "Enough. You need to work on them more. Now that you're a secundus and free to travel off Imagisle, you need the ability to protect yourself."

"Sir, I don't want to sound presumptuous or like a trouble-maker, but what happens if . . . well . . . if I'm in a position where shields aren't enough?"

"I'd say that you'd probably acted unwisely." Dichartyn laughed genially, but the laugh died away quickly. "Still . . . there are times when ruffians will attack a single imager, particularly a younger one. We do lose some who are not careful. The rules for defense are simple. You must have exhausted every practical way to avoid attacking, and it's preferable that you leave no traces of what you have done."

"How can I avoid . . ." I paused. "Should I practice imaging rain or shadows or fog or mist?"

"I'd try it at night in secluded corners of Imagisle. You'll get a splitting headache if you try rain, fog, or mist in your room, and you won't see the shadows right inside. For those efforts, you have my permission, but only when no one is nearby."

"Thank you, sir."

"You'll face other trials, as well, Rhenn. I can't say what they are or where they'll come from, and it's best that I don't try to guess, because those trials are different for every imager and if I give you details, then . . . it's like naming— you'll fixate on those. I can only say that if your life is truly threatened, no matter where you are, you have the right to use any imaging ability to defend yourself. Obviously, it's better not to kill attackers unless absolutely necessary, and every situation facing you has a weakness that can be exploited—if you think quickly enough."

The implication was that I well might be injured or dead if I did not think swiftly.

"Now . . . off to the laboratories." He gestured toward the door.

I picked up my bag and books and slipped out, closing the door behind me. I wasn't sure, but I thought I heard him mutter under his breath. It might have been ". . . Nameless save me . . ."

In reflection, as I walked down the corridor toward the door onto the quadrangle, I pondered one phrase Master Dichartyn had said. Why had he said "no matter where you are"? Did he mean that absolutely?

How could you disable someone effectively and reliably— using imaging? You would need something so painful and yet so small that it would be easy to image. And it would need to be comprised of substances common everywhere. On the way across the quadrangle toward the building that held the laboratories, it came to me. Common lye—imaged into someone's eyes. They certainly wouldn't be able to see or easily move, and it was made of relatively common substances.

With that revelation, I'd hoped to visit the kitchen and

scullery before lunch, but Maitre Chassendri was in the laboratory, and, for some reason, she decided to personally instruct me. If I'd thought that Master Dichartyn had been picky, his strictness was lenient compared to hers.

"No! Do not ever place the beaker in any position where the fumes can rise to touch you or your skin . . ."

"The glass must be absolutely dry!"

I wouldn't have said that I was shaking by the time I escaped from Maitre Chassendri's tender instruction, but I felt that way when I walked into the dining hall for lunch.

Johanyr waved, and I walked over and took the seat across from him and Diazt.

I usually drank something cool at lunch, but I was more than ready for tea, as much to settle my stomach as to warm me. The beef ragout helped as well.

"What was your morning like?" Diazt asked Johanyr.

"Master Ghaend was pounding away at the structural differences of materials."

I managed to keep from saying anything, but merely nodded. Master Dichartyn had moved me past that, and Johanyr had been at the Collegium far longer than had I.

"Old Schorzat wasn't even around," offered Diazt, "but he left word that I still didn't understand section five of the science book well enough. I'll have to go back over that."

"What sort of questions does Master Dichartyn ask you?" Johanyr's tone was idle, but he watched closely.

"This morning he was asking about the Council and why it was structured the way it was. He wasn't happy that I hadn't memorized the actual structure."

A faint smile crossed Diazt's face.

"What about science?"

"He sent me to the laboratories to learn some basics. I got some very direct instruction and too many warnings about handling beakers and how to clean equipment." I shook my head. "What about you?"

"I didn't have to go to the laboratories." Johanyr laughed. "That's always good. Sometimes the stenches there turn my guts."

"Has Master Dichartyn said anything more about what happened in Westisle?" asked Diazt.

"He was gone for two days, but he hasn't said anything."

"You ask him?"

"I've already learned that, when he says he doesn't want to talk about something, he gets unpleasant if you bring it up again. I don't think I can afford to make him angry."

"No . . . I wouldn't think so," said Johanyr in a musing tone. "There are more than a few you don't want to anger, and it's sometimes hard to tell who's really important to your getting along and staying at the Collegium."

"I'm working at understanding that."

"We're certain you are." Johanyr smiled, then stood. "I need to get to the workshops."

"Me, too," added Diazt.

I'd definitely gotten their message, and I really would have liked to visit the scullery after lunch, but there wasn't time. I had to get to the workroom to see if I could work out an even less exhausting way to image those aluminum bars.

The workroom was empty, except for the barrels, but it looked to me that most of them had been replaced with other barrels. So I sat down on the stool and thought about imaging, and began to try yet another way of doing it. A half glass or so later, Grandisyn barely looked in, then just nodded and ducked out.

Right after the Collegium bells struck the fourth glass, I headed for the scullery on the level below the main dining hall. The steps leading down were the same gray granite, and just as clean as any other staircase or corridor I'd seen on Imagisle. I'd taken no more than ten steps down the lower hallway when an older woman, an obdurate from her muted black shirt and trousers, appeared.

"Sir, you can't be looking for anyone down here. Nobody here but us ob sculls."

"Then, you're the ones I'm looking for. My master gave me a project, and I need a little common caustic."

She just looked at me.

"Lye, the soda you clean with. I only need a little, a half cup?"

After a moment, she nodded. "We could spare that little, but best you be careful. It burns fearful when it's wet. You just wait here, sir."

I stood in the underground hallway, half-wondering if she'd return with a master.

When she returned, alone, she handed me a battered and chipped crockery mug a little more than half filled with off-white lumpy caustic. "Here you are, sir."

"Thank you." I inclined my head. "Where would you like me to return the cup?"

"You can keep it. There are enough that get broke or chipped that we got plenty."

"I appreciate it." With a nod, I turned and headed back upstairs, and then outside.

While trying not to look over my shoulder, because I worried that someone might follow me, I walked to the west river wall, and then south across the causeway leading to the Bridge of Stones, and to the park-like grove of ancient oaks between the causeway and the grounds of the Anomen D'Imagisle. The oaks were showing traces of green and had not leafed out, but the trunks were massive enough that I felt largely concealed, at least from casual observers.

Then I got to work. Imaging the caustic wasn't all that difficult. Imaging it in small quantities was harder, and image-projecting some of what was in the cup was even harder. Image-projecting it head-high on the oak trunks was yet more difficult. But I persevered . . . because I knew I had no real choices.

It was close to six before I was confident that I had mastered what I could with the caustic, but that was only half of what was necessary. I needed to work on shields more. I wouldn't be in much shape to image lye into someone's eyes after I'd been hit with a bullet or bashed with a cudgel or run through with a stiletto. According to Master Dichartyn's rules, effectively I had to be able to withstand an attack in order to prove self-defense. After what I'd seen with Floryn, I definitely wanted to be sure it was self-defense. That meant far better shields.

At the same time, I was exhausted by the time I took the rest of the cup of lye to my room. That left just enough time to wash up and hurry back to the hall for dinner. When I walked in, I could see Diazt and Johanyr. I didn't really want to sit near them, but I didn't want to create the impression I was avoiding them. There was a seat empty to the left of Shannyr so that he would be between me and Johanyr. Since Diazt was seated to Johanyr's right, neither could press me at the table, and I wouldn't be obviously avoiding them.

There was a momentary look of surprise on Shannyr's face as I stood behind the chair next to him, waiting for the masters at the head table to seat themselves.

Once we were seated, I asked him, "How was your day?"

"Like any other. I went to work at the armory machine shop, had lunch, and went back to work."

It hadn't occurred to me that many of the seconds, perhaps most of them, had finished all their instruction and were working for the Collegium. It should have, but it hadn't. "I suppose they'll assign me somewhere once I get caught up on what I have to learn."

"Could be worse than the armory. They had me in the engine room of one of the riverboats. Wet and cold most of the time."

I shuddered at the thought of being cramped into a riverboat engine room. "What do you do in the armory? Can I ask? I mean . . ."

Shannyr laughed. "You can ask. I can even tell you. I image the special powder for the percussion caps that the four-digit naval guns use."

"You image it right into the cap?"

"That's right. There's no metal touching metal, no chance of a spark, and no explosions."

Another one of those special services provided to the Council by the Collegium, I realized. How many were there?

"What about you?" he asked. "When you're not under instruction?"

"Making metal bars."

He winced. "That's work."

"I can only do so many, and I have to rest a lot." I paused. "You know I'm new here . . . I was thinking about girlfriends. I used to have one, and some imagers are married . . ."

"They're the lucky ones." Shannyr shook his head. "Lots of women will give you a fling, even married ones, but not many want to marry an imager."

"Why is that?"

"We scare 'em a bit. That interests 'em, but they won't marry someone who scares them."

I could see that, but I had to wonder if that happened to be true with all imagers, or if that had just been Shannyr's own experience.

"You want to have fun with the women, when you're free, don't stay around Imagisle. Take a hack out to Martradon or out to some of the bistros on Nordroad or Sudroad . . ."

I listened politely, although I could see that I knew far more about where the women were in L'Excelsis than he did.

That night, after dinner, I had another idea. I went outside and imaged rubber, a thin layer of it, along the inside of a small cloth bag. Then I poured some of the caustic I had left into the bag, which I tied shut. For a while, anyway, until I was more confident in my abilities, I could carry that with me.

Then I tried to practice shields—and shadows—until I was truly exhausted. The shadows weren't very good, and I was more than ready to climb the stairs and collapse into my bed.

28

*Those in a family may well share the same dwelling,
but not the same home.*

Both Vendrei and Samedi mornings were hard because
Master Dichartyn kept pressing me on my shields. No matter
how much I improved, he kept insisting that my efforts were
not adequate. Then he offered an onslaught of questions, not
only on what I read, but on how it all related to the Collegium
and its role in Solidar. I kept those questions to myself and
told Johanyr and his group of seconds only a few of the easier
and more purely academic or technical ones.

On Samedi afternoon, I was waiting on the east side of the
Bridge of Hopes a good half glass before three. The day was
sunny, with the faintest haze, but there was a hint of chill,
and I wore my cloak. On the roughly triangular space where
the boulevard intersected the East River Road stood a flower
seller with a weathered face, but a pleasant expression.

"Flowers, sir imager? Flowers for a lady, a friend, or family?"

For a moment, I couldn't help smiling. "No, thank you."

The tempting aroma of fowl roasting over charcoal on a
cart across the boulevard wafted around me. For all that, it
might as well have been gray and gloomy, given the way I
felt. I shouldn't have. I was healthy and had a profession, if
not what I'd expected, that earned decent coins. Mother and
Rousel certainly wanted to see me, and probably Remaya
did. Even Father did, I suspected, even if he'd never admit it.

Two women, one in bright green and the other in scarlet,
eyed me speculatively as they neared, but I wasn't in the
mood for either of their favors, even if I could have afforded

them. After they passed, a mother in a worn brown coat dragged two children toward the wall separating the sidewalk from the narrow boulevard gardens in order to put as much space between the three of them and me as possible. Was she a malleable, or did she just fear imagers?

As the time neared three, the coach, with its glistening brown body and polished brasswork, appeared on the Boulevard D'Imagers. Before long, Charlsyn pulled up next to the curb, but well short of the flower seller, easily reining in the two matched chestnuts.

"Good afternoon, Charlsyn."

"Good afternoon, sir."

I climbed in and closed the coach door. Because of all the coaches and riders on the Boulevard D'Imagers, I surmised, Charlsyn took Marchand Avenue back to Sudroad, and then to the Midroad. It was close to half past the glass before the carriage pulled up at the side portico of the house, where Mother, Rousel, and Remaya were waiting as I stepped up under the portico.

"Good wool in that cloak and waistcoat," observed Rousel, if with a grin.

"Mother already noticed that. Did she tell you?"

"She told me to look," he admitted.

"You look dashing in that gray," added Remaya with a smile. She had become rotund, and even chubby in the face, but her eyes sparkled, especially when she looked up at Rousel.

"Much more businesslike than when he was an artist," added Father from the doorway where he stood. "Come on inside, all of you, especially you, young woman," he added to Remaya. "The breeze isn't good for my grandson."

"She might be a granddaughter," said Khethila from behind Father.

"Grandson!" yelled Culthyn from inside the family parlor.

Rousel just laughed. "He or she will be what he or she is."

In moments, everyone was in the parlor, and Nellica was passing a tray with spiced wine, or chilled white or red. After slipping out of my cloak, I took the white.

Father had settled into his favorite chair. He didn't wait for anyone else to sit down before he asked, "What can you tell us about this imager business?" As always, everything was business. Before I could answer, he added, "You know that last weekend a young graycoat was killed near the Nord Bridge." He shook his head. "Shouldn't have been there."

I hadn't seen that in either *Tableta* or *Veritum*. "I wouldn't go anywhere like that."

"I would hope not."

"The Collegium at Imagisle is like a guild for imagers." I settled into the straight-backed chair across from his uphol-stered needlepoint armchair. "When I started, I was an im-ager primus. Now I'm a secundus. Most imagers are tertius, I suppose just like most crafters are journeymen. There are four classes of masters."

"Names . . . names . . . what do you do?"

"Chenkyr . . ." murmured Mother.

"It isn't what you're called that matters," he replied amia-bly. "It's what you do and what you earn."

"I'm still learning," I replied, "in the mornings, anyway. I have to learn more about science and about government and history. In the afternoons, I work."

"What do you *do*?" A hint of exasperation colored his words.

"Imager things. I can't tell you."

"Can't or won't?"

"Chenkyr . . ." Mother's voice was firmer and louder.

"I could, but I'm not allowed to. Since I don't want to spend the rest of my life doing imaging drudgery in the workshops, I won't. I get fed better than at Master Calio-strus's and have a chance at earning a comfortable living." I smiled politely. "How is the wool business?"

"Very well," interjected Rousel cheerfully. "We've more than tripled sales and shipments out of Kherseilles this year. That won't last, but with the shipping embargo levied on Caenen by the Council and by Ferrum and Jariola, we're do-ing well."

"If shipments to Caenen are embargoed . . . ?" I asked.

"We just ship to factors in the Abierto Isles. They sell to

Caenenan factors. We had to advance them a little credit, but the Caenenans send their own bottoms there."

"Why won't it last?"

Rousel shrugged. "I had a feeling things would get tense with the dual-godders. So I opened up trade with some cloth factors in the isles. They usually don't deal that much in wool, and I had to give them . . . some considerations . . . last year, but no one else shipping out of Kherseilles had any arrangements in place. They're all hurrying and scrambling, but for now, we're doing nicely. More than nicely, and I've got an arrangement for some high-quality Caenenan cotton coming back the other way. We didn't have that even before the embargo."

"The Council won't object?" I asked.

"How can they?" Rousel grinned. "We're not selling to Caenenans. We're selling to Abiertans. We can't control who they sell to."

"You can't stop trade with laws," added Father. "Even embargoes and warships aren't effective. People want to buy what they want to buy, and they want to pay as little as possible."

"Unless it's rare, and then they bid up the price." I paused. "Is there a difference in the tariff rate between what you'd pay if wool went directly to Caenen and what it costs going through Abierto?"

"You're still sharp enough to be a factor," said Rousel. "There's only a one percent tariff between Solidar and the isles, and we have a reciprocal agreement."

"And the difference in shipping costs?"

"The landed price per hundredweight is almost the same."

I had to wonder why the Council bothered with the embargo.

"Can we talk about something else?" asked Mother. "Have you met anyone we know?"

"Not that I know of. There aren't all that many imagers in all of Solidar."

"What does that have to do with anything?" demanded Culthyn.

"It's mathematics, stupid," replied Khethila. "If there aren't many imagers, then not many are born—"

"That's enough . . . I understand, and I'm not stupid."

I looked to Rousel and Remaya, sitting on the settee. "See what awaits you?"

"We'll manage," he replied.

"Are there any women imagers?" asked Remaya.

"Only a few." Forestalling the inevitable, I quickly added, "I haven't met any my age, but there might be one or two."

"I hope you do."

Behind her smile and the kindness of her words, I could sense the pity. I'd never wanted her pity, and I quickly asked, "How are you finding Kherseilles?"

"It's charming," she answered. "It is not too large, and we have a lovely small villa on the hills overlooking the harbor, with a pleasant breeze . . ."

After more chatter, mostly about Kherseilles, Mother rose. "Dinner is ready."

As people began to move toward the dining chamber, Mother eased up beside me. "We're going to have a dinner here on the thirty-fifth of Avryl. I think you'd like the people."

"Who is she?" I couldn't help grinning.

Mother did have the grace to blush. "She's nice, and quite pretty, but very shy. You actually have met her younger cousin."

"I have?"

"Quite a number of times." Her face had a mischievous expression. "Aeylana D'Weidyn is her cousin. You painted her portrait. Her father is the renowned cabinetmaker, and his brother Tomaz is the largest produce factor in L'Excelsis. Tomaz is also a friend of your father, and we've invited them for dinner."

"And the shy young lady? What's her name?"

"Her name is Zerlenya."

I couldn't say that I'd met or remembered anyone named Zerlenya, and that was probably good, because few of the girls or women I'd met over the years had impressed me. Only a handful had—Remaya, Kalyssa, Larguera, and

Seliora—and I hadn't heard anything about Kalyssa in years, and Larguera had married some heir to a brewery fortune or something like that.

"I'll be here, and I'll be as charming as I can."

"More charming than that, please, dear." Her smile was affectionate. "Now . . . enjoy the dinner. It's one of your favorites—the apple-stuffed pork crown roast."

It was one of my favorites, and I did enjoy it. The conversation at dinner was pleasant. Even Father stopped being the businessman and told stories, including one I'd never heard about the time when he'd first been buying wool and didn't know that sangora was coney hair.

When I left and Charlsyn drove me back to the Collegium—or the east side of the Bridge of Hopes—it was close to the eighth glass of the evening. I did realize one thing when I stepped out of the carriage just short of the Bridge of Hopes that night. For some people, home is always there. For others, while the structure and the family may still be there, and they may all still care for you, it's no longer home. I was one of those. Was it that I was an imager? Or had it been that way from the time I'd wanted to be an artist?

I walked across the bridge quickly, alert for whatever or whoever might be around, but I saw no one, except a few figures in gray from a distance. Although Artiema was full, the faint haze dulled her luminous light. To the west the quarter disc of Erion seemed redder than usual, as if the lesser hunter were somehow lying in wait for the greater huntress. Was that because I felt that someone, or more than a single person, was watching? Yet no one appeared as I neared the quarters building.

I had time to work on my shields, and that I could do safely in my chamber. I'd already done the reading assigned by Master Dichartyn.

29

~

The greatest curse is to inherit wealth or position
without ability.

There was nothing to keep me from leaving Imagisle on
Solayi, except no one I wanted to see and no desire to spend
my few silvers in L'Excelsis merely for the sake of spending
them. Besides, I was still worried about my imaging shields,
especially after having had the feeling of being watched the
night before. So, after breakfast, which I ate near several
thirds at a table with less than ten people scattered along a
length that could hold close to a hundred, I walked back to
my chamber and read my assignments, trying to think of the
kind of questions Master Dichartyn might ask. After every
few pages, I stopped and worked on my shields.

By late morning the overcast had lifted, and I decided to
take a break from the indoor studying and try to work on fog
and shadows. After leaving my room, I made my way down
the steps to the main level and then across the quadrangle
and southward to the grove north of the chapel. Once more,
not only was someone watching me the entire way, I felt, but
he or they kept watching while I struggled with concealment
projections. Fog proved to be easier to create, but it tended
not to last long, vanishing shortly after the sun struck it. It
did linger in the shadows, but I had trouble making it thick
enough to cloak me. What I created might work at night . . .
maybe.

Shadows were something else. After perhaps a quarter
glass, I figured out how to create shadows—an imaging shield
that blocked sunlight without being visible—but that didn't
help much, because in any light bright enough to create shad-

ows, I'd still be visible, and that meant I needed another approach. Even after a long glass of experimentation, I couldn't think of one.

When I walked back north to the dining hall from the grove, just before the ten bells of noon began to strike, I saw Diazt and Johanyr talking some ten yards outside the main entrance. Johanyr's voice was low and intent, but he stopped for a moment and glared at me, then snorted, before returning his attention to Diazt.

What had I done to make him angry, except try to avoid him? Or had they been the ones observing me? If they were, there wasn't much I could do about it. So I went inside and sat next to Shannyr, who, unlike Diazt and Johanyr, gave me a friendly smile.

"Johanyr's not in a very good mood," I said quietly.

Shannyr shook his head. "He's not. Hasn't been since Vendrei. Stewing in his own sweat. Master Ghaend told him that he'd never make tertius if he didn't study. Also said that if he didn't learn more, he'd have to go to work with the seconds like me." Shannyr's tone was totally without rancor or bitterness.

"Master Ghaend said that?"

"No. Master Ghaend told him he couldn't play at being a student, and that he'd have to learn or go to work. I heard Johanyr telling Diazt that. He was so angry that anyone in ten yards could have heard."

"Why doesn't he just study?" I had an idea why, but I wanted to hear what Shannyr said.

"He was born Johanyr D'Ryel. Might have something to do with it."

"He comes from the High Holders, and he's an imager?"

"Doesn't matter where you come from." He laughed softly. "Me, I'm one of the fortunate ones. Till I came here, never knew when I'd eat next. Ma was happy to know I'd get fed and happier to get the gold."

"You don't mind working in the armory?"

"Why'd I mind? I'd be slaving for some factor, lugging barrels and the like, or I'd already have been press-ganged into the Navy or conscripted." He smiled. "Much better to work as a common imager. Diazt doesn't see that. He thinks he's so much smarter than Floryn. He's just the same, but not as smart."

"Did Diazt come from the taudis?"

"The hellhole."

That was the worst slum in L'Excelsis, except that—unlike the taudis below South Middle—it wasn't actually in the city, but off the highway that Sudroad turned into some five milles south of the Avenue D'Artisans. "He's better off here."

"He doesn't think so. He ran a ganglet—kids doing stuff for the elvers and stealing from the sansespoirs."

"He was in control, and he doesn't like it when other people are." I paused, then added, "It sounds like Johanyr doesn't much like it, either."

"No matter who you are," Shannyr said, "there's always someone else tougher. Saw that growing up."

"Or brighter or better-connected . . . or whatever."

"You miss painting?" he asked.

"Sometimes," I admitted. "But, in a way, imaging's like that. I don't know that I'd have ever discovered I could image if I hadn't been a portraiturist. Did you ever . . ." I wasn't quite sure how to ask whether he'd worked at anything. ". . . want to do anything besides be an imager?"

"Fieldwork or the mines—those were the choices out in Tacqueville. Didn't care much for either, but I was working a ditch crew when I imaged a lousy copper for Ma. So bad that she knew I'd made it. Hadn't seen that many." Shannyr laughed. "Armory's better any day."

Diazt was the type who'd rather run a gang in the hellholes of Solidar than answer to anyone in twice the comfort. But weren't more than a few people like that?

When I left the table and Shannyr, Diazt and Johanyr were standing beyond the archway. Neither looked at me as I passed, and I even offered a polite smile. Behind me, though, I could hear a few muttered words.

"Stuff's too easy for him . . ."

"Rodie . . . got to be a rodie . . ."

Me? A rodent, a snoop, reporting back to the senior imagers? That didn't make sense. Why would I give up being a portraiturist to become an imager, and then an informer for Master Dichartyn or any other master? I almost turned and snapped back that they were imbeciles and master imagers didn't need toadies, but my guts told me that would only make matters worse.

Besides, if I didn't react, they couldn't be sure if I'd overheard them.

30

Arrogance makes a man stupid,
and stupidity can make him even more arrogant.

On Solayi evening and at breakfast on Lundi, Johanyr and Diazt stood outside the entrance to the dining hall and looked hard at me. I just smiled back. They didn't return the smile, nor did they choose to sit anywhere near me. I sat with Shannyr. He was good company.

After breakfast, when I was finally admitted to Master Dichartyn's study, he didn't test my shields at all. Instead, he concentrated on asking me questions about the Council and governing. Once he'd determined that I'd read the pages he'd assigned, he smiled.

"In Jariola, the Oligarch rules absolutely, but the oligarchy votes every five years whether to replace him or not, and he can be replaced at any time if forty-six of the fifty members of the council vote to remove him. Forty-five members of the council are the wealthiest High Holders in the land and the other five are the high prophet of Khanahl and four others appointed by the ruling oligarch. The Abierto Isles are governed by an assembly, and the members are elected by a vote of all property holders, whether those holders are men or women, regardless of where they live or were born, and the assembly elects a speaker who makes day-to-day decisions. In Caenen, the high priest of their Duality is the ruler of the country. You know how we are governed. Which means do you think is more effective, and why?"

My immediate reaction was to prefer our system, but to say so would just invite more questions. "I'd say that the Caenenan system is the worst, because they are governed by one man, and there is no effective way to remove him—"

"Killing him would remove him effectively, but I don't think that's what you meant. Be more careful in your choice of words."

"There are no accepted rules for removing him in the event that he proves a bad ruler."

"That is true, but what is a bad ruler?" asked Master Dichartyn. "If taxes are high upon the crafters and low upon the landholders, is it not likely that the landholders will praise him and the crafters will declare him a bad ruler?"

"Yes, sir."

"Go on."

"I'd say that the Jariolan system is the next least desirable, because power is held in the hands of so few men, and that is not good—"

"For all the rhetoric and common talk, government is not about good and bad, Rhennthyl. Nor was that what I asked. What is it about?"

"Creating the laws and rules under which people live."

"Why is government necessary?"

"Things don't work well among people without some form of government."

"That's true. Why not?"

"People would try to do whatever they could get away with. Unless you had golds and power, you couldn't trust anyone. Even then . . ."

Master Dichartyn nodded slowly. "Effective governments set rules and limits on how power is used in a country.

Now . . . that means some who have greater power must accept limits on their power. Why would they do so?"

"Because, otherwise, those with less power will band together and restrain or eliminate them?"

"That's one possibility. Can you think of another?"

At that moment, I couldn't.

"If you were High Holder Almeida, would you want to spend tens of thousands of golds on maintaining a private army to defend your lands or would you rather pay a few thousand golds in taxes to a government that generally protected them?"

"If the government rules weren't too burdensome, I'd prefer the taxes."

"So do most High Holders of Solidar. What does that tell you about government?"

"It provides a balance of power at a lower cost for the wealthy and greater order and freedom for those with little power."

"An effective government does. If most people want effective government, why do governments vary so much from land to land?"

"They have different ideas about what is effective and how to make things work?"

"Do you think that a chorister of the Nameless and a priest of the Duality would think of power in the same way . . ."

Master Dichartyn's questions seemed endless. I was all too happy to leave when he finally dismissed me, despite his assignment of the additional reading.

Again, at lunch, Johanyr had positioned himself where he could watch me, although I didn't see Diazt. I walked over to him and asked, "How are you doing? I haven't seen you around, except outside the dining hall."

He didn't say anything for a moment, clearly taken aback by my addressing him. Then he replied, "I'm fine. There are some things that have to be settled."

I didn't feel like saying anything to respond to the implied threat. "I'm sure things will settle out if you give them time."

"I'm not very patient, Rhenn."

"Most of us aren't. I'm not, either, but I've learned that sometimes rushing things creates more problems than it solves."

"Don't threaten me."

"I'm not threatening anyone," I said, managing to smile. "It's not wise, and it's not polite. I hope you feel better later." I nodded courteously and turned toward the dining hall.

I could still feel his eyes on my back, and I still didn't understand why he was so angry. Was it just that he was angry and needed a target? I certainly hadn't told anyone about what he thought or his nastiness to me, except telling Shannyr once that Johanyr didn't seem happy.

I took a chair between Gherard and Whaltar and across from Shannyr.

Whaltar was speaking to Gherard. ". . . got Naquin Samedi night . . . warned him about the Nord quarter, but he said that was where the girls were . . ."

"Did someone get hurt?" I asked.

"Naquin. He was a third. They found his body on the street yesterday morning." Whaltar shook his head. "Have to be twice as careful if you're a graycoat."

I didn't quite know what to add. I hadn't known Naquin.

"How is Master Dichartyn treating you?" asked Gherard, clearly wanting to change the subject. "Some of those assignments looked difficult."

"The reading isn't too bad," I admitted, "but the questions he asks about what I've read make the reading seem easy."

"Most of the thirds haven't made it as far as you have," Gherard said.

"I'm sure that they're doing better elsewhere." I decided on tea, filled my mug, and took a long sip. "That's why they're thirds." The longer I'd been at the Collegium, the more I wondered why Gherard was still a secundus. "If you don't mind . . ."

Gherard laughed. "I don't. You've waited longer than most to ask. I have trouble reading. The letters don't make sense to me, and I'll never be a great imager. I can remember anything anyone tells me word for word, and Master Dichartyn tells me that I have a good feel for incoming imagers."

Put that way, his position made sense. "Is Petryn still help-ing there?"

"No. He's a second now, and another junior prime took his place—Beleart. You know . . . you scared the Namer out of Petryn."

"I did? I was the one who felt scared."

All three of them laughed, and Shannyr just shook his head.

They all thought it was funny that I'd felt scared? Did I re-ally project that much confidence? I didn't think so. I cer-tainly hadn't known that much about imaging when I'd arrived at the Collegium.

After lunch, when I went to the workshops, Grandisyn es-corted me to another workroom, one also with barrels, and showed me a small bar of metal no bigger around than the body of a pen and no more than a digit in length.

"If you're really good, you ought to be able to do four of these, but if you get really tired after two, stop. We are not certain of the concentration in the ore." He paused. "Do you understand?"

I understood. I remembered what had happened to Mhykal.

After he left, I fingered the silvery metal, which seemed as heavy as gold. Platinum?

In the end, I managed three small bars, and decided against trying for a fourth. That took less than a glass, and Grandisyn said I was free to go. When I returned to my room, I took a short nap—and I'd never taken naps since I'd been small, not until I came to the Collegium.

At dinner, Johanyr and Diazt sat at the end of the table, with two other seconds I'd barely met. Johanyr never looked in my direction, but Diazt did, and did so more than a few times.

"What did you do to Diazt?" asked Clenard, one of the older seconds who was a friend of Shannyr.

"I asked Johanyr how he was doing. He wasn't happy that I spoke to him." My words came out a shade ironic.

"That's because he likes to ask the questions," Shannyr added dryly.

"What do you work at?" I asked Clenard.

"I help the machinists. It's easier to image blanks than to cast them, and then they machine them down. Don't have to have a furnace, either, but it works best for small parts. . . ."

Every time I thought I'd learned most of what happened at the Collegium, I found out something more. But at least I had a good conversation at dinner.

Afterward, I talked a bit with Shannyr, then walked through the deepening twilight across the quadrangle back to the quarters building—one of two, I'd also learned. Again, I had the feeling of being watched, but I didn't see anyone. I wasn't imagining things, and that suggested that whoever was watching and following was a very good imager.

When I got inside, I hurried up the stairs. No more had I stepped off the landing on the second level and into the corridor leading to my room than I heard heavy steps coming up the stairs behind me. I moved away from the staircase, but looked back.

"If it isn't the painter boy." Diazt stepped out of the staircase landing and stopped. He carried a metal bar.

Walking down the hallway in the other direction was Johanyr. He held some sort of blade, a sabre perhaps. He didn't say anything. I moved toward him, because I didn't want to be that close to Diazt. My fingers brushed my trousers. I still had the bag of caustic, but I couldn't very well attack first. Master Dichartyn had made that very clear. Were the two of them trying to provoke me into attacking? That way, I'd be totally at fault—if I even survived whatever defenses and retaliation they had in mind.

I could hear several low sounds—door bolts snicking closed. Did Johanyr and Diazt have all the seconds cowed? At that point, I realized that most of the wall lamps in the corridor had been wicked off—or imaged out.

"How are you doing this fine evening?" Johanyr's voice was sarcastic. "It's dark out now, and that's the best time for rodents."

"I'm no rodent. You're just looking for excuses."

"All rodies say that they're innocent."

"So do all innocents." I moved slowly toward Johanyr in order to avoid the metal bar Diazt carried, although I couldn't move too far before I'd be in range of the sabre.

"You're no innocent. We didn't have any trouble before you showed up."

"You mean that no one complained," I suggested.

He stiffened.

Then I staggered back as *something* slammed into my shields. Before I could recover my balance another blast struck me from behind, and I staggered in the other direction.

I couldn't see what they'd imaged at me—but it was something that was designed not to leave any traces, because nothing had dropped to the stone floor. I would have heard it, even if I couldn't see it in the low light.

"Rodie's got shields . . . how sweet." That was Diazt. "That will just make it so much easier."

I didn't know what he meant until the iron bar slammed against my shields, and I ricocheted off the wall. By beating on my shields, they could wear me down and still punish me, and leave few if any bruises.

Johanyr struck with the flat edge of the sabre. That rocked me, but not enough to unbalance me.

"You'd better stop," I said.

"We'd better stop? You have a strange view of things, rodie."

The iron bar hit my shields again, and I had to take several steps toward Johanyr to keep my balance. He struck with the sabre, and I was forced back toward Diazt. They weren't going to stop. That was all too clear.

I managed to square my feet and look straight at Johanyr. I concentrated on imaging caustic, just like that in the bag, behind his shields, right in his eyes.

There was a moment of resistance—that was what it felt like—and then he blinked. "Kill him! Diazt! Ohh . . ." He collapsed on the corridor floor.

The iron bar struck the back of my shields with such force that I stumbled and had to take three or four steps and could barely stand before I whirled to face Diazt—imaging even more caustic into his eyes.

The bar flew toward me, and I ducked, and then Diazt was screaming, but only for a moment before he went limp.

Master Dichartyn and Master Ghaend both appeared from somewhere.

Ghaend looked to Dichartyn and nodded. Two obdurates in black hurried down the hallway toward us.

"What happened? What did you do?" demanded Master Dichartyn. "Spare me any niceties about accidents and the like."

"They cornered me, and everyone on the floor locked their doors. I could hear the bolts snick shut. Then they claimed that I was some sort of spy and that the Collegium had no use for rodents like me. They began to image things at me—"

"What did you do?" Master Dichartyn's question was hard and urgent.

"I imaged lye—caustic—into their eyes."

"Through their shields?"

"Yes, sir."

"Ghaend! Get them to the infirmary and start washing their eyes out with clear water. Have the staff keep doing it for at least half a glass. Get some water and a little of the basic elixir in them."

"Yes, sir."

Each of the hulking obdurates hoisted one of the two fallen imagers, and before I could say anything, Master Dichartyn and I stood alone in the corridor.

"You come with me, Rhennthyl."

"Yes, sir."

I followed him back to his study, hoping that his coolness didn't presage even more trouble, but fearing that it did. I didn't understand why Johanyr and Diazt had collapsed. I could understand burning or pain in their eyes, but they'd barely uttered anything before they fell.

Master Dichartyn said nothing until he had closed the door to his study behind us and offhandedly imaged the wall lamp into burning brightly. "Go ahead and sit down. You probably need to get off your feet."

I sat. My legs were shaking. I didn't want him to start in with more questions. So I spoke on what had been bothering me on the walk from the quarters. "I don't understand why they collapsed. I was only trying to blind them so that they couldn't attack."

"Think about it, Rhenn. Where were you?"

"In the corridor."

"You said all the doors were shut. What's behind—"

"Oh, shit . . ."

"Exactly. Where do you think that caustic came from? You pulled some of it out of their own bodies. If they're lucky, they'll live, but they'll never see well enough to image again."

"What will happen to them?"

"They'll be sent to Mont D'Image. It's a pleasant place, if isolated, and if they recover, they can take duties there. If not, they can live on a stipend in the village adjoining the Collegium. Master Ghaend and I both thought that this would happen. Neither of those two has been exactly a model imager, and you threatened them both."

"I threatened them, sir?"

"Whether you know it or not, and you'd better learn to accept and train it, not only do you image, but you have a talent for projecting whatever you feel—or want to feel. That talent means that, given time, you can be very effective in managing people. Let me ask you this. When you want to be alone, does anyone ever bother you? When you feel friendly, does anyone not respond?"

I hadn't thought about that, but I was still thinking about Johanyr and Diazt. Why had Master Dichartyn let them go so far? I almost blurted that question. Almost. Instead, I asked, "Was it a test of sorts? Or will I face a hearing?"

"Self-defense is always allowed, and you did attempt not to kill them. There will be no hearing. You will be restricted to Imagisle for the next few weeks, not as punishment, but as protection, of a sort, and you will spend one glass every evening practicing with shields and imaging against one master or another. That's another form of protection, both for you and for others." He smiled sadly. "You need to learn a few less lethal ways to use your abilities."

Why hadn't he taught me those before?

"Because, unless you could protect yourself in some way or another, or talk your way out of it, doing so would have been a waste of everyone's time, because you'd have been crippled or died in the first confrontation. Tonight, we would have stepped in, if you'd managed to hold them off, or even if you'd reacted well, but not had the skill. You moved so quickly that all we could do was help them."

"You *knew* they were planning something?"

"It was obvious. You knew, didn't you?"

"Yes, sir. I didn't know when, but I had the feeling that it wouldn't be long."

"We have a shade more experience, Rhenn. Now, gather all your gear. You're moving over to the wing with the other thirds."

"The other thirds?"

"What do you think distinguishes a second from a third? Or one factor, anyway."

"The ability to use shields?"

"Let's make it more general. Seconds don't become thirds at your age unless they have very useful skills. Some seconds will never develop their skills beyond a certain point, but they will often become thirds later on when they have more life experience."

"Seconds like Shannyr or thirds like Grandisyn?"

Master Dichartyn nodded. "And others. Experience in the Collegium is also valued, and sometimes it is more valuable than imaging skills alone." He smiled, briefly. "Another matter which I'm sure you'll appreciate is an increase in your weekly stipend to a half gold."

Five silvers a week? That was more than all but the best master portaiturists made, and certainly more than journeymen made.

"You will more than earn it." He rose, and his words were a promise close to a threat.

I got up more slowly than he had.

Tertius

31

The more exalted the position, the heavier and yet less obvious the burden of responsibility and the greater the expectations of others.

One thing I noticed immediately about my new quarters. They were larger and actually consisted of two rooms—one that was both parlor and study and a second smaller sleeping chamber that held a much larger armoire as well as a separate chest of drawers. The other thing was that I was totally exhausted. I could barely put away clothing and books before I collapsed onto the unmade bed beside the clean linens I was too tired to use.

The next morning I was up early, arranging my new quarters. They were not only much more spacious, but the bed also had a larger headboard of golden oak with simple carving. In the sitting room were an armchair for reading and a desk chair in front of a writing desk.

Once I washed, shaved, and dressed, I stepped out into the corridor and started toward the stairs down to the main level.

An older third came out of the next doorway and smiled. "You're Rhenn, aren't you?"

"Ah, yes." I was surprised by the friendliness in his voice, because everyone in the other quarters section had been far cooler.

"Claustyn. I heard that you took care of Johanyr and Diazt."

"I was just trying to disable them. I didn't do a very good job of it."

Claustyn laughed heartily. "The way I heard, you did a very good job of it, and the masters were most relieved."

"Because Johanyr was disabled when he was attempting to injure someone badly?"

"And because you're the son of a noted factorius."

Unhappily, that made sense. In the past, I suspected, most of Johanyr's victims had parents of little status, and Johanyr had assumed that my inability to remain as a portraiturist had meant that my family had effectively abandoned me. That assumption had doubtless been strengthened by the fact that I had nothing of value with me, no golds, no pillows or bedding or anything that I could have brought. I had no doubt that as the son of High Holder Ryel, he had brought everything permitted. Because his assumption was incorrect, the masters could simply report to his father that his son had broken the rules of the Collegium and attacked another imager, one who was the son of a noted factor, and had been injured by my attempts to defend myself against an unprovoked attack.

I also realized something else. Master Dichartyn had known exactly what was likely to happen, and he and Master Ghaend had waited just long enough to make sure that neither Johanyr nor Diazt would be able to image again. "Has he been a problem for a while?"

Claustyn shrugged. "For long enough. High Holder Ryel is not on the Council, but a number of those on the Council are beholden to him. The factors on the Council are not."

That would make my personal situation more difficult in the future, although I could not have explained why. So I just replied, "They attacked me, and I really didn't have much choice."

"That's all the better."

Claustyn and I walked to the dining hall together and sat with several other thirds—Reynol, Menyard, and Kahlasa.

Kahlasa was plump with bright light brown eyes and curly sandy-blond hair, and she was the first to speak after we sat down near the foot of the table and Claustyn introduced me. "You really were a portraiturist?"

"A journeyman, not a master."

"Could you paint my portrait?" Her lips and face conveyed an expression that was half grin, half smile.

"I could . . . if I had paints, brushes, supplies, canvas, and the like, but I couldn't take coins for it. If I did, the guilds would bring it before the Council, and I doubt that's something the Collegium would look favorably upon."

Reynol laughed. "The Council doesn't look favorably upon much."

"They favor more golds in the treasury," suggested Menyard.

"But not those taken in taxes from their guilds or peers . . ."

All in all, it was one of the more enjoyable meals I'd had at the Collegium. After eating, I made my way to Master Dichartyn's study, where the door was open.

"Come on in, Rhenn. How are you feeling?"

"Fine, mostly. I was so tired I collapsed last night." I closed the door and slipped into the chair across the desk from him.

"That's not surprising. Holding shields and imaging behind lead can be very tiring. As your technique improves it will get easier, but working in a restricted area is always more difficult."

"Are Johanyr and Diazt all right?" I didn't want to ask, but felt that I should.

Master Dichartyn shook his head slowly. "Johanyr will live. He's likely to remain with such poor sight that he can barely make out shapes and light and dark, and he won't regain all his strength, but he can have a productive life in Mont D'Image, if he chooses. Diazt died shortly after he was taken to the infirmary."

I swallowed. "I didn't intend—"

"That was most obvious, Rhenn. You allowed them to pummel your shields viciously, and you tried to tell them that they had no grounds for their attack. When you did attack, it was only after great provocation, and your intent was only to disable. Had they attacked you outside, they both would have lived. In that sense, they chose their own fate."

I had a strong sense that Johanyr had lived and Diazt had died because of who their parents were and were not. I also had another suspicion that I wanted to voice. "Shannyr kept you informed, didn't he?"

"Did he?" Master Dichartyn raised his eyebrows. "Does it matter now?"

That was as much of an acknowledgment as I was likely to get. "No, sir."

"You realize that your duties will change? You won't be going to the workshops anymore. Instead, you'll be working with Clovyl for the next few weeks. He's a senior imager tertius, and he will teach you the use of various weapons, but most important, how to defend yourself without imaging and without weapons. You'll meet him in the exercise room at the first bell of the afternoon, every day except Solayi and Samedi, and you will spend two solid glasses with him, if not more. Before you do, you will obtain some exercise clothing from the tailoring shop. You will need it. Then at the seventh glass you will return here. Either I or another master will be here every night from Lundi to Vendrei, and we'll be working harder on developing different kinds of shields and other imaging techniques. You'll also need those."

Before I could think much about the implications of his words, he went on, as if nothing significant had occurred. "Now . . . what is the primary purpose of taxation and tariffs?"

"To raise funds to support government services."

"Is all taxation used for such purposes?"

"No, sir."

"Why not?"

Again, the text hadn't mentioned much about other uses of taxation, but Master Dichartyn expected an answer beyond that. "Because governments are comprised of men, and men do not always do what they say they will or what may be best for those they govern."

"That will do, but only for now. For what other purposes might taxation be used?"

"Some rulers and others in governments have used taxes to increase their own personal wealth. Others have used tariffs to protect the commerce and trade of their people."

"How does increasing the cost of a good through tariffs protect commerce?"

"It often doesn't. It benefits some people and hurts others."

"Can you provide an example?"

At that moment, I was glad I had listened to Father and Rousel. "Caenen imposes a tariff on our textiles, and that increases the cost to their people. . . ."

Master Dichartyn kept the questions coming for close to a glass before he stopped and looked at me. "That's enough for now. Read the appendix to the history, the one that outlines the development of Council precedent and procedures. You'll need to go to the tailoring shop before lunch. Wear one of the exercise suits you get there when you meet with Clovyl. Also, in addition to the exercise suits, you'll need special black and gray garb identifying you as a messenger." He smiled. "One of the duties of imager thirds is to serve as silent guards in the Council chambers." He smiled. "You might carry one or two messages in the course of a day, but the uniform allows you to walk anywhere in the Chateau. You won't be assigned there for another month, depending on your training, but your uniforms will be ready when you are."

"What exactly are the duties of silent guards?"

"You use all your skills in ways to protect the councilors and their assistants, in such a fashion that no one will even know exactly how they are being protected."

"People faint, or trip, or slip . . . things like that?"

"As well as a few others that are even less obvious." Master Dichartyn frowned momentarily. "You'll also have to learn the procedures by which the Council operates, because anyone intent on disrupting Council business will also know those and time their acts based on what is happening in the chambers. That is why you need to study the appendix, but that only provides the barest outline."

"Does that happen often?"

"Disruptions seldom occur. Attempts are quite frequent because our defenses are so invisible that all too many who oppose Solidar think that there are none."

That seemed strange to me. It was almost like encouraging attempts.

"I can see that puzzles you. I would like you to think about that and provide me an essay tomorrow explaining why the Collegium's secrecy in this is either wise or unwise." He stood. "Now . . . off to the tailor's shop. I've left word that you're to be fitted."

I rose quickly. "Yes, sir."

As I walked away from Master Dichartyn's study, I saw Gherard coming the other way. "Good morning."

"Good morning, sir." His voice was pleasant, and he inclined his head slightly as he passed me and headed toward the study I'd just left.

Sir? I'd been Rhenn the last time we'd spoken. Why was he being so deferential? Did everyone know what had happened? Or was it my advancement to tertius?

I was still pondering those questions when I reached the tailoring shop, but I wasn't given much time for musing.

"Ah, yes, you must be Rhennthyl, the new third," began the graying, thin, and stooped imager who greeted me. "Must say you look innocent enough. Always an advantage in what you'll be doing. Off with that waistcoat. We need to measure you, yes we do. . . ."

Before I could say more than a few words—at least that was the way I felt—I was headed back to my new quarters with an armful of exercise clothes and the promise that my other garments would be ready for a fitting on the following Meredi.

Back in my rooms, I inspected more closely the exercise clothes. They were gray and consisted of loose-fitting trousers and a thick collarless tunic made out of soft but heavy cotton. I also ended up with lace-up high ankle boots.

At lunch, I didn't see Claustyn, but I sat with Reynol and Kahlasa. I mostly listened while Reynol talked about his position as one of the assistant bookkeepers for the Collegium.

". . . and before I leave on detached assignments, I make sure every entry in the ledgers is up to date and documented. Jezryk's a fine fellow, and the heartwood of any tree, but you should see the entries he's left for me to make when I return. Now, sharing a position is fine, and rotating collateral duties is an evil we all live with, but fair is fair . . ."

I had the feeling that one didn't inquire about detached duties, but since he was talking about bookkeeping, after taking a mouthful of a fowl ragout, I asked, "Is it because he's uncertain about how to make those entries?"

Reynol laughed again. "No . . . it's because those are the ones that require supplementary documentation in the masters' review ledgers, and that takes care in writing."

"He's good at what else he does," Kahlasa said.

"When are you leaving again?" Reynol asked her.

"Not until the twenty-seventh of Mayas. There were some difficulties."

"When you're dealing with the Caenenans, there always are." Reynol turned to me. "Do you know what your new assignment will be yet?"

I shook my head. "Master Dichartyn just said I had some training ahead of me."

"There's always training." Reynol nodded. "Have you heard about the new bistro on Beakers' Lane off the East River Road? It's called Felters. You both might like it."

"Beakers' Lane?" asked Kahlasa.

I knew that, even if I didn't know the bistro. "That's the second lane south from Boulevard D'Este."

"Thank you. I still don't know all I should about L'Excelsis."

"Where are you from?"

"Shastoilya. No one has ever heard of it. . . ."

"How long have you been here?" I asked.

"Not quite four years. It took me a while to get adjusted to the Collegium."

"She was a Nameless chorister in training," Reynol interjected.

"Do you have to tell everyone?" Kahlasa's voice carried a tone of mock irritation.

"Do all the women imagers have their own quarters?"

"We have the north end of the lower level of the tertius quarters building, and that's all the women who aren't maitres. When we're here, of course."

From what the two of them said in passing during lunch, I

had the definite feeling that imagers did far more than I'd realized—and in many more different locales.

After eating, I hurried back to my quarters and changed into the exercise clothes, then hurried back to the exercise rooms. I had to look at a copy of the map, because I didn't remember where they were. I still made it to the foyer outside the rooms before the first afternoon bell rang.

A muscular figure in the same sort of exercise clothes appeared. He looked closer to my father's age, although he was far trimmer, but his black hair was streaked with gray.

"You're the latest savior of the seconds?"

"I'm Rhennthyl, sir. Are you Clovyl, sir?"

"Most polite. I can see why Johanyr overstepped himself." He nodded. "Have you ever been physically trained?"

"No, sir, except for grammaire."

"You're going to have a difficult few months ahead. The reason for this is simple, but I won't make you guess. The duties Master Dichartyn has planned for you will take a great amount of physical strength and conditioning. You understand that imaging is work, don't you?"

"Yes, sir."

"Then let's get started." He turned abruptly and went through the middle door.

I hurried after him, closing the door behind me.

He gestured to the exercise mat. "You'll see more of that than you'd like. After the first two weeks or so, you'll join the other thirds in their workouts, but right now, all you'd end up doing is hurting yourself and getting frustrated. I'm going to show you a series of exercises, and you're to do them exactly as I show you them. Exactly."

"Yes, sir."

"The first set is limbering and stretching. That's so that the later ones don't hurt you . . ."

When Clovyl said exactly, he meant exactly. At the end of the first half glass, I was soaked in sweat, and he'd corrected me a score of times.

"Your legs stay straight!"

"Keep your heels on the floor!"

I was trying to do the best I could, but I'd never even seen any of the exercises he showed me and then ordered me to do.

"You need a break." His expression was close to disgust. "Follow me."

I would have liked to say that I scrambled off the exercise mat, but my movements were more like a stagger to my feet as I walked after him and through a doorway into the adjoining exercise room.

What looked to be a cloth-covered mannequin hung from a rope attached to an iron ceiling bracket. Certain areas were marked in red, and several in maroon. Clovyl walked over to the dummy and pointed. "The red marks the places where, if you strike a man hard enough, you will disable or kill him. When I am finished training you, you should be able to know exactly how and where to strike without looking and without having to think about it—either through imaging or with hands or anything else. You will also have the strength to do so, even if you have just run a mille at full speed." He paused. "Why do you think this is necessary?"

"Because I'll be assigned to places where I may not be able to image or where it will not be wise to do so, and I won't have any weapons at hand? Or even if I can image, I won't have time to think about where."

Clovyl nodded solemnly. Then he said, "That's enough of a break."

The first set of exercises had only been warm-ups compared to what followed, and I tottered back to the quarters building slightly before the fourth glass. My exercise clothes were soaked, and so was I. With a chill spring breeze blowing across the quadrangle I was shivering, even before I took a too-cold shower to clean up. After I dressed, I tried to read the appendix to the history, but the procedures were so dull that I fell asleep.

I woke at the fifth bell and managed to read some more . . . and I *thought* I might remember some of what I read.

At dinner, Kahlasa introduced me to two other thirds— Dierkyl and Sonalya. They asked me about portraiture, and I asked them about exercises. They laughed.

At the seventh glass, I was once more outside Master Dichartyn's study.

He arrived shortly and opened the door.

"Clovyl says that your coordination and skill aren't bad, but that your conditioning needs work. For him, that's almost a compliment. How do you feel?"

"I'm tired."

"You'd better get used to it. Or as Maitre Deloityn said to me when I was about your age, 'Welcome to the real world, where you never have enough time, energy, or golds.'" He paused. "You're too tired to deal with shields tonight. So we'll work on precision imagery." He lifted a wooden ring about fifteen digits across, and then set four small wooden cylinders on his desk. "I'm going to hold this ring up, and I want you to image one of the cylinders into the open center of the ring."

"Yes, sir." That I could do, but I had a feeling that worse was coming.

He held up the ring.

I concentrated and imaged a cylinder. One vanished from the desk and appeared in midair in the middle of the ring. Master Dichartyn reached out and caught it with his free hand. "Now I'm going to move the ring back and forth slowly. You still have to put it in the middle of the ring."

It was going to be a long glass—that I knew.

32

The difference between an explanation and an excuse lies with the one receiving it.

I'd had to write the essay on the reason for the Collegium's secrecy in protecting councilors after working with Master Dichartyn on imaging skills on Mardi night. That was more than a little difficult, because, first, I was so tired that I could hardly think and, second, I knew nothing about how the Collegium actually handled protection. Because I could not keep my eyes open any longer after writing the essay, I went to bed. Then, I'd had to get up early on Meredi to read the appendix on Council procedures and precedents. I had to read it twice, and I doubted that I understood a fraction of what I read, because it seemed so arcane. While I waited outside Master Dichartyn's study, I even read the first ten pages of the procedural appendix again, but I still wasn't sure I understood it any better.

Once he summoned me into his study, Master Dichartyn didn't waste any time. "Let me see your paper on imager secrecy."

I handed it over and sat in the chair opposite him while he read it.

Finally, he looked up. He did not look pleased. "This is not a good essay, Rhennthyl. There are mistakes in grammar and in logic, and your scrivening is sloppy."

"Yes, sir. I know, sir."

"If you know, why did you turn in something so bad?"

"I didn't have enough time to do it better last night, and I was so tired that I couldn't think straight, sir."

"You will redo this and hand in a more acceptable effort

tomorrow—a much more acceptable effort. Now . . . on to your reading assignment. What is the ostensible purpose of a call for quorum in the Council and what is the real purpose?"

The first part I recalled. "A call for quorum is made to ensure that a majority of the Council is present so that important business may be brought before the Council."

"That is indeed the procedural purpose. What is the real purpose?"

I had not the slightest idea. "I don't know, sir."

"Don't you think that most members of the Council would be present if truly important matters were to be discussed?"

"I would think so, sir."

"Then why would anyone need to require a call for quorum?"

"To keep someone from bringing up something else?"

"That is partly correct. It's most generally used, however, to delay proceedings so that members can persuade others or reconsider strategy, or so that the entire Council can avoid making a decision."

Avoid making a decision? Couldn't they just not vote or decide? "Would that be to avoid even bringing up something that they were not ready to decide upon?"

"I think I just said that." Master Dichartyn's voice was sharp.

"I'm sorry, sir. What I was trying to say was that they might use it even to avoid the appearance of avoiding making a decision."

"That's more accurate, far more accurate." The sharpness faded from his voice. "Now . . . is a point of order a procedural stalling tactic or a valid objection?"

"Ah . . . both?"

"Rhenn . . . you don't seem all that certain about what you read. Why not?"

"I read that section twice, sir, and part of it a third time."

"Surely, with that much perusal you could remember with more certainty."

What did he want? I was doing the best I could do.

Master Dichartyn's face turned even more stern.

"Rhennthyl . . . you may have talent, but you definitely do not understand one basic thing about the Collegium and the world. No one cares whether you are tired, whether you had a hard day, or whether you have trouble thinking straight. In fact, if you let anyone know when you feel that way, it may well result in either your death or your immediate retirement to Mont D'Image with your friend Johanyr."

I did hide a swallow at that.

"Being a fully trained imager is one of the most difficult professions to master, and failure to master it will mean either that you will end up in the machine works or the armory or some lesser position or that you will be injured or die." He paused for a moment. "I have the feeling that you do not wish to spend your life doing something beneath your potential. Am I wrong?"

"No, sir."

"Then you will need to use your time more effectively. If you cannot think after a long day of effort, you need to rise earlier and do your reading and assignments then. Short naps also help. Long naps are worse than no naps, because they disrupt your sleep, and you end up more tired than ever."

"Yes, sir."

After that, he was *slightly* less sharp, but his questions were as probing as ever, and I felt like I knew almost nothing.

Finally, he stopped examining me on the procedures appendix and said, "Read the appendix again, and think more about it. I also want you to read the next section in the science text, the one about anatomy." He paused. "Master Draffyd overheard something about your wanting to paint portraits."

"No, sir. Not exactly. Some of the thirds asked if I could paint their portraits. I said that I couldn't do that for coins . . . but I suppose I could let them give me supplies and brushes. Would there be anywhere I could set up a small studio?"

"You want to do more? You just told me you were having trouble doing what has been assigned to you."

"I didn't mean right now. It would take weeks even to obtain everything, and I wouldn't even think of trying it unless

I was doing well enough that you approved. But I wanted to know if it might be possible. If it is not, I understand, and I will not bring up the matter again."

Master Dichartyn frowned for a moment, then suddenly smiled, and nodded. "I hadn't thought of that, but it might be well for you to keep that skill. It could be most useful, and some of the masters here have not ever had portraits . . ."

That was the best part of the day.

I had to go back to my quarters and rewrite my essay on secrecy and then pore over the procedural appendix yet again. Lunch was one of the few meals I could barely eat—a strong liver and onion ragout whose smell nearly turned my guts inside out. Even the bread tasted like onions and liver to me. I hurried to get into my exercise clothing. Clovyl worked me hard for a glass with exercises, and then took me on a run—twice all the way around Imagisle, close to four milles. He was barely breathing hard, and I was panting and gasping and sweat-soaked when I tottered to a halt outside the exercise rooms.

Then came my first instruction in hand-to-hand fighting, where Clovyl demonstrated a move, and I had to mimic it exactly. Exactly.

After his instruction, which lasted well past the fourth glass, and left me almost as sweat-soaked as the run had, I showered again, and took a short nap and then read the next section of the science text, the one on human anatomy. Dinner was better, a rice and cheese dish with some sort of fowl.

Then I had to return to Master Dichartyn's study by the seventh glass and work on imaging with and passing items through moving objects. At that point, my muscles were getting sore, very sore, and I tried not to think about the fact that I had a month of this sort of training ahead of me . . . if not more.

I did force myself to hang up my clothes and put everything in my quarters where it should be before I climbed under my blankets.

33

⟨⁓⟩

*Those who speak of "good people" with great conviction
are to be feared.*

The next two and a half weeks followed the same pattern of
that first full day as an imager tertius in training, a day that
could well have been called a Day of the Namer—except that
each day except Solayis was more difficult than the day
before, and it would have been repetitious to attribute the trials of each to the Namer. Along the way, I managed a visit to
the barber, prompted by Master Dichartyn. By the time the
morning of Vendrei the twenty-seventh of Avryl had arrived,
I had to admit that I was developing muscles I hadn't realized
I had, and I could certainly run farther and faster, and I was
so tired every night that I had little trouble falling asleep. The
muscular soreness had also abated, and Clovyl had grudg-
ingly admitted the afternoon before that my skills in defending myself had improved.

"You might be able to take down most common footpads
now, but your knifework needs work." Clovyl had shrugged.
"You're getting there, but don't go getting any ideas."

Most evenings I worked with Master Dichartyn on shields
and specialized imaging, including the differences in handling powders and liquids, and even air itself.

After much more reading and rereading, and more than a
few pointed questions from Master Dichartyn, I did understand the rules and procedures of the Council, finally. "Better than some of the councilors," he admitted.

Still, that morning, he asked me another question that I'd
never heard, just another in a seemingly endless series of
such. "Do you know the 'good people' fallacy?"

"That wasn't in anything I've ever read," I said, adding quickly, "I don't think."

"That wasn't a bad recovery," he replied with a smile, "but I'd suggest saying something like, 'There are a number of fallacies involving good people. Which one did you have in mind?' Of course, to say that, you'd best have a few in mind."

I didn't have any in mind, and he knew it.

"The fallacy is that someone who is good cannot do evil. I get rather suspicious when someone talks about another as being a good person. A man may do good in every small way on every day, and yet be a part of great evil. Even a land cannot be accurately judged by the number of good or bad people within it. All lands have good and bad individuals. The goodness or evil of a land is determined by what that land does as a whole. A handful of evil leaders can pursue hatred and destruction, while the majority of so-called good-hearted souls do nothing. Less frequently, but still occurring, are the instances where good-hearted leaders lead a populace whose individuals are predominantly selfish and cruel, and the acts of such a land under such leaders are praiseworthy. All too often, the term 'good people' is used as an excuse, as in the phrase 'but they were good people.'"

I could see that, and I'd even heard words like that from my parents.

"How would you judge Solidar, Rhenn? Is it a good land or less than good?"

"Compared to what, sir? I know only what I have read about other lands, and I haven't even met that many different kinds of people in L'Excelsis. I've never really met a High Holder or many from the taudis or other countries."

"That's a fair answer. Not helpful, but honest. Shall we say . . . compared to what you think it could be."

I wasn't at all certain why Master Dichartyn pressed such questions, although I could understand his efforts to get me to think and to point out errors in my facts or thinking. "Ideally, any country could be better than it is, if people acted as well as they could, but they often do not. Solidar is like that, but I don't see the kinds of cruelties that I read about in places like Caenen."

"How do you know what you read is accurate?"

"I don't, not for certain. But the reporters aren't locked up for what they write, not often, anyway, and that would indicate there has to be some truth in what they write."

"There is some truth in what you say, but your logic is weak. What if the reporters know what is acceptable to the Council and what is not? Then what?"

"I'd say that what is acceptable could not be totally inaccurate, because, if it were, then word would get around. It's hard to hide something that's wrong."

"The first part of what you said is absolutely correct. The second part is half true. Can you tell me why it is only half true? Based on your own life and experience?"

For a moment, I had no idea what he meant. Then I did—Master Caliostrus and Ostrius. I managed not to show any reaction. "Some things, perhaps isolated events that few care about, can be hidden, but large and repeated patterns of evil cannot be kept secret forever?"

"That's a fair approximation, although I would be leery of using the term 'patterns of evil.' Evil can be in the eye of the beholder. Some of what is evil to us is not to the Caenenans, and the other way around. Patterns contrary to the sensibilities of a people cannot be repeated without being noticed."

That was a way of expressing it that I wouldn't have thought of.

"How much, then, do you think that the Council controls what appears in the newssheets?"

"I don't *know,* sir, but I would guess that there is very little direct interference."

He nodded. "I'd like you to think about that and write a paper on it. You'll have some time because I'll be away for the next few weeks, beginning this afternoon." He reached to the side of his desk and lifted a black-bound book, which he then handed to me. "Read the first two sections before Lundi."

I opened the heavy tome to the title page—*Jurisprudence.*

Now I was going to have to learn the actual legal code of Solidar?

"While I'm gone, you will work on learning more about the laws and how they work with Master Jhulian, but at half past seventh glass in the morning, starting on Lundi. His study is at the end of the hall on the right. You will meet with Maitre Dyana next Mardi evening and on whatever other evenings she sets. She asked that you wait outside the dining hall for her."

"Yes, sir. Am I still restricted to Imagisle?"

"No, but I would suggest you avoid the more dangerous areas of L'Excelsis. Clovyl says you should be able to handle common dangers, but not large groups, or more than a pair of hired bravos. What did you have in mind, if I might ask?"

"I thought I might call on my family, and perhaps eat a meal in a bistro, things like that."

"Those I would recommend. You need to see L'Excelsis again."

I didn't realize how strange those words were until after I left him to go study.

34

Too often friends fall away when one rises.

For the first time since I'd left my parents after the fire, I had more than a few coins, and that meant I could take a hack out to visit my parents on Samedi. Since Master Dichartyn was gone, I could also leave Imagisle earlier than on most Samedis. Even so, because I enjoyed taking my time, it was past the ninth glass when I walked across the Bridge of Hopes. The sun warmed the air, heralding late spring, and there was just enough of a breeze for comfort, and not enough to blow away the fragrances from the spring flowers blooming in the narrow gardens flanking the Boulevard D'Imagers. There weren't many coaches for hire, but I found one and arrived at my parents' house just before noon. I could only hope that someone happened to be there, because I hadn't known I'd be able to come in time to dispatch a note and receive a reply.

Nellica's eyes widened when she opened the door and beheld me in all my subdued imager glory.

"Is anyone here, Nellica?"

"Your sister and Madame Chenkyr, sir." Her eyes avoided mine.

"If you'd tell them I'm here."

"Yes, sir. If you'd come in, sir." Nellica ushered me into the foyer and hurried off.

In moments Khethila appeared, wearing a severe green that made her face look far too pale. "Rhenn! You don't have to wait in the foyer. You're still family. Come into the parlor."

"Are you still reading Madame D'Shendael?" I offered teasingly as I followed her.

"Father disapproves," she said strongly, before glancing around and lowering her voice. "I have her treatise on *Civic Virtue*."

"I wasn't aware that there was such a thing." I tried to keep the irony out of my voice.

"Neither is she. She claims those who profess a civic virtue are cloaking their self-interest in morality."

"She doesn't believe in virtue?" I kept my voice pleasantly curious.

"She espouses virtue as an individual value."

"So we abandon virtue whenever we're with others?"

"Rhenn!" Definite exasperation colored her voice. "That's not it at all. Virtue or morality cannot be practiced by a group, but only by an individual. Each individual is different from every other individual, but a group pressures each individual to be the same. Otherwise, there is no group. The same is true of a society. The values of the strongest or most persuasive become the values of the group. The larger the group, the fewer the values those in the group share. In time, groups become mobs."

"I think your logic is lacking there."

"She says it better than I do."

I hadn't read Madame D'Shendael, but Khethila's inter-pretation suggested that Master Dichartyn and Madame D'Shendael had considered the same questions and possibly shared some of the same views. Logically, that shouldn't have surprised me . . . but it did.

At that moment, Mother bustled out of the kitchen. "Rhenn! What a pleasant surprise. We were about to have a small lunch in the breakfast room. You will join us, won't you?"

"I hoped so." I offered a grin.

Mother studied me. "You've lost weight."

"A little." I hadn't, not really, but Clovyl's exercises and running had turned any softness I'd once had into muscle.

"Aren't they feeding you enough?"

"They're feeding me very well, Mother." I started in the direction of the breakfast room, hoping to forestall any more detailed interrogation.

"He looks stronger," suggested Khethila.

"Laborers need to be strong, not imagers."

"Imaging does require strength, more than one might think." I stepped from the back hallway into the breakfast room, where Nellica had added another place to the table. Even with the two wall lamps lit, the breakfast room was gloomy, because the windows were on the east wall and al-lowed no sunlight past late morning. Lunch had been clearly informal, with the plates set on green place mats, rather than on one of the linen tablecloths used for guests—or family when one or more men were present. "Where's Culthyn?"

"He's with Father," Khethila replied. "Father says he needs to learn the business."

"That's why we're having leftover fowl in pastry," Mother added from behind me. "Neither your father nor Culthyn cares much for it."

Since I'd always liked fowl in crust and sauce, I had no

objections. Then, as I turned, I saw my chess study, mounted in a far more ornate frame, on the always-shaded south wall. For a moment, I just looked. It was every bit as good as I remembered, if not better.

"It goes well there," Mother said.

What I realized as well, and what she had not said, was that it was placed so that she could see it from her customary place at the table. It was behind where my father sat.

"It does," I finally said. "Thank you for reframing it."

Mother looked puzzled. "That was the way it arrived."

"Oh." Who had reframed it, and why? It had been in a simple black frame for the competition, as was required, so that no painting had an advantage. "I must have forgotten."

Khethila gave me a sideways glance, as if to suggest that wasn't something I'd forget. She was right, but what else could I have said?

Once she was seated, Mother looked at me. "You could have sent a note, saying you would be coming."

"I honestly didn't know that I would have this afternoon free until it was too late."

Mother just raised her eyebrows.

"I was given more training, and while it was going on, I couldn't leave Imagisle. I finished it more quickly than I'd been told it would take. This is the first time I've left the Collegium since I had dinner with you the last time."

"Even if you didn't let us know, it was good of you to come here first. You'll stay for dinner, won't you?" asked Mother.

"Not tonight." I could have, but it was the fourth Samedi of the month. I hadn't seen any of my friends since I'd become an imager, and it was a certainty that some of them would either be at Lapinina or at the Guild Hall later in the afternoon. "I'll be more free from now on, since I won't be spending quite so much time in training."

"Your father will be disappointed."

"I can stay for a while after we eat."

"He said he'd be later today."

"Does the extra time off mean that you got advanced again?" asked Khethila.

I smiled. "I did get nicer quarters—two rooms to myself, a sitting room or study, and a sleeping chamber."

"Perhaps everything is turning out for the best," said Mother brightly. "But your father will be sorry to have missed you."

"I think you've mentioned that before," I said dryly.

"Rhenn . . . I know you two do not see the world in the same way, but that does not mean that he doesn't care for you."

"I know." I still had the feeling he'd care for me more had I chosen to become a wool factor, but I wasn't about to say that. I turned to Khethila. "What are you going to do now?"

"I'm learning to be an assistant clerk for Father, the one who makes all the daily ledger entries."

There was a hint of a frown from Mother. "Until she finds a proper young man, anyway."

"What happened to Armynd?"

Khethila laughed. "He discovered I was reading Madame D'Shendael. He didn't put it quite that way, but when he said that it was clear we had interests too different for harmony, that was what he meant."

Mother frowned, if briefly, and I knew she'd hoped for the match, as much for Khethila's comfort as anything.

I managed a pleasant smile, although what had already happened confirmed that anyone Khethila felt interested in would not be someone for whom my parents would care much. "Do you find working at the factorage interesting?"

"You just have to be careful and thorough," my sister replied. "What's interesting is the way in which certain number patterns show up in the accounts. I'm studying Astrarth's *Theory of Numbers* on my own, and seeing if any of what he postulates shows up."

"Has it?"

"Not yet, but I've only been working on the ledgers for the last two weeks. Rousel thinks it's a good idea that I know more about business."

"So does your father," added Mother.

"How are things going with Rousel?" I asked quickly.

"He and Remaya are doing well." Mother smiled briefly. "He writes occasionally."

Khethila shifted her weight in her chair, ever so slightly.

"And how is the wool factoring going in Kherseilles?" I looked to Khethila.

"I couldn't say, because so far I'm only doing the ledgers for the factorage here, and not the master ledger that merges both accounts."

Mother looked sharply at Khethila, who smiled pleasantly.

In short, matters weren't going quite so well in Kherseilles, but Khethila wasn't about to say or was guessing from what she'd seen so far, and Mother wasn't about to say anything negative about Rousel . . . or allow anyone else to.

"Do you know what you'll be doing as an imager?" Mother asked. "Can you tell us?"

"They say I may have some duties working for the Council, but very minor ones at first. No one's given me any details, but I have had to learn all the Council procedures."

"Your father would be very pleased if you became a Council advisor."

"That's not going to happen any time soon," I replied with a laugh. "How is Aunt Ilena?"

"As stubborn as ever. I'm thinking of visiting her in Juyn, on the way to Kherseilles . . ."

From that point on, I just asked questions and listened. Although I stayed almost to the fourth glass of the afternoon, neither Father nor Culthyn appeared, and I took my leave. The late afternoon remained pleasant, and while it was more than two milles, I walked the entire distance to the Guild Square, taking my time.

Because I didn't see anyone I knew around the square, I made my way to Lapinina. When I stepped into the bistro, the couple at the table nearest the door looked away. Rogaris and Sagaryn sat at a round table for four, and I stepped toward it.

"How are you two coming?"

Sagaryn's eyes widened as they took in the gray waistcoat, shirt, and trousers. "Is that you, Rhenn?"

"The same."

"You're . . . an imager?"

I nodded. "Might I join you?"

"Oh . . . yes . . ." Rogaris said hastily.

Sagaryn nodded, a trace reluctantly, but I eased into the seat across from them.

Staela appeared. "What would you like, sir?"

I looked up at her. "I'm still Rhenn, Staela."

Her expression didn't change at all. "Yes, sir."

"Just a glass of the Cambrisio white, if you have it."

"Yes, sir."

"We don't see imagers up here very often," Rogaris offered.

"You're the first," added Sagaryn, taking a swallow of dark beer.

"I'm probably the only portraiturist who's ended up an imager."

"That well could be."

"How are you two doing?"

Rogaris glanced at Sagaryn, who remained stone-faced. "The same as always."

"Have you heard anything about Madame Caliostrus?"

"She's all right. He had some sort of assurance annuity or something . . . some patron paid for it, and the masons' guild is rebuilding the place."

"Lucky at that," added Sagaryn. "You know anything about it?"

"No." I shook my head. "He never talked coins with me— except to explain why he'd docked my pay."

Staela reappeared with a glass of amber-white wine, which she placed before me with far greater care than she ever had when I'd been a journeyman. "Your Cambrisio, sir. It's four."

Almost as soon as I'd put a silver on the table she scooped it up and had six coppers back before me. Then she was gone. I took a sip of the wine. It was cool, and not that bad, but I realized that what I'd been drinking at dinner at the dining hall was just as good.

"How is Master Jacquerl treating you?" I asked Rogaris.

"Nothing's changed." He sipped the dark red wine.

"And you?" I turned to Sagaryn.

"The same as always."

Neither spoke for a time. Nor did I. Then I looked to Rogaris. "How is Aemalye?"

"She's fine."

"Are you still planning to get married a year from this Agostos?"

"Something like that."

After a few more questions, I smiled and stood, leaving most of the Cambrisio. "It was good to see you both. Take care of yourselves."

"You, too," replied Rogaris.

Sagaryn only nodded.

It was just past the fifth glass as I stepped out of Lapinina, wondering why I had come at all, when a voice called from behind me.

"Rhenn!"

I turned.

There stood Seliora, beside a taller, red-haired woman. This time Seliora was wearing a rich green skirt with a black blouse and a matching green jacket. She smiled at me.

"Seliora." I couldn't help but smile back, especially after the coolness of Sagaryn and Rogaris.

She took another step toward me, and another, stopping almost close enough that I could have reached out to embrace her. I thought about it, but didn't.

"I'm glad to see you," she began, her words warm. "You just disappeared, and no one heard anything. I heard that you couldn't find a position. I worried about you."

I was glad someone worried, but I didn't want to say that. "I couldn't leave Imagisle for quite some time," I explained, adding, "You know that's where I went?"

"I can see that. The gray looks good on you. I thought . . ."

"You thought what?" I looked at her. "Foretelling?"

She flushed, but kept her eyes on me. "I saw you in gray a long time ago. I didn't know what it meant. Sometimes . . . it's like that."

I didn't want to press her, and my smile turned wry. "It

was either become a wool merchant or try to become an imager."

She tilted her head, and her eyes sparkled, almost impishly. "I couldn't see you as a wool merchant. I think you weren't meant to be one. Are you an imager yet?"

"If they accept you, you're an imager right away. You're just a very low imager who's restricted to the isle until you learn more."

"I don't imagine you'll stay lowly that long."

"I've been advanced since I've been there." I could say that much without being boastful.

"I'm not surprised." She smiled, tentatively. "Will you come to the dance with me?"

"I'd be pleased to . . . if you don't mind being escorted by an imager."

"Rhenn . . ." She shook her head.

"I'm sorry. I went in to Lapinina to talk to Rogaris and Sagaryn, and they barely said a dozen words. Staela kept calling me 'sir,' as if I'd never been in her bistro, and I've been coming there for almost five years."

"I'm not them." She smiled once more.

"I'm very glad."

"Oh . . . Rhenn . . ." She turned and gestured to the tall redhead. "This is my big cousin Odelia."

"I'm pleased to meet you." I inclined my head to Odelia. She was definitely tall, within a few digits of me, not heavy, but muscular. Was everyone in Seliora's family muscular?

Odelia smiled back politely. "I've never met an imager."

"Three months ago," I replied, "neither had I."

Seliora looked at me, and I offered her my arm. "Shall we proceed?"

"You sound so formal."

"It comes with the gray."

She giggled—a sound so totally false that I knew she was jesting—and I laughed.

"That's much better."

Odelia stepped up on my left. I would have offered my other arm, but that didn't feel right, and she didn't seem to mind as we made our way across the pavement to the Guild Hall. In the west Artiema was about to set. I wondered if it was just coincidence, or if the silvered moon happened to be a patroness of Seliora or Odelia. But that too was silly.

The guard who stood inside the hall looked at my grays, and then at Seliora and Odelia, then resolutely turned his head.

"You see," I murmured.

"It doesn't matter. You're with us, and we're still guild members."

"I paid my fees for the first half of the year," I added with a smile. "Doesn't that still make me a guild member?" I didn't think Guildmaster Reayalt would agree, but he wasn't anywhere around, and, besides, Seliora was quite correct. She could bring anyone she pleased, although there were usually few outsiders.

The musicians were getting ready to play, and Odelia nodded to Seliora and slipped away.

"Kolasyn is over there with his friends," Seliora said, "but he won't be long."

"Odelia gets her way?"

"We all do." She offered that charming but mischievous smile. "You'll see."

By "all" I assumed she meant all the women in her family, but that wasn't something I was going to ask. Maybe meeting her again under Artiema wasn't exactly a coincidence, although that was just a superstition.

The music started, and I placed my right hand gently on the small of her back and took her right hand in my left. We began to dance. Seliora was a far better dancer than I was, even though Father had insisted that I learn the basics—even providing a dancing maitre, Madame D'Reingel—my last year in grammaire.

When the musicians paused, so did we.

"You dance better now," she observed.

"I don't know why. I haven't danced since the last time we were here."

"Did you think of me?"

"Yes. More than a few times." That was certainly true.

She offered a false pout. "You tell all the girls that."

"Only you," I replied, immediately wishing I hadn't phrased it quite that way.

"You only lie to me?" She flashed the mischievous smile.

"No. You're just the only one I thought of—except women I'm related to, like Mother and Khethila."

"I don't know as I'd like to be considered a sister."

I just groaned. "I can't say anything right, can I?"

"At least you recognize that." This time she laughed, softly, but not cruelly.

The music started up again, and I decided that silence was the better part of valor. We swirled out into the double handful of couples dancing.

"You're stronger, too," she said, after I twirled and lifted her, then set her back on the floor.

"That's part of the training," I admitted.

"It suits you."

"What have you been doing, besides designing and embroidering and needlepointing chair fabric designs?"

"We don't do the needlepoint by hand. We have several looms, including a small jacquard loom, but I have to punch out the cards once I work out the design. I'm also the one who keeps it running. Father isn't all that mechanically inclined."

"How tight can you get the weave?"

She looked up at with another smile. "How tight do you want it?"

I almost flushed at her words. "I guess I recall more of wool than I thought, or enough for you to pull it right over my eyes."

She squeezed my fingers, just slightly.

We danced and talked until the musicians stopped playing for the evening. Then, I let go of her hand, reluctantly, I realized.

"Do you think I could persuade you to come next month?" she murmured.

"You could. I have Samedi afternoons and nights and Solayi afternoons off." I realized I didn't want to wait a month to see her again. "I've heard there's a new bistro called Felters . . ."

"It's quite good, Kaelyn said. I haven't been there."

"Next Samedi?" After I asked, I realized I was supposed to go to my parents' for their dinner, but I knew I'd far rather spend the evening with Seliora.

"I'd love to, but Father is taking us to see his sister."

"The seventh, then?"

"I'd like that very much. . . ."

"At fifth glass at your place?"

"That would be good." A twinkle in her eyes accompanied the next words. "My parents will expect to meet you."

"I'd be pleased." I wondered if they would be, though. I didn't know if all Pharsi families were as accepting as Remaya's family had been of Rousel.

I did end up spending silvers—on a hack to drive her and Odelia back to the large building on the corner of Hagahl Lane and Nordroad that was clearly home and business to her and her family, and then to take me back to the east side of the Bridge of Hopes.

I was still smiling when I walked into my quarters.

35

Law is necessary because, without it, no one willingly reins in self-interest.

Throughout the day on Solayi, as I struggled through the pages of *Jurisprudence,* my thoughts kept drifting back to Samedi. Why had Sagaryn and Rogaris been so distant? We'd been friendly for years, and I certainly hadn't changed that much. Yet they'd been edgy and uncomfortable, as if they were suddenly afraid. Was their reaction one of the reasons why Master Dichartyn had said that I needed to see

L'Excelsis again? But . . . Master Dichartyn had said that I projected what I felt, and I'd only felt friendly to them. Did that mean that they were so afraid that it didn't matter that I was friendly? Yet Seliora had seemed happy for me, and Odelia had been more than pleasant.

The dining hall was nearly deserted at the noon meal, but I did see Reynol, and we ate together and talked pleasantly before I headed back to my room and the heavy pages of *Jurisprudence.*

By the time I rubbed my eyes and collapsed into bed on Solayi night, I thought I understood most of what I'd read, but I wasn't so certain when I woke after a night filled with dreams of advocates and jurists uttering phrases that had no meaning at all to me.

On Lundi, after breakfast, and after half a glass spent reviewing the assignments in *Jurisprudence,* I left my quarters and headed across the quadrangle, wondering what Master Jhulian would be like in person.

Two seconds—Whaltar and one I didn't know—were walking toward me.

"Good morning," I offered.

"Good morning, sir," returned Whaltar. The other secundus murmured the same.

I could hear a few low words after they passed.

"He's the one . . . took Diazt down . . ."

". . . was always friendly to me," said Whaltar. "Never pushed his way around."

". . . good to know . . . helps to have friends like that . . ."

Friends like what?

I only waited something less than a quint of a glass before Master Jhulian opened his study door and beckoned for me to enter. His study was almost identical to that of Master Dichartyn, save that he had two chairs set before his desk. I took the one closer to the window.

Master Jhulian was more slender than I had thought, and his hair was almost white-blond, but I had only seen him from a distance, either in the dining hall or at the hearing for Floryn.

"Rhennthyl," he began after closing the study door, walking to the window, gazing out, and then settling himself behind his desk on a chair covered by a wide and worn gray cushion, "Master Dichartyn has told me about you. He states that you are relatively direct and generally honest. I will attempt to be both with you." He cleared his throat before continuing. "I would prefer that you ask me about those things you do not understand. Otherwise, you will waste my time and yours because I will assume that, if you have no questions, you will know the material." He smiled politely, waiting for me to reply.

"Yes, sir. I will try to ask such questions, but some of what is in the text is so complex that . . . well . . . even though I've read all of it several times, I'm not sure that I understand enough to ask a question."

"That is a fair statement, Rhennthyl, and if . . . if you tell me where you had trouble, even if you cannot articulate exactly what you do not understand, that is acceptable. Please begin by explaining what jurisprudence is and why it is of particular import to Solidar and the Collegium."

"Jurisprudence is the study of the law itself, in terms of both its precedents in case law and in terms of the philosophical basis behind both laws enacted by the Council and those derived through the example of case law."

"Close enough. What roots of traditional jurisprudence, indeed of law itself, did the establishment of the Juristic Courts of Solidar deny?"

I actually knew that. "Many scholars outside of Solidar claimed that the law historically had four basic roots—eternal, natural, human, and divine. Because the Nameless does not distinguish by appellation"—those words were not mine, but from the text—"but by function, the first judges of the Juristic Courts divided all legal precedents and existing codes into two basic categories, those of human and natural . . ." I went on explaining.

"What is the problem with the idea that laws are to promote good and restrain evil?"

I didn't see a problem with that idea, and yet Master

Jhulian was suggesting that there was. I had to think. "The idea isn't bad, sir, but it seems to me that one could have problems in defining what is good."

"Oh?"

"Each person . . . well, most people . . . would tend to see good as what benefits them and evil as what does not. What benefits the High Holders most might not benefit the common folk nearly so much, and what benefits the factors—"

"All of that is true, without a doubt . . . *but* . . . what is the specific problem that this conflict engenders with the formal fundamentals of law itself?"

The term "formal fundamentals of law" jogged my memory. "Oh . . . one of the formal requirements of law is that the laws of the land must be impartial and apply equally to all, and if laws define good to benefit one group at the expense of another, they can't be impartial."

"*Jurisprudence* doesn't discuss this, taking it as a given, but why must laws be impartial?"

I took a chance with my answer. "They don't have to be, sir. That's the ideal, but there are other countries that have lasted without impartial laws."

Master Jhulian nodded and gave me a wry smile. "Master Dichartyn said that you might offer some . . . insights. Let me rephrase the question. Why must the laws in Solidar be as impartial as we can make them?"

"Because people are happier when the laws are fair and will obey them more readily?"

He just laughed. "People are probably less happy with impartial laws, but they will obey them because they see that others do not gain what they know are unfair advantages. Remember that each man perceives an advantage to himself as fair and deserved and any advantage to another as unfair and undeserved." He smiled.

I didn't like the expression because I suspected a difficult question was about to follow.

"With all the emphasis on fairness, why did the Council allow the High Holders to retain the right to low justice on their holdings outside any city or large town?"

I'd read about low justice, which basically referred to the process of dealing with petty theft, assault without weapons, criminal trespass when no other offense was involved—crimes like that—and I'd wondered why the High Holders had retained those rights and the ability to confine offenders for less than half a year or to apply corporal punishment within limits. Until I'd read the text, I hadn't even realized that such rights existed. "I don't know, sir."

"Then guess."

"Ah . . . because who else could enforce that on large holdings?"

"That's partly true, but there is another reason. On whose side were the High Holders in the transition from rule by rex to the rule by the Council?"

"They supported the guilds and factors, didn't they?" I paused. "Was that their price?"

"Whether it was their price, or whether the guilds and factors felt that that they could only push so far, it had to be something along those lines. Also, the guilds and the factors have always been more concerned about what happens in the cities and larger towns."

That also made sense.

"Back to the essential questions of fairness, since we do operate largely in the cities. There is another reason why we as imagers have a great interest in ensuring that the laws are fair and impartial. In point of fact, the penalties for imagers who break either the laws of Solidar or the rules of the Collegium are far stricter than any received by others. Why is this unfairness to our advantage? Or less to our disadvantage?"

I had no idea.

"When times are bad and things are going badly, people do not seek the causes. They seek someone to blame. Who do they blame? The first target is almost always the group that appears to be favored, that has more than they do, and whose numbers are small. Only if those in that group are powerful do they seek another group to blame, but even so their resentment and anger remain." He looked to me.

"By subjecting ourselves to stricter rules and by not displaying overtly our prosperity and power, we attempt to avoid being a target?"

"As you will discover, anyone who attacks an imager is an enemy of the Collegium, and yet, as you will discover, while measures are taken to ensure that such attackers or those who hired them do not survive, the Collegium seldom acts in a way so as to create an impression of might as an institution. Even so, while we occasionally are not successful in finding the attackers, we seldom fail in discovering those who hired them, although it may occasionally take years. Consequently, most attacks are not planned by those in L'Excelsis. But there are some." He paused. "What does this mean in the context of the question I asked you?"

By the time I left Master Jhulian, there were so many thoughts flying through my head that nothing seemed quite as it had been. Equally disturbing were the two short papers he'd assigned, along with the reading. How was I going to prove or disprove that natural law was a contradiction in terms? Or that the second formal requirement of law—that laws must be knowable and understandable to all who are capable of understanding them—was in conflict with the first requirement?

And why did I need to know all that? Just to be a silent guard for the Council? That didn't seem likely, but it also didn't seem likely that I was being groomed to be a jurist or advocate for the Collegium either.

36

*A true imager sees beyond the eyes and hears beyond
the words.*

On Mardi night at dinner, I was sitting with Kahlasa and
Menyard, exhausted in both body and mind, because Clovyl
had continued to increase the severity and intensity of my
physical training, both in terms of exercise and running and
in learning greater physical self-defense skills. In order to
gain weaponless combat skills, I was now sparring with several other thirds, all of them older and more experienced.
Not only was I exhausted and bruised, but that had come on
top of another long morning with Master Jhulian.

"You look a little dazed, Rhenn," Kahlasa said. "You
haven't said much this evening."

"I'm sorry. It's been a long day. I had my first session with
Master Jhulian yesterday, and he gave me two essays and
more than fifty pages of reading in the *Jurisprudence* book.
Today, he criticized those essays and told me to rewrite them,
and added another longer one, and forty pages more." I
wanted to take a long swallow of wine, but I only sipped. I
had to work with Maitre Dyana later, and I didn't want my
senses or abilities wine-dimmed.

Menyard looked as blank as my mind felt, but Kahlasa
nodded knowingly.

"And Clovyl has me doing a half glass of exercises and
running six milles before we even get into everything he's
trying to teach me."

That surprised Kahlasa. "They're pushing you hard. That's
not good."

"You're telling me it doesn't feel good? I hurt most of the time." I finished my last bite of the crumb pudding.

She shook her head. "You're not the only one. They're stepping up training on several levels, and they're cutting short return leaves for field imagers. That suggests troubles ahead."

"The newssheets reported that emissaries from the High Priest of Caenen and from the Oligarch of Jariola were meeting in Caena last week," Menyard interjected. "The Abiertans have been refitting some of their merchanters with heavy weapons, and bought several old cruisers from Ferrum that they're also refitting."

"Tiempre and Stakanar have signed a pact for mutual defense," added Kahlasa.

"Do any of them really think they'll end up gaining anything?" I'd read about all the pacts and the arming and rearming. Tiempre and Stakanar bordered Caenen, and both worried about the High Priest and his efforts to spread the gospel of Duality. My thought was that the gospel was merely a front to get his people to support a war of expansion, but maybe I'd been too steeped in the more practical religious approach of the Nameless. Then the Otelyrnan League, composed of the smaller nations on the continent of Otelyrn, had agreed to allow the Tiempran forces rights of passage on major highways and waterways. That had incensed the High Priest of Caenen, and one thing was leading to another. But I still didn't understand why; wars almost always cost the winner more than the winner gained, and the loser—and its leaders—could lose everything, including their lives. But most leaders clearly didn't believe they'd be the losers.

"The High Priest wants to save the world from the damnation of the Nameless and any other faith in conflict with Duodeus, and make a profit while doing so," suggested Kahlasa.

"And Ferrum wants to make a higher profit by selling arms to both sides, and the edgy neutrals," said Menyard.

"And our factors want to sell to everyone, I suppose?" I added.

"Of course, but these things can get out of hand," replied Kahlasa. "That's why the Collegium is preparing."

"For what?"

She just smiled. "For whatever may be necessary. Right now, I don't know, but Master Dichartyn will tell you, and Master Schorzat will tell me."

"And neither of you will be pleased," added Menyard. "I'm just glad I don't have to do what you two do."

"What do you do," I said, "if I might ask?"

"I'm an equipment designer and imager. Very special equipment. At some point, Master Dichartyn may send you to me. I've worked with most of his imagers."

"Do you two know what I'm being trained for?"

"No," replied Kahlasa. "Except in general. You're being trained by Master Dichartyn. He's in charge of Collegium and Council security, but he never tells imagers in training what their final assignments will be until they're through training, or until he's sure that they will get through training. He's in charge of the Council guard force, the Collegium security section, the covert/overt section, and imager reception."

I couldn't help but frown at the last. "Reception?"

"What better way to find out what we do than send an imager spy into the Collegium?"

Put that way, it made sense. I decided against asking about the covert/overt section, not because I didn't wish to know, but because I knew I wouldn't learn any more.

As I left dinner, I thought about a term Kahlasa had used—"field imagers." The fact that she came and went from the Collegium suggested that she was one of them. The handbook on the Collegium didn't mention specifics. It just said that imagers had a wide range of duties, both at the four Collegia and elsewhere. But Kahlasa didn't report to Master Dichartyn, and that meant field imagers weren't directly connected to Master Dichartyn.

I almost started out the dining hall doors to my quarters, out of force of habit, then stopped. It was still before seven, and I was supposed to wait for Maitre Dyana.

Everyone had left the corridor, and the first bell was striking when I saw her step through the rear door and walk toward me. I just watched, politely, as she approached, taking in her iron-gray hair and bright blue eyes. She wore imager grays, but in addition, she had draped herself with a brilliant blue scarf that matched her eyes. The skin on her face was pale and smooth, younger than her hair would have suggested, and she offered a pleasant smile.

"Rhennthyl . . . you're Dichartyn's protégé." She nodded. "I can see why. You look like a well-mannered young fellow, could be a junior son of a High Holder or a merchant heir or, with a beard, a struggling artist. That's not so surprising, since you've already been two of those."

Except I'd never had a beard. I'd tried, once, but it came in curly and itchy, even though my hair only had a slight wave in it.

"There's a small conference room off the entrance. That will do."

She turned, and I followed her. She walked briskly, for all the gray hair and her almost fragile frame. When I entered the room with the oval table and six chairs, she was standing by the window, looking out into the twilight. She said nothing.

I closed the door and moved closer to the conference table. Finally, she looked at me. Those blue eyes were as cold as lapis, yet seemingly without judgment.

I waited.

"Good. I detest unnecessary chatter. Conversation is useful only in certain settings, and for certain purposes. Master Dichartyn has requested that I attempt to teach you how to improve your shields. I do not know how you developed your shields. So . . . I will make several brief attacks, and we will proceed from there."

"Yes, maitre." I inclined my head slightly.

The first attack was more like a jab, so light that my heavier secondary shields did not spring into play. The second was harder, but easy enough to repulse. The third was strong enough that I was forced backward a step. The fourth and last was aimed more at my shields, but was powerful enough—even though off-center—that I had to move back once more.

Maitre Dyana looked at me sadly, as though I were a truant grammaire student. "Finesse, dear boy . . . finesse. You'll exhaust yourself in a fraction of a glass defending yourself like that. The last attack was at an angle. You used your entire shield to stop it. Almost all attacks come from an angle, if a small one. When you can, let your shields collapse a little. Let the attacks slide off. The object is to protect yourself with the least effort possible. Imagers are too few in number as it is. We don't need to lose more because you spent too much energy defending yourself unnecessarily vigorously." She waited for a response.

"Yes, maitre."

"We'll start over again. This time I'll stand over here and image force at you. It will be direct. Please make an effort to slide it past you . . ."

I wouldn't have said my efforts were a total failure, but my successes were few and far from complete.

As the outside bells struck eight, Maitre Dyana raised her hand. "That will be all for this evening. Now that I've gotten your attention and you understand your deficiencies, dear boy, tomorrow evening I will expect a better performance from you."

She offered a brief and perfunctory smile, then nodded and walked past me, leaving me standing in the conference room, sweating and exhausted once more. So far as I could tell, the seemingly frail maitre had not even raised a drop of perspiration while wearing me out.

37

*The best traders weigh their words
as carefully as their goods.*

The week ended as it began. No matter how hard I worked
for Master Jhulian, Clovyl, and Maitre Dyana, and no matter
how much I improved or learned, there was always more to
learn and do. By Samedi, I was more than ready to leave
Imagisle, even for a dinner at my parents with a factor I hadn't
seen in years and his daughter, a young woman I'd never met.

I didn't leave at ninth glass or even noon. Instead, as the ten
bells of midday struck, I was seated in my study poring over
Jurisprudence, the section dealing with tort claims. According
to the text, the Council itself was immune to juristic claims
of damages, as were the Juristic Courts, and all branches of
government. Individual councilors, or anyone in any branch
of government, could be subject to a suit under tort law. At that
point, I closed my eyes and rubbed my forehead.

After several moments, I opened my eyes and looked
down at the listing of acts for which an official was not liable,
followed on the next page by a listing of those where he
might be. I slipped a leather bookmark in place and closed
the book.

I still had another essay to write for Master Jhulian, this
one on the theoretical and practical limits of sovereign im-
munity as exercised by the Council and the government over
which it presided, and I had to explain why the first Council
had created the malfeasance and misfeasance sections of the
Juristic Code.

I'd asked Master Jhulian why imagers needed to read
about law, and his answer had been direct and troubling. "All

imagers need to know some of this. Anyone who works with Master Dichartyn needs to know more than I can teach. I have to prepare you to keep learning." Then he'd smiled. "*After* I'm satisfied, Master Dichartyn will explain why what you are learning is applicable. That's because, unless you do learn it, you won't keep working with him, and you won't need to know why."

From the time I'd first come to Imagisle, I'd known that there was a darker side to the Collegium, and with every day that passed, I was getting the feeling that I was getting closer to it. Finally, I began to reread the pages in *Jurisprudence*. I stayed at my desk, more or less, until just before the fourth glass, when I hurried out of my quarters.

Even so, I was at my parents' door at half past four, where Nellica ushered me in.

"Sir . . . everyone will be meeting in the formal parlor at five."

"Is anyone there?"

"No, sir."

"Then I'll slip into the family parlor and wait there."

She wasn't totally pleased, but she didn't have to be. I settled into one of the armchairs—not my father's—but I didn't have to wait long before Culthyn appeared, a slightly sullen expression on his face.

"What's the matter?" I asked.

"Father says I'm not invited to dinner. Khethila isn't either."

"Where is she?"

"She went to Brennai's for the evening. Brennai's her best friend. This week, anyway."

"You're cynical."

"That's what Mother says." He looked at me. "What do you really do as an imager?"

"At the moment, I'm studying the laws of Solidar and L'Excelsis."

"You're going to be an imager advocate? That's freezing!"

"We all have to study law . . . and science, and history, and philosophy."

"Oh . . . Can you do imaging? Can you show me?"

"Not yet. I can do it, but the masters don't let us do it off Imagisle until we're more experienced."

"Come on, Rhenn. No one would know."

I offered a smile. "I would, and sooner or later, so would Master Dichartyn. He's my preceptor. He's very perceptive."

"What good is being an imager if they don't let you image?"

"Culthyn," I said slowly, "imaging is more dangerous than I ever knew or dreamed. That's why almost a third of all imagers die in training."

That stopped him, but only for a moment. "You haven't died."

"That's because I've paid attention to those who know better than I do."

"That's a lesson you still need to learn, Culthyn," announced Mother as she entered the family parlor. "Off to the kitchen. Your dinner is on the table in the breakfast room. Don't bother Nellica or Kiesela. When you're done, up to your rooms."

"Yes, Mother." He looked to me. "Someday, will you show me?"

"I will. It might be a while."

After he left through the archway into the rear hall, Mother asked, "Show him what?"

"Imaging. Right now, I'm not supposed to image off Imagisle."

"I can see that." She nodded. "Zerlenya and her parents are most anxious to meet you."

"Rhenn!" My father's voice boomed across the parlor. "You're even early!" He looked at me. "You look more like a guard officer every time I see you."

"He looks just fine, Chenkyr."

"That's what I meant. He stands taller."

Shortly, there was another knock on the front door, and the three of us moved to the formal parlor while Nellica ushered the guests into the house.

In moments, Tomaz was stepping toward me. He was a

short and stocky man with an engaging smile. "You're Rhenn, I take it, and an imager to boot. Wager your father never planned on that."

"No, sir, he didn't, but he's fortunate to have Rousel and Culthyn to carry on." After I'd said that, I realized I should have mentioned Khethila.

"Oh!" Tomaz turned and gestured. "This is my daughter Zerlenya." He beckoned again. "Zerlenya, come and meet Rhennthyl. It's not every day you get to meet an imager that you know personally—or his father, anyway."

Zerlenya stepped forward, offering a tentative smile. She was thin, almost painfully so, but she had wide cheekbones, and a clear pale complexion, with tight-curled jet-black hair that would have dropped to midshoulder had it not been swept up and curled into a swirl at the back of her long neck. Her eyes were pale gray, and in the off-white gown and shoulder scarf, she gave the impression of a beautiful swan, if one ready to take wing at the slightest danger.

"I'm pleased to meet you." I offered a smile with my words.

"Father has spoken of you. I've never met an imager."

"You have now. I'm a very recent imager, though."

"What can you image?"

"So far I've managed a copy of my brother's wife's comb, a box, and all sorts of small objects in training, including a metal bar or two."

"That doesn't sound terribly dangerous." Her voice was thin and bright, the kind that could be heard across a room.

"I hope not. Time will tell."

"It always does."

I just nodded to that.

"Do you like being an imager?"

I hadn't really thought about that, unlike being a portraiturist. I'd wanted to paint, but since I'd never considered being an imager until I discovered I had the talent, it hadn't been a question of liking, but of doing the best I could. "I hadn't thought about it. It's not an occupation you dream about as a child."

"But do you like it? Father's always saying that you cannot be good at something unless you like doing it."

"Do you believe that?"

"I do. That's why Uncle Weidyn is so good a cabinetmaker."

"I haven't met him. I've only met Aeylana."

"Oh . . . yes. You did the portrait, didn't you? It's very pleasant."

I couldn't help but bristle inside. When someone refers to a work of art, even one that is not superb, as "nice" or "pleasant," it means that they don't know art or that they think it's terrible. "She seemed to like it."

"I'm sure she did."

"She was very good at the sittings."

"She's very good, and very well mannered."

Before long, Nellica rang the dinner chimes, and we repaired to the dining chamber, where we stood behind our chairs. The dinner settings were not strictly formal, because Father was flanked by Madame Tomaz and Zerlenya, while Mother was flanked by Tomaz and me, but with just six it really didn't matter. Anyone could converse with anyone else.

Father rested his hands on the back of his chair and offered the blessing.

"In peace and harmony," we all murmured when he finished, then seated ourselves.

Father carved the side of beef with his usual dispatch and efficiency, and before long, plates and goblets were full.

"How is the produce business these days?"

"Slow . . . so slow, Chenkyr. We're almost through our stored stocks of root vegetables and the like. The spring vegetables and fruits from the South won't be in for another month, three weeks if we're fortunate. You can sell cloth at any time."

"Ah . . . my friend . . . I can sell at any time, but I have to buy the wool and arrange the weaving almost a year in advance, and pay much in advance, and if I judge wrong . . ." Father shrugged expressively. He always showed more emotion when he talked about business.

"You can always sell wool; it does not spoil."

"The price. It is always the price at which one buys, not the price at which one sells."

I looked at Zerlenya and offered a helpless shrug.

A ghost of a smile was her reply.

"Father is most at home talking business," I added, "wherever he is."

"Business is what supports the home," said Tomaz enthusiastically. "Why shouldn't we talk about it? We're not High Holders who talk about music no one can understand or books no one has read."

Khethila would have disputed that, but I doubted that Tomaz had ever seen a copy of Madame D'Schendael's book. I looked to Zerlenya. "Do you follow the produce business?"

"It would be difficult not to. Father insists we know everything."

"And why not?" replied Tomaz. "If anything happened to me, the Nameless forbid, if you didn't know the business, how would you all get by? Even you, Zerlenya, know more than I did at your age, and a good thing it is, too."

"Are all of your children following in the business?" asked Mother.

"All but Thurlyn," answered Madame Tomaz. "He's an ensign in the Navy. He's stationed on the *Rex Charyn*. He's always loved the water . . ."

From there the conversation remained firmly fixed in the areas of the mundane, and no one said anything about imagers and Imagisle.

Once the guests had left, nearly two glasses later, Mother closed the front door and turned to me. "What did you think of Zerlenya?"

"She's very nice."

"You didn't like her, then."

"She is pretty, in an ethereal way. I don't think she'd be happy with me."

"That's not the question," interjected Father. "Could you be happy with her?"

"It is the question, Father. Imagers cannot marry those who are not happy with them."

"Marriage isn't just about lust."

"No, it's not," I agreed. "I didn't say that. It's just that it's very important that an imager and his or her spouse get along well. More important than with other couples."

There must have been something in my voice. They exchanged glances.

After a moment, Mother said, "You know best."

Her tone suggested that I knew anything but. "It's something that all the senior imagers have stressed, Mother. I might not know, but I have to trust that they do."

"I see." This time, there was resignation in her voice. "I hope you find someone."

So did I, I reflected as I left.

At least they provided Charlsyn and the coach for the ride back to the Bridge of Hopes. For better or worse, Artiema had set and Erion—the grayish red lesser hunter—stood almost at its zenith, ruling the night sky.

38

*One cannot love truly without loving truly
the words of one's lover.*

The second week with Maitre Dyana was even more rigorous than the first, but I felt that I was learning a great deal, especially in how to focus imagery and to use the least amount necessary. But she still kept demanding more and more finesse.

"Dear boy, you are but one imager, and at times, you could face far more than a ruffian or two. Without precision and finesse, you will be lost."

Precision and finesse! How often I heard those words, but

I could take consolation in the results, even if my performance was seldom to the level she demanded. The same was true of my work with Clovyl. I could feel my skills improving, steadily, if not dramatically.

With Master Jhulian, I had no such consolation. As soon as I learned one aspect of the law, we pressed on to the next. The assignment that had concerned me the most had been on murder, as defined in the Juristic Code. Master Jhulian had examined me in great detail on that. When I had asked why, his response had been direct.

"Contrary to your unstated belief, I am not trying to make a nomologist out of you. I am trying to instill the knowledge you may need to survive. Because any unexplained death in these times tends to be laid at the feet of the imagers, it is important for every imager to understand what murder is, in both real and legal terms, and to make sure that he or she is never involved in something that could be termed murder, either by the newssheets or the civic patrollers."

Because I felt every word meant something, I committed the phrase to memory and wrote it down as soon as I returned to my room that Vendrei. "Never involved in something that could be termed murder" was a phrase that could cover a myriad of meanings—and sins.

By the time I returned from the dining hall after lunch on Samedi, I was more than ready to leave Imagisle. I'd been looking forward to that afternoon and evening, particularly after the long evening the week before at my parents' house. I had written them a short note thanking them for their thoughtfulness and kindness, and the wonderful food— which it had been. I doubted that would much appease my mother, who definitely wanted her eldest son married to someone from the "right" background, certainly not another Pharsi girl, and before all that long . . . and never mind the imager business.

Ready as I was to depart Imagisle right after lunch . . . I didn't. Instead, I sat down and attempted to organize my thoughts on my final essay for Master Jhulian—an analysis of the applicability of the Juristic Code to imagers. Two glasses later I had three pages of notes and an outline—as well as a profound desire to leave Imagisle as soon as possible. Since I had the feeling that I might be meeting Seliora's parents, I did wear my best uniform and make sure that my boots were well blacked and shining. I had also squeezed in another haircut on Jeudi.

Outside, the day was pleasant, if overcast, with a slight breeze out of the northwest. I did have to wait almost a quarter of a glass before a hacker stopped to pick me up.

"Nordroad and Hagahl Lane, on the east side."

He nodded, and I stepped up into the cab. The inside was clean, but threadbare.

When I descended onto the pavement close to a half glass later, I found that the building that served Seliora and her family as factory, factorage, and dwelling was far larger and more impressive in the daylight than in the lamplit gloom of late evening. The walls rose three stories, and the yellow brick was trimmed with gray granite cornerstones. Even the wood of the loading docks at the south end was stained with a brown oil and well kept, and the loading yard itself was stone-paved. The entrance on the side street to the north was the private family entrance, and it had a square and pillared covered porch that shielded a stone archway.

The hacker looked at me, and my grays, then at the stone entryway, but he said nothing. I gave him two coppers extra, then made my way up the steps. In the middle of the wide eight-panel door was an ancient and ornate brass knocker. Both the knocker and the plate had seen much wear, but both were brightly polished. I gave the knocker one hefty blow, then prepared to wait, but the door opened immediately.

Odelia stood there in the modest foyer, dressed in a pale green dress and darker green shawl that set off her coloring well. "Do come in, Master Rhennthyl." She grinned at me.

"Thank you, Odelia, but I won't be a master for some time."

The only exit to the foyer was the polished oak staircase behind Odelia, and she turned and gestured toward it. "Everyone's waiting upstairs."

"Then I'll let you lead me." I added, "Who's everyone?"

"Besides Seliora? Uncle Shelim and Aunt Betara, of course, and there's Hanahra and Hestya—they're the twins, my sisters—and Methyr, Seliora's younger brother. Bhenyt's off somewhere. Then, there's my mother. You'll recognize her."

"She's Aegina?"

Odelia nodded, adding, "And there's Shomyr. He's Seliora's older brother, and he very much wants to meet you."

I found myself squaring my shoulders as I followed Odelia up the steps.

The staircase, ample as it was, with its carved balustrades and shimmering brass fixtures, opened at the top into a large foyer or entry hall, a space a good eight yards wide and ten deep. The walls were paneled in light golden oak, and the floor was an intricate parquet, mostly covered with a lush carpet of deep maroon, with a border of intertwined golden chains and brilliant green leafy vines. Set around the foyer were various chairs and settees of dark wood, upholstered in various fabric designs. At the far end was a pianoforte.

The group standing in a rough circle at the edge of the carpet, beside a long settee, all turned as Odelia announced, "Rhennthyl D'Imagisle."

I had barely picked out Seliora, in a crimson dress with a black jacket, when a broad-shouldered, black-bearded young man a half head shorter than I was stepped forward. "I'm Shomyr. I'm Seliora's brother, and she's said so little about you that I wanted to meet you."

Said so little?

"Now, now, Shomyr, you'll have confused him totally." A dark-haired and wiry woman in green silk trousers and a matching jacket, who could easily have been Seliora's older sister, moved toward us. "The less my daughter says to us, generally the more she's interested, and the less we know." Her smile was identical to Seliora's.

I inclined my head. "I'm very pleased to meet you, Madame D'Shelim."

"Betara, please. Please. We're not that formal here."

They could have fooled me, given the furnishings in that grand upper entrance hall.

Seliora eased forward and around the others. She took my arm gently, as if to suggest a certain restrained possessiveness. "Rhenn is very talented. He's an outstanding portraiturist as well as an imager, and his family owns Alusine Wool."

"Ah . . . you're Chenkyr's boy, then?" asked Shelim.

"He's my father. My brother Rousel runs the factorage in Kherseilles." Even as I explained, I wondered how Seliora had known. I'd never said more than that my father was a wool factor, and there were more than a few in L'Excelsis, and even more throughout Solidar.

"How did you get to be an imager?" The question came from the single boy in the group, standing beside the red-haired twins, who looked to be two or three years younger than Khethila.

"Methyr," someone murmured.

"When I discovered I could image, I walked across the Bridge of Hopes and told the imagers. They tested me and decided I was an imager."

"It couldn't have been that simple," suggested Shomyr.

I managed a short laugh. "It was just that simple. Everything that came after that wasn't at all that easy. They didn't let me leave Imagisle for over a month."

"Are there any girls?" asked one of the twins.

"Some. One of the maitres I've been studying with is a woman, and there are others."

"Can imagers marry?" That was Odelia, and the question was delivered with a grin.

I could feel Seliora stiffen just slightly, and I had a definite sense that the question hadn't pleased her. "They can. That's if anyone wants to marry them."

That brought smiles to several faces, including to the face of the older and taller redheaded woman who had to be Odelia's mother.

"Generally, they usually live on Imagisle after they're married," I added.

"What exactly do imagers do?" pressed Shomyr.

"Whatever our duties are." I paused for a moment. "I've worked at certain things, but right now I'm being trained for a position at the Council Chateau."

"With the Council?" asked Shelim.

"I haven't been given all the details, but young as I am, I suspect it's far more like working for them." I tried to keep my tone wry.

"Do imagers make lots of coins?" asked Methyr.

"More than journeymen, and a great deal less than your father makes."

At that, Betara nodded slightly, and there was a quick set of glances between Seliora's parents. Before anyone else could ask another question, Betara spoke up. "Rhenn came here to take Seliora to dinner, not to see all of us. I think we'd best let them go."

Seliora gave her mother a quick glance that I wasn't about to try to decipher, then turned. Since she was still holding my arm, we turned and moved toward the steps, and then down them.

More surprising, there was a hack waiting outside, and a youngster standing on the steps. He grinned at Seliora.

"Thank you, Bhenyt," she said.

"My pleasure," he replied, nodding to us both.

"Felters, sir?" asked the hacker.

"If you would," I replied, looking at Seliora.

"Bhenyt is Odelia's younger brother," she replied, taking my hand as she stepped up into the coach. "I just thought it might be nice not to wait for a coach. You were very gallant," she added.

"Thank you." Had I had any real choice?

Once we were settled in the coach and moving south on Nordroad, I turned to her. I couldn't help but notice that, despite the similarity in colors to what she had worn the night we had truly danced for the first time, the dress and the jacket looked fresh—and had probably just been tailored and delivered. "How did you know who my father was?"

She laughed. "I didn't. Mama was the one who wanted to

know about your family. She had you investigated as soon as Odelia admitted I'd spent all of that Samedi with you."

"Is Odelia your guardian?"

"We're close, but she likes you."

"You know I'm not likely to ask for money or anything else from my parents. So why do they matter?"

"The money doesn't matter, even to Mama. She was impressed that you made journeyman and then became an imager. She says that you come from solid stock." Seliora squeezed my hand. "I could tell that."

"How could you know that from meeting a journeyman artist a few times?"

"You were always neat, clean, and with short hair and no beard, and after I saw the study you painted, I could tell you had talent to go with that ambition. I worried that you had too much ambition for a portraiturist."

"Too much ambition?"

"I didn't say that right." She tilted her head slightly. "Too much honesty for a portraiturist with that much ambition."

A faint scent of flowers emanated from her, not too much, a light scent.

Before that long, the coach stopped, we stepped out, and I paid and tipped the hacker.

Felters was ensconced in what had been a graystone row house on the south side of the lane that angled off East River Road. The oversized lamps that flanked the door were already lit, although the sun had not quite set.

The harried-looking server who greeted us looked at Seliora, then at me.

I did my best to mentally press friendliness upon her. "For two, please."

"Ah . . . this way."

We ended up at a small window table, crowded between two much larger tables, one occupied by three older men in suits of a cut I did not recognize, and one empty, but the smaller table was fine with me.

"What would you like to drink?" asked the server.

I inclined my head to Seliora.

"Do you have a white Sanellio?"

The server nodded.

"Cambrisio, white," I added.

The server left a slate on which the three specialties of the evening had been written in small script—Chicken Asseroiles, Pork Samedi, and Flank Steak Especial.

"Are any of these favorites of yours?" I asked.

"I think I'd like the chicken. You?"

"The steak. I'm partial to both mushrooms and parsley."

When the two goblets of wine came, right after two couples were settled in at the table behind me, I ordered for us, adding a crab bisque as an appetizer and choosing the walnut and shaved apple and cheese salad. They were probably winter-kept apples, but it was worth a try.

After the server left, Seliora looked at me. "You don't have to impress me."

"I just wanted to have a good meal with you and enjoy it. That's not something I get to do often."

"If you do it often, you won't be able to afford anything else." But her words were said warmly.

I lifted my wine goblet. "To you and to a delightful evening."

She lifted hers. "I'll return that. To you . . . and the evening."

The Cambrisio was good, but looking at Seliora was better.

"Why did you ask me to dance, that first time?" I asked.

"I wanted to. Rogaris told Odelia that you were too serious for me."

"He didn't know you well, then."

"Do you?" A hint of mischief colored her words.

"No, but I know that there's more to you than meets the eye . . . and I'm interested in learning more about you."

For just a moment, her eyes flickered past me, looking outside.

"What is it?"

"Nothing. Someone going past, but he was looking this way."

"Do you know him?"

She shook her head. "From what I saw, he's not someone I'd wish to know."

The server arrived with the salads. I took a bite, gingerly. "The salad is good, especially the cheese."

A faint smile crossed Seliora's lips, but she nodded, before saying, "It is."

"Why did you smile?"

"Not that many men would worry about the salad. They'd either eat it or ignore it."

I shrugged. I wasn't about to say I'd wanted it to be good for her. "I enjoy a good meal."

"You couldn't have eaten that well at Master Caliostrus's house."

I hadn't. "Why do you say that?"

"Last summer, I was with Odelia, and Ostrius was talking to her escort—the one before Kolasyn—about how he skipped as many meals as he could."

"He could afford to. I couldn't. It wasn't that bad."

"I like that about you."

"What?"

"You're not the complaining type. You do what's necessary until you can make things better. That's why you'll do well as an imager."

"Complaining doesn't do any good," I pointed out. "If the person you complain to is the kind who would listen, they've already done what they can, and anyone else either won't listen, doesn't care, or can't do anything."

"Most people aren't that practical."

I'd never thought of myself as that practical. How practical was trying to be a portraiturist when you came from a family of wool factors?

The server reappeared, took the empty salad plates, and placed the entrees in front of us. I cut into the flank steak, and then ate several bites, enjoying the combination of mushrooms, buttered parsley, and seasoned tender beef. "How is your chicken?"

"Very tender, and tasty. It reminds me of Aunt Aegina's."

"Odelia's mother?"

"Yes. She's a good cook, better than Mother. That might be because she enjoys it."

"Your mother eats because she has to."

"You noticed."

"She has a certain . . . determination, like someone else, I suspect."

Seliora flushed, just a touch. Then she stiffened and looked up and out the window. "That man . . . out there, in the dark brown cloak and a square beard. He's walked past twice, and he's looked at you."

"At you, I'm most certain. You're the one worth looking at."

"You're kind, but he wasn't looking at me."

If Seliora said the man wasn't, then he wasn't, but why would anyone be looking at me? From what I'd seen so far since I'd become an imager, no one gave imagers more than a passing glance—and that more to avoid us than anything else. "There's not much I can do about it now."

"I suppose not."

"Enjoy your chicken." I almost added that she should enjoy my looking at her, but that would have been too forward.

"And what else? You were about to add something."

"The company, if you can."

"I'm enjoying that very much."

"I'm glad."

After several more bites and another swallow of wine, I asked, "Do you like designing the patterns for the upholstery?"

"The designing I like very much." Seliora's smile turned wry. "Working with some clients is sometimes less enjoyable."

I kept asking her questions through the remainder of dinner and through dessert—an apple cream custard—and the tea that followed.

Finally, as much as I'd enjoyed the dinner, both the food and the company, there were people waiting outside, and the server kept looking at us.

"I suppose we had better go. I wouldn't want to be accused of keeping you out too late."

"You would have been anyway, even if we'd left a glass ago," she replied.

All in all, the dinner cost four silvers, counting what I left for the server.

We stepped out of the bistro and were walking toward the pair of hacks waiting for fares, when Seliora stiffened again, glanced to my right, and then tugged my arm.

"Over there," she whispered. "It's the same man."

I turned my head and saw the glint in the bearded man's hand, and then what looked to be a spark or flash. I was too slow in trying to throw up shields, and something smashed into my shoulder. Despite the pain, I was furious. I concentrated on imaging caustic into his eyes and inside his chest, around his heart, or where I thought his heart was.

There was a single shriek, and he pitched forward onto the pavement of the sidewalk.

I stood there dumbly for a moment.

Seliora looked at me. "You're bleeding."

Before I could speak, she'd started to open my waistcoat and shirt and had jammed something into the wound.

"You!" Her voice penetrated the night as she pointed toward the lead hacker of those waiting outside Felters. "We're headed to the Bridge of Hopes. Now."

"But . . . that's . . ."

"Someone's shot an imager. Do you want the imagers after you?"

Getting into the coach wasn't too hard. I didn't even need Seliora's help.

Once we sat down on the hard seat of the coach, she resumed pressing the handkerchief against and into the wound. "You're still bleeding too much. I can't stop it all." She turned her head and yelled, "Faster!"

I tried to image something like a shield around the wound.

"Whatever you're doing, Rhenn, keep doing it. The bleeding's almost stopped." She didn't lessen the pressure on my shoulder, though. To keep the pressure on the wound, she had to be very close to me, and if it hadn't been for the pain—and the fear—I would have enjoyed that closeness a great deal more.

The ride toward the bridge seemed to take a long time, and no time at all, in a strange way, but before that long the hacker called down, "I'm not supposed to cross the bridge, Mistress!"

"Cross it!"

"But . . ."

A small pistol appeared in her gloved hand, and she leaned out the open coach window, pointing the pistol. "Cross it."

The clatter of hoofs on stone was almost reassuring.

"Where should he go?" asked Seliora.

I was having trouble thinking, and maintaining the shield over the wound, but it had to be the infirmary. Someone was always there. "The right . . . lane after we cross the bridge. The second building, and the first door, the one . . . staff and a green leaf on the door."

Seliora shouted the directions to the driver, then turned back to me. "Hold on. Keep doing that."

Then, the hacker brought the coach to a stop.

"Hold this in place, Rhenn." She pressed my hand against the wadded handkerchief and the warm dampness, then pushed open the coach door and darted out, snapping something at the hacker.

I kept trying to stay awake and alert, trying to push back the encroaching darkness, as I heard doors opening and voices, but then . . . darkness was all there was.

. . . except a darkened twilight that I was carried through . . .

The room where I woke, if becoming vaguely aware of one's surroundings meant awakening, was small and gray, and I lay on a hard and narrow bed or pallet. I had a vague recollection of being carried somewhere, and then someone standing over me, and pains shooting through my shoulder.

Seliora was standing there beside the bed. So was someone else, but she was closer.

"You're here . . ." My voice was barely a whisper.

"I'm here. Where else would I be?" She reached out and squeezed my fingers—the ones on the hand of my uninjured side.

"Thank you." I had to squint to see the figure behind her. "Master . . . ?"

"Draffyd," he supplied. "I took care of the wound, but you'll have to lie still for a time. You won't have a choice. You're strapped to the bed, but that's so that you don't do anything to rip open the stitches and reopen the wound. Please don't try to move against the restraints. Later, we'll remove them, but for the next few glasses, you'll need to be still."

I didn't like that at all, but there were both dull and sharp pains in my shoulder and chest, and both felt like I'd been run over by a draft horse with spiked shoes.

Master Draffyd turned to Seliora. "You cannot stay here for the evening."

She just looked at him as if to ask why not.

"In Rhennthyl's case, it wouldn't be safe for either of you. There are imager reasons why this is so."

She turned her head back to me.

I had to think for a moment before I realized why. Who knew what I'd do in my sleep? Or in a delirium. "He's right . . . wish you could stay . . . but . . ."

"We'll send you back home in a Collegium carriage. You'll be quite safe," added Master Draffyd. "We're very thankful you were there, and both the Collegium and Rhenn owe you a great deal."

"What about Rhenn?"

"He'll recover. You got him here while he still had enough blood. If he were going to die, he'd already be dead. He'll be very weak for a few days, but he'll recover. You stay with him while I send for the carriage." Master Draffyd nodded to Seliora, then slipped out of the room.

She moved closer. "That man outside Felters . . . I knew he was after you."

"I . . . won't dispute you . . . again."

"You killed him, didn't you?"

I started to nod, but even that hurt. "Yes. I think so . . . anyway . . . tried to disable him . . . Hurt too much . . ."

She bent over and brushed my forehead with her lips. She was so close I could see the redness in her eyes. She still looked lovely.

". . . be all right . . ."

"I expect it. Now . . . you be quiet. You don't need to talk. Save your strength." She squeezed my fingers again as she straightened, but she did not let go of them, not until Master Draffyd returned.

"The carriage will be outside in a few moments."

"So soon?" she asked.

"There's always one ready, at any glass."

I hadn't known that, not that it would have made any difference. The hacker had gotten us to Imagisle as fast as anyone could have. "The hacker . . . ?"

"I had him paid," said Master Draffyd. "The Collegium paid, actually. We also gave him a goodwill token. It's worth a gold when he renews his medallion." He paused. "I hear the carriage outside. It's rather late, Mistress D'Shelim, and I'm certain your family has been worried."

"They will understand." Seliora bent over and kissed me, gently, but on the lips. "Take good care of yourself." Then she stepped away.

After she left the room, Master Draffyd stepped closer. He held a small vial. "I'm going to give you something to deepen your sleep a little. You'll have to open your mouth."

I did, and he poured close to a cupful into me. Despite a mint-like scent that wasn't unpleasant, the liquid itself tasted like acidic peppermint laced with cheap plonk, and I couldn't help but grimace.

"It tastes terrible. I remember. You don't forget. " He stoppered the vial and slipped it into a pocket of his waistcoat, then looked back at me. "You wouldn't be alive without the young woman, you know?"

"Nor . . . without you, either."

"That's true, but she had the presence of mind to get you here. How did she know?"

"I gave her directions." I realized that I was a little stronger. Not much, but a trace.

He frowned. "You were awake?"

"Until after we crossed the bridge and got to the infirmary door. I was holding a shield tight against the wound . . . until the end when I got too light-headed to concentrate."

"In that case, it did take both of you. She said so, but . . . it's still amazing."

That irritated me, weak as I was. "If Seliora said so . . . it's true."

"No. I'm certain she told the truth. I meant your holding a shield against a wound like that. Most wouldn't think of that."

I wouldn't have thought of it without Seliora's suggestion, but I wasn't going to tell Master Draffyd that. "You imaged the bullet out, didn't you, and then imaged some sort of dressing or patch in there."

"It's more complicated than that, but something like that." He paused. "What about the man who shot you?"

"He's dead, I think. I imaged caustic into his eyes and chest . . . inside his chest, near the heart. That was hard. He screamed and dropped over." I could feel my eyes trying to close.

"You need to rest. Don't worry. Someone will be watching."

I was worried, but that didn't stop my eyes from closing.

39

No one survives in the world without wounds; the lucky and the determined are unfortunate enough to survive more of them.

When I woke on Solayi, barely after dawn, with gray light seeping into the gray room, I ached all over, and my head was pounding. I'd barely opened my eyes when an obdurate in a plain black uniform appeared, holding a tall glass filled with clear liquid.

"Master Draffyd said you are to drink all of this." He held it to my lips.

I drank. So far as I could tell or taste, the liquid was just water, but water with no taste whatsoever. Water or not, in less than a quarter glass, the worst of the pounding in my head had subsided to a dull ache. That was a mixed blessing, because I was still strapped in place, and most uncomfortable, as well as able to think about it.

Before all that long, thankfully, Master Draffyd appeared. "I'm going to remove your restraints, but please don't move until I tell you to."

"Yes, sir." I would have agreed to anything to get clear of the straps.

I forced myself to look down as he changed the dressing. There were two wounds, less than four digits apart. The area around each was bruised. Both were sutured with wide stitches.

"So far, so good. You'll have some interesting scars there, Rhennthyl."

Whatever he used to clean the area stung. Then his face tightened in concentration, and I could feel stinging in my chest, then stabbing pain that slowly subsided.

"You were carrying some shields, weren't you?"

"Just ones with triggers against imaging. I tried to raise full shields, but I was too slow."

He nodded. "The shields you did have saved your life. Those bullets would have gone right through you, and the exit wounds would have bled even more."

"I wouldn't be alive if we hadn't come here."

"No, but please don't test your luck again."

I had no intention of that—except I hadn't been testing anything.

"Obern will be here and help you clean up and get into a set of dry sleepwear and get you some clean bedding. Just lie here quietly for at least a glass. After that, you can move, but only slowly and carefully and not often. And don't use the arm on your wounded side. Not at all. You'll get something to eat in a while."

"Yes, sir. When I can return to my quarters?"

"That won't be for several days, possibly a week."

After Master Draffyd left, Obern—the very same obdurate who had given me the water earlier—reappeared with linens, sleepwear, and bedding, and before too long I was cleaner and drier. I tried to rest, but too many thoughts kept running through my head. Who could possibly have wanted me dead? The most likely possibilities were the High Holder Ryel or some former friends of Diazt, but how would they have known where I was? That left someone to whom Seliora had talked . . . or someone that Odelia had talked to . . . or . . . someone they had talked to who had talked to someone else . . . That was pointless. Gossip in L'Excelsis went everywhere.

Another thought struck me. If I'd really wanted to get clear of the restraints, couldn't I just have imaged them elsewhere? That thought alone told me that I still wasn't thinking as clearly as I thought I was. I also realized that I would have been safer against an imager, because I'd have gotten full shields without thinking. I needed more work on shields, so that I barely had to think to get them.

Why was it that I could figure out things afterward, when

it would have been so much better beforehand? I didn't have an answer to that question either, but then Obern came back with breakfast on a tray, actual egg-fried toast with a syrup and tea. I ate all of it.

I was feeling better—until I saw Master Jhulian walk into my infirmary room.

"Good morning, Rhennthyl."

"Good morning, sir."

"You had quite an evening, I hear. I've heard quite a bit from everyone else, but it might be best if you told me exactly what happened. Talk slowly, please, and take your time. Stop whenever you want. I've asked Obern to bring you more tea. That will help relax you, and it will also help the healing." He pulled up the single chair beside the narrow bed. "Whenever you're ready."

"I had taken a friend—Seliora—to dinner at Felters . . ." I went through the entire story, including Seliora's notice of the man in the brown cloak, and ended when I lost consciousness outside the infirmary.

"Did you ever see the man closely?"

"No, sir. Well . . . just for a moment. He didn't look familiar."

"Did the young woman know him? She saw him more clearly, didn't she?"

"She didn't know him. I teased her about him looking at her, not me, but she said she didn't know him."

"Rhennthyl, keep this in mind. No matter how pretty the woman at your side, if a man looks in your direction, the odds are that he's looking at you or for you. Don't ever forget that."

His voice was firm, almost cold.

"No, sir. I won't."

"Did you say anything to the man?"

"No, sir. Seliora saw him and whispered that he was there, and I turned and saw him raise the pistol. That was when I tried to increase my own shields. But I never said anything."

"Someone in the bistro saw it, and they summoned the civic patrollers. They had close to the same story." He frowned.

"You said you imaged caustic at him. He died in great agony. He might have been blinded, but that doesn't usually kill someone. What exactly did you do?"

I started to answer, then coughed, and almost doubled over even more in pain before I could reply. "I guess I wasn't clear, sir. I imaged caustic into his eyes and somewhere into his chest. At least, that was what I was trying to do."

"You did it well enough to kill him." Master Jhulian held up a long-fingered hand. "There's no question that it was self-defense, and the man you killed was already being sought for two other murders, and is thought to have committed a number of others. The civic patrollers were happy not to have to keep looking for him. So is the Collegium."

"He killed another imager?"

"A very junior one over a year ago. That is what we know. There have been two other killings of junior imagers over the past three months, and his act against you might raise several other questions, except for one thing. He was definitely looking for you. Do you know why?"

"The only thing I can think of is the business with High Holder Ryel—you know, with his son Johanyr?"

"Oh . . . that?" Master Jhulian frowned. "That is possible, but most unlikely. The High Holder would not wish there to be any traces to him, and that particular assassin was one . . . not suitable for someone like Ryel. Nor would Ryel act so quickly."

"At the moment, sir, I really can't think of anyone . . . well, except Diazt came from the taudis, I think, and I suppose it could have been some relative or friend of his." I couldn't think of any other possibilities, but that might have been because I was still most uncomfortable at best, and in some considerable pain at other times.

"That is more likely, but still unlikely." He stood and closed the small black book in which he had been writing. "Once you can write, you will owe me that final paper." He set a book on the chair. It was a copy of *Jurisprudence*. "I took the liberty of retrieving this from your desk. Your outlines are tucked inside. I would suggest that you consider that

there are two meanings of 'presumption.' The legal definition is not the same as personal presumption, and your notes
do not reflect that."

"I'll . . . keep that in mind, sir."

"After you get some rest." He nodded and slipped out of
the room.

Obern entered immediately with a large mug of steaming
tea. "The master said . . ."

"I know. I need to drink it." I felt like there were so many
things I needed to do . . . but I wasn't feeling up to doing any
of them.

40

Attempting to teach forethought is a thankless task.

Master Dichartyn did not appear until Lundi morning, since
he'd been away. He showed up in my infirmary room after
Master Draffyd's ministrations and my breakfast.

"Good morning, Rhennthyl." He settled onto the chair.

"Good morning, sir."

"I have a letter for you." He set the envelope on the bed, as
his eyes took in the *Jurisprudence* book I'd laid aside when
he had come in, although I'd only reread a few pages after
eating. "Hard at work, I see."

I hoped the letter was from Seliora, but I couldn't tell from
the writing. I'd never seen her hand, but the script looked
feminine, and it wasn't Khethila's, or Mother's. I wanted to
pick it up, but I didn't. "Master Jhulian reminded me that I
still have an essay due to him. I'm not supposed to do anything like writing for another day or so, but I can read and
think."

"Thinking is always useful, especially if you do it before you get into difficulties." He fingered his chin. "I've talked to both Master Jhulian and Master Draffyd."

I winced slightly, even if his words had been delivered gently.

"Rhenn, because imagers work alone, of necessity, great necessity, we need to pay attention to what others say, what they see, and what they hear. Even someone who is trying to deceive you will reveal much that he does not intend. Those who favor us will do far more."

"I should have listened to Seliora more closely."

"You should have, and that is a lesson you will not forget."

I knew. The lessons I remembered best were the ones that hurt, in one way or another.

"I have some other questions for you."

After nodding to him, I waited.

"You were wounded, and in a great deal of pain, weren't you? Yet you stood against two bullets and then imaged caustic into the attacker's eyes and heart. Might I ask how?"

"I didn't want him to hurt Seliora, and I wasn't by the Nameless going to let the bastard escape, and I couldn't have restrained him in the condition I was in."

"Quite a lot to think about in a few moments, I'd say. Did you, really?"

"Not that logically, sir," I admitted, "but I knew all that even as I was imaging at him."

Master Dichartyn nodded. "Admirable . . . and effective. How did you know that caustic would cause his heart to swell and stop?"

"I didn't know. I just thought it would, or that if it didn't, he'd be blind and in so much pain he wouldn't be going anywhere." Besides, I hadn't known any other quick way to react, because I hadn't practiced any kinds of imager attacks—just defenses. "Will this keep me from being a field imager?"

"If you'd been trained for that, no . . . but that's not what your position is likely to be. This incident will help you understand just how important what you'll be doing is, and it will also give you a feel for the dangers and consequences that no amount of training will. For you, since you've survived it, that's probably for the best, but we certainly didn't intend for anything like this to happen." He frowned. "There's been a bit too much of this sort of thing recently, but as Master Jhulian and I discussed, this assassin was after you and no one else."

As sore as my shoulder was, I was still irritated that Master Dichartyn hadn't said what I was being trained for. "So what will I be? An imager who tracks down those in L'Excelsis who might harm the Council and the Collegium? One who kills as necessary?"

"Only if ordered to—or in self-defense," he agreed. "We work as what you might call counterspies, although our group has no name and does not officially exist in the records of the Collegium. We're all technically assigned as part of Council security. There are only around ten of us who work as counterspies. There's no limit on the number, but imagers who meet the requirements are extremely hard to find. They show up only every few years, and we lose close to a third of them before they become masters."

"What made you decide on me?"

"A number of things." He smiled. "I will tell you. That I promise you, but not now. Since it's your left shoulder, and you're right-handed, you can write while you're recovering. Write me an essay explaining what qualities you think an imager counterspy should have."

"Yes, sir."

"Take your time. Not forever, but say, a week." He paused. "Oh . . . by the way . . . all the paints and oils and canvases arrived this morning . . . as well as all the other things you'll need. Once we have a studio set up in the workshop area and you're up to it, I'll have Master Poincaryt sit for you. If anyone deserves a portrait, he does."

"Is it also that it's safer to have an imager do it?"

"That certainly is something that makes it easier, but there's never been an imager trained as a portraiturist, and we're vain enough that we'd like an accurate resemblance."

That was a compliment of sorts. "I can see that."

"Keep following Master Draffyd's instructions. He says that if all goes well, by Jeudi or Vendrei, you can return to your own quarters. You'll still have to see him every morning, but I trust you'd rather not be here."

"That's true, sir."

He smiled, then turned to go. After he left, I realized that he hadn't even asked me if being a counterspy was what I wanted to do. I also realized that he hadn't needed to.

Only then did I pick up the cream-colored envelope and look at it closely. On the front was my name—Rhennthyl D'Imager—and below it, simply Imagisle. I turned it over. Even though I knew from whom it had come, I couldn't help but smile as I saw the name—M. Seliora D'Shelim, Nord-Este Design, Nordroad.

I opened it carefully, but the wax seal still broke and sprayed wax across the blanket. I read slowly, taking in each word.

My dear Rhenn,
I trust that you are recovering. I hope that you will be well before long. Can you have visitors? If you can, and if you can let me know, I would like to see you.

Until the last moments, I enjoyed dinner so much. I have never had a dinner so exciting. You will understand if I say that I hope never to have another. The next time, you must come to our house and have one of Mother's special dinners.

I look forward to hearing from you.

The signature was a simple "Seliora."

I couldn't help but smile. The letter was so like Seliora—direct and warm. I certainly could have visitors, if only after I could leave the infirmary. As soon as I could, I would write her to suggest Solayi afternoon.

My eyes dropped to the *Jurisprudence* book. I would have

more than a little other writing as well, and that would not be nearly so enjoyable.

41

Some men change their principles as frequently as their linens, and others never do; both are in error.

The next several days were slow, long, and tedious. Master Dichartyn checked on me briefly each morning, as did Master Draffyd. Besides that, all I did was some walking, with Obern accompanying and watching me, some reading, some eating, and more than a little dozing and sleeping. On Jeudi morning Master Draffyd and Master Dichartyn both arrived at the same time. That could not have been coincidence.

First, Master Draffyd examined me and changed the dressing on my upper chest and shoulder. "It's already healing well. You can leave here, but stay on Imagisle and keep the dressing dry. No strenuous exercise, only walking, and no exercise with that arm except for light things. Don't pick up anything heavy . . ."

The way my shoulder felt, I wasn't about to lift anything more than a pen. Certainly not anything as heavy as the *Jurisprudence* text.

". . . If there's any sudden pain or soreness, or redness or swelling, come back here immediately. If I'm not here, Obern or one of the others will find me. Is that clear?"

"Yes, sir."

Master Dichartyn waited until Master Draffyd left.

"You're very fortunate. I need to make one thing very clear. Until you're fully healed, and I do mean fully, you are not to leave Imagisle. Do you understand why?"

"Anyone with enough coin and desire to hire someone to kill me won't likely stop at losing one bravo."

Master Dichartyn nodded. "We—you, actually—will put a stop to it, but you won't be able to until you're well, and that is likely to be at least a month, according to Master Draffyd."

"A month?"

"The outward wounds and the worst of the damage will heal in another week, two weeks at the outside. Then you'll have to regain strength in that arm and shoulder, and you'll work with Clovyl on that—he knows what happened. He'll be the one working with you to rebuild your strength and conditioning. Maitre Dyana and I will teach you a few more techniques when the time comes. For now, you are not to do any imaging—except in emergencies, and I do hope you can see your way to avoiding those. I'll see you tomorrow at eighth glass. I won't need your essay, but I want you to review the anatomy section of your science text, especially the section on the human chest and heart."

I did force myself to walk back to my own quarters slowly, and I carried the *Jurisprudence* book in my right arm. I couldn't help but worry over his words about my being the one to put a stop to matters.

When the time approached tenth glass and lunch, I made my way to the dining hall slowly and deliberately. Even so, I saw that Claustyn had gotten there earlier. He waved for me to join him at one end of the long table. When I reached him, so had Menyard and Reynol.

I was more than happy to sit down.

"We haven't seen you for almost a week," said Claustyn. "Word is that some assassin attacked two imagers, and killed one. Was that why we haven't seen you?"

Two imagers? "I don't know about anyone else. I did get shot—right outside Felters. Do you know who the other imager was?"

"Some are saying it was Jacques," Reynol replied. "No one's seen him, either, but you never know for a while when these things happen. The Collegium doesn't like to acknowledge publicly that any imager was attacked—or killed, especially."

"Did he get away?" asked Menyard.

What could I say to that? After a moment, I laughed, gently. "I managed to disable him, or that was what I tried. He died, though."

"If I might ask," ventured Reynol, "how badly . . . ?"

"Two shots. Here and here." I pointed with my good hand. Claustyn and Menyard looked at each other.

"You imaged him *after* you were hit?" asked Claustyn.

"I didn't know he was shooting at me until I got hit." That wasn't quite true, but close enough.

Claustyn nodded and said to Menyard, "That's why."

"Why what?" I asked.

"Why Master Dichartyn is your preceptor. He only takes imagers who have that kind of reaction. None of us can figure out how he knows that, but he seems to sense it whenever a new imager who has that ability arrives. Do you have a duty assignment?"

"I know what it will be, once I recover and finish my training."

"Did you like the dinner at Felters—before what happened?" Claustyn asked. "Was it as good as people say?"

Obviously, some questions were pursued only so far—another of the unspoken rules. "I had a marinated flank steak stuffed with buttered parsley and mushrooms. It was excellent, and they had a Cambrisio that was very good."

"Was it that expensive?"

"It wasn't bad . . . four silvers, I think, but we had salads, and dessert and wine."

"That's not too dear," reflected Reynol, "if you don't do it too often." He grinned. "Was she worth it?"

"How would he know?" asked Menyard. "He got shot before he could find out."

I smiled. "She was very worth it. She was the one who got me to the infirmary in time."

"That's very worth it," said Claustyn, "if not exactly what Reynol had in mind." He laughed.

So did we all.

"Where's Kahlasa?" I asked after several bites of a fowl casserole.

"She got called back to field duty early," said Reynol. "She didn't say why, but a Caenenan cruiser sank one of our merchanters on the high seas—more than fifty milles off the Caenenan coast. The Council ordered a blockade of Caena, and the Fourth and Fifth Fleets are steaming south now. That's what they say, anyway."

"What are the Jariolans going to do?"

"The Council sent a strong message suggesting that they keep out of it," Menyard added. "But their Oligarch—Khasis III, I think, is his name—is supposedly massing forces on their border with Ferrum. That's because Ferrum has been arming Caenen, and has been receiving favored trade."

"So we're looking at war in Cloisera and in Otelyrn?" I asked.

Claustyn shrugged. "It's possible. We control the seas, but we don't have an army big enough to fight in both places."

"Couldn't we help Ferrum and just blockade Caena?"

"That's up to the Council, but . . ." Reynol drew out the words: "Ferrum doesn't like Solidar, and particularly the Collegium, much more than Jariola does, and if we blockade Caena, the High Priest is likely to turn on Tiempre to get some of the resources he needs because he knows we don't want to invade Caenen . . . or any country in Otelyrn."

Why Tiempre? I almost asked, but then realized why. Tiempre had banned imagers almost a century earlier. That had ended up driving out many of the wealthier and more creative types. More than a few had come to Solidar. I doubted that Tiempre could stand up to Caenen and the High Priest's religious hordes, and I couldn't see the Council sending troops to Otelyrn.

"So . . . if we blockade Caena . . . we'll start a war between Tiempre and Caenen, and if we don't, the Caenenans will feel free to keep firing on our merchant ships?"

"I'd venture to say that about sums it all up," said Claustyn cheerfully. "Unless the High Priest changes his mind."

"That doesn't seem likely," I pointed out.

"No," Menyard said. "True believers—or those who depict themselves as such—seldom change their minds. They'd rather die first, and, if they do change their minds, someone else in the hierarchy is likely to see that they die."

"Did you get that from Master Dichartyn?"

"Master Jhulian. For all his legal knowledge, he's almost as cynical as Dichartyn."

In the end, our discussion led to nothing more, and afterward I returned to my quarters and wrote a note to Seliora thanking her and asking if she could visit on Solayi afternoon . . . and telling her where to meet me if she could. After that, I wrote a shorter note to my parents, telling them I'd been injured and that, while I was healing well, I wouldn't be leaving Imagisle soon.

Then, after taking them both to the administration building to be sent, I walked slowly back to my room, once more, and stretched out—gingerly—on my bed to rest. *Jurisprudence* and the two essays would have to wait.

42

Achieving true excellence risks all that holds happiness.

Well before third glass on Solayi afternoon, I was sitting waiting on the second graystone bench—the one shaded by the oak that was finally leafing out—near the Imagisle side of the Bridge of Hopes. I'd brought the science text, because Master Dichartyn had not been pleased with my lack of visualization of anatomy when we had met on Vendrei. While he had been slightly happier with my performance on Samedi morning, he'd asked more questions, and then pointedly suggested that I finish my essay for Master Jhulian in order to have my mind clear to finish the essay I owed him.

On Solayi morning, I had finished a draft of the essay on the Juristic Code's applicability to imagers. Because the Code recognized the discretion granted to civic patrollers, anyone actually charged was presumed guilty. Since patrollers tended to defer to imagers, the Code provided for a review hearing on any matter involving an imager—provided the Council approved. That also explained why Master Jhulian and Master Dichartyn had emphasized that imagers should never be even remotely associated with the appearance of violence and murders. Such a petition to the Council, even if rejected, might well raise issues better left unexamined.

As I could feel the time nearing third glass, I finally closed the science text, because I was not reading it. My eyes were merely skipping over the page in front of me and then glancing toward the nearer end of the bridge. Just moments after the third bell rang, two figures came into view, walking casually, but not dawdling, along the south side of the bridge, Seliora and a taller figure—Odelia. Seliora wore a long flowing dress, a pale green, with a cream silk jacket. Odelia was in a brighter green.

I stood and stepped toward them.

Odelia smiled but dropped back to let her cousin move toward me alone. Seliora stepped forward and took my hands. She smiled, an expression of both concern and warmth. "You look better than the last time I saw you."

"I feel much better."

She inclined her head toward the shaded bench I had just left. "You're still pale, and you need to sit down."

I didn't argue, and we sat down in the shade. Odelia took the other bench, close enough to watch, but far enough not to hear, although I doubted she would have passed on anything.

"I'm glad you came." I couldn't help smiling at her.

"Should you be up?"

"Master Draffyd said that gentle movement would help, but I'm not supposed to lift anything heavy with my left arm or hand."

"I told Mother where you were shot," Seliora said slowly. "She said most people would have died right there."

"I almost did. If you hadn't gotten me to the infirmary that quickly, I would have."

She looked directly at me. "You're fated not to die young. That is what Mama said." Then she smiled. "She told me to tell you that's from the Pharsi side."

I frowned. "I thought that was your father's side."

Seliora flushed. "Actually . . . there's full Pharsi on both sides."

I laughed. "That doesn't surprise me. Can you tell fortunes as well?" I wished I hadn't asked the question, because, belatedly, I remembered that she'd already told me that she'd seen a vision of me in gray before I'd become an imager.

"I do better with people I don't know."

"People you don't know or people you're not . . . close to?" I hesitated over the words.

"Those I don't care about. When you care, it's difficult to separate what you want to see from what you do see."

I wanted to put my arms around her. I didn't. "Your parents weren't upset?"

"Why would they be upset?"

"Because you were with someone who got shot. That could be upsetting."

"Papa said he was happy you were going to be well and that . . ." She shook her head.

"What?" I spoke before I realized she had that glint in her eye.

"He didn't want his daughter to be interested in a man who wasn't worth shooting. Someone shot him when he was courting Mama. It was only in the arm, and it didn't even break a bone."

"Did he ever say what happened to the man?"

Seliora shook her head. "He did say that the fellow wouldn't bother anyone again."

"I thought it might have been something like that. I don't think I'll cross your father."

"Be nice to me, and he won't say a word." She grinned.

"But I think Grandmama had more to do with it. She didn't like anyone interfering with her family. She still doesn't."

"Did you get the pistol from her?"

That brought a sheepish look to her face. "I bought it when I was fifteen. Grandmama knew before I took three steps into the house. She spent every day for a month teaching me to use it. She told me that you never bought anything you couldn't use or didn't learn to use."

"I didn't meet her," I said.

"She has a bad leg. She also told me that she didn't want to meet anyone I thought much of in a crowd, and the family was definitely a crowd." There was the faintest pause. "She knows about you, though."

"Oh?" I wasn't certain I liked that.

"I've told her. She said that if you were talented and honest, you'd never amount to anything as a portraiturist."

Even as I winced, I had to admit that the grandmother I'd never met was right. "Does that apply to furniture and designs?"

"Absolutely! We're talented, but we're not totally honest. We cheat anyone who tries to cheat us . . . and we're better at it."

That also surprised me not in the least.

"Will you be able to come to dinner before long?"

"I want to, very much, but Master Dichartyn has confined me to Imagisle until I'm totally well and better able to take care of myself. That could be almost a month." I smiled, if faintly. "He also said that I'm to listen to you."

The last words did bring the faintest hint of that mischievous smile I liked so much.

"I'm glad they think I'm of worth to you."

"Master Draffyd said I owe my life to you, but I already knew that." I paused, then added, "I can't think of anyone I'd rather owe it to."

"Rhenn . . . I know what you're doing must be dangerous. Please don't take risks you don't have to take."

"That's what they're trying to teach me." Among other things.

"Then listen to them."

I smiled broadly at her. "Shall I tell Master Dichartyn you ordered me to listen to him."

"If it pleases you." The words were not quite coy, but there was a hint of chill.

"I'm sorry. I was teasing. I didn't mean to offend you."

"Teasing is fair," she replied. "Condescension is not."

I almost said I hadn't been condescending, then thought better. "That's fair, but I probably don't recognize it all the time when I'm being condescending. If condescension isn't fair, then you have to accept my apologies for inadvertent condescension." I offered a mournful face.

Either the expression or the words brought a laugh, and I laughed with her, if very gently. Too many things hurt too much for enthusiastic laughter.

"Have you seen Rogaris or any of the others?"

"No. There's no reason to, and we've been busy. I had to come up with an entire new design for High Holder Esquivyl. He decided that the rendition of the family crest that he approved two weeks ago wasn't what he wanted after all. Or his new child bride decided that."

"Did you meet her?"

"She simpers and bats her eyelashes, but she has more brains in the little finger she beckons to him with than he has in his skull."

"Have you ever met High Holder Ryel?"

Seliora frowned, thinking. "No, but you never know. Why?"

"Just don't mention my name. That's all. His son attacked me."

"What did you do?"

"I defended myself. Actually, there were two of them. They were both imagers who were senior to me. I partly blinded Johanyr—he's Ryel's son, and he was transferred to Mont D'Image to recover. He won't be allowed to return to L'Excelsis. But I can't imagine High Holder Ryel would look upon anyone connected to me in any way favorably."

"Did the senior imagers try to stop them?"

"They did, but I didn't know that they were trying to protect me. I didn't know they were even around, and when it looked like Johanyr really meant to harm me, I tried to disable him. I disabled him a bit too much. That's another reason why I can't leave Imagisle for a while. I need to learn better control of what I do."

"It isn't just that, is it?"

I'd known that Seliora was perceptive, but her perception could make it hard for me. "No. The masters think that someone is hiring assassins to kill me, and they don't want me to leave until I'm fully recovered and I've learned some more techniques."

"High Holder Ryel?"

"They don't know, and one doesn't charge High Holders without a great deal of proof."

Seliora nodded. "I won't tell Papa and Mama. I'll just tell them that all imagers run the risk of being targets at times . . . especially the good ones."

"I'm just a junior imager third."

"That's like a journeyman imager, isn't it?"

I supposed it was. I nodded.

"That makes you good. How many imagers become journeymen in less than half a year?"

Things had happened so fast I hadn't considered that. "I don't know, but you're probably right. I just didn't think of it that way."

"You haven't told your parents, either, have you?"

"No. I won't say a thing unless I become a master."

"You're as proud as any Pharsi, Rhenn." Her smile was warm, sympathetic, and sad, all at once. "There must be some of that blood somewhere in your background."

I could only shrug . . . slightly, and I still had to hide a wince.

She took my hands again. "I can't stay long. Not today. We're having a birthday dinner for Grandmama." Another smile followed. "Could we have a picnic here next Samedi?"

"Are you sure you want to go to that trouble?"

"I wouldn't have asked if I didn't. You wouldn't mind if Odelia brought Kolasyn, would you?"

"I can't see that as a problem. I am allowed visitors when I'm free, and there's no restriction, except common sense, I suppose."

"Half past fourth bell?"

"I'll be here."

"So will I." She leaned forward and brushed my cheek with her lips, squeezing my hands.

After a moment, we stood. Then we walked toward Odelia, who rose.

When they headed toward the bridge, I just sat down on the bench and watched the two of them walk back across the bridge to L'Excelsis, a reminder of sorts that the city I'd grown up in was now a foreign land, at least in some ways.

43

Seeking fame can be as deadly as poison.

On Lundi, I handed in the essay for Master Jhulian. He read it, then nodded. "It is acceptable, and that is all I could expect from an imager who is not a legal scholar."

I knew the essay wasn't outstanding, but just acceptable?

On Mardi, I handed in the essay on the qualities of a counterspy to Master Dichartyn. He took his time reading through the four pages. Then he set it down on the writing desk.

"You have noted in some detail the obvious points, that an imager counterspy should be accomplished in technique, be in excellent physical condition, and be able to anticipate what may happen." The coolness of his words suggested that

Master Dichartyn was less than pleased. "Tell me, Rhennthyl. Besides your need to recover, why are you being confined to Imagisle?"

"You had indicated, sir, that was to protect me until I learned enough to defend myself and until the Collegium and I could deal with the perpetrator of the attack."

"That is true. Why is the perpetrator of the attack seeking you?"

"Because I did something that offended or upset him, or her."

"That is also most probably true. In connection with your assignment, what conclusion should you draw?"

"Never let anyone know what you are doing, have done, or might do?"

"That is also true, but that is a behavior pattern, not a quality, if you will. I will give you a hint. How did your first meeting go with Maitre Dyana?"

I thought back. Her initial appraisal of me had been strange, because she'd said she could see why I was Master Dichartyn's protégé. "She said I could be any number of things."

"Rhennthyl! Think . . ."

"Oh . . . the quality of being anything except an imager agent?"

"Precisely." He shook his head. "The last thing you want is to be noticed—or noticed for what you really are. Any time anyone notices you as excessively capable and bright, you endanger yourself, and sometimes the Collegium."

That made sense. I wasn't certain I liked the idea of being invisible, but I couldn't argue.

"Do you want to be married someday—to the young lady who saved your life or someone like her?"

"I'd hope so, sir."

"Do you want to have children and live for years with her? How could that happen if everyone in L'Excelsis knew that you were a feared counterspy? No matter how good you became as an imager, would you want to carry heavy shields all the time, never knowing who might be looking for you every time you set foot outside, or even every time you awoke? Or worry whether you would wake up?"

A cold jolt ran down my spine. In a way, I *had* been thinking of myself as becoming a feared and respected counterspy.

"Do you ever again want to see someone firing a pistol at you a moment too late for you to shield yourself?" pressed Master Dichartyn.

"No, sir." My words there were firm and heartfelt.

"Then . . . you'd better think about how not to stand out." He smiled wanly. "It's not about slinking and slouching, either. That's an even bigger sign of someone up to no good. The most feared counterspies are the ones no one knows, because they could be anyone in any place. You want to appear so perfectly in place that no thought of offense occurs. Call it first among seconds. Like the lesser moon."

That made no sense to me.

"Erion was a feared hunter, at least mythologically, but who writes poems to the lesser hunter? Except in a deprecating fashion? Yet no one ever wished to offend Erion in person." Master Dichartyn smiled. "Say you have three High Holders in a room, and three assistants. You want to be the assistant who's both perfect and most deferentially confident, so much so that none of the other assistants would think about offending you, and none of the High Holders would either, because you're deferential and an assistant."

I didn't like the idea of being the best second . . . at anything.

"It takes a very confident and superior man to be an imager counterspy, because you have to be better than anyone else, except the few others in your group, and you can never let anyone know how good you are or show it. You have to be able to take pride internally, without needing the recognition of others. Most men can't live without overt praise and recognition. Lack of praise and recognition can turn them into twisted angry souls, converts of the Namer, if you will, wanting a name and fame beyond anything."

I had to think about that, and Master Dichartyn let me have time to consider his words.

"What if I said that I couldn't do that?" I finally asked.

"I'd turn you over to Master Schorzat for field training. You'd make a good field imager. People suspect who field imagers might be, but they can't ever trace how they do what they do." He shrugged. "They do get more recognition, but more of them get killed."

"You think I could be good as a counterspy?"

"If you work at it, you could be very good." He paused. "There's an advantage and a drawback."

"Beside being . . . under-known?"

He laughed. "That's a good way of putting it. Under-known." The smile vanished. "Because what we do trains imager capabilities more deeply and widely, imager counterspies get advanced more quickly, and that includes field pay . . . but your public grade is left lower, at least in most cases, until later. If you work, you could become a Maitre D'Aspect fairly soon, but while you would get the pay, your rank wouldn't be known beyond the maitres of the Collegium. You'd still be viewed as a third. When you master Maitre D'Structure, you will be listed as a Maitre D'Aspect. After that, you can be listed at whatever level of mastery you wish. Most have remained publicly as Maitres D'Aspect until they have left day-to-day countering duties."

I could see that.

"What do you want to do?"

"Continue with you, sir, if that's acceptable."

"I'd hoped you would . . . but it is a matter of choice." He fingered his chin. "Because of your injuries, and because we're shorthanded, I'm going to change your training schedule. Starting next week, you'll spend a glass with Clovyl, right at first afternoon bell, and he'll give you just the right amount of exercise to help you heal. After that, you'll report to Maitre Dyana. She will teach you how High Holders behave and some of their particular customs and mannerisms, and what they signify."

"She was raised a High Holder, wasn't she?"

"You noticed. Good." He lifted a long rolled tube—rather large papers rolled to form a tube a yard long—and handed it to me. "These are the plans for the Council Chateau. By the end of next week, I expect you to be able to draw every floor from memory. Keep them out of sight in your room, and don't take them out of it until you bring them back a week from Jeudi." Then he stood. "I will see you this Jeudi morning. We will work on some imaging skills that will not take much strength. They're a matter of technique and knowledge."

After leaving his study, I carried the Chateau plans back to my quarters and began to study them. In less than a quarter glass, I understood why he'd given me a week. There were rooms and passages that no one could ever have guessed were even there.

I took my time getting to the dining hall, but Menyard and Reynol were the only ones I could see of the group with whom I usually ate.

"You're looking healthier, Rhenn," said Reynol.

"I'm feeling better."

"Where's Claustyn?"

Menyard shrugged. "On assignment. Field imagers don't say where, and we don't ask. He left sometime yesterday."

"You'll say less than that," observed Reynol.

"Even if I wanted to," I replied, "I'll have far less to say. How can one say anything about what never happens? That would be like writing a history of a place that never existed."

Both of them laughed.

At that moment, one of the seconds sitting an empty space away from Reynol handed over a platter of chops, and I could see a dish of stewed and spiced apples following. "I haven't picked up one of the newssheets. What's happening in Caenen or Cloisera?"

Reynol shook his head. "We probably won't hear until someone actually invades, and the news will be a good week late, if not two."

"Who's stronger, Ferrum or Jariola?"

Reynol frowned. "That's hard to say. Ferrum has more heavy equipment, and they've even got something called a landcruiser—an armored thing powered by steam that can travel over land without rails. The Oligarch has more trained troops . . ."

As Reynol went on, I got the feeling that a war between the two would be long and bloody and in no one's interest, but wasn't that true of most wars?

44

There is a hidden advantage to imaging what appears to be nothing.

Jeudi morning was damp, raw, and drizzling. I was back in Master Dichartyn's study, more than a little curious about the imager techniques I would be learning. Instead of saying anything immediately, he looked at me and fingered his chin, a sign that a lecture, a question, or something else to make me think was about to be delivered.

"Rhennthyl . . . have you ever considered the governmental uniqueness of Solidar?"

"Compared to other governments?"

"Against what else did you have in mind in comparing Solidaran government?"

I winced. I hated asking stupid questions. "Solidar offers the greatest representation of crafters in its government."

"With only three guild representatives?"

"Sir, you know far more than I do, but nowhere in anything I have read does it mention that other lands allow any craft participation."

"Not as crafters. But in most lands, those who possess a certain amount of wealth do have a voice in government, and some of those are the more successful crafters."

"There's a difference. The wealthy individual represents

his coins, while the crafters represent the interests of those to whom they must answer—other crafters. Also, there is an imager on the Council, and the councilors have to represent different parts of Solidar."

"What does that mean, Rhenn?"

"The Council has to represent more than those in power in L'Excelsis."

"Does that matter when the Council has power in and of itself?"

I forced myself to stop and think before replying. "A Council member has power because he is a member of the Council that governs Solidar. As a representative of a guild or as an imager, such a member may not have had power to influence government before being selected as such a representative and may not have such power after he ceases being a Council member. Those with wealth can almost always purchase influence in one fashion or another."

"What does that mean for the average person in Solidar?"

"I would judge that the average person in Solidar has less to fear from government than in other lands, and more of them have a chance to voice their concerns without fear of retribution."

"Most carefully worded, Rhenn, and generally accurate. Now . . . what government structure in the world has changed the least over the past four centuries?"

"Ours. You're suggesting our power and stability rest on wider representation of power?"

"I'm trying to get you to make the connection. Why would this be so?"

"Because we have to spend fewer coins in things like putting down revolts and in having more patrollers in the cities?"

"Or in collecting tariffs and taxes," added Master Dichartyn. "This creates a long-standing and real problem for the Council. Some both within Solidar and in other lands do not like the example that Solidar presents to the world. Those here feel that their own power is limited by such diversity. The outsiders understand that our power rests on the diversity of our political structure because it allows us to tax our people less and devote more of those taxes to maintaining and expanding our power. They have spent centuries trying to undo what the first Council began, both by external threats, such as attacks on our shipping and merchants, and by internal attacks, such as attempted assassinations of councilors and others in Solidar.

"If no organization in Solidar did what we do, Solidar would long since have returned to despotism or mercantile oligarchy centuries ago—or we would have been forced to spend tens of thousands more in golds every year on non-imager counterspies and secret patrollers and more, and that would have destroyed what Solidar is. If any group under the Council's control—or anywhere in the government—did what we do, they would eventually control Solidar, with close to the same result. That is why the standards set for imagers are so high. That is another reason why you need to know the laws as well, if not better, than any city justice or civic patroller. Now . . . can you explain why we can do this without being corrupted by power—as an institution?"

That seemed direct enough. "Because the Collegium has a structure to minimize the dangers of corruption."

Master Dichartyn nodded. "That is part of the answer. The second part is equally simple. We also can never hold power because the people would not stand for rule by imagers, and we weed out any imagers who do not understand that. Above all, you need to remember that. Sometimes . . . let us just say that once or twice in the past, certain masters failed to realize that basic truth, and disaster for both the Collegium and Solidar was narrowly averted."

Conviction ran through every word Master Dichartyn had spoken. Even so, I wasn't certain I would have been convinced had it not been for the events that had befallen me over the past months—from the total change in attitude by Rogaris and Sagaryn and even Staela to being shot by someone I didn't know for reasons I also did not know.

"Now . . . you need to work on a particular imaging technique." As he spoke, Master Dichartyn placed a bowl of water on the desk and then lifted a short glass tube from somewhere. He submerged the tube, covered the ends with his fingers, and then held up the water-filled tube. "You see the tube. I want you to image air, just a little of the air around you, into the middle of the tube. Not enough to fill the entire tube—that well might break it—but enough to create a bubble about one digit wide in the center."

Image air into water? I'd had to image things into the middle of the air, unsupported, but the other way around? I wondered why, but I'd learned that I seldom got the explanations until after I mastered a technique.

It took me almost a glass to manage it consistently.

"That's enough for now. We'll work on doing it to a moving tube tomorrow." At that point, Master Dichartyn set down the tube. "Now . . . besides studying the plans of the Council Chateau, you need to set up your portraiture studio. Grandisyn has cleared out a small workroom with northern light and moved all the equipment and supplies in there, but you need to arrange it so that it suits you. If you need other items, just tell him."

I almost laughed. I'd worked for not quite ten years, trying to get to the point where I could become a master portraiturist and have my own studio, and now that I was an imager, I was being given a studio with all the equipment and pigments I would have had difficulty affording—almost as an aside and a cover.

45

~~~~~~

The excellence of the cuisine is but half the meal.

In between some resting and meals, it took me the rest of Jeudi and all of Vendrei, besides the time with Master Dichartyn, to organize a studio in the workroom set aside for me. It was a good thing no one expected me to begin painting immediately, because a number of items were missing, including a grinder, a mortar and pestle, certain oils and waxes, and a burner and old pots, not to mention a chair for whoever would be sitting for me. Still, Grandisyn assured me the missing items would be there by Lundi. That was fine with me.

Samedi morning, after another session with Master Dichartyn, I spent poring over the plans of the Chateau and then trying to draw each floor from memory. I had lunch, but with some thirds I knew only slightly, before returning to my study. I tried to take a nap, but all I did was lie there. So I alternated studying anatomy and the Council Chateau. By the time the four bells rang, I couldn't concentrate on plans or texts any longer. I washed up and walked down to the main level, and then out and across the quadrangle.

Two of the seconds headed toward me eased onto an adjoining path. I recognized the second behind them, who did not avoid me. "Shannyr, how are matters with you?"

"Well, thank you. I'm getting married in two months. Master Dichartyn has approved quarters for us on the north end. They're small, but far better than either of us ever hoped."

"That's wonderful!" I was truly happy for him—and them. I'd always felt that Shannyr was a good and solid person. "Would I know the lady?"

"I don't think so. Her name is Ciermya. She works as a drafter for a naval architect."

"You're a fortunate man."

"I am that." He paused. "Sir, some of the seconds asked me to convey their thanks if I saw you."

"Diazt and Johanyr were that hard on them?"

"Word is . . . some of them had sisters . . . and Johanyr . . . he'd threaten the sisters . . . say that he couldn't be responsible for what happened to their brothers."

"The masters didn't know this?"

"No, sir. I didn't know it, not till last week. Johanyr and Diazt threatened to hurt the sisters if their brothers said anything."

I hadn't realized just how much of a bastard Johanyr had been . . . and how clever, because his schemes had all rested on threats, and the implication of force, and probably minimal use of imaging. I also realized how calculating Master Dichartyn had been. He'd made sure Johanyr couldn't image, but would live, and the way events had transpired deprived High Holder Ryel of any official recourse. That just made it more likely, despite what Master Dichartyn had said, that the dead assassin had been sent after me by Ryel . . . or more unfortunately, that I had something worse to look forward to. "I'm glad I was able to do something about it, but I didn't know that was happening. I just didn't trust them." I paused. "I hope no one is trying to take their place."

"Not that I know." He smiled. "But I won't be worrying about such much longer."

"That's true, and you shouldn't have to." I thought for a moment. "Poor Gherard."

Shannyr looked surprised.

"Who else is there right now?" Shannyr had kept as close a watch as he could on those imagers who would be seconds for most of their time and life at the Collegium. Master Dichartyn had rewarded him, and probably the same would be true of Gherard.

"There is that, I'd guess, sir."

"You have my thanks, Shannyr, and give my best to Cier-mya."

"That I will." He gave me a broad smile and continued on.

I turned eastward and made my way to the benches on the west side of the river, where I sat down on one shaded by the late-afternoon sun to wait for Seliora, Odelia, and Kolasyn.

Before that long, three figures appeared on the bridge. Each carried a wicker basket. Seliora was attired in a maroon skirt, a cream blouse, and a shimmering gray vest. As she neared, I realized that she was actually wearing split skirts, far more practical for a picnic.

I bounded to my feet, surprised that I had . . . and that nothing hurt.

Seliora hurried to meet me, setting down the basket she had carried. She gave me a gentle but brief embrace and a dazzling smile. "You're looking much better."

"That's because you're here."

She blushed ever so slightly.

"I told you he was gallant," Odelia murmured to Kolasyn.

"Oh . . ." Seliora half-turned. "You've never met Kolasyn, have you?"

"No, I have not. I'm pleased to have the opportunity." I inclined my head to him. "Both Odelia and Seliora have spoken well of you."

"You have the advantage, then." Kolasyn laughed. "They refused to say anything about you." He was clearly older than I was, but I doubted he was quite so old as Odelia, who I suspected was a good five to six years older than Seliora. Like Odelia, he was rangy and redheaded, slightly taller than she was, and he had a short and neatly trimmed beard. His eyes were dark brown, and his smile was pleasant. I couldn't help liking him.

Seliora picked a shaded spot, but one that had been sun-warmed earlier in the day, so that, while the grass was cool, it was not damp, given the rain earlier in the week. Then, from her basket came a blanket and an oilcloth, along with four heavy glasses and two bottles of wine—a white grisio and a red Cambrisio. From Odelia's basket came an array of covered wooden bowls and baskets, more than I believed could ever have fit into it. Then Seliora took the basket that Kolasyn held and laid out cutlery and utensils, and four enormous napkins.

When everything was set on the cloth, Seliora looked at me and smiled. "It is here for us to eat, you know?"

Kolasyn was deft with a corkscrew, and I had a glass of the Cambrisio, as did Odelia, while he and Seliora had grisio. There was more than enough food, from crispy rice fries and almond-stuffed peppers to a honey-sour crispy baked chicken and apple and cheese strips, and a warm peach and berry cobbler.

"This is excellent." I turned to Seliora, sitting not quite beside me. "Thank you."

"You're welcome, but Mother fixed most of it. I did the chicken, and Odelia did the rice fries. Mother did everything else."

"I thank you and Odelia, and if you would convey my thanks to your mother?"

"We can do that."

Everything was good, but the chicken and the cobbler were my favorites, and I did have a small second helping of the cobbler, but only after everyone else had eaten some.

"What are you studying now?" Seliora asked.

"More about the Council and about imaging. What about you?"

She shook her head. "Nothing changes. The people do, and the details do, but the work doesn't. I just finished a design for the upholstery on a set of dining chairs for a High Holder near Mont D'Artewelle. It's rather . . . bright."

Odelia laughed. The design and colors had to be more than just bright.

"What are you working on, Kolasyn?"

"Ornamental bronze fire-screen castings, and the fire tools to go with them for a hunting lodge, as well as a number of garden bronzes."

We talked for a while, or rather I asked about their projects, and then listened. As I did, it struck me that all of them were involved in creating things—as I once had been—and now I was being trained, in a way, to keep Solidar and others from being uncreated.

Odelia stood. "Is it all right if Kolasyn and I walk over to the river?"

"On this side, near the bridge," I replied. They'd be safe anywhere, but I didn't like the idea of their being too far away, although I couldn't have said why. I turned to Seliora and lifted my glass, which held but a small remnant of wine. "I can't tell you how much I appreciate this."

"I enjoyed putting it together."

"I'm looking forward to the time I can leave Imagisle," I began, "but that is likely to be a good three weeks." It was hard to believe that spring had departed and that it would be full summer by the seventh of Juyn.

Seliora nodded, but I could sense that there was more.

"What is it?"

"Father and Aunt Aegina are sending Shomyr and me with Grandmama on a trip to Kherseilles, Asseroiles, and then for a month at the beach near Pointe Neimon. The heat of the summers here is hard on Grandmama. Mama thinks that we can also visit a number of the textile mills we order from. They're within an easy trip on the ironway from Pointe Neimon."

"An easy trip?" Even I knew that wasn't so. "Compared to what?"

"The trip to Asseroiles and Kherseilles." Her smile was half wry, half mischievous.

"When are you leaving?"

She smiled faintly. "We depart next Jeudi. Father was able to arrange a compartment on the Express."

Somehow I had the feeling that there was more to it than that. "I'm not Pharsi, but I have a feeling about this trip."

"So does Grandmama. She says that it will be better this way."

Better for whom?

"She also says that you're more Pharsi than you think."

"So are you," I replied dryly.

For the briefest of instants, Seliora looked stunned. Not hurt, but truly surprised. "Why did you say that?"

"Because you are. You see things. How many Pharsis would have sensed enough to look out the window at Felters? You didn't see the assassin. You felt him first. Isn't that right?"

For a moment Seliora didn't say anything. "When did you notice?"

I smiled, although I didn't feel much like it. "In a way, I saw it then, but I didn't realize or understand what I'd seen."

"They're not trying to separate us, Rhenn. Mama had planned to have you over for dinner this week. She did most of this." Seliora gestured at all the dishes and bowls on the oilcloth. "That's because she likes you. As soon as we return, and you can leave Imagisle, Mama wants you to come for dinner. She said a real dinner."

I could tell that Seliora meant every word, but still . . . "What do they—or you—see?"

"I'd rather not say."

"Is it that bad?"

She shook her head. "I'm trying to keep it from being bad. You have to understand, Rhenn. There's a . . . it's a curse of sorts that comes with the sight. Too often, we've found, if things are bad, but not too bad, and we warn someone, especially someone we care about, in their efforts to avoid what we saw *might* happen, they make it worse."

I didn't like what she said, especially about things being bad, but I could see how that could happen. If I'd been warned about Johanyr, I might well have tried to be less harsh, and I might have been the one headed to Mont D'Glace. "You didn't know about the assassin?"

"It's harder with you. I told you why. Mama just told me to be very careful." She paused. "You have to understand. I wouldn't be telling you this now if you weren't an imager."

"Because people think of Pharsis and imagers in the same way?"

She nodded. "People don't like those who do things they can't understand."

I'd already seen that. "Does having the sight help in your business?"

"Sometimes. At times, I can see someone who's pleased and even get a glimpse of the design. Mother and Grandmama are better at sensing what people like."

"Between all three of you, that gives you a great advantage."

"Only because Papa and Shomyr are fine crafters. The craft of the furniture and the design together . . ."

"Are all the most sighted Pharsis women?"

Seliora smiled and tilted her head. "Mostly, but that's because you have to trust your feelings. Most men think too much."

I took her hand in mine.

"That's the one area where they don't think enough." But she was smiling, and her words were soft and warm.

"And women do?" I grinned at her.

"When we find what we know and feel is right, we don't keep looking. Any woman who does hasn't found what's right." Her lips quirked. "There's always the problem that the right man won't recognize that she's the right woman."

Her words shivered through me, because they made me think of Remaya, who had seen Rousel and never let go. What if Rousel hadn't seen? Was Seliora the right woman for me? Or was I merely the right man for her? The two weren't necessarily the same thing. I'd certainly wanted to be with her, but . . . how would I know? Really know? And was I thinking too much?

"Yes. You are thinking too much." She laughed.

"Do you read thoughts as well?"

"Only when they're written on your face."

I laughed. We might be close to the same age, but in one area, at least, she was far older and wiser. So I said just that.

"It's a good thing you know your weaknesses, Rhenn," she replied. "You don't have many, and that can make you most vulnerable. Too many men with few weaknesses delude themselves into believing they have none."

"Oh . . . I have weaknesses, and you're definitely one of them."

We talked for a long time, not saying all that much, but enjoying the banter and the early evening, and it was well past the seventh bell when I finished helping Seliora and Odelia pack everything back into their wicker baskets and then walked to the bridge with them.

There, on the edge of the bridge, Seliora turned to me and slipped her arms around me, then lifted her head and lips. We did kiss, and it was anything but brief.

When we finally released each other, she looked up. "You *will* come to dinner when we come back." Her words were anything but a question.

"I promise."

I stood on the bridge and watched until the three of them caught a hack, and I was glad that Odelia and Kolasyn were with Seliora, competent as she was.

46

A wink is not as good as a well-chosen phrase;
in intrigue, it's better.

The next week and a half gradually got harder and harder, both in terms of my lessons with Master Dichartyn and the interrogations that resulted from those studies; the exercises required by Clovyl, which were designed to increase my strength and stamina without straining unduly my recovering injuries; and the sessions with Maitre Dyana.

I thought about Seliora, more than a little, but generally during the day, because I was so tired at night that I fell asleep quickly.

Maitre Dyana had me read and memorize a set of handwritten notes and observations on High Holders, and then she would quiz me. On the first Jeudi in Juyn, she took the notes back. "By now, you should understand that conversation is more than mere words. It is a combination of inflections, innuendos, gestures, and dry wit. Few not born into that culture ever master the intricacy of conversing well in that style, but someone such as you could certainly learn enough to interpret what lies beyond the words."

"Especially as a merchant-born young man never expected to be more than an aide?"

She ignored my question, clearly deeming it rhetorical and unworthy of a reply. "The difficulty faced by the High Holders is that many of them equate intricacy and complexity with intelligence. The difficulty faced by those who do not understand intricacy and nonverbal complexity is that they often cannot distinguish between mere complexity for the sake of complexity and complexity that masks motives and intelligence often far greater than is usually encountered."

I thought for a moment. "The more powerful High Holders would not remain so without both wealth and intelligence, but the web of complexity that veils all High Holders can shield the actions of the more intelligent and deadly, often until it is too late to discern the pattern and results."

"Dichartyn believes you can see beyond the complexity." Maitre Dyana raised her right eyebrow, a gesture far more effective than words could have been.

"You have great doubts, but you're willing to make the attempt." I smiled politely. "I can't do a gesture like that, but even if I could, wouldn't it be out of character for a man?"

"For any man thought to be interested in women."

I had doubts that I'd be terribly convincing as any other type of man.

"Maintain that pleasant, close-to-but-not-quite-supercilious smile through everything, young Rhennthyl, and it will save you many words and much difficulty. Do not ever forget that on their actual holding, High Holders retain the rights of low justice, and that can be quite painful." Her face changed slightly, in a manner I could not have described, but could

certainly have painted, and there was pleasant interest, behind which was a hint of cold predation.

"Is that the expression one receives just after swallowing
poison or getting a knife in the back?"

"No." Her voice was sweetly pleasant. "That is the expression used when someone has just received word that they
have ruined you. It's an expression of triumph over someone
who used to be an equal. The High Holders seldom kill each
other . . . or those who have done them great wrong. That is
far too kind."

What was left unsaid was that a High Holder who did not
dispose of an underling who needed it was considered weak,
as was one who actually had to attempt to kill an equal,
rather than ruining him and his family. But it also suggested
that High Holder Ryel might well have worse in mind for me
than assassination . . . and over a long time.

Her face changed again. Now, behind the smile lay contemptuous pity.

"That's disposal of inferiors?"

"Good."

That was my introduction to the conversational patterns of
the High Holders, but Maitre Dyana was just beginning. At
the end of our session, she handed me a book. "This is a
novel. Read it. Part of it is accurate. Part is not. We will discuss it on Mardi."

That was on top of Master Dichartyn's latest assignment—to
describe with a supporting proof the easiest ways to enter the
Council Chateau and reach the private studies of the councilors without being detected. I had the feeling that the weekend would be long, both because of the work I had to do . . .
and because I would not be seeing Seliora.

Messenger/Guard

47

Silence is not golden; it is only a tool like any other.

At the end of the following week, Master Draffyd examined me and said that I could go back to a stronger conditioning regimen, and whatever imaging Master Dichartyn had in mind. I had not received a letter from Seliora, but I couldn't say I was totally surprised, not when she and Shomyr were still traveling. I did receive a letter from my mother, expressing concern and wanting to know if and when she could visit. I wrote back that because of the nature of my training it would be several weeks yet. I just didn't want to have to explain. Some of what had happened I knew shouldn't leave the Collegium, and Mother didn't respond well to my refusing to say much. I also didn't want to mention Seliora, not yet. Not until after she returned from her trip. It had taken Mother years to accept Remaya, and I wasn't about to raise that issue until I was absolutely certain that Seliora and I belonged together.

The next Lundi—Juyn sixteenth—I had barely settled into the chair in Master Dichartyn's study when he said, "Your messenger uniforms arrived, did they not?"

"Yes, sir. They fit comfortably."

"They should. It's time for you to go to work. You'll be going to the Chateau every morning for the next three weeks. In the afternoons, Clovyl will still work with you, and I'll occasionally give you instruction and exercises. When the Council resumes meeting officially on the second of Agostos, you'll be there all day, every day, and some evenings." He paused. "But you will be expected to continue the physical conditioning. After you begin full-time at the Chateau, you'll be joining the group that exercises at fifth bell every morning but Solayi."

What could I say to that but "Yes, sir." Then I asked, "With everything going on between Caenen and Ferrum and Tiempre, the Council's not meeting?"

"The Executive Council is still there. Effectively, they control the government. The full sessions deal more with laws and problems." He cleared his throat. "At the Chateau, Baratyn will brief you on your duties. He's in charge of the messengers, both the imagers and the non-imagers who handle most of the messages. All of the imagers are listed as part-time messengers and security aides. The regular messengers aren't supposed to know that you're imagers, but they all know you've been trained to deal with weapons and attackers. Now for Baratyn—he's a Maitre D'Aspect, but he's listed on the official public Collegium records as a tertius."

"Yes, sir. Am I supposed to know who the other imagers are?"

"You are, and they're supposed to know you. Baratyn will introduce you. You wear the messenger uniform here at the Collegium only when you're on your way to and from the Chateau. All of you travel using a duty coach that's generally indistinguishable from a hack. If necessary, you can take a hack back, but only so far as West River Road. The Council members know that some of the messengers are imagers, and, soon enough, most of the sharper ones will be able to pick you out, but they don't say anything because their safety rests on you."

"What about the High Holders?" I knew that there were five High Holders on the Council, and I was glad that Ryel was not one of them. He had been, years earlier, but councilors were limited to two consecutive five-year terms. If they wished and their appointing body agreed, they could return after standing down for a full term.

"Even if Ryel were a councilor, you'd be quite safe for now, and always in the Chateau. Your situation isn't the first time that sort of thing has occurred. High Holders never act precipitously. Often they wait months or even years."

That didn't reassure me.

"There's one other matter. Usually some new messenger, or occasionally a relative of one of the councilors, generally a young woman, will ask if you're an imager or insist that you must be. You are to say you are assigned to serve the Council. If they get very insistent, you may say that they can believe what they wish, but the truth is that you are assigned to the Council. That is what you are to say, and all you are to say. Is that clear?"

"Yes, sir."

Master Dichartyn stood. "Go put on your messenger uniform. I'll meet you at the west duty-coach station behind the dining hall in half a glass."

I walked quickly back to my quarters and changed. The messenger uniform was made of a fine lightweight black wool, trimmed with a gray piping so faint in color that it was almost white. Fine as the wool was, and thin as the pale gray shirt that went under the short-waisted jacket was, I did hope that I didn't have to spend much time in the sun, not in the summer.

My changing was swift enough that I was walking up to the duty coach at almost the same moment as Master Dichartyn. He said nothing, but gestured for me to enter the coach.

Because he had not spoken, I waited until the coach began to move before I asked, "Do you know what is happening with our fleets and the Caenenans, sir?"

"No more than is in the newssheets, Rhennthyl."

That was little help because neither *Veritum* nor *Tableta* contained anything but vague speculation. "What do you think will happen?"

"The Caenenans and their High Priest will do something foolish out of pride, and, hopefully, we will do something less foolish to keep open warfare from flaring up." He fingered his chin, then lowered his hand.

I waited. Sometimes silence was a better way to get a response.

"Life is always about power. When men or nations talk about honor, what they mean is how others perceive their power. When a man claims his honor has been affronted, what he is saying is that another's actions, if unchallenged, may diminish his power in the eyes of others. The same is true of nations. The Collegium does not care about the popular perceptions of power, unless those perceptions actually diminish Solidar's power. Often our duties require redressing the balance of power without any overt use of military or economic force. That is all I will say for now, but I trust you will consider my words carefully as you watch the Council and those who move around it, prating of honor when they are in reality merely seeking to have the Council increase their power or diminish that of another."

I already understood that. A wool importer benefited when import tariffs were lowered, and I had heard my father rail on about the lack of honor in the Council in not tariffing certain finished fabrics, but that was because those fabrics went to other factors.

My eyes strayed outside as the coach carried us over the Bridge of Desires, not the other bridge on the west side of Imagisle, which was the Bridge of Stones, because that was used almost entirely for heavy wagons and the like. We rode west past the modest spires of Council Anomen, so named because it was the anomen closest to the Council Chateau, not because the councilors necessarily attended services there, and then down the Boulevard D'Council a good mille and a half to Council Hill, ringed by a wide avenue, with the Square of Justice on the plaza to the south. Eight avenues or boulevards radiated from the ring road, but none of them were all that heavily traveled, not the way those east of the river were. The coach turned south on Council Circle, then came to a stop on the east side, just opposite a small postern gate in the white alabaster wall. I got out and waited for Master Dichartyn.

He walked up to the black iron gate. I followed him. The guard standing behind the chest-high grillwork wore a black uniform similar to mine, except for a thin black cotton waistcoat rather than a full coat. He also had a large pistol in a belt holster and a truncheon.

He nodded. "Another messenger, Master Dichartyn?"

"Yes. This is Rhennthyl. He starts today."

The guard studied me, then nodded. I realized that he was an obdurate, but that made sense. He opened the iron gate.

Behind the wall and gate was a narrow stone walk—also white, but white granite—that led to an equally narrow set of steps leading up the side of the low hill on which the Chateau sat. Even so, there were more than a hundred steps before we reached a stone terrace surrounded by a waist-high alabaster wall. By then I was sweating, but I wasn't breathing hard, and that I owed to Clovyl. Neither was Master Dichartyn, either, and he'd set a quick pace up the steps. The terrace had but two exits—the steps and a door in the wall of the Chateau.

"This is the way you always enter—unless you have specific instructions otherwise." Master Dichartyn opened the door, and we stepped out of the glare of the blazing sun into what seemed cool gloom, although I knew that was only by comparison.

Inside was another armed obdurate guard. Master Dichartyn nodded in my direction. "This is Rhennthyl. He's the newest messenger."

"Yes, sir."

Beyond the guard was a circular foyer with narrow corridors leading out of it both to the left and right. Master Dichartyn took the right corridor. The walls were plain white stone, old but spotless, each block precisely cut, with but the thinnest line of mortar at the joins. The floor tiles were of polished gray slate. Despite the immaculate appearance, there was a sense of age, perhaps because there were no embellishments or decorations.

The short corridor ended at a wider one, the main corridor running north and south on the east side of the ground level of the Chateau. There, Master Dichartyn turned left, stopping at the first door, which was open.

"Baratyn . . . I've brought you your new messenger."

The study was small and without windows, although there was a ventilation grate high on the east wall, and held a modest desk with drawers and a wooden file case on one wall.

Two chairs stood before the desk and one, with arms, behind it.

"Master Dichartyn." Baratyn stepped forward and beckoned for us to enter. He was a few digits shorter than I was, with short-cut brown hair, a squarish chin, and eyes that seemed to change colors, from brown to hazel to light green, even as I looked at him. Like me, he wore the gray-trimmed black uniform, except on the short stiff jacket collars were two small pewter triangles—one on each collar. "You'd be Rhennthyl."

"Yes, sir." I inclined my head.

He nodded, then turned toward Master Dichartyn.

"That's all. Rhennthyl will be here mornings until the Council reconvenes officially."

"That should be long enough to get him squared away."

Even before Baratyn finished speaking, the senior imager was gone.

Baratyn looked to me. "Basyl will be here in a moment. He's one of the senior regular messengers. He'll show you around. If he asks where you're from, tell him where your family lives."

I was spared having to answer because at that moment we were joined by Basyl, a thin, almost frail man, a good ten years older than me by his looks, with wide gray eyes under brown hair so dark it was not quite black and a narrow chin. "You sent for me, sir?"

"I did. Rhennthyl here is the new security support messenger."

"I'm pleased to meet you," I offered.

He nodded politely. "The same."

"I'd appreciate it if you'd give Rhennthyl a tour of the Chateau, particularly the routes and places he'll need to know as a messenger once the Council reconvenes."

"Yes, sir." He nodded somberly. "Are you ready?"

"Yes."

As soon as we stepped out of Baratyn's study, Basyl gestured down the long corridor. "On this level are the studies for the advisors to the councilors. They have the bigger studies, the ones with the windows. The smaller studies are for the staff, like Baratyn and Pelagryn."

"Pelagryn?"

"He's in charge of the maintainers. Of course, Chasylmar has the northeast corner study on this level."

"I haven't met Chasylmar."

"He's the Chateau steward, and his study is the big one in the northeast corner. The corner studies are the best, because they've got windows on two walls and you can get a breeze there. Up on the Council level the three Executive Council members have three of the four corner studies, and the most senior guild representative has the other—that's Councilor Ramon."

Basyl led me all the way around the main corridor on the ground level, pointing out everything, from whose study was where, the waiting room for messengers, and where the staff jakes were and the two circular staircases. We took the one in the northeast corner down to the lower level, which held the kitchen—and a dumbwaiter that ran directly up to the upper pantry off the Council dining chamber. Then there were storerooms for everything, various workrooms, and other spaces for the maintainers and their equipment. From there we took the northwest staircase up to the third and topmost level, which held the main Council chamber, the smaller Executive Council chamber, the councilors' lounge, their dining chamber, and all the studies.

Basyl stopped at the top of the grand staircase that led down to the foyer holding all the artwork, which he had not shown me, but which I recalled. "How did you end up here?"

"I was a journeyman portraiturist. It didn't work out. After my master's death, none of the masters in the guild wanted to take on another journeyman, especially one so old."

"You're not that old."

"I'll be twenty-five shortly, and that's old to begin with another master in portraiture."

"Your family . . . they must have . . . must know people."

"My father is a wool factor. He wishes I had that talent. What about your family?"

"He's a tinker of sorts. He has a small shop. People bring things to him to be fixed or sharpened. I'm not that good with my hands, but I'm quick, and I never forget anything anyone tells me. That's useful for a messenger." Basyl nodded slowly, then turned and led the way down the grand main staircase—the one I had last beheld more than ten years earlier. We'd barely reached the bottom when Baratyn appeared holding an envelope.

"Basyl . . . I need this run to Chasylmar. He's not in his study, and I don't have time to track him down."

The senior messenger nodded and took the envelope. "Yes, sir."

"You come with me, Rhennthyl."

Baratyn didn't say anything until we were inside his study. "If you'd close the door . . ."

I did, then sat down after he'd seated himself behind the desk.

"You answered Basyl's questions accurately and yet without revealing anything."

How had he known that? "Was that a test? Are there listening tubes everywhere?"

"Of sorts. Only in the corridors. That's one of the other things we monitor. You will, too, in time. With what we do and you will be doing, everything is a test. But then, most of life is. Most people just don't realize it—or don't want to think about it. At the moment, even with you, we're shorthanded." He laughed. "We're always shorthanded. There are three of you as messengers and silent guards . . . and me. In an emergency we can call on one or two others, but that includes Master Dichartyn, and he's not always available. The other two security messengers should be here any moment. While we're waiting, do you have any questions?"

"How many regular messengers?"

"Just four. That's enough to allow one or two to be sent off Council Hill, if necessary."

At the knock on the door, Baratyn called out, "Come on in."

I stood. I didn't like being seated when meeting other

people, particularly when they were standing. The door opened, and two men stepped inside. The second one closed the door. Both of them were about my size, and at least several years older. They looked almost politely nondescript, yet I could sense that behind that facade, they were formidable. Was that the kind of impression that Master Dichartyn was seeking—someone who could blend into any group, yet who, if you looked closely, you really didn't want to encounter in dark corners?

"Rhennthyl, meet Martyl and Dartazn. Martyl is the blond one."

Martyl smiled politely. "Be good to have some help here."

"Especially the way things look to be going," added the dark-haired and dark-eyed Dartazn, who was just a shade taller than Martyl.

"I had Basyl give him the general tour," said Baratyn. "You two can show him all the places he really needs to know. He'll only be here mornings for the next few weeks. They're rushing his training so that he'll be as ready as possible when the Council goes back in session."

Dartazn looked at me, his brows furrowed. "You usually sit with Kahlasa and the other field operatives, don't you? At the Collegium, I mean?"

"I do. That was because I got to know Claustyn when I became a third."

"You're the one who took a bullet near the heart and managed to image-shield it until Master Draffyd could take care of it."

I hadn't realized the bullet was that close. "Two bullets, actually, but I didn't know it at the time. And I passed out a little bit before I got to Master Draffyd."

"Claustyn hoped you'd go field," added Martyl.

"That would have been my second choice," I admitted.

"You three can talk later," Baratyn said, "at the Collegium, not here."

"Yes, sir," replied Martyl genially. "All the walls but those here have ears. We hear and understand."

"Go!" But Baratyn was smiling.

We left.

By the time I climbed into the duty coach at ten bells, with Martyl and Dartazn, my head was swimming with the effort of trying to remember all the hidden nooks and passages.

"We get lunch at the Collegium when the Council's not in full session," Martyl explained. "That's because they close down the kitchens to give the staff their summer break. The Chateau's practically deserted now."

That was fine with me. I'd need all three weeks to really learn where everything was—and that was in spite of my study of the Chateau's plans.

48

Implying guilt in writing is like eating food held too long, providing neither satisfaction nor savor.

On Mardi, two letters were waiting in my box when I checked after lunch, but I was running so late that all I did was to see that one was from Seliora. I didn't open it, because I wanted to enjoy reading it, and I didn't have time for that. The other was from Mother. I had immediately recognized her handwriting. I didn't open it, either, if for very different reasons, before I hurried back to my quarters and changed into exercise clothes and heavy boots.

Clovyl was waiting outside the exercise hall, with his usual patient smile, a smile that—I was convinced—concealed a hidden glee at the thought of how hard he'd make me work.

"Good afternoon, Rhenn. You still have a lot more catching up to do."

I followed him to the chamber, where I began on the loos-

ening-up exercises, although my eyes did stray to the corner
that held the free weights. It wasn't that they were so heavy,
but my muscles burned after I went through that routine—
and I still had to look forward to another two glasses of special treatment.

Once he had worked me over thoroughly for slightly more
than two glasses, Clovyl told me to stop by Master Dichartyn's study after I cleaned up.

The one advantage of an afternoon shower was that the
water was merely cool, rather than ice-cold, and before long
I was sitting on the bench outside Master Dichartyn's study.
If I'd known that I'd be sitting there for close to half a glass
I would have brought Mother's letter, but I'd been hurrying
so much that I hadn't thought about that.

The study door opened, and a secundus stepped out. I
stood, and his eyes flashed to me and then away.

"Good day, sir." He fled as much as walked away.

I knocked.

"Come in, Rhenn."

Once inside, I shut the door and sat down, waiting to see
what else Master Dichartyn had scheduled for me.

"Clovyl says that you're doing well, and that, if you keep at
it, you'll be close to where you should be by the time the
Council reconvenes . . . where you should be in terms of
physical training and conditioning. You're still lacking in finesse in your imagery, but we need to get you some experience. On Jeudi morning, you're to meet me here in the
morning at half before fifth bell. We'll be going to the prison
for an execution."

"Practice, sir?"

"Two kinds of practice. Subtlety and effectiveness. That
night, you'll have to work with Master Draffyd. Mostly,
you'll just be watching him do a dissection. Too much of
your knowledge is text knowledge. That's not your fault, but
it's something we need to remedy." He stood. "You have to
excuse me, but matters are pressing."

"Caenen and Jariola, sir?"

"Partly. That's mostly Master Schorzat's headache. It doesn't help much that imaging is banned in Tiempre, and that its practice, if discovered, is punished by execution. Ferrum doesn't ban it, but known imagers face great difficulties. That makes working in either land even more difficult, the Nameless knows, although neither Ferrum nor Jariola is a place we'd normally want to be. You'd think that we were the disciples of Bilbryn." He shook his head.

Bilbryn? It took me a moment to recall the name. When Solidar had been warring states using bronze weapons, he'd been the imager champion of Rex Caldor, and his enemies called him the great disciple of the Namer, declaring him evil incarnate.

"I'll see you on Jeudi," Master Dichartyn said.

Our meeting had been short enough that I had a good glass left before dinner, and I hurried back to my quarters. Once there, I recovered the letters, opening Mother's first, knowing full well what awaited me. I forced myself to read the words carefully.

Dear Rhennthyl,
I had hoped that we would be able to host a birthday dinner for you this Samedi and perhaps invite Zerlenya or another suitable young lady, if you did not find Zerlenya to your liking. I do hope that you are feeling better, but I cannot help but worry, since we have not heard from you since your last letter. I do hope that we have not done anything to offend you. I had only invited Zerlenya because she is a beautiful and intelligent young woman, and you had mentioned that there were few women at all on Imagisle . . .

I paused in reading, then shook my head.

. . . and you are now reaching the age where it will become more and more difficult to find someone suitable, as the most attractive ones from a suitable background will already have been spoken for. . . .

A suitable background was a polite way of saying some-one who was at least from the factoring or full merchant class and most preferably not Pharsi.

. . . That is, of course, a matter with which you must deal, but we were only trying to be helpful.

That was doubtless true, but I didn't need to be reminded of it.

We would still very much like to have a belated celebra-tion of your twenty-fifth birthday. I do hope that this finds you in good health and that you will let us know when we may expect you or when I may visit you.

The last thing I wanted to do was write a reply, but doing so quickly would reduce the amount of guilt Mother would attempt to lay at my feet. I set aside the still-unopened letter from Seliora and wrote a quick reply to Mother, based on the truth, stating that while I had recovered physically, I was still restricted to Imagisle until certain aspects of my training were completed, but that, if she wished to visit, she was now more than welcome on either Samedi or Solayi afternoons, and should drop me a note to let me know when to expect her, and that I looked forward to seeing her.

Then I finally sat back in my study chair and opened the letter from Seliora.

Dear Rhenn,
At last, we have arrived in Pointe Neimon. The trip was hard for Grandmama, but she is in good spirits. She sends her best to you. So does Shomyr.

We have already toured four textile manufactories, and we have improved arrangements with two. Their fabric is ex-cellent. One other is satisfactory. The other we will not use, but it is good to see what each can do.

I trust that you are well and will be fully recovered and able to leave Imagisle by the time we return. We have tickets on the Express for the fourth of Agostos. Grandmama says that we should invite you to dinner on the fourteenth. If you know that you can come then and let me know, I can write Mother and tell her to plan for it. If you do not know, then we can work out a time once we return to L'Excelsis.

You would find Pointe Neimon refreshing and beautiful. I do wish you could be here, but you must do what you must. I only ask that you take care in your duties, great care.

At the bottom was an address in Pointe Neimon, and, again, the signature was just her name, but the last two words before her signature, and the kiss when we had last parted, suggested far more than friendship.

I smiled. I did have time to write a response.

49

Death always leaves some stories incomplete; and some are better left so.

Getting up well before dawn on Jeudi was not exactly to my liking, especially with what lay ahead, as much as I knew the necessity. I struggled to Master Dichartyn's study, early enough that I sat slumped on the bench for a time before he appeared.

"Buck up, Rhennthyl. You're not the one being executed."

I jumped to my feet. "It's early, sir."

"Every morning's early." His voice was dry.

I walked quietly beside him as we made our way to the duty coach, which had drawn up outside the administration building. He said nothing to the black-clad obdurate driver.

Mist rose from the river as we crossed the Bridge of Stones, the hoofs of the two horses clattering on the pavement. The route to the prison was fairly direct—south on the West River Road to the intersection with the Avenue D'Artisans just after it crossed the Sud Bridge, and then more than a mille on the avenue and across the bridge over the ironway tracks, after which the coach turned onto a short street that ended at a gatehouse. Behind the gatehouse rose the gray flint walls of the Poignard Prison.

The duty coach halted by the gatehouse. No sooner had we stepped out onto the ancient cobblestones, damp from the light rain of the evening before, than two men in blue and black uniforms emerged. The one with the four-pointed star on his collars bowed to Master Dichartyn.

"Maitre D'Esprit."

"Warden . . ."

The warden's eyes flicked to me, just for a moment, before he and the guard escorted us through the gate and along a windowless stone-walled corridor until we reached an iron door, where another guard turned a black wheel to unlock it. We stepped into a small courtyard. I glanced up. The sky was beginning to lighten, just slightly, but I could still see clearly the reddish crescent that was Erion. At the far side of the courtyard was a scaffold. There were three nooses rigged from an overhead beam.

The warden stepped away, and the guard remained, a pace to one side.

Master Dichartyn leaned toward me and spoke softly. "The man to be executed will be led onto the platform, to one of the traps where there is a noose. He will be hooded and blindfolded. The executioner will put the noose over his head and adjust it properly. Then the executioner will step back. His next move will be to pull the lever to release that trap. As soon as he steps back and puts his hand on the lever, you are to act. If you image properly, the man will die and start to slump, and the executioner will pull the lever. The guilty man will be dead or dying before the noose breaks his neck.

"There will be three executed this morning. If you are successful with the first, try another technique with the second, and another with the third."

Left unsaid was that I had practiced none of the techniques on living people—for obvious reasons.

The first technique was simply to image a moderate amount of air into the convicted man's heart, vena cava, and aorta. Master Dichartyn had pointed out that, given the pressure of the heart pumping liquid, I would have to image some of the blood elsewhere for the effect to be near-instant.

The first prisoner was a heavyset man. Not only was he blindfolded, but his hands were tied behind his back, and his feet were manacled so that he could only take short steps. Two guards had to hold him, and a third wrapped a strap around his legs before the executioner could put the noose in place. As soon as the executioner stepped back, I concentrated.

The prisoner gave a sudden jerk, as if burned all over, then started to slump. The executioner pulled the lever. The prisoner was shuddering and twitching for that long moment before he reached the end of the rope and the noose snapped his neck.

"Not enough air in the aorta," observed Master Dichartyn. "He would have died, but not quickly. Try that again."

The second prisoner was thinner and shorter, and probably older. He didn't struggle, just walked listlessly to the noose. This time I tried to follow the procedure more carefully.

The convicted man only jerked once, then slumped.

"Good. He felt one jolting pain, and that was it. Try something else now."

I wasn't ready for the next prisoner. She was a woman, tall and with a shapely figure, even hooded and in the prison drab.

Master Dichartyn sensed my reaction. "If she's up there, whatever she did must have been horrible. Otherwise, she'd be drugged and used as a comfort woman by the Navy."

That didn't help, because I'd never heard of drugged comfort women. I swallowed and tried to concentrate. Fortunately, the convicted woman, who had taken her first steps almost demurely, literally jumped with both manacled feet, trying even while hooded and blindfolded a form of snap-kick at the leg of one of the guards. She struck hard enough that he went down, but so did she, and another guard dashed forward and wrapped a leather strap around her ankles. The three were not gentle as they forced the noose over her head and around her neck.

"Concentrate." Master Dichartyn's voice was low and hard.

I fixed my eyes and concentration on that part of her skull—or the spot beneath it—where the pitricine had to go. Contrary to that long-ago rumor promulgated by Seleus, it wasn't swift if imaged to the heart or stomach—and most physicians could detect that kind of poisoning.

Just before the executioner touched the lever, I imaged.

She folded and slumped, but the executioner was ready, so much so that I doubt if anyone who did not know what had happened would have guessed that she was already dead.

"That was well done." Master Dichartyn's voice was again low. "Especially under the circumstances."

The executioner stepped forward. "Evil as they may have been, they had lives and hopes, and we commend them to the Nameless. Let their example remind us all that kindness and honesty to others are the roots of harmony."

For a moment, all was silent. Then the warden crossed the courtyard to us, and without speaking led us back the way we had come.

When we reached the coach, Master Dichartyn nodded to the guard and the warden. "We thank you."

Both bowed slightly, and the warden replied, "As always, we appreciate what Imagisle does for us, and we wish you both well." There was a slight, but distinct emphasis on the word "both."

"As do we you," I replied, as I'd been coached.

Once we were in the duty coach and on our way back to

Imagisle, Master Dichartyn cleared his throat, then said, "I'd like you to think of another way to accomplish what you did this morning, one that is equally undetectable—if done properly."

I managed a polite smile, even after the last three words, which were a reminder that I had not handled the first prisoner as well as I should have. "Yes, sir."

"You are not, obviously, to write this down, but you are to think it out thoroughly." He paused. "Why am I asking this?"

"I would judge, sir, that if everyone I must stop from doing harm seems to suffer either a heart stoppage or a brain seizure, there might be more questions than I or the Collegium would like to answer."

He nodded. "On Lundi night, we'll work on slowing and disrupting stratagems. Most times, those are to be preferred, but they're easier and quicker to learn, and your injuries have necessitated training you in a different order to ready you in time to assume your duties."

I was getting an ever-stronger feeling that Master Dichartyn was anticipating great troubles before long. "Who will strike first?"

He laughed, and there was a bitterness I had not heard before. "Who will not?"

I had to think for a moment. "The Abiertans? Or the Ferrans?"

"The Abiertans are afraid that we will annex them to keep the trade routes open. Any councilor who suggests such will be a target, and several already have survived attacks, not that they know it. Especially Councilor Reyner. The Ferrans are so touchy and arrogant that they believe their machines will allow them to fight both the Oligarch and Solidar. We don't want any of those wars, and if councilors are attacked, wounded, or killed, there will likely be war. An important part of your job—and that of Baratyn and all of you working with him—is not to give anyone on the Council the excuse for fighting a war."

Before all that long, we were back at the Collegium, but I was still late for breakfast, and Martyl and Dartazn, even

Reynol and Menyard, were already finished. All through my hurried meal, I had to wonder what the woman had done that was so horrible that she had been sentenced to die. Then I had to rush to the duty coach that took the three of us to the Council Chateau.

"You were late for breakfast," Martyl said as I climbed into the coach.

"I was with Master Dichartyn. We finished late—not late last night, but late with what we were doing this morning."

The coach pulled away from the Collegium. Outside, it was still misty, but getting brighter, and that suggested a hot and sticky day to come.

"Prison stuff?" asked Dartazn.

I just nodded. I still worried about the woman, then I wondered why I was more concerned about her than about the men. There was no reason why a woman couldn't have killed someone . . . or worse. "I had to drag myself over to meet him before we left. He looked as if he'd been awake for glasses."

"He doesn't ever sleep much, they say," replied Martyl.

"If I had to deal with what's on his mind," added Dartazn, "I wouldn't sleep much, either. He's got to think of his work and supervise Master Schorzat as well."

I hadn't fully realized that Master Dichartyn was over Master Schorzat, although I should have, because Master Dichartyn was in charge of all Collegium security.

After reaching the Chateau, we met with Baratyn just before eighth glass, as had been the practice, although that would change to half past seventh glass once the Council reconvened.

"This session of the Council, we will be making some changes," Baratyn said. "The first one is that when the Council is in session, one of you will always be near the doorway from the councilors' lounge to the private passageway that leads to the chamber. As always, you will say nothing unless you are delivering a message or if you are addressed personally."

"Even if you want to make Councilor Ramsael trip and crack his skull," added Martyl, almost under his breath.

"Especially if you want that," Baratyn riposted. "We're not here to like them. We're here to preserve them so that we don't end up with something worse."

I knew Ramsael was a High Holder from Kephria, but I'd never seen him. I had the feeling that one of the hardest things was going to be matching councilors' names with their faces.

"In addition . . . at least one of you will be available to escort and act, if necessary, against anyone here to see a councilor."

I could see that. Although every visitor allowed into the Chateau had to be on a list compiled from names provided by the councilors—or their aides—there was no assurance that the person who showed up at the gate was the person actually expected. Anyone could claim he was Raphael D'Factorius or Jorges D'Artisan. That didn't mean that they were.

After Baratyn's briefing, Dartazn took me on a tour of the outer grounds, pointing out all the places where assassins and intruders had tried to climb the walls or hide. Needless to say, as soon as we had gone outside, the sun broke through the mist, and I began to sweat.

Halfway along the west side, he pointed out the heavier foundation wall. "They call this the wall of life and death. The name dates back to Rex Regis."

"Why?"

Dartazn shrugged. "Because it meant life for some and death for others."

By the time Dartazn had finished taking me through the upper and lower gardens and the inner walks bordering the walls, we were both perspiring even more heavily. We were quite thorough in studying and inspecting the fountain court, with the cool created there by the various sprays of water. Then we returned to Baratyn's study.

"Rhennthyl . . . you're to spend the next glass studying a list of the regular visitors so that at least you know their names. After that, you can join Dartazn and Martyl in finishing the inventory of security equipment."

Neither trying to learn names of people I had never seen

nor comparing equipment in cases, racks, and boxes to a listing was terribly interesting, and all three of us were more than happy when it was time to return to Imagisle for lunch.

After lunch, I found a letter from Mother in my letter box. I read it quickly on my way back to my chamber to change into exercise clothes for my afternoon torture session with Clovyl.

> *Dear Rhennthyl,*
> *Your father and I are both glad to hear that you are recovering, but sorry that you are being limited to Imagisle for the near future. We had hoped that you would be able to accompany us to Kherseilles. We are leaving on Jeudi to see Rousel's and Remaya's son. They have decided to name him Rheityr, after your great-grandfather.*

I couldn't help but shake my head at her assumption that, if I hadn't been injured, of course, I'd be able to leave Imagisle for more than a week.

> *We will not be back for more than a week, since your father needs to go over the factoring in Kherseilles with Rousel, but as warm as it has been here in L'Excelsis, it is bound to be more pleasant there, and it will be good to see our grandson. Khethila will be at the house, and she will be spending each day at the factorage in your father's absence, but we will take Culthyn with us.*

I smiled at that. Neither of them wanted to admit how competent Khethila was getting to be. So far as the handling of coins went, I'd prefer to have her in charge, rather than Rousel. Rousel could sell anything, but coins had always had a way of dropping out of his wallet.

> *I will write once we have returned, and we will see about that dinner. By the time we are back and you are free, it may be well into harvest, but then, it will be cooler, and you might even have the name of a marriageable young*

*woman that we could invite, inasmuch as you did not seem
to find Zerlenya to your taste.*

I winced at that, but just laid the letter on my desk as I entered my quarters. I had to change quickly and then hurry back to the exercise chambers.

After the warm-ups and the weights and the conditioning run, Clovyl resumed the training with knives, then followed that with a session with truncheons—or any relatively short length of wood or pipe or the like.

After a quick dinner, at seventh bell, I met Master Draffyd in the anteroom of the infirmary.

His face was grave. "This is not likely to be terribly pleasant for you, Rhennthyl. It will, we trust, make you a better imager. I'm going to dissect one of the bodies from this morning's execution, in order to show you the exact placement of certain organs. I will also ask you to attempt certain precise imaging from time to time during the process. Some of it will improve your abilities to protect the Council. Some of it will help you protect yourself."

"Yes, sir." His words suggested some would improve my ability to kill, and some to heal, or at least limit bleeding or trauma, although he had not said those words.

He turned, and I followed him into the infirmary and down the corridor to a small room with a table. On one wall was a rack of shimmering instruments. On the table was a figure half covered with a thin gray blanket.

The body that lay faceup on the table was that of a woman with long flaming red hair, naked and uncovered from the waist up. She had been beautiful. Even in death, there was some attractiveness, but her face still bore a trace of pain or agony. Then, that might have been my imagination.

"This is the woman executed this morning. From her expression, your effort was relatively good."

Relatively good?

He pointed to the top back of the woman's shoulders. "You can see here the edge of faint white scars, and some newer welts. She's been beaten. I reported that to the chief of patrollers and the justice, but the last beating took place before she was apprehended. The welts almost had healed during the time she was held for her hearing." He shook his head. "I don't always trust all the patrollers, but the degree of healing supports the chief's story. I suppose we'll never know what happened." He pointed to her neck. "We're using her body because it requires more precision. I'd like you to image a small plug of wax into her carotid artery." He gestured to a white oblong of wax on the narrow shelf beneath the instrument rack.

The initial imaging wasn't too bad, nor were the ones that followed, except I had to push away the questions about the welts on her back.

The dissection was another matter. It took every bit of willpower to keep my guts from turning inside out once Master Draffyd lifted back the scalp and began to peel away various areas of skin, muscle, and bone to show me most clearly what he had in mind, illustrating where I could use imaging for what, and how it could be effectively used and where . . . and where it was useless, and why.

He also checked the accuracy of my imaging at almost every step of the dissection. I'd been accurate with the wax in the neck artery, and far less accurate with some of the other placements, particularly those deeper in the body or in the spinal column.

It was close to midnight when I made my way from the infirmary. Even a thorough washing didn't help too much with my thoughts.

After I reached my own study, I first lit the lamp—with a striker and not by imaging—and then just stood there. Finally, I sat down at the writing desk and took out the letters from Seliora. I needed something to take my mind off what had happened during the course of a very long day, especially the beginning and the end.

50

◠

All ask where the river goes, but few study how it flows.

The rest of the week went somewhat better, although I had to decline going out with Martyl and Dartazn on Samedi because I was still restricted to Imagisle. That night and again on Solayi, I spent the time with my thoughts and the anatomy section of the science text, trying to come up with another silent and deadly technique for stopping an attacker. That was difficult because, at times, I could still see in my thoughts the woman I'd executed.

In midafternoon on Solayi, I walked to the north end of Imagisle, past the workshops and the park, and then past the cottages and dwellings. There were more than a few dwellings that looked to be spacious and gracious. I supposed those were for the masters with families. I sat on a shaded bench overlooking the river for a time. Even in late summer under a clear sky, the water was gray.

That night, of course, I went to services, and one section of Chorister Isola's homily on Solayi did remain with me, when she was speaking of luck and fortune.

". . . Good fortune can fall upon the evil, and evil upon the good. Chance and time befall us all. Do not rail against such, for such vain protests can only make matters worse and you less able. Do not grant the Namer more power over you by giving names to your misfortunes or declaring your fortune as if it were a named quality that is an integral part of you . . ."

Her words made me think about Rousel. Had I named luck and charm as part of who he was? But were those really part of him, or my appellations, offered out of envy?

Then, when I left the service, as I saw the wives and children of the older married imagers also departing with their husbands, I was reminded that the Collegium was indeed a city within a city, and I actually saw Master Dichartyn with an angular brunette and two daughters. I couldn't help wondering about what he saw in her until I saw her smile at him, and his smile in return. I was glad he didn't see me studying them.

Lundi was like all the weekdays, beginning with a hurried breakfast and a rush to the duty carriage. The morning was long, because I had been tasked with writing a fair copy of the inventory we had done the week before. The good part was that lunch was a good ragout with dark bread, and the three of us had a chance to talk before they returned to the Council Chateau.

Once more I had to hurry to get ready for Clovyl, although I had come to enjoy those afternoon sessions and learning skills that were largely physical in nature and technique. I couldn't help but think that, had I known what he had taught me when I'd been at grammaire, my years there would have been far less painful.

Lundi evening I met with Master Dichartyn, and he actually agreed with my "new" technique—imaging aleyan into the back of the eye—but he pointed out that it was not new, and that pitricine would work as well, although aleyan was harder to detect. After that, it was actually enjoyable to learn about various delaying or disabling tricks, many of which were so obvious after being told, but not something that I would necessarily have thought of without prompting, things like imaging oil and wax onto a step or pavement under a boot or shoe, or tar, for a slowing effect on someone running. I particularly liked the powdered chilis in the nose.

When we had finished with that, he fingered his chin, and I knew something was coming.

"Now that you are about to become a true working imager, I need to repeat some things. There are other unwritten but very real rules for imager counterspies. I am certain that Master Jhulian has intimated what they are, but I will lay them out directly. First, except in cases of publicly witnessed self-defense, anyone you kill or otherwise dispose of must appear to have died through an accident or in some fashion that cannot be said to be murder. Second, such removals must always take place when you are unobserved and someone else is present to honestly testify that no one else was present. Third, you will report every such incident, and failure to do so could result in severe consequences. Fourth, you tell no one but me or the head maitre of the Collegium what you have done in accomplishing those duties, and such reports are to be only verbal. You are never to write down anywhere the actions you have taken or the charges that you have been given. Do you understand that?"

"Yes, sir."

"I have some reading material for you." He smiled wryly. "It's not text. It has to do with one of your assignments."

"Don't I already have my assignment, sir?"

"You do, but we all have multiple assignments. The Council generally only meets some ten glasses a week, usually from ninth glass until second or third glass of the afternoon. In the later afternoon, not all of you are required. Everyone has some additional assignments, and at times when the Council goes out of session early, Baratyn will decide who will remain at the Chateau and who will be released to work on the assignments I've given." He handed me several sheets of paper.

I glanced at them, then looked again. The first was the civic patroller report on the death of Master Caliostrus, and it contained the names and addresses of all of Caliostrus's relatives in L'Excelsis. The second was a sheet listing information on Johanyr, and the third dealt with Diazt.

"Someone was hired to kill you. Your assignment is to see if you can discover who hired that assassin. Once you have evidence of that, you will report to me before acting against that person. If you encounter other assassins, you can dispose of them, provided you do so either quietly or in a well-witnessed instance of self-defense. The most likely suspects are relatives of the late Master Caliostrus, but Diazt also had friends from the hellhole who engage in such matters as removing enemies. I would suggest not visiting there, because there would either be a great number of dead taudismen or we'd have to find and train another imager to replace you."

I hadn't thought of visiting the hellhole, or any of the taudis. "Does this mean I'm no longer restricted to Imagisle?"

"As of tomorrow, you're not. You certainly have the skills to defend yourself, but what you still lack is an awareness of everything around you. That is something you will need to practice all the time until it becomes as natural to you as breathing, until you know all that may impact you without ever having to think about it. Only time and practice will grant you that." He smiled sadly. "Please be cautious. As I told you months ago, there are no bold old imagers."

Now that I was finally free to leave . . . none of the people I really wanted to see, except Khethila, were presently in L'Excelsis, and it didn't make sense to see her until the weekend, because there really wasn't enough time to take a hack out and back during the week.

"And one other thing—on Samedi morning, at the eighth glass, Maitre Poincaryt will be at your new studio so that you can start his portrait." Master Dichartyn smiled. "This is an example of being careful in what you ask for, Rhennthyl. If you get it, you have to deal with the consequences."

That meant more work to squeeze in somewhere, because the studio wasn't set up for me to actually start painting. Still . . . I did look forward to it. "It will be a good portrait, sir, but it may take a little longer with the press of carrying out other assignments."

"Master Poincaryt understands that all too well." Master Dichartyn stood. "Go get some sleep. You'll need it."

"Yes, sir." I nodded. Would I find sleep that easily after all that had happened, and the additional assignment that I'd just been given?

51

When you seek, do not seek only that which
you can accept or believe.

By the time I walked across the quadrangle to dinner on
Vendrei evening, I was tired, but not overly so. I was just glad
the majority of my intensive training had come to an end. I'd
received a brief letter from Mother on Mardi, and another
one from Seliora just that afternoon. Mother informed me
that the three of them would be arriving back in L'Excelsis
on Lundi, the second of Agostos, and hoped that I could
come on the following Samedi for dinner—a small family
birthday dinner, since I had made it more than apparent that
her choices of female companions did not appeal to me.

Seliora's letter was cheerful. She hoped I was well and
apologized that dinner would have to be on the fourteenth
because her mother had already planned a birthday celebration for Aunt Aegina on the seventh. She also wrote that they
all felt that I'd probably be tied up with my family on the
seventh. Was that a good judgment . . . or Pharsi foresight?
Either way, it worked out better for everyone, and I wrote her
back immediately, saying that I understood, but hoping that I
could at least call on her on Solayi afternoon—the eighth.

Although Master Dichartyn hadn't said anything since
he'd given me the information sheets dealing with the background on my shooting, I knew I had to start working on that
assignment as well, but I had to start on Master Poincaryt's
portrait first. That was why, on Samedi morning, I was up
before breakfast and over at my "studio," making arrangements and checking the light. After hurrying over to the din-

ing hall and eating, I returned to the studio and set up the easel and the chair.

As the first of the eight bells struck, Master Poincaryt stepped through the open door of the small converted workshop. He wore exactly the same gray garb as I did, with the addition of a small silver four-pointed star circled in silver and worn high on the left breast of his waistcoat. The silver circle only touched the star at the points, and the spaces between it and the star were open, showing the gray wool of the waistcoat. His eyes took in everything in a single sweep and came to rest on me. Despite the lines carved into his face, his hair was jet black, as were the heavy eyebrows. The squarish shape of his face was offset by a chin that was almost elfin and a glint in his eyes as he moved toward me. "Rhennthyl."

"Master Poincaryt."

"You know that you're the first imager that's been a painter? That seems strange to me, because imaging is a visual skill, as is painting."

"I wouldn't be surprised, sir, if there were painters with small imaging abilities who have kept those abilities to themselves."

He offered a lopsided smile. "Between us, neither would I. Didn't you, for a time?"

"Yes, sir." I decided against explaining that it was because I'd thought my abilities so modest. I gestured toward the chair. "If you wouldn't mind sitting there, sir?" I smiled. "You won't be portrayed as sitting in anything quite that severe."

"I'd appreciate it if you didn't show me in one of those upholstered thrones." He settled into the chair, then looked at me. "It feels strange to be sitting here."

"Sir . . . I would think that you deserve a portrait."

"I don't, but the head of the Collegium does." He smiled. "That's what Dichartyn claims. He says that having portraits of the heads of the Collegium will reinforce tradition."

That gave me an idea. "Sir, is there anything that might suggest the Collegium?"

"Only the star, and that doesn't really suggest the Collegium by itself."

The four-pointed star of Solidar was symbolic, with the points representing the High Holders, the factors, the artisans, and the Collegium. I'd work out something. I always did.

The first thing I did was sketch Master Poincaryt's face. Rather, I did a series of quick rough sketches in pencil until I had the sense of what would be both accurate and flattering.

Those took almost the entire glass, and there wasn't much point in asking him to stay longer, because I'd need to think about the entire portrait and set up the design before his presence would be necessary again. "That's all I'll need from you now, sir."

"Could I look at the sketches, Rhennthyl, so I won't be too shocked?" His voice was gently humorous.

"Certainly, sir. I would ask that you remember that these are very preliminary. They're as much to enable me to set up a design that's appropriate." I brought over the sketches and began to go through them. "Your profile from the left . . . the right . . . full face here . . ."

After he'd looked at the them all, he stood. "The Collegium is fortunate to have you." He smiled. "If we are to have portraits, they should be accurate. My family may not agree, however." He paused. "Next Samedi at this time?"

"Yes, sir, if that is convenient."

After he left, I put away the sketches and the pencils, closed the workroom, and walked back to my quarters. Then I headed out on what would probably be a long Samedi, walking across the quadrangle and then toward the Bridge of Hopes.

I'd thought at first that the easiest part of looking into who had targeted me would be talking to those I knew in the guild, but after the reception I'd gotten from Rogaris and Sagaryn, I didn't want to start with them. But where could I start? I racked my brain before I remembered the old man who had liked my study—the former portraiture master. I finally recalled his name—or names—and what Master Estafen had said. Everyone called him Grisarius, but he was really Emanus and he had some rooms off the Boulevard D'Imagers.

Surely, it wouldn't be that hard to find him. People did notice odd characters, and Grisarius was anything but usual in appearance. I also could talk to Madame D'Caliostrus or Shienna.

As I crossed East River Road, at just after half past nine, I was glad there was a faint haze and a slight breeze. Even so, the day would be hot, and then some, by midafternoon. I wasn't quite certain whether to walk up the Boulevard D'Imagers or take a hack to see Madame Caliostrus. I noticed a man talking to the flower seller, the same weathered woman who seemed to be there most every Samedi I'd crossed the bridge. I didn't look in their direction, except for that first glance, but I did listen.

". . . don't some of the imagers buy your blooms?"

"Not many. Most of those who cross here are young, and they don't have that many coins. They don't understand the power of flowers."

"Here comes one," said the man in a low voice.

"Young sir . . . what about a bouquet or a flower? Just a few coppers . . . just a few . . ."

I couldn't help thinking that I'd be perverse and buy some. I certainly had enough coppers for a few flowers, and it might be fun to take some to Khethila. Even if she wasn't home, Nellica would be, and could arrange them—and they'd be a pleasant surprise. I stopped and stepped into the shade of the green and yellow, but slightly faded, umbrella that covered the flower seller's small cart. "I just might. How much for the tulips—the red and yellow ones?"

"Three coppers a bunch, sir. Just three."

"I'll take them."

As I handed her the coins, she didn't conceal the surprise on her face—not so much that I had bought them, I thought, but that I hadn't haggled over the price.

The man who had been talking to her eased away, but not before I caught a better glimpse. He wore a wash-blue workingman's shirt and yellow-tan leather vest. His features were regular, and his brown hair was well trimmed. His beard was also neatly trimmed, but his eyebrows were bushy. The only distinguishing feature was the fact that the bottom of one ear was slightly shorter than the other, as if the lobe of his left had been removed.

"Thank you." I inclined my head slightly to her.

Buying the flowers made a decision for me. I'd need to take them to Khethila first. So I hailed a hack. "West lane off of the circle at Plaza D'Este."

The hacker, one of the few women drivers I'd seen, looked at the tulips, but said nothing beyond, "Plaza D'Este, west lane it is."

When I finally reached my parents and knocked on the door, Nellica opened it. "Oh . . . Master Rhenn . . . there's no one here but Mistress Khethila, and she wasn't expecting anyone."

I eased my way in, closing the door behind me so that the heat of the day didn't flood into the foyer. "Just tell her that I'm here. I can't stay long, but I wanted to see her."

Before Nellica could even turn, I heard Khethila.

"Nellica? Is someone here?" She caught sight of me and rushed past Nellica. "Rhenn! How are you? How badly were you hurt? Did someone stab you or something?"

I extended the small bouquet. "I brought these for you."

"For me? You shouldn't have."

"You're the one who's working while everyone else is holi-daying in Kherseilles."

Khethila took the tulips, then immediately handed them to Nellica. "If you'd arrange them . . . in the middle pale green vase?"

"Yes, mistress." Nellica smiled and headed for the kitchen.

"Tell me what happened." Khethila motioned toward the parlor. "It's cooler inside, right now." She was wearing a se-vere straight dark blue dress with long sleeves.

"I see you're dressed for bookkeeping."

"I just got home." She dropped into Father's armchair. "Tell me what happened."

"Actually, I got shot. I'm fine now. The masters didn't want me leaving Imagisle until I was completely well. This is the first weekend I've been off the isle in almost two months."

"Mother thinks you're mad at us, at her, really, because you didn't like that Zerlenya bitch."

I couldn't help laughing. She laughed, too.

"I didn't know she was a bitch," I finally said. "I just wasn't interested. After I got shot, well, I wasn't in shape to go anywhere for quite a while."

"She is. At the grammaire, she was the High Holder of all holders, but she'd play sweet for any boy she was interested in, and when any parents or adults were around. None of us could understand why the boys didn't see through her."

"She's attractive enough," I said.

"The sweetest-scented roses have the sharpest thorns."

Since Khethila and I agreed about Zerlenya, and there was little more to be said there, I asked, "How are you liking keeping the ledgers?"

"It's much better than dealing with the people who want to buy the wool. They all want it for less than it cost and can't understand why it costs what it does. The figures in the ledger, if they're entered properly, remain the figures in the ledger. I like making sure everything balances." For an instant, her expression changed.

"You're far better at that than I'd be, or than Rousel will ever be."

This time she frowned, if briefly.

"Is Rousel having trouble with his bookkeeping?" That was a guess, but not a wild one.

"I think so." She shook her head. "I hated telling Father, but some of the accounts didn't work out. They couldn't. That's one reason why he went with Mother. He hadn't planned to."

"It's also why he could leave. He knows you'll keep the accounts here straight."

"Old Chelink did fine, but when he died . . ."

"He died? When did that happen?"

"In late Maris . . ."

We talked for a glass or so before I stood and excused myself, telling her that I had some imager tasks to do. I managed to catch a hack two blocks short of the Plaza D'Este and had him drop me off at the corner of North Middle and Bakers' Lane, about two blocks from Master Caliostrus's place. There were some people along the lane, about what I'd have expected on a summer afternoon. Several looked at me, then looked away. Most didn't pay much attention.

Even before I reached the gate to the place where I'd spent nearly ten years, I could hear the clink of stonework and chisels, and the murmurs of workmen.

"Mortar! Up on the top course . . ."

The gate had been removed. Inside the walls, a larger version of Master Caliostrus's dwelling had mostly risen on the foundations of the old, and this one was entirely of stone. The shed against the rear wall had been demolished, and there was no sign of the garden.

I eased toward the gray-bearded man in charge of the masons. "Pardon me."

He turned, his mouth open, as if to upbraid me—until he took in the gray. "Imager . . . what can I do for you?"

"I was looking for Madame D'Caliostrus . . ." I offered. "I knew her husband had died."

"You won't find her here. She sold the place to Master Elphens . . ."

Elphens had made master? Even as a representational artist? I wanted to shudder and scream at the same time. My study had been far superior to his mist-covered gardens with all the wrong lighting, and he was now a master—and I hadn't been able to get a journeyman's position. And where had he gotten the coin to purchase the place, let alone rebuild such a dwelling?

". . . Even with all the damage, I hear, she didn't do badly. Plot this large is hard to come by here in the Martradon district."

"Do you know where she went?"

"Word is that she went back to where her parents came from." He frowned. "Little place near Rivages, don't recall the name. She got some money from an annuity or something from a patron of Caliostrus. She said there was no reason to stay here and plenty to leave."

"You wouldn't know anyone who might be able to tell me where she is now?"

"Might be someone at the Portraiture Guild. I don't know anyone."

"I see. Thank you." I nodded and departed.

Because it was more than a little warm, I used more of my coin to take another hack, this one down to the Guild Square. From there I could walk down the Boulevard D'Imagers and make my inquiries. I had the hacker drop me on the east side of the square. As always in late summer, the sidewalks were less crowded than earlier or later in the year, partly because of the heat, and partly because those who could left L'Excelsis in the hottest weeks of the year.

After less than twenty yards, my forehead and shirt were damp, and I had the feeling that someone was looking at me. I turned as if to study the display items in the silversmith's window, so that I could look at those around me, but I couldn't see anyone clearly looking at me, or anyone that I knew. That didn't mean someone wasn't looking at me, only that I wasn't skilled enough to pick them out.

I continued on, walking slowly toward Lapinina, coming abreast of the coppersmith's, except that his shutters were closed. He was on holiday. As I passed the bistro, I glanced in through an open window. There were people at only two tables, and I didn't know any of them. The cooper's place was open, but there was no one in I could see there.

I crossed Sudroad and walked back toward the boulevard, slowly, looking down the two lanes I passed to see if there were any hidden boardinghouses or the like. I kept getting the feeling that someone was staring at me, but whenever I glanced around, I couldn't detect who it might be—or whether it was just my imagination.

There was another bistro a block west of the square on the Boulevard D'Imagers. I knew some of the older artists went there, although I never had. The name on the signboard was

Axotol. I had no idea what that meant, but I stepped in under the light green awning toward a serving girl.

She looked at me, her eyes wide. I could almost feel the fear. It had to be the imager uniform, because I'd never seen her before. "Yes . . . ah . . . sir?"

"I'm looking for an artist, white-haired, with a goatee. He's usually called Grisarius."

The girl just stared at me blankly, as if frozen.

An older woman hurried over. "Might I help you, sir?"

"An artist named Grisarius, or Emanus . . . white-haired with a goatee. I'm looking for him. He hasn't done anything wrong, but he might know something."

"He's sometimes here. Not now. You might try Reynardyl, three blocks toward the river."

"Do you know where he lives? It's supposedly close by."

"I couldn't say. He doesn't talk much."

"Thank you." I offered a smile.

As I stepped back out into the heat, I could hear the older woman talking to the younger.

". . . won't do anything to you here. Best to answer their questions and get them out. They stay, and people won't come in. That'll get Rastafyr in a black mood faster 'n any imager . . ."

Reynardyl was a long and hot three-block walk from Axotol, and I almost missed it, because it really wasn't on the boulevard but down an unmarked lane off the main walk, with a signboard so faded that I couldn't read it until I was almost under it. Although the place was twice the size of Lapinina, there was no one inside except a gray-haired server.

"Anywhere you want." Her smile was tired.

"I'm looking for someone, an older artist named Grisarius. He has a white goatee—"

"He hasn't been in today . . . probably won't be. It's the end of the month."

"Do you have any idea where he might be?"

"You might find him in the public garden, you know, the one south of the Guild Square . . . lot of older types there."

I had my doubts, but it was worth a try. "Thank you." I paused. "If I don't, I understand he has rooms near here. Do you know where they might be?"

She shook her head.

I waited a moment, still looking at her.

"Well . . . sir, I can't say as I know, but he did mention going to Mama Lazara's once."

"Is that a boardinghouse?"

"Yes, sir."

"Do you know where it is?"

"Not the street, but it's somewhere south of Marchand not too far west of Sudroad. That's what Makos told me."

"Thank you." I gave her a pair of coppers and headed out the door. Since I knew where the public garden was, and I didn't know exactly where Mama Lazara's boardinghouse was, I headed back up the boulevard toward the square.

It was too short a distance to take a hack, and there were few around, and too long for the walk to be comfortable under the now-sweltering afternoon sun. I wished I'd stopped for something to drink, but I marched onward. When I reached the public gardens, I strolled along every pathway, checking all the benches. There were perhaps fifty people there, and outside of two women with infants talking to each other, I don't think that anyone else in the gardens was under thirty, and not a one bore the slightest resemblance to Grisarius. As I reached the north gates, where I had begun, I again had the feeling of being watched.

Since Grisarius wasn't in the public garden, and since I felt the observer was on the boulevard somewhere, I turned and walked back through the gardens to the south gate. From there, I walked three blocks south to Marchand, crossed it, and came to the next street, much narrower and meaner. The faded letters on the corner wall read LEZENBLY. There was no boardinghouse or pension anywhere among the older and moderately well-kept stone dwellings situated on the two blocks that led north to Sudroad. So I retraced my steps and headed back southward on Lezenbly. At the end of the first block on Lezenbly south of where I'd started, I saw a white-haired figure sitting on a shaded side porch. So I opened the gate and walked around to the side.

"Grisarius? Or should I call you Emanus?"

The older man jerked in the chair. I hadn't realized that he hadn't been reading, but dozing, still holding the book. He just watched as I took the stone steps and then pulled up a straight-backed chair across from him. My feet ached, and I was more than a little hot.

The old man squinted at me. "Imager. Ought to know you, shouldn't I?"

"Rhennthyl. I was a journeyman for Caliostrus before I became an imager. I did a study in the journeyman competition in Ianus that you liked. A chessboard."

He frowned, then nodded slowly. "You're the one."

That suggested something. "Has someone been asking about me?"

"Not as such. Staela—the bitch at Lapinina—she was saying that some imager had stopped by a month or so ago, said he'd been an artist, but he scared off a bunch of people."

"That was me."

Grisarius nodded again.

"I went to see Madame D'Caliostrus. She'd sold the place and left. There was something about an annuity. The mason working on the walls said Elphens had bought it."

"Ah, yes . . . young Elphens . . ."

"How could he afford to purchase it? How did he make master so quickly?"

A crooked smile appeared above the wispy goatee. "Might have to do with his father."

"Who is his father?"

"A High Holder from Tilbora . . . Tillak or some such."

"A son on the back side of the blanket?"

"Something like that."

I shook my head. That figured. "That must have brought the guild a few golds."

"The masters who voted on him, anyway." Emanus snorted.

"I never knew Caliostrus had a patron who would have purchased an annuity on his life."

"He probably didn't. That's always what they say when someone makes a settlement."

"But who . . . why?"

"Rumor was that the fire wasn't natural-like." The old artisan shrugged. "It could be anyone. For any reason. That son of his was trouble all the way round. Could be that the fire was meant for Ostrius, and the settlement was because Caliostrus got caught accidentally. Or it could be that it was just easier to send the widow packing so that questions didn't get asked. You're young, for an imager. You'll see."

"You've seen a great deal, haven't you?" I hoped he'd say more.

"There's much to be seen, if you only look. Most people don't see things that are right before them because it goes against what they believe or what they want to believe."

"You know that I could never find a master to take me on as a journeyman."

"That doesn't surprise me." Emanus offered a twisted smile. "I don't think it happened that way, but it wouldn't have surprised me if someone went after Caliostrus because you'd have made master if he'd lived, and half the portraiture masters in L'Excelsis don't have your talent."

"Were you forced out of the guild?"

"Let's just say that it was better that I let it happen. Didn't have much choice, but I got to watch the mess Estafen and Reayalt made when they took over."

"You were the guildmaster?"

He nodded. "I prided myself on being fair. Most people don't like that, and when they found out a few things . . . Like I said, it was better that I let them trump up a scandal than what might have happened." There was a wry smile. "What might have happened remains my business, and I can at least take consolation that I wasn't the cause of anyone getting hurt."

"Except yourself, sir."

"That's a choice we sometimes have to make." He shook his head. "That was a long time ago, and there's nothing that anyone can do now."

It might have been my thinking about Johanyr and the tactics he'd used, but I couldn't help asking, "Was it someone in your family you had to protect?"

"Why would you ask that, young Rhennthyl?"

"I watched a High Holder's son do something like that not too long ago."

"What did you do?"

"Blinded him enough so that he'll never image again."

"And you're still alive?"

"So far. I've been shot once."

Emanus looked at me, then leaned back in the chair. "Why did you seek me?"

"I thought you might be able to tell me if someone was hiring bravos to go after me, or if I needed to look elsewhere."

"You seem to think I know more than I do."

"You've seen a great deal, and far more than I have."

"You flatter me with my own words." Emanus laughed. "Estafen, Reayalt, and Jacquerl wouldn't go after you, not once you became an imager. Caliostrus's and Ostrius's deaths benefited them, and they'd not wish to have any cloud drawn to them."

I frowned, but waited.

"Caliostrus had a brother. Thelal. He was a tilesetter, journeyman. Liked the plonk too much. Caliostrus gave him silvers. Madame Caliostrus didn't like it. If I had to wager, I'd say Thelal was involved. Either him or that High Holder." He frowned. "High Holder's not likely. Most High Holders would make you suffer for years."

"Do you know where I might find Thelal?"

"From what I've heard, I doubt Thelal knows where he'll find himself tonight."

After that, while Emanus was pleasant enough, I didn't learn much more, and I began to have the feeling that someone was watching us. So, finally, I stood. "Thank you. I appreciate your talking to me."

"Best of fortune." His face quirked into a strange smile. "You might remember that truth has little to do with the acts and decisions of most folks."

Rather than leave by the front gate, I went down the porch steps and then hurried to the alleyway behind the pension, making my way eastward. I was back on Marchand, almost to Sudroad, when I caught sight of a man almost a block behind me. I couldn't make him out clearly, because he was on the shadowed side of the street. I turned northward on Sudroad toward the Guild Square, and kept checking. He was still following, holding to the shadows, but I could make out that he wore a light-colored vest. I stopped to look at a crystal decanter in the glassblower's window. He halted to talk to a man selling kerchiefs and straw hats.

There had to be some way to separate him from the Samedi crowds around the Guild Square. I passed one alleyway, but it was a dead end. The second one ran clear through, if at an angle, to Carolis, and the entire alleyway was cloaked in shadow. I ducked into the alleyway, then hurried down the north side. I didn't hide behind the first pile of broken crates, because that was obvious, but instead slipped into a niche where the rear walls of two buildings joined. Once there, I created a brownish shadow shield that matched the painted plaster walls.

Then I waited in the shadows behind the shield that I had imaged, as the man peered this way and that. I also raised shields against a bullet or a blade, but since the bravo—or possible assassin—hadn't done anything but follow me, I really couldn't do much more. Not yet. He kept moving and peering, but before long walked past me. As he passed, I got a good look at him. He was the same man in the yellowish tan vest and wash-blue shirt who had been talking to the flower seller, making small talk while he'd been waiting for me to leave Imagisle. He finally vanished into the orangish late-afternoon sunlight at the end of the alley.

Recalling the conversation that had drawn me to the flower seller, I did not follow him, but retraced my steps, still holding shields. I decided against staying or eating in L'Excelsis since I had no idea who had been following me, or why, and not when I really didn't know what to do next. I wanted to talk to Master Reayalt and Master Estafen, but not until I talked to Master Dichartyn.

On the way back to Imagisle, I looked for the flower seller, thinking she might be able to tell me more about the man who had been tracking me, but the cart, the green and yellow umbrella, and the flower seller had all left. By the time I reached my quarters, I was tired, and my feet were sore . . . and I wasn't sure that I knew that much more than when I'd left that morning.

52

What is seen can tell one what is not.

Predictably, on Samedi night, I had a nightmare about someone I couldn't see clearly following me everywhere. After breakfast the next morning, I crossed the Bridge of Hopes, looking for the flower seller with the yellow and green cart and umbrella. I covered a fair area, both on the Boulevard D'Imagers and along the East River Road, but I saw no sign of her, or of any other flower seller. I even tried later, in mid-afternoon, with no better luck. Apparently, flower sellers didn't find much trade on Solayi. I also didn't see the man with the yellow vest, but in the afternoon I did see a number of families picnicking in the gardens off the boulevard.

Especially after what Emanus had revealed, I didn't want to approach anyone else in the Portraiture Guild, not until I'd talked to Master Dichartyn, but he wasn't around on Solayi, and I wasn't about to track him to his dwelling.

On Lundi, I got up earlier because the duty coach to the

Council Chateau left at a fifth past seventh glass. I climbed out of bed, washed, dressed, and managed to gulp down breakfast and stop by Master Dichartyn's study. He wasn't there. Even so, I was the first one to the duty coach, but Baratyn was but a few steps behind me, and then Dartazn and Martyl followed.

Once we were all in the coach, I asked, "What will happen today with the Council?"

"Almost nothing," replied Martyl.

"That doesn't mean we won't be busy," added Dartazn. "All sorts show up insisting that they need to see one of the councilors, and some of them do."

"Others are junior guild members or merchants who claim that they have the right to visit their representatives."

"It's a long day because they want to see those people before anything happens?" I asked.

I knew that they had the right to request a meeting, that the regular messengers conveyed those requests to the councilor, and that, if the councilor agreed to see them, one of the three of us had to escort them and listen to the whole conversation, at least until we were dismissed by the councilor. But we still had to wait outside in the corridor to escort them out.

"That's right," said Baratyn. "That way, the councilors can claim they listened before they did what they were going to do anyway."

Once the coach pulled up outside the Chateau, Baratyn led the way through the side gate and up the narrow steps. Harvest season it might well be, but early as it was, the morning air was as hot and close and damp as on any summer morning. I blotted my forehead with the back of my hand once I stepped into the comparative cool of the stone structure.

"Martyl . . . go get the visitors' request sheet. Dartazn, if you'd get the night guards' reports." Baratyn turned to me. "Rhenn, for the moment, just wait in the messengers' study."

"Yes, sir." The messengers' study was a spare room with two benches and two writing desks and chairs adjoining Baratyn's study. I hadn't spent a half glass there in the past three weeks.

"Don't worry. You'll be more than a little busy. There's already a queue outside, all with passes or claims." With a nod he hurried off.

Martyl grinned at me, and Dartazn raised his eyebrows before they both left.

I walked to the messengers' study. Boulyan and Celista—she was the only female regular messenger—were already there, sitting on one of the benches.

". . . can't believe the crowd out there, and only six of the councilors are even here yet. Councilor Etyenn probably won't show until Meredi . . ."

"Or Jeudi. That's when the first full Council meeting is."

Both looked up at me. Then Boulyan spoke. "Palyar says the petitioners out there are already complaining. We've carried requests to everyone who's here."

"They're mostly traders, I'd wager, worried about what all the tariffs and embargoes and blockades are doing to their business." From what I'd seen at home and from what I'd heard and learned at the Collegium and the Chateau, that was as good a guess as any. "And they're from nearby." That wasn't a guess. Most traders wouldn't take a long ironway journey on the chance of seeing a councilor, and those that could would already have arranged appointments.

Celista grinned. "You have that right. The next two days are when they listen to all the complaints so that they can tell their guilds or the factors' associations that they've heard from scores of good honest citizens. Councilor Haestyr is the worst. He's a High Holder, but he likes to think he's a friend to merchants and crafters, and he sees scores of them."

"All of whom want to fill their strongboxes without a care about their competitors, or how many sailors will die in keeping trade open."

"Very true." Baratyn's voice came from the open door. "But we all play our part in the process." He looked to me, extending a pasteboard square. "You get the second lot. They want to see Reyner. Martyl is already escorting some factors to see Councilor Glendyl."

Glendyl was the factorius on the Executive Council, and

his business produced most of the steam engines for the iron-way and the Navy.

I took the pasteboard and looked at the neat script—Tuolon D'Spice and Karmeryn D'Essence. Under them was the name and seal of Councilor Reyner.

"When you've finished, return here immediately," Baratyn said. "You'll likely be running all day. There's a long line out there."

"Yes, sir."

I headed out along the east corridor and through the grand foyer, out the main entrance past the guards stationed there, down the two sets of steps, and then along the main side stone walkway. The mixed mutterings of the petitioners carried over the wall, suggesting a long queue. When I reached the visitors' gatehouse, through the grillwork of the heavy iron gate I could see a line stretching a good hundred yards. I concealed the frown I felt beneath a pleasant smile. With only three of us acting as escorts, even if each meeting took less than a quarter glass, we'd only be able to escort half—or less—of those waiting. Given the deliberation I'd seen from Master Baratyn and his experience, he had to have known that.

While I could see two guards stationed outside the gates, there were three just inside, and another four in the shaded alcove behind the gatehouse. Basyl was leaving with a white pasteboard in hand, presumably another request to meet with a councilor. He nodded.

Once he passed me, I stepped forward and handed the pasteboard with the two names and Councilor Reyner's name and seal on it to the receiving guard.

He took it, studied it, and turned toward the gate, calling out, "Tuolon D'Spice and Karmeryn D'Essence, to see Councilor Reyner."

Two men stepped up to the gate. The taller and black-bearded one brandished a letter or sheet of something. "Here we are. It's about time."

The guards opened the gate and let them step through, as each wrote his name on the entry ledger. I studied the pair, watching the ledger as well. The taller one signed as Tuolon D'Spice, the shorter and younger as Karmeryn D'Essence.

"The messenger will escort you there and back." The guard's voice was even and firm, but carried a note of boredom, as if he'd made the same statement time after time.

"This way, honored traders," I offered, gesturing to the side walkway.

"About time," muttered Tuolon.

Because I had to lead them, I carried back trigger shields, ones that would spring full if either moved too close to me. Baratyn had assured me that there was minimal danger to me on the walk to the councilor's study, because all unescorted strangers were suspect and detained. Once we were inside the Chateau and out of the already uncomfortably warm sunlight, I led them through the foyer and up the grand staircase past the two winged angelias of Pierryl the Younger. I still thought their proportions were ridiculous, especially after several months of anatomy studies. When we reached the top of the staircase, I paused to check over the two traders.

The younger one had come up the steps quietly, and that bothered me. So did the fact that neither was breathing any faster. I edged to one side, and gestured. "To the right, traders."

"Go on!" snapped Tuolon. "We're not here to admire empty stone walls."

I raised full shields before I led them down the east corridor to the fourth doorway, where I stopped and stepped aside. I rapped on Councilor Reyner's study door. "Messenger Rhennthyl announcing Tuolon D'Spice and Trader Karmeryn D'Essence to see Councilor Reyner."

"You may escort them in, messenger."

"You can go now, fellow," said the heavyset and dark-bearded factor.

"I'm to stay with you until you leave." I smiled politely.

"My golds pay for whatever you make, fellow, and I say that—"

At that moment, I turned slightly and did my best to image-project absolute strength.

The other trader's elbow went into the bigger man's ribs,

and he said quietly. "They're guards, Tuolon. To protect the councilors."

"My business is with the councilor, not for everyone to hear."

"That is for the councilor to decide, honored trader," I replied.

Because I didn't like Tuolon, I was prepared with two possible imagings as I opened the study door. As taught, I stepped half inside, but to one side, my eyes on the two traders.

"I'd appreciate it if you would remain, messenger." Reyner's light brown hair was shot with gray, and he wore the pale blue stole-vest of a councilor over a thin but fine cotton short jacket. His eyes never looked in my direction, but at the tall spice trader.

Tuolon bowed, and his hands went to his waist.

I imaged an invisible shield between the two and the councilor. Even angled as it was, a lesson from Maitre Dyana, I was jerked off balance by the impact of the bullet on the shield.

The smaller man had not even looked at Reyner but was lunging at me with a knife. I wasn't quite fast enough, and the blade hit my shields. That stopped him short, and the hesitation was enough for me to image caustic into his eyes and the lower part of his heart. He doubled over in agony.

Tuolon had turned the pistol in my direction, but I imaged iron into the barrel, and my shields channeled the metal of the explosion across his chest. He toppled forward.

"Guards to Councilor Reyner's chamber! Guards!"

I didn't move toward the taller figure or the shorter one, who was still writhing on the floor, but just held my shields to separate them from me and the councilor.

Reyner took out a cloth and blotted his forehead. He inclined his head. "Thank you."

The shorter figure stopped twitching, but he was still breathing.

"The taller one looks like Tuolon. He even acted as obnoxious as Tuolon did."

Two huge black-clad obdurate guards burst through the door, followed by Baratyn. He glanced at the councilor, then at me, then at the pair on the floor. "Take them below."

In instants, both figures were trussed and carted away.

The councilor blotted his forehead again. "I'd heard . . . but never . . ." He shook his head.

"By your leave, Councilor."

"You have my leave."

Baratyn said nothing until we were out in the hall. "You sensed something, didn't you?"

"Yes, sir . . . but they didn't do anything until the door was open."

He nodded. "Professionals. We'll be seeing more of them." He studied me. "What you did takes strength, and I'd wager you didn't eat enough breakfast. Go down to the kitchen and get something to eat. Otherwise you'll be shaking all over in a glass."

I didn't argue. I already felt unsteady.

"When you feel stronger, come find me."

"Yes, sir." I headed down to the kitchen, by the northeast circular staircase.

As I entered, one of the servers looked at me. "Sir . . . you can sit over there. I'll get something for you right away."

I could hear her as she said to another server. "Must be trouble upstairs . . . come down here that pale . . . has to be the new security . . ."

". . . times when the Council comes back, something happens . . . don't say anything . . ."

In moments, there was a platter before me, with a slice of beef, an end cut already cooked enough to eat, with bread and cheese, and a mug of ale. "Sorry there's not more hot, sir."

"I understand, and I thank you."

After she left, I began to eat, and within a few mouthfuls the shakiness vanished. Even so, I ate everything on the platter and finished the ale. By then, I felt normal, and I made my way back up the stairs to the main level. I knocked on Baratyn's door, but he didn't reply. So I went to the messengers' study. It was empty, and I was glad for that, since I didn't want to explain what had happened.

Basyl was the first to return, and he sat down on the other bench and nodded. "Busy out there . . . and hot."

I nodded back. "Warmer than I'd like, especially outside."

I couldn't have been sitting there more than a tenth of a glass when Baratyn peered in. "Rhenn . . . good." He gestured.

I followed him to his study, where he closed the door and turned to me. "Don't worry about it. There's an attempt like that about every other time the Council returns from recess."

"I don't know that I handled it that well. I thought I was ready."

"You were ready enough. You kept the councilor from being hurt, and no one knows what really happened. If anyone asks, the story is simple. You knocked one assassin into the other and when he fired, his gray pistol exploded."

That was true enough, so far as it went. "What about the one who was alive?"

"He's still alive, but he was just a hired blade. He's already admitted that he'd been paid to kill the assassin if it looked like they'd be captured. His fee went to his wife. He claims she's crippled, and he won't say where he's from. So far." Baratyn studied me. "You ready?"

"Yes, sir."

He handed me a pasteboard. I took it. The name on it was Khatyn, Master D'Artisan, and the name and seal beneath were those of Councilor Sebatyon, a lumber factor from Mantes.

I walked back out to the gatehouse, at a deliberate pace, but not rushing.

Master Khatyn was a gray-haired man who only came to my shoulder, but he was wiry and moved with a spring in his step. Before all that long I was standing at the second door on the upper level in the west corridor announcing Master Khatyn. Despite my feelings that Khatyn was not a danger, I was more than ready as I opened the door and escorted him in.

"Honored councilor." Khatyn inclined his head, although his eyes flicked toward me.

"The messenger stays. I prefer not to hear anything that cannot be said before him," added Sebatyon. "What is your concern?"

"My family has made fine furniture for generations, but those who wish the finest also wish the finest in woods, and many of those woods do not grow in Solidar."

"That's true," replied the councilor.

"Honored councilor, there is an embargo against any woods from Caenen." Khatyn shrugged helplessly, as if his point were more than clear.

"This is also true. We prefer not to reward Caenen when the Caenenans fire upon our ships. They've sunk two merchanters."

"Honored councilor, the wood itself costs but a fraction of what we make, and even of the taxes we pay. I would not wish our merchanters to be endangered, but what harm is there if I buy wood from an Abiertan trader, or from a Solidaran who bought it elsewhere? The timber is there. It is already cut. It will be sold somewhere. No additional golds go to Caena."

"Can you not make fine furniture with other woods?"

"I can make fine furniture out of many woods, honored councilor, but without the finest of woods, I cannot expect it to sell, no matter how good the crafting."

"You are asking me to seek an exception to the embargo?"

"Only for the rare fine woods, sir. Without those, much of our work will not sell, and we will not be able to purchase the fine woods from here in Solidar that go with imported woods."

"You are telling me that there is no way . . ."

Khatyn shook his head. "There are smugglers, but the tariff agents of Solidar know that any rosewood or ebony comes from Caenen, and those fines and the years in prison would destroy me."

"I understand your concerns, Master Khatyn, but if I support an exemption for you, how could I not support one for the spice merchants, or the essence traders, or satinrope makers? Before long, there would be no embargo, and Caenen would suffer nothing."

"Honored councilor," replied Khatyn, "they suffer little or nothing now. Those goods are still sold, and we must make do with less. We are the ones who suffer."

"I can only promise that I will make sure your points about the suffering of the crafters of Solidar do come before the Council. That is all that I can offer now."

"That is all that I will ask, then." Khatyn's smile was ironic. "I thank you for hearing me out, honored councilor."

After I escorted Khatyn back to the main gate, I took an essence importer to Reyner. The councilor did not even acknowledge me, except by title. The second visit was far more like that of Khatyn to Sebatyon, with a written petition, this time against the embargo of tropical oils.

That was how the remainder of the day proceeded, escorting master crafters, traders, and factors to various councilors. Along the way, I got a quick lunch, and during a brief respite in midafternoon, Celista told me that a petitioner headed to see Councilor Glendyl had slipped outside the councilor's study and cracked his skull on the stones. I wished I'd been that quick-thinking, and wondered whether Dartazn or Martyl had managed that.

When fourth glass rang, the Chateau was closed to petitioners and all outsiders, but it was a good half glass later before they had all been escorted from the Chateau, and close to fifth glass before Martyl, Dartazn, and I took the unmarked duty coach back to Imagisle.

"A little more action today," said Martyl, "at least for you two."

"Complaining or relieved?" asked Dartazn.

"Relieved. There's always the chance that matters won't go as they should."

They certainly hadn't with me, but I just nodded. "This will go on until Jeudi?"

"Tomorrow will be about the same," replied Dartazn, "but Meredi will be slower."

"That's if it's like the last few years," added Martyl.

As soon as I got back to the Collegium, late that afternoon, I hurried to Master Dichartyn's study and rapped on the door. There was no response. While that didn't surprise me, I did want to talk to him. So I headed back to the reception foyer.

A young imager was at the desk, and he looked up as I neared. "Sir?"

"Are you Beleart?"

"Yes, sir."

"I'm Rhennthyl, and I was looking for Master Dichartyn. I needed to convey some information to him."

"Yes, sir. He didn't say when he'd be back."

"If you'd tell him. I'll keep trying."

"Yes, sir."

I'd barely walked into my chambers and seated myself at the writing desk when there was a rap on the door. I decided on full shields before I opened it. A very frightened, very young fellow in imager gray looked up at me. "Sir . . . if you'd not . . . mind . . . Master Dichartyn is in his study and will be for a short time . . ."

"I'll be right there."

The young prime trailed me all the way back, then slipped away when Master Dichartyn opened his study door.

"Come in, Rhenn."

Stacks of papers filled Master Dichartyn's desktop. I couldn't help looking. I'd never seen more than a paper or two.

"Yes?" His voice was curt, as he settled back behind the desk. He nodded toward the door. "You had something urgent?"

I leaned back and closed the door.

"Puzzling, sir, and you've always stressed caution. I was working on my other assignment over the weekend, sir . . ." I explained what I'd done and what I'd discovered, and described the man who trailed me. ". . . and you'd said that I should eliminate suspects as I could. I'd thought if I could meet this Thelal . . ."

"I'm glad you talked to me. We do have an arrangement

with the patrollers for certain kinds of information. They may be able to locate Thelal more quickly than you can, especially if he indeed does have a weakness for the plonk. I'll have them see what they can tell us." He paused, and jotted down a few words on a sheet of paper. "Tell me what you've learned by trying to track down who shot you."

What had I learned? "It's not easy, and it takes time. And one thing leads to another."

"Why do you think you've been assigned to look into your own shooting?"

"Because I'll have a greater interest in it?"

"Partly. Also because if you don't, that indicates a certain weakness in dealing with the unpleasant. When it's your life that's involved, you're more likely to learn as much as you can. If you don't, then you're not meant to be a master. Even if you are, you don't know enough yet. That's not your fault. No one of your age does."

After the experience at the Council Chateau, I was beginning to feel that I didn't know enough about anything.

Then he nodded. "You weren't with the morning exercise group, Clovyl told me."

I swallowed. I'd totally forgotten about that addition to my schedule.

"Don't forget it tomorrow." Master Dichartyn smiled faintly. "It's more for your protection than anyone else's. Much more."

"Yes, sir."

"One more thing, Rhennthyl. You know that the world doesn't stop when you leave the Council Chateau? There are still people in L'Excelsis, if you need to talk to them." He held up a hand. "Not until I get word from the civic patrollers. I just don't want you to get into the habit of thinking that Samedi is the only time you have to deal with other assignments."

"Yes, sir."

How long would it be before I fully understood what I needed to know, what was necessary, and how to do it?

53

Beware men in power who praise principles; they're either without them or lacking in perception.

Mardi and Meredi were much the same as Lundi . . . with the exception of getting up each morning a glass and a half earlier to join Martyl, Dartazn, Baratyn, and four other imagers I'd never seen before—as well as Master Dichartyn—for a vigorous two-thirds of a glass worth of exercises and sparring led by Clovyl. He followed that by sending us on a three-mille run. I didn't finish last in the run, but I wasn't anywhere close to being first. Dartazn left us all well behind.

Jeudi started the same way, but once I got to the Chateau, there was a considerable difference. For one thing, there were only a handful of petitioners waiting, and all of them actually had letters from councilors granting them appointments at specific times. They all were also far better dressed and groomed, which confirmed more than a few of my suspicions.

I'd no sooner arrived than Baratyn handed me a pasteboard. "Factor Alhazyr has an appointment at eighth glass with Councilor Caartyl."

I nodded and headed for the visitors' gatehouse. I had to wonder what a factor wanted in dealing with the representative of the masonry guilds, but it could have been that Caartyl was the only one of the executive councilors who would grant Alhazyr an appointment.

Alhazyr was waiting, smiling pleasantly. He stepped forward and through the gate when his name was called. He wore a thin silvery vest—open and without buttons—over a pale green linen shirt and carried a thin leather folder, tucked under his left arm.

"This way, sir," I offered.

He nodded in reply and followed me. We had climbed the outer steps and were crossing the grand foyer before he said another word. "You're new." His statement was not a question.

"Yes, sir."

"There's not much change in the staff, I understand."

"No, sir." I kept a quick pace, but managed to lead the factor by so little that we were close to abreast. Shields or no shields, the more I could see, the better I felt.

"That can be very good, or very bad."

Since he hadn't asked anything close to resembling a question, and we weren't supposed to volunteer information, I just said, "Yes, sir." Then I gestured for him to walk between the guards—and the angelicas—at the foot of the grand staircase.

He laughed softly.

As one of the three executive councilors, Councilor Caartyl had his study in the northwest corner. When we reached the door, I rapped and announced Factor Alhazyr.

"Escort him in, messenger."

I opened the door, watching Alhazyr the entire time. He held an amused smile on his face, as if to indicate he knew I was more than a mere messenger. Once Alhazyr was inside, I closed the door and took a position beside it, ready to depart if the councilor wanted that. I hadn't brought any petitioners to see Caartyl before, and while I knew his face, I hadn't been all that close to him. I was surprised to see that he had stood when the door opened and that he was a good ten years younger than my father and wiry, with jet-black hair and a hawk nose. He gave me a quick glance before his eyes settled on Alhazyr.

"Honored councilor." The factor inclined his head respectfully, but kept his hands in plain view, the left one still holding the thin leather folder. "I have brought the proposal I had mentioned earlier. I trust it will satisfy the concerns which you raised." He stepped forward and carefully laid the leather folder on the edge of the desk, then stepped back.

Caartyl smiled faintly. "They were not my concerns, Factor Alhazyr, but ones raised on behalf of those whom I represent."

"That speaks well of you. Not all in power would put the concerns of others above their own."

"Most in power in Solidar must do so if they wish to retain power."

"That is true, but it does not make your position less admirable," replied Alhazyr.

"Nor yours, when most factors think only of this year's golds." Caartyl paused, then asked, "How do most factors feel about the embargo on Caenenan goods?"

"Those who are affected complain. Few believe it is a good idea or effective. It only raises the costs of goods in Solidar without hurting Caenen."

"And makes the Abiertan merchants wealthy?"

"That, too."

Caartyl nodded at the folder he had not touched. "I will study that."

"That is all we could ask." Alhazyr bowed again. "By your leave, honored councilor."

Alhazyr said nothing the entire trip back to the gatehouse. There, he turned to me. "Thank you." Then he left.

I handed the pasteboard back to the receiving guard and hurried back to the messengers' study. I had barely seated myself on one of the benches when Baratyn peered in.

"Rhenn . . . has Factor Alhazyr departed?"

"Yes, sir." Baratyn hadn't asked that all week. Who was Alhazyr? What had been in the leather folder? It could have contained anything from letters of credit to who knew what.

"Good. You take the post in the east corridor off the councilors' lounge. That way, all of them will get familiar with your face. Martyl is already at the post in the west corridor. When the councilors break for midday meal, so do you two, but afterward, switch places. Remember, if a councilor offers you a message, you say you'll take care of it, but you can't be out of sight of your post. If it's farther than that, use the speaking tube to summon me or one of the regular messengers. Most of the councilors won't ask you because they know that, but sometimes they're in a hurry, and they know we'll get the message or package delivered. You only take messages from the councilors themselves. Their aides have to bring letters or packages to the clerk next to the messengers' study."

I'd barely reached the corridor doorway to the councilors' lounge and turned so that I could watch the corridor in both directions when Councilor Reyner hurried up past and entered the lounge. He didn't even look at me.

A short time after that, one of the councilors' aides appeared—they all wore pale blue waistcoats with a silver triangle embroidered over the left breast. He hurried into the lounge, and perhaps a half glass later left carrying a short stack of papers. Two other aides came and went in the same period. Then Dartazn escorted a factor past me to Councilor Haestyr's study.

For the rest of the morning, that was the pattern—an occasional councilor coming or going, and aides carrying papers and folders in and out, and a scattered petitioner or two. I didn't see Caartyl, but since his study was on the other side of the Chateau, he doubtless entered the chamber by the west entrance.

During the lunch break, Martyl and I gulped down a rice and lamb dish, and some lager, and then hurried back up to the Council level, where I moved to the west corridor. During the rest of the afternoon, I saw a few more councilors and a few less aides. About a fifth of a glass before four, the Council adjourned for the day, and the councilors returned to their studies or left the Chateau. For the next glass we stood by to escort any visitors. There were only two, and Dartazn took both. Then each of us accompanied a pair of obdurate guards as they inspected and closed down all the public rooms and the outside gardens of the Chateau. After that, Martyl, Dartazn, and I caught the duty coach back to the Collegium.

Once we were headed back, I asked, "Do you know what the Council was doing today?"

"No," replied Dartazn. "We seldom know until later, not unless something special is scheduled, and we have extra duties."

"The head clerk's office prints a digest at the end of each week. It lists any laws or rules that affect Solidar or other lands. There will be copies in the messengers' study on Lundi. Copies go to the newssheets, too," added Martyl.

"Most of it's pretty dull, and even the exciting stuff sounds dull the way they report it," said Dartazn.

When we stepped out of the coach at the Collegium, another prime was waiting. "Tertius Rhennthyl?" His voice quavered slightly.

"Yes?"

"Master Dichartyn would like to see you immediately, before you go to dinner."

"Lucky you," murmured Dartazn. But he did grin.

I walked quickly across the quadrangle, ignoring the looks from several primes and seconds, and made my way to Master Dichartyn's study. The door was closed, but when I knocked, he opened it immediately and ushered me in.

I did sit down. I'd been on my feet most of the day.

Master Dichartyn did not. He stood by the open window in the light breeze that didn't seem to cool the late-afternoon air at all. "Rhennthyl, we have several matters to discuss. First, how often did the councilors have you leave when you escorted a petitioner to their study?"

I had to think for a moment. "There's only been one time so far."

"What does that tell you?" His words were slightly sardonic.

"Their minds are already made up, and any considerations they might entertain have already been determined or will be somewhere besides the Chateau."

"Did any petitioner state anything you thought would have been of value to Solidar?"

"One furniture maker pointed out that the embargo on rare timbers from Caenen did not make much sense because the value of the logs was low and the value added in furniture-making here in Solidar was much higher."

"That's probably true, but embargoes are not just about value. They're also tools to allow our ships to board or even attack suspect merchanters . . . among other things. Were there any conversations that puzzled you?"

"There was one today. A factor named Alhazyr visited Caartyl and left a proposal. Both talked in generalities. . . ." I went on to explain, ending with, ". . . suddenly, they talked about the worthlessness of the trade embargo against Caenen, and then Caartyl dismissed Alhazyr."

"Hmmm . . . I would have thought he'd have gone to see Haestyr. We'll have to keep watch on that. I'll have to talk to Baratyn about it."

"About what, if I might ask, sir?"

"When politicians and factors congratulate each other on their principles, almost anything but principles are involved. Just keep your eyes open, and you'll see in time."

That didn't answer my question, but that was Master Dichartyn's way of indicating that he wouldn't.

"More interestingly, your inquiries last Samedi stirred up something."

"Sir?"

"The civic patrollers located Thelal. There was a brawl at Antipodes on Lundi night. Someone knifed him. He was dead when the patrollers got there. Even more intriguing is the fact that Emanus died in his sleep the same night of the day you visited him."

"That couldn't be natural."

"It could be," replied Master Dichartyn, "but it's rather unlikely."

"Could it have been another imager from somewhere else?"

"It's very possible. If so, he must be very accomplished, and in the pay of, and probably attached to, some foreign embassy."

I didn't follow that logic at first, until I thought about it.

"What will you be doing on Samedi?" asked the head of security.

"I was going to have dinner with my family—a belated birthday dinner."

"What time were you planning on leaving?"

"Not until about fourth glass."

Master Dichartyn nodded. "I'd like you to depart earlier, say about third glass. You'll walk across the Bridge of Hopes and up the Boulevard D'Imagers on the south side. You will be holding full shields. Someone will be following whoever's following you."

"What if someone isn't?"

"Count yourself fortunate, but there will be. There couldn't be two deaths and someone following you last week without someone being there this week."

While I had my own ideas about what was happening, I wanted to see what Master Dichartyn might say. "Do you have any idea why all this is happening?"

"I have several. It could be that someone happened upon something and wants to link Caliostrus's death to the Collegium. Or it could be that you were simply one of the imagers targeted by whoever is trying to kill imagers, and it's a matter of pride. . . ." He shrugged.

"What about High Holder Ryel?"

"We can't rule him out, but High Holders are usually more subtle and more vicious."

I could hardly wait. People had tried to kill me already, and others were following me, and the only man I'd talked to who'd given me any useful information was dead—and the High Holder wasn't even involved yet?

"I assume you don't want me to talk to anyone else until after Samedi."

"That would be best." He gestured toward the door. "You need to change before dinner."

As I hurried back to my quarters to change into imager grays, questions swarmed through my mind, and at the moment, I had answers for none of them.

54

Violence is everywhere, but most will see only that which they must.

Vendrei was slower than Jeudi, with only a handful of visitors and petitioners for the councilors. Whoever was not on corridor patrol handled those few. Even so, I found time dragged when the corridors were empty more often than not. We were all pleased when we returned to the Collegium late on Vendrei afternoon.

The brightest spot of the day was a short note from Seliora that was waiting in my letter box when I checked just before dinner. She apologized for being so late in replying, but explained that her grandmama had insisted they leave Pointe Neimon early in order to stop by another textile manufactory, this one in Kephria, and Seliora had found no place to post a letter until she had returned to L'Excelsis. She also wrote that she looked forward to seeing me on Solayi and that she hoped I could come at the first glass of the afternoon.

I couldn't help smiling at that.

When I finally climbed into my bed on Vendrei night, I was still smiling, thinking of Solayi. That was before I realized I still had to get up early the next morning for Clovyl's exercise session, and then be at my studio to work on Master Poincaryt's portrait.

I did manage to make it to the exercise area on Samedi morning—and not be the last. Dartazn was. One good thing was that it was far cooler that early. I tried not to think about what that might mean in winter. Of course, Dartazn outran us all again.

After showering and dressing in my grays, I had breakfast

and hurried out to the workroom studio, where I set up the canvas and materials. Then I began to sketch designs. I should have done that earlier, but there never seemed to be enough time. The second one seemed to fit, with the chair angled slightly, and Master Poincaryt looking not quite forward. I'd decided to make the background indistinct, both for practical and symbolic reasons. Just before the bells began to ring, he walked into the studio and sat down. I could see immediately I'd need to shift the angles, and I changed the faint outlines on the canvas.

For almost a quarter glass, neither of us spoke, as I worked on the general shape of his face, concentrating on the broad cheekbones and wide forehead.

"Rhennthyl, what do you think of the Chateau? Is it close to what you had expected?"

"It is, and it isn't, sir. I was taught so much . . ." How could I say what I meant without seeming stupid? I didn't want to seem ungrateful, but I didn't want to lie, either.

"But what you've been taught almost seems meaningless or irrelevant? Is that it?"

How could I answer that? Finally, I shrugged. "I know it's not, but sometimes . . ."

"Watching corridors and escorting petitioners seems most uneventful, even boring."

"At times, sir," I admitted.

"That suggests that you are not observant enough, and that you are letting your mind lie fallow. Because you are an artist, I imagine that you could draw a fair likeness of the other imagers with whom you work, could you not?"

"Yes, sir." My words were cautious.

"Could you describe exactly how each of them walks, or carries their hands, or what gestures are so habitual to them that they do not even notice themselves making such gestures? Or how they wear their garments, as much as what they wear? Or, more important, how they use words and arguments and even body postures to inform or dominate others?"

"No, sir."

"You should practice that skill with every person you meet, until it becomes second nature. If you do so, you will find that there are times when it has saved your life. If you do not, your life may well be that much shorter."

I couldn't help frowning.

"Rhennthyl . . . think of it this way. What distinguishes those who are successful from those who are not is what they know and how they apply that knowledge. Because the world is governed by men, should you not endeavor to learn as much as possible about men? If you study men with the same diligence as you have studied art and the texts with which Master Dichartyn has plied you and examined you, you will gain great knowledge about how best to apply all you know." He smiled. "That is my homily for the day, but I would ask you to consider it."

Master Poincaryt was true to his word and did not offer a single other piece of advice, only thanking me for my diligence just before he departed and confirmed that he would be present the following Samedi at the same time.

As I cleaned up the studio, I realized something about Master Poincaryt and his advice. He'd only given me one suggestion. Because he had offered nothing else, I was likely to remember that suggestion far more than if it had been buried among a wealth of ideas. What he said certainly made sense, and I could certainly practice during the slow times at the Chateau.

After cleaning up the studio, I wandered back to my quarters before making my way to the dining hall for lunch. Once there, I spied Reynol.

"Could I join you?"

He looked to both sides—where both chairs were empty—then raised his eyebrows dramatically and grinned.

"I think you made your point." I settled into the chair on his left. "Have you seen Menyard lately?"

"He's out visiting some cousin today. That's because he's interested in her best friend. Whatever happened to the lady who saved your life?"

"She's been away and just got back. I'll see her tomorrow."

"It must be nice to leave L'Excelsis in the summer."

"It was a mixed blessing. She was accompanying her grandmother and her brother."

"That could be a very mixed blessing." Reynol passed a platter of cool fowl slices, and then one of rice fries.

I poured some of the red wine. "Would you like some?"

"Please."

"What do you think about what might happen in Caenen?" I asked.

"Haven't you seen the newssheets?"

"Not today."

"The High Priest was leading some ritual meeting. He declared that we were whatever the Caenenan equivalent of the Namer was, when he dropped dead. Apparently, his heart stopped."

"Oh . . . I see." I had a good idea how that happened. "What's likely to happen next?"

"We or Tiempre will be blamed." Reynol shrugged, then added, "One would hope his successor would see the error of his predecessor's ways. Sometimes they do, sometimes not."

"Has anyone heard from Kahlasa or Claustyn?"

"We would have heard if something went wrong, unless it happened in the last few days."

"Oh?"

"Their names would go up on the plaques of those lost in the line of duty. Those are the tablets on the wall to the right of the main entrance."

I'd seen the plaques, and the names, but I had thought of them more as memorials to much older imagers. Until that moment, it hadn't really struck me that the names of those I knew near my own age might appear on them. After a moment, I asked, "What about Jariola?"

Reynol laughed. "The death of the High Priest of Caenen won't matter to the Oligarch. He's the kind that thinks nothing could possibly happen to him. Besides, it won't. When their entire government is composed of a small number of people who think exactly the same way with the same interests and prejudices, what difference does it make to Solidar who's nominally in charge? The Oligarch dies, and the next one acts just the same."

Again, I hadn't thought of it in quite that way.

In the end, we came to no real conclusions about what might happen. Afterward, I picked up copies of both newssheets and sat on a shaded bench in the quadrangle and read them. I didn't learn much. After that, I watched the younger imagers walking back and forth and tried to practice what Master Poincaryt had suggested. It was far harder than it had sounded.

At slightly before third glass, I crossed the Bridge of Hopes under a sky that held a high silvery haze that might have kept the day cooler, except that there was no breeze at all, and the air was still and sodden. Following Master Dichartyn's instructions, I was holding full shields and hoping that I could do so for as long as necessary. Despite the warmth of the afternoon, the streets were crowded, and so were the sidewalks. I had to wait several moments before I could cross East River Road, weaving my way through carriages and wagons, and the occasional rider.

The flower lady with the green and yellow umbrella was on the south side of the Boulevard D'Imagers, if a half block farther east, near the east entrance to the boulevard gardens. I saw no sign of the man who had been in the yellow vest— but there were scores of people moving along the broad walk bordering the gardens.

"Fresh flowers . . . the best for you, sir." She turned toward me.

"How much are the daisies there?"

"For you, sir, a mere three coppers."

I didn't feel like haggling, but I did want to know a few things, and I tried to concentrate on observing the flower seller. "Last week you were talking to a man in a pale blue shirt and a yellow vest . . ."

"I talk to those who buy or those who might. That'd be scores every day." She smiled, but her eyes remained tense and worried, and her shoulders stiffened. "Last week? I'd find it hard to remember who I saw this morning."

I handed over the three coppers. "I just wondered because he's a bravo. He could even be an assassin."

There was the faintest twitch at my words.

"I see you do know him."

"No, sir. Not by name. Everyone knows him as the Ferran. He talks just like you and me. He's been on the streets here longer 'n me, and that's longer 'n I'd like to count."

"After all those years, no one knows more than that?"

She shook her head. "Even the streetwalkers avoid him. They say one of 'em learned something about him, and she washed up against the barge piers downriver two days later."

"Then I won't press you." I took the daisies. "A good day to you."

As I turned away from her, stepping out from under the umbrella and into the direct sunlight, the faint crack and the sharp impact against my shields were nearly instantaneous. I was pushed around, back toward the cart. A second crack followed.

The flower seller sprawled beside her cart, the dark redness of blood welling across the thin blouse. She shuddered several times, and was still. I managed to turn, but I saw absolutely nothing out of the ordinary—except a handful of people staring in my direction.

Then, from behind the wall, Master Dichartyn and a civic patroller appeared and hurried toward me.

"Are you all right, Rhennthyl?"

"I'm fine." I glanced down at the dead flower seller, then back at Master Dichartyn and the patroller. He was older, graying, and that definitely bothered me. "Did you see him? Whoever shot her?"

Master Dichartyn shook his head. "He shot from the garden on the other side. He waited for an opening in the traffic."

"You were talking to her. Did she tell you anything?" That was the patroller.

Before I said a word, I looked to Master Dichartyn. He nodded.

"Not much. I asked about the man in the yellow vest. She

only knew his street name, and she didn't want to know more. People who discovered anything about him ended up dead. They called him the Ferran. She didn't know why because he talked like everyone else."

The patroller looked to Master Dichartyn. "Your man here has enemies with expensive tastes and wallets to match." He glanced around the stone of the wide sidewalk, as if searching for something, then hurried westward where he picked up something. I had the feeling it was the bullet that had hit my shields.

"You're going to get a great deal of experience with shields, Rhennthyl." Master Dichartyn kept his voice low.

What he didn't say was that, if I didn't whenever I left Imagisle, I'd soon be dead. "Do you think this was . . . linked to Johanyr?" My voice was equally low.

"No. This is something else. I don't know what."

From his lack of expression, I could tell he didn't like not knowing.

The senior patroller returned. He looked at me, then at Dichartyn before holding up the bullet. The end was squashed at an angle.

I didn't say anything. Neither did Master Dichartyn.

"Nasty business," the patroller finally said, adding conversationally, "I don't think anyone in headquarters would look into matters much if this Ferran were found dead."

"Possibly not," replied Master Dichartyn, "but if he died now, whoever hired him would just hire someone else."

As we stood there, a Collegium duty coach pulled up. Master Dichartyn gestured. "It's to take you to your parents' house. There's nothing more you can do here."

I didn't argue.

In the coach on the way to my parents', I thought about what had just happened. Why was Master Dichartyn so convinced that the Ferran had not been hired by High Holder Ryel? Based on what I'd learned from Maitre Dyana, the likely answer was that the High Holder regarded mere murder as too kind, but there had to be other reasons. I just didn't know what they were.

When the driver took the South Middle Road, rather than staying on the Midroad, I started to worry, until he took Sangloire, and then the back lanes, ways to the house that I'd only seen Charlsyn use. That familiarity raised other questions, but there was no one to ask. The driver did wait after he pulled up outside the house, watching as I walked up onto the portico.

Khethila opened the door before I even knocked. She rushed out and threw her arms around me. "Rhenn!"

At that moment, I realized I'd left the flowers behind, but I managed to grin as I disentangled myself. "I did see you last Samedi, you know?"

"It's been a long week, a very long week. Come in!"

I glanced back and saw the coach pulling away.

Khethila followed my glance. "That's no hack."

"No. I was fortunate to get a ride in a Collegium coach."

"I think I've seen one like that before," mused Khethila, "but I don't remember where."

"That's possible." I closed the door behind us and managed not to sigh as I released full shields, leaving only the anti-imager trigger shields in place.

"The rear courtyard porch is cooler, and Father and Culthyn are already out there."

Since it was sheltered and walled, that was fine with me, and I followed her through the house. Father was sitting in the most shaded corner, looking over what appeared to be a ledger.

Culthyn was sitting at the small table with a deck of plaques, playing at solitaire. He looked up after a moment.

"How did you like Kherseilles?" I asked Culthyn, taking the other corner chair.

"It was like any other place." His tone conveyed boredom.

"Did you do anything interesting?"

"Not much."

I paused as Nellica appeared and placed a cool glass of some sort of white wine on the side table beside my chair.

Father cleared his throat, loudly enough to catch Culthyn's attention.

"Well, Rousel did arrange for me to do sailing a couple of times. It was cooler on the water, and once we saw a sea sprite."

"They don't usually get close to people."

"We were pretty far away."

"Not many people see them," added Khethila. "You were fortunate."

"Fortunate indeed," snorted Father. "You threaten them, and they're worse than a necrimager."

"There haven't been any necrimagers since the bad old times," Culthyn asserted.

"Not any *known* ones," I said.

Khethila glanced at me, surprised. "You aren't saying there are some at the Collegium?"

"Of course not." Not that I knew, anyway. "What I meant was that just because someone hasn't seen something doesn't mean it doesn't exist, especially when you're talking about something like imaging life force into a dead or dying person. You can't do that, anyway, but I suppose other things . . . are possible." I realized that I'd almost revealed something I shouldn't have, and I kept talking to change the subject. "People see things that they don't understand, and they claim it's caused by something, usually what they want to believe. There are cases where people have fallen into such a deep trance everyone thought they were dead. Then they wake up. I suspect all the old legends about necrimaging are based on misunderstandings like that."

Khethila raised her eyebrows, but did not question me.

"You make it sound so dull." Culthyn gathered together the deck of plaques laid out on the table and shuffled them, then began to deal them out into the six piles for solitaire once more.

"Most things are," Father offered dryly, "until you understand them even more fully." He closed the ledger with a thump. "To an observant man, the figures in any business ledger can tell an interesting story."

I wouldn't have gone that far, but he did have a point. I also had a glimmer of an idea why Khethila had said it had been a long week. Like Father, she could read behind the figures, but unlike Father, she had no real authority in the factorage.

Mother appeared at the porch door. "Dinner is ready."

"I'm famished!" Leaving the plaques half dealt on the table, Culthyn bounded up and into the house, past Mother, who had stepped back as if to avoid a charging goat.

"Famished?" I looked to Khethila.

"He heard about what you said to Rousel years ago when he said he was starved."

"Famished is just as bad." But I couldn't stop smiling as we rose and followed, far more sedately.

Once in the dining room, we waited for Father, who finally entered and placed his hands on the back of his armed chair. He looked to me, standing to the right. "Since it is in celebration of your birthday, belated as it may be, you should offer the blessing."

I nodded. "For the grace and warmth from above, for the bounty of the earth below. . . ."

"In peace and harmony," came the reply.

"You still offer the artists' blessing?" asked Culthyn. "You're not an artist anymore."

"Actually, I'm still painting. Besides, there isn't an imagers' blessing." I poured Father's wine, then Mother's, then my own, before sitting and then handing the carafe to Khethila.

"You can't paint, can you?" Culthyn looked surprised.

"I can paint. I just can't get paid for it. I'm actually doing a portrait of one of the senior imagers. That's when I have time."

Kiesela carried in a platter with three fowl upon it. Each was halved, and the scent of orange and spices filled the air.

"Naranje duck," Mother announced. "Rhenn's favorite, with cumin-cream rice."

I smiled.

"Worth a small fortune now, cumin is," Father announced.

"Why?" asked Culthyn.

"It comes from Caenen, mostly," Father explained as he served half a duck to Mother and then to himself. "They still smuggle it in, but it costs more, and all the spice merchants raise the price even when they have large stocks."

"Couldn't you get it from Remaya's father?"

Mother glared at Culthyn. "One does not take advantage of relatives, nor ask for special favors that will cost them. It's unfair to impose. Besides, it's ill-mannered."

Culthyn squirmed in his chair.

I took a bite of the duck. It was excellent, the orange and the bitters and the apple reduction all turning the meat succulent. The crispy skin was good, too.

"This would be perfect," Mother offered, "if Rousel and Remaya were here, and . . ." She deliberately left her sentence unfinished.

"But I don't," I said, managing a smile, "and I won't for a while, it's likely." I wasn't about to mention Seliora, not yet, although I suspected it wouldn't be long.

"He's still young yet, Maelyna."

"Not for that long." She glanced toward Khethila, but said nothing.

Khethila flushed.

"So . . . what did the Council do this week?" asked Father.

I couldn't help laughing.

"It's that amusing?"

"No, sir. It's just that my duties keep me from knowing, in most cases, what the Council is doing. What I find amusing is that I spend most of the day within twenty yards of the Council chamber, and I don't know much more than when I spent the entire day at the Collegium." I'd also laughed at Father's valiant, but transparent, effort to get the subject away from whom Khethila and I might marry and when. But I did appreciate the attempt.

"Just what is it that you do, dear?" asked Mother quickly. "I don't believe you've ever said or written anything about it."

"We escort petitioners to see councilors. We help make sure people don't intrude upon the councilors. Sometimes we carry messages from the councilors to other councilors or to their aides, and we do other things that I can't mention."

"Are those scary and dangerous?" asked Culthyn.

I laughed. "Usually they're boring. Once or twice they could have been dangerous."

"Do you see factors petitioning the councilors?" asked Father. "Anyone I might know?"

"It's possible. I don't know everyone you know. Councilor Etyenn is a cloth factor. I didn't encounter him, but some of the regular messengers were jesting about the fact that he spends as little time as possible in L'Excelsis."

"That doesn't surprise me," Father replied. "He has the largest cloth warehouses in Solidar. It's a wonder that he has any time to devote to the Council."

"Do you know him?"

"We've met a few times, and we've provided some special wools to him on a few occasions. He was never early with payment, but never late, either."

"What is he like personally?"

"He seemed pleasant enough, if a bit preoccupied. Who else have you seen?"

"More than a few spice and essence factors and traders, and a factor named Alhazyr . . ."

"Oh, him. He's the one who wants to change the Council and put more traders on it—and even two public councilors. Next, he'll be advocating women councilors." Father snorted.

"That might not be a bad idea," suggested Khethila. "They couldn't manage things any worse."

"Solidar hasn't done badly under the Council," Father replied. "Would you want to live in Jariola or Caenen? Women are serfs in one and slaves in the other."

"Father . . ." Khethila paused, then spoke slowly and deliberately. "I agree with you that Solidar is a far better place to live than almost anywhere else. It was a better place to live than Caenen was even when we were ruled by a rex, but it's better now with a Council, and a more widely representative Council would be even better than that."

"More widely representative? I suppose you'd want that Madame D'Shendael making laws, then?" Father's tone was more than merely ironic.

"Why not? She's intelligent and a High Holder. She has been known to think, unlike most of them. But then, I suppose that's a flaw for a woman. Not thinking, but letting it be known that we can think, like that poor Madame D'Saillyt. Her High Holder husband beat her and confined her for contradicting him in public, and did who knows what else to her, but when she shot the beast, she was condemned and executed."

"Likely story," Father snorted. "You don't think she couldn't have gone to the patrol?"

"No," she couldn't," I interjected. "Not if it happened on his lands. The High Holders retain the right of absolute low justice on their own lands. He could beat her and confine her on the grounds that she assaulted him. She could only have avoided that if she had managed to flee his lands, and that might have been difficult if he kept confining her. Even so, she'd probably have lost everything, because he could cite her for desertion."

"No honorable man would do that," Father huffed.

"Chenkyr, dear," Mother said sweetly, "few men are as honorable as you are."

I managed to keep from breaking out in laughter at the way Mother had cornered Father.

In that moment, she stood. "Who would like the fresh peach cobbler and who would like the almond cake?"

"I'd like the cobbler, but with a small slice of the cake." I offered the words with a grin.

"I will follow Rhenn's example, with a slight modification, dear," said Father. "I would prefer a small slice of each."

"Me, too," said Culthyn, "except could mine be bigger?"

Khethila shook her head. "Just a small slice of the cake."

After that, I listened, saying as little as possible as Mother rhapsodized about their visit with Remaya and Rousel and how beautiful young Rheityr was and already how bright he seemed.

A little after eighth glass, I excused myself.

Mother had arranged for Charlsyn to take me back to the Bridge of Hopes. I did take the precaution of raising full shields on the walk from the coach to the quadrangle. As I walked, I couldn't help but think about Madame D'Saillyt. Had she been the one I'd executed? Or had the woman who had died at my imaging been another woman condemned for something similar? The second possibility, I realized, was worse than the first.

55

Love never presents a true image.

After breakfast on Solayi, I did take some time to write a thank-you note to my parents for the dinner and their thoughtfulness. It was long, at least for me, and I tried to make it warm. I set it on the writing table so that I'd remember to post it on Lundi. Then I took my time in getting ready to call on Seliora.

It was still before one when the hack pulled up outside the private entrance to the NordEste Design building. I didn't want to stand in the hot sunlight holding full shields, waiting until one, although I was wearing the lighter-weight summer imager's waistcoat and a thin gray cotton shirt. So I stepped up to the door and lifted and dropped that ancient and well-polished bronze knocker, shaped much like a stylized upholsterer's hammer, I realized for the first time.

Young Bhenyt opened the door. "Master Rhennthyl, sir. Please come in."

"Bhenyt . . . did Seliora send you down to act as greeter? Or your sister?" I was curious and couldn't help wondering.

He grinned at me. "Odelia ordered me to, but Seliora paid me." Then, abruptly, he gulped. "I wasn't supposed to tell anyone."

"I won't let anyone know." I concealed my own swallow, wondering if he were slightly mal. "Lead on." I stepped inside and let him close the door, then followed him up the stairs to the second level.

Fortunately, Seliora stood alone in the upstairs entry foyer, wearing flowing black trousers and a cream blouse with a short but filmy red vest. Her entire face lit up as she saw me. Mine probably did as well. I took her hands, and then found my arms going around her.

Hers were around me, but only for a moment, as she whispered in my ear, half laughingly, "These walls have both eyes and ears."

I did let go of her, if after a brief kiss. She was still smiling. "I have so much to tell you, but it's warm here, and . . ." Her eyes flicked to one side, then the other.

"I see." I didn't see anyone peering into the foyer, but that didn't mean anything.

"There's a bit of a breeze on the third-level east terrace . . . and it's more private. Everyone else is on the north terrace." She smiled. "I will have to take you there before we slip away."

I sighed, more for effect than because I had expected anything different.

"It won't be that bad. Everyone will be glad to see you." She led me to the side of the foyer and through the archway that led to a narrow staircase.

From the landing at the top of the stairs, we emerged from another archway into a narrower hall or foyer.

"Everyone's sleeping and personal chambers are up here," Seliora explained as she turned and led me though an open set of double doors onto the terrace, a tile-floored and covered expanse that ran the entire width of the building, close to twenty-five yards, and extended northward from the doors a good ten yards. Heavy iron grillwork, waist-high, enclosed the terrace, whose roof was supported by square masonry pillars. Exposed as it was to the air on three sides, the terrace was far cooler than the interior foyer or the streets below.

At a glance, I could see the extended family had gathered

in groups—Seliora's parents and aunt around a table near the iron railing on the east; the young adults in wooden chairs around a table holding arrangements of plaques that suggested a game of Regian in progress, and the younger children listening to a story being told by a graying woman too old to be an aunt or cousin, and too young to be Seliora's grandmother. "I don't see your grandmama."

Seliora frowned. "She was here. She might be taking a nap. She did want to meet you." She shook her head. "Grandmama always does things her way." There was a mixture of ruefulness and respect in her tone, as she gently guided me to the table where her parents sat.

"Madame," I began, inclining my head to her mother.

"Betara, please. You make me feel like my mother."

I offered a smile. "My own mother would give me a very long lecture on being too informal and not showing respect if she ever found out that I used your given name."

Betara smiled in return. "Then we will make certain she never finds out."

"She is quite capable of that," Shelim added, with a fond look at his wife.

"I understand all the women in this family are most formidable."

Both Betara and Aegina laughed. Shelim offered a wry grin, but his eyes crinkled in amusement.

"I understand you are learning your way around the Council Chateau," offered Shelim.

"Around is a very good description. There's a great deal to learn."

Betara had been studying me. Then she nodded. She wasn't agreeing with her husband, and I would have liked to know exactly what I'd somehow confirmed for her.

"His eyes are older," she said abruptly, looking to Aegina.

"He has seen what most never will."

I hadn't thought of it quite that way, but it was true. Not many men of any age have looked into the barrel of a gun that will almost kill them, and that was only part of what had happened since they had last seen me.

"You understand, I see," observed Betara.

I inclined my head. "I suspect so, madame." I could not make the statement without the honor of the formality.

A faint smile crossed her lips, but not an unpleasant one. I thought there might have been a hint of sadness behind it.

"We'll be on the east terrace," Seliora said.

"I'll bring you something to drink in a while." Betara looked to me, the somberness gone as if it had never been. "What would you like? We have some cool Sanietra, most wines, or Alusan gold lager, or some naranje juice."

"The Sanietra sounds very good."

"I'd like that, too," said Seliora, "but I could get it . . ."

"Nonsense. You young people have a summer to catch up on."

"You're most kind." I understood the unstated but informal chaperoning involved. "Thank you."

Seliora turned, and I moved with her.

As we passed the game table, Odelia looked up from the plaques of the game and grinned. "Enjoy yourselves."

"Concentrate on the game," returned Seliora, "or Shomyr will take every coin you have."

Once we left the north terrace, Seliora took my arm, much more possessively, and guided me along the wide hallway until we came to a doorway that looked like all the others. She pressed the door lever, pushed the door back, then used a brass catch to hold it open. A very short hall—less than four yards—ended in another door, which she also opened. The east terrace was much smaller, no more than five yards by four, almost as if it had once been a room and someone had replaced the outer wall with the iron railing and grill-work.

Seliora bent and moved a stone pony to prop the door between the short hallway and the terrace open, then stepped to one side of the door. "It gets too hot and still here if we don't leave the door open." I could see that, because there was no other way for the air to flow.

Then, she was in my arms, and there was no hesitation with the embrace and the kiss.

After a long time, she looked up at me. "I missed you. I worried."

I kissed her again, gently. "I missed you . . . and I'm here."

After a time longer than I had hoped and shorter than I wished, she eased out of my arms, and we settled in on each side of the circular table on the right side of the terrace, since the terrace had no settees that might accommodate two. Looking eastward, I could see the incline, filled with buildings and houses, that formed the southwest part of Martradon. I thought I could pick out where Master Caliostrus's studio had been.

"You've had a long summer, haven't you, Rhenn?"

"So have you," I replied lightly. "How was Pointe Neimon?"

"Quiet . . . pleasant in a dull way. It was much cooler than here. One whole week it rained almost all day every day. We played plaques until I didn't want to look at another plaque again."

"What about all the textile manufactories?"

Seliora tilted her head slightly. "Grandmama was right. We did need to visit them." She laughed, softly, throatily. "At every one, she entered dressed like the wealthiest of factorians."

"Isn't she?" I accompanied the gentle question with a smile.

Seliora paused. "We don't think of it quite that way because we've avoided the factoring associations. We've kept ourselves as part of the woodcrafters' and cabinetmakers' guild."

"This building, with all the shops and quarters and everything—it's larger than most factors' warehouses." Also, remaining as crafters avoided the prejudice against Pharsis who tried to join the factoring associations.

"It's all family. Almost, anyway."

"That may be true, but the number of people who work here, from what I can tell, is larger than those employed by most factors." I grinned. "When she walked into those manufactories, I imagine your grandmama put them all in their place without saying a word."

Seliora nodded. "They all know her. She didn't say so, but part of the trip was to get them to know who Shomyr and I are. She said we'd do another trip in the late fall, if she felt up to it."

"Where did you stay?"

"At not very good hotels, except at Pointe Neimon. There, Grandmama has friends—or acquaintances. They have a cottage on the west side of the point. It overlooks the water. It's very rocky, and the water's rough, even in summer. It is beautiful, though, and very pleasant. There's only one small cove where it's safe to swim, and the water isn't that warm. We could walk to a market. There aren't many hacks, but you can rent a carriage if you need one . . ."

I listened and offered questions, just enjoying being with her and looking at her.

Then there were footsteps on the hardwood floor of the hallway from the main corridor.

"Seliora . . . ?"

Betara's words were as much a warning as an announcement.

"We're here," Seliora said. "We've just been talking."

Betara stepped onto the terrace carrying a small tray. On it were two glasses of sparkling crystal-clear Sanietra, one of my summer wines of choice, although I hadn't had any for a while, and a small platter holding thin slices of apple and peach, along with two napkins.

"I thought you might like a little light refreshment."

"Thank you," I offered.

"Oh . . . Grandmama sends her apologies. She says that, in this heat, she's not feeling her best, but she promises she'll meet Rhenn next week." Betara looked to me. "You are coming?"

"I wouldn't miss it for anything."

She laughed. "With all that has happened to you, let us hope that it doesn't come to that." In moments, she was gone.

I took a sip of the Sanietra. It was as cool and dry as it looked and slipped down my throat easily, leaving a faint hint of sweet lime and lilac behind. "This is good."

"It is." After a moment, she said, "You haven't said what you've been doing."

"Until a little more than a week ago, all I did was work on learning everything the Collegium thought I needed to know for my duties at the Chateau." I smiled. "Then I went to work and discovered that most of it was very routine, escorting petitioners to see councilors, standing corridor watches, taking a message or two . . ."

She raised her eyebrows. "What else?"

I didn't want to answer that directly. "You said that your family had ways of finding out things. Can you or your mother or grandmama find out about a bravo called the Ferran?"

"Was he the one who shot you?"

"No . . . and yes."

She frowned, then asked, "They hired someone else to go after you? You didn't tell me?"

"I couldn't have written you, and . . . well . . . I didn't want to come here and announce that people were still shooting at me. At least, it seems that way. Last week he—that's the Ferran—followed me when I was trying to find out who hired the first killer. I avoided him, but I'd found out that Master Caliostrus's brother might have been involved. So, I suspect, did he, because Thelal—that was the brother—ended up knifed dead in a tavern brawl two days later."

"Master Caliostrus? What did he have to do with this? He's been dead for months."

"Some people think that the explosion that killed Master Caliostrus wasn't an accident. I've heard guesses that it was intended for Ostrius, or at Master Caliostrus because Madame Caliostrus was trying to stop Caliostrus from giving coins to Thelal. She sold the ruined house and the land to Elphens. Did you know that he made master?"

"I didn't. I'm not surprised. He always had more coins than a journeyman should."

"His father is a High Holder, I was told."

"Since he is not one, Elphens must be the son of a mistress . . . or less."

"A mistress, I would guess, because High Holder Tillak

wouldn't shell out so many golds for a bastard son unless he felt something special about him or his mother."

Seliora nodded. "What else? You still haven't told me why people are shooting at you. When did all this happen?"

"I don't know why. No one else seems to know, either. Yesterday, when I was on my way to my parents for that belated birthday dinner—"

"You didn't tell me it was your birthday."

"It happened while you were gone. It would have sounded wrong . . . to write and mention my birthday, especially after you've been so good to me." I smiled apologetically.

"Oh . . . Rhenn. You don't . . ." Her headshake conveyed a mixture of affection and exasperation. "Go on."

"I'd just crossed the bridge and was getting some flowers to take to my sister. I had just asked the flower seller about the Ferran, because he'd said a few words to her the week before. That was when he was talking to her so that he could follow me—but I didn't know that until later. Yesterday, she told me that he was the Ferran, and right after that he shot at us both. He killed her. There was a civic patroller not ten yards away, and he couldn't even see the shooter. Neither did I, but it had to be him."

"Are you sure?"

I shrugged. "It's either him, or I'm in even bigger trouble than I thought."

"Do I understand that a week ago this person—the Ferran—was following you and yesterday you think he shot at you and killed the flower woman?"

"He was trying to kill us both. Me because I'm the target and her because she told me about him."

"Why would anyone want to kill you?"

I had to shrug. "I don't know. No one at the Collegium does, either, but it must be tied to Emanus—"

"Rhennthyl D'Imager." Her voice was stern. "You're only telling me bits and pieces. Tell the whole story from the beginning."

So I did, leaving out what might reveal too much about the Collegium and my real duties.

Afterward, she looked at me and shook her head. "It has to have something to do with High Holder Ryel. A connection with Emanus doesn't make sense. You only talked to him twice, and the first assassin tried to kill you before anyone could have known you were going to talk to him the second time."

"I just don't know. Master Dichartyn is convinced that's not the way High Holders do things. That's why I wanted to know if you could find out about the Ferran."

"I can ask Mama. I don't have those contacts, but Grandmama is . . . involved in many things."

I'd already gathered that.

Then, I heard the four bells ringing. "I need to go." I stood.

So did Seliora, gliding around the small table and putting her arms around me. I didn't need any more encouragement.

It was a bit before we stepped apart.

"You're coming next Samedi at half past four." Her words weren't a question.

"I said I wouldn't miss it."

"If it's too hot, we'll eat up on the north terrace. We often eat there in the summer and early harvest."

"And I might meet your grandmama?"

"She said she would meet you when the time was right. I thought she meant today."

We walked slowly down to the second level and then down to the main entry foyer. Seliora stood at the top of the steps as I made my way down the last set of steps. Someone had sent Bhenyt down and out into the street, because, by the time I stepped out of the door and walked down the steps, a hack was waiting, and Bhenyt was standing beside the stoop.

"Thank you, Bhenyt."

"My pleasure, Master Rhennthyl."

The ride back to the Bridge of Hopes was uneventful, but I did hold full shields when I left the coach and walked across the bridge.

Dinner was also without incident, and Dartazn and I sat with Menyard and Reynol, and we all speculated about what might happen with Caenen and Jariola, not that there was anything new in the scandal sheets. And, of course, we went to services, where, as was often so, Chorister Isola had some interesting things to say in her homily.

". . . one of the deadly sins is that of Naming. We all talk about the snare of the Namer and praise the life and works of Rholan the Unnamer, but how often do we consider why Naming is indeed a deadly vice? There are two kinds of hunger in life. One is physical. That is based on the need for bodily nourishment, and eating too much becomes the sin of gluttony. The other hunger in life is for self-worth. All men and all women need to feel that they and what they do are of value. But just as eating to stop hunger can become gluttony when carried to excess, so the seeking of ways to show self-worth can quickly turn into Naming. A proud factor builds more and more factorages to prove his worth, and then he engages in practices to undermine other factors and drive them out of business. Will being the wealthiest factor in Solis, or Westisle, or even L'Excelsis prove to be enough? A High Holder, already wealthy and respected, still schemes to bring down and even ruin other High Holders to prove he is among the more powerful High Holders. A nation, such as Caenen, or Jariola, or in the past, even Solidar, wants to prove its power—and that is an extension of self-worth—and uses that power to humiliate or defeat other lands. All these are examples of Naming, seeking to exalt one's name and reputation above others, not through honest effort, but by trying to undermine, ruin, or defeat and destroy others . . . and this is why Naming is the greatest sin of all, because the unbridled hunger for greater esteem can never be satisfied . . ."

I couldn't say that I really believed in the Nameless, but so much of what surrounded and infused the services made sense. Could I believe in the doctrine without believing in the deity?

56

Seemingly unrelated tiny pieces comprise images;
whoever sees those pieces as a whole earliest
comprehends first.

Lundi, like Vendrei, was a slower-paced day, at least after the
morning exercise and run, and I did have time to slip my letter to my parents into the outgoing post in between my duties
at the Council Chateau. Besides escorting two very condescending factors from Estisle to see Councilor Diogayn and
carrying sealed messages from Councilor Reyner to Councilor
Glendyl, all I did was watch the corridors and try to sharpen
my observation skills on the few who did come my way.
Councilor Glendyl had a tic in his right eye when he spoke,
but not when he listened. Councilor Alucion still had massive calluses on his palms and walked with the swaying gait
of a man who must have carried great weights when he was
younger—as he might have, since he was the representative
of the Stonecutters' Guild. Councilor Haestyr was younger
than I'd realized and was cheerful to everyone, but I thought
his green eyes were cold.

Because Lundi was such a slow day, we were released before fourth glass. I'd already decided that I needed to talk to
more people in the Portraiture Guild, if only to see if someone
had been talking to them about me . . . and because I had no
idea where else to continue in trying to track down who was
after me. Seliora's family would probably find out more than I
ever would, but I had to try. Rogaris might tell me something,
if for no other reason than to get me to leave, because he had
been clearly uncomfortable the last time I'd seen him. Could
that have been because he and Sagaryn knew something?

When we reached the Collegium, I didn't even have a chance to get to my chambers to change, because a fresh-faced prime was waiting for the duty coach. "Imager Rhennthyl, sir? Master Dichartyn would like to see you immediately, sir."

Both Dartazn and Martyl shook their heads as they slipped away. I'd have wagered they were just glad they hadn't been summoned. I followed the dutiful youngster to Master Dichartyn's study, where the door was open.

"Come on in, Rhenn," he called.

I entered and closed the door, then took the seat across the desk from him.

"Rhennthyl, there are some other items which the Civic Patrol neglected to mention to me." Although Master Dichartyn's voice was pleasant, his eyes were cold.

"Yes, sir?"

"Is there anything you can add to what you've told me—anything at all."

"Sir, I thought I told you what I knew, but there may be more that I thought I told you and did not." That was the safest answer.

He nodded. "Please let me know if you recall more after I tell you what else I have discovered. The rooms in the pension where Emanus lived were modest, but his savings were not enough to pay for them and food. I had some investigations made. He was receiving a monthly stipend from the Banque D'Excelsis, but the funds came blind from the local branch of the Banque D'Abierto, and we have no way of determining the sender." He looked at me.

"I cannot say I'm surprised, sir. I did ask him if he had allowed himself to be removed as guildmaster—"

"He was a guildmaster?"

"Didn't I tell you that, sir?"

"It could be. Matters have been less than serene. Go on."

"He said he had been, and thàt he had allowed a scandal to be trumped up because it was better that way, and no one else got hurt. I asked if he'd allowed it to protect someone in his family. He didn't answer except by asking why I'd ask that. I think he was protecting someone."

"That might well be. The other thing that the patrol found, hidden inside a leather case made to look like a book, was a miniature portrait of a young woman. Since Emanus had no other known family, they let me have it for the moment." He held up the portrait of a dark-haired young woman, set in a simple oval ebony frame, no more than five digits from the top of the oval to the bottom, then extended it. "Do you know her . . . or recognize the artist?"

I studied the unfamiliar image of a dark-haired girl perhaps the age of Khethila, also looking closely at the surface texture. "I'd guess it's close to twenty years old, sir, but I don't recognize her. The technique is outstanding. I'd judge that Emanus painted it himself, because I don't recognize the technique, because it's better than anyone painting in L'Excelsis today, and because it's unsigned. All works that are sold have to be signed. This was never meant for sale, not with that frame." I paused. "I'd say that he knew the girl very well. This wasn't done just for golds. The detail is too good, almost loving."

"Almost loving . . . of course!" He held out his hand for the portrait. "We need to keep this safe."

"Might I ask?" I handed back the miniature.

"You may, but I'd rather not say right now. If I'm wrong, it could be rather . . . embarrassing for the Collegium."

"Oh . . . that has to be his daughter," I blurted. "That's why."

That brought Master Dichartyn up short. "Why do you say that?"

"The portrait is twenty years old. At least, I think it is. Grisarius—Emanus—had to be more than sixty. I got the feeling, from all the serving girls I talked to, and from when I talked to him, that he had never pursued any of them. Yet he was friendly to them, and there were no rumors about male lovers. That means either a wife, a mistress or lover, or a daughter. You said he had no family, and no one has ever mentioned a family. Since he would have been over forty when this was painted, a daughter fits better than a lover, especially when he talked about not wanting to see anyone hurt. Usually people talk about children more that way than about lovers."

A wry smile crossed Master Dichartyn's face. "That's a rather interesting speculation. What else might you think about this daughter?"

"She's probably married, and probably, from the clothes, either from a very wealthy merchant . . . no . . . the cloth . . . that has to be, I'm just guessing, from a High Holder household."

"You think that was why he was killed?"

"No, sir. If the painting is of a daughter, and she was close to eighteen when it was painted twenty years ago, it couldn't be a husband's vengeance or another lover's revenge. He was too visible to have avoided a killer for so long. It had to be something more recent."

"So why do you think he was killed?"

"I have no idea, but it has to tie in to my visit. Otherwise, why would it happen then, and in that way? A renegade imager doesn't come cheap, and that suggests a High Holder or someone with great wealth and connections."

"It may," replied Master Dichartyn, "but there's not a shred of proof."

"You know who she is, don't you, sir?"

Master Dichartyn sighed. "Every once in a while, Rhennthyl, I can see why others might have a reason to murder you." He paused. "I have not told you who she is. That should tell you that I have a reason for not telling you. Such a reason is either for my safety or yours, or because it might endanger someone else. When such an occasion occurs, keep the speculation to yourself. And spare me the old canard about no question being stupid. Some are."

"Yes, sir." That spiel told me he was worried—more than worried—and that I should be even more concerned, because it indicated that more people wanted to get rid of me than I even knew. "Your messenger reached me just before I was going out to talk to acquaintances in the Portraiture Guild. What would you recommend I do, given what you know that I don't?"

"That's much better. I would suggest that you talk to more than a few people about Emanus's death—if only to protect them."

I did understand that. If I talked to one person, that person was at risk. More than a handful, and it would be difficult . . . I almost smiled, because I had a very nasty idea.

"Can I tell people I'm following up on something for the Collegium?"

"What would you tell them?"

I'd already thought that out. "Wasn't there some speculation that the first bravo, the one that shot me, had shot some other junior imagers?"

"And you want to tell them that you thought Emanus might have known something?"

I nodded.

"Since he's dead, he can't very well contradict you. But you'll have to use full shields, and you'll be on your own this time. I don't have to tell you to be careful."

"I will be, sir."

"Oh . . . take the duty coach for your first stop. That way, if anyone's watching the bridge they won't see you cross it. I'll have Beleart let them know." His eyes flicked toward the door.

I stood immediately. "Thank you, sir."

"Best of fortune."

As I walked back to my quarters to change into imager grays, I wondered why Master Dichartyn was suddenly so interested in people who were trying to kill me . . . and who the woman was. She couldn't just be anyone, or it wouldn't have mattered if I knew. She also was still alive, for the same reasons.

After changing quickly, I hurried back to the duty-coach stand and found two coaches there.

"Imager Rhennthyl?" asked the wiry obdurate driver of the first coach. "I'm to take you wherever you want to go, all evening if necessary. Master Dichartyn decided it would be quicker and safer that way."

Not to mention giving me greater authority, but I forbore mentioning that. "I appreciate it."

"It's not a problem, sir." The driver smiled. "Where to?"

"Daravin Way, off Duoeste Lane to the east of Plaza D'Nord. It's about the third dwelling from the corner, heading east."

"Yes, sir."

I'd already thought that I'd begin with Sagaryn, since Chasys's studio was the farthest from the Collegium, and then work back as I could. I climbed into the coach. The driver took the Bridge of Desires, then the West River Road north to the Nord Bridge before crossing the river and heading east. That route made sense, because there were far fewer coaches and wagons on it than on the Boulevard D'Imagers. It also might throw off anyone looking for me.

Even so, it was close to a quint before fifth glass when the driver stopped the coach in front of the small two-story dwelling. This time, when I used the bronze knocker on the outside studio door, Sagaryn was the one who greeted me, if a surprised look and an open mouth amounted to a greeting. Finally, he stammered, "Rhenn . . . I didn't . . . you're the last person . . ."

"It isn't a personal visit, Sagaryn. I'm here on imager business."

"Chasys isn't here."

"That's fine. You're the one I came to see, at the behest of the Collegium." I thought that was a correct, if indirect, way of putting it.

"Ah . . . come in."

"Thank you." I still held my shields as I stepped inside and he closed the door.

In the studio beyond, I could see a portrait on the easel, barely outlined. "New portrait, I see?"

"Yes. I'm sure you didn't come about that. Not on imager business."

"No. I'll make it as quick as I can. You might recall Emanus . . . the old artist who sometimes came to the hall. They usually called him Grisarius."

"I saw him. I never spoke to him." Sagaryn's eyebrows knit in confusion or puzzlement.

"He's dead. It's very likely because of what he knew. I don't know if you'd heard, but there have been several shootings of junior imagers over the last few months. I was one of those shot, and where I was shot was known to only a few people, most of them connected to the guild. We don't think anyone in the guild had anything to do with the shootings, but we do think that whoever did must have talked to several people in the guild." I smiled. "So I'm here to see who outside the guild asked you about me."

There was the slightest movement at the corners of his mouth, and for a moment, his eyes flickered away from me. I just waited.

"Ah . . . it's been a while, maybe as far back as around the beginning of Mayas—it could have been the end of Avryl. Rogaris and Dolemis and I were at Lapinina. I think it was a Jeudi night, and we were talking about how Seliora and her cousin took you to the Samedi gathering, and how the guard's eyes near popped out when you walked in with them. There was this fellow, and he'd just sat down at the next table, with another fellow. He said something like, 'Was that the imager who used to be a portraiturist journeyman?' Rogaris asked him what business it was of his, and the fellow smiled and said that he'd supplied things to Caliostrus, and that he'd remembered that you'd become an imager because there weren't many who'd been artists." Sagaryn shrugged. "That was pretty much it, except I did hear the other fellow mention something about NordEste Design—the furniture people—and how it was where Seliora worked. They stayed a bit and then left."

"What did they look like?"

"That was two months ago, Rhenn. Both of them, they just looked like anyone else."

"Did either one of them wear a yellow vest?"

"No. One fellow had a square-cut beard, old-style, you know, the way some of the old representationalists did."

A square-cut beard. Not many men had square-cut beards anymore, and the man who had shot me had one. That could be a coincidence. Or it might not be. "Do you remember anything else?"

Sagaryn shook his head. I kept asking, but he couldn't add any more.

Before that much longer, I left, and the driver made his way through some back lanes even I didn't know to get us to Sloedyr Way, where Rogaris opened the brown-painted door to Jacquerl's studio.

"Rhenn . . . what are you doing here?"

I gestured back at the gray coach waiting for me. "Imager business. Might I come in? It shouldn't take too long."

"I hope not. Madame Jacquerl is serving quail tonight in celebration of a new apprentice."

"I see," I said dryly. "The wealthy son of whom?"

He did flinch, if slightly. "A grain factor. He's the youngest son. Jacquerl did drive a hard bargain." Rogaris stepped back and gestured for me to enter.

I did, even as I doubted that Jacquerl, for all his politeness, would take any other kind of bargain.

"What is this about?" asked Rogaris.

"You know Grisarius . . . or Emanus . . . the old artist . . ." I gave him the same explanation I'd given Sagaryn and the same opening question.

"I don't recall anyone . . ." He shook his head.

"Sagaryn did, and he said you and Dolemis were with him, two months ago at Lapinina."

Rogaris frowned, tilted his head, then looked down. Finally, he spoke. "Oh . . . that, but they didn't really ask any questions. Well . . . we'd been talking about girls, and Aemalye, and Sagaryn said that you were lucky to have Seliora interested in you because a lot of imagers had trouble with women. One of the fellows at the next table made a comment about you being one of the few artists to become an imager, but it wasn't a question. It was like he already knew."

"Did he ask anything else?"

"He made some comment about imagers not having much time for women, and Sagaryn said that you were the type not to let one like Seliora pass by. That was it."

"Do you remember what they looked like?"

Rogaris shook his head, then stopped. "Just one thing . . . the one who talked had an old-style beard."

"What about the other one?"

"He never said anything to us." There was a pause. "I remember . . . he had sort of thick bushy eyebrows, because I was thinking you could almost define him in a portrait by them."

And that was about all I got from Rogaris.

As the driver headed the carriage toward Beidalt Place, just beyond Bakers' Lane, I thought over what they had told me. The square-bearded man *might* have been the first assassin, and the bushy-browed fellow could have been the Ferran, but there was certainly more than one man in L'Excelsis with an old-fashioned square beard—and more than a few with bushy brows.

The same apprentice who had opened the zinc-green-trimmed white door to Master Estafen's studio the last time did so again. He looked at the imager grays and turned pale.

"I'm here to talk to Master Estafen on imager business."

His eyes flicked past me to take in the gray coach, drawn by the pair of matched grays. If anything, he turned even more pale. "Yes, sir. If you'd come in . . ."

I did, and in less than a few moments, the rotund master portraiturist appeared. He looked at me, then nodded. "I might have guessed. What sort of imager business is this?"

"I'm part of a group trying to track down assassins who have killed several junior imagers, Master Estafen. I was fortunate enough to survive the attack on me, and the Collegium thought I might be of use in looking into this, especially since the guild appears to be involved, at least indirectly."

"The guild? Involved? How could that be? If it is, shouldn't you be talking to Master Reayalt?"

"The guildmaster is next, but you were closer. The reason I came is that last weekend I talked to Emanus because it had been brought to my attention that he might have knowledge that might be helpful. The next day he was dead, but he did provide some interesting insights."

"Interesting does not mean accurate, Imager Rhennthyl.

Nonetheless, how might I help the Collegium?" His words were smooth and assured.

"Has anyone asked you about me since I became an imager?"

"Why would they?"

I offered a smile. "That's what we're trying to discover. Several members of the guild were approached and observed by one man who fit the description of one of the assassins. It's possible that others were approached, and since I do have some knowledge of the guild I was asked to follow up on it."

Estafen nodded, and I had the sense he was not quite so tense. "I can assure you that no one, except Master Reayalt, has even so much as mentioned your name to me."

"Do you have any idea why someone who has been assassinating junior imagers would be interested in Emanus?"

"I have no idea. Emanus made a few enemies, but those I know of are long dead, and even were they alive, they would not have associated, even indirectly, with common killers."

I asked questions for almost a quarter glass . . . and learned nothing more. Again, I took my leave, feeling I had learned little, and returned to the Collegium coach.

By the time I left the coach at Guildmaster Reayalt's dwelling, on the south end of the Martradon area, three blocks south of the Midroad, the sun was just above the rooftops and casting a long reddish light across L'Excelsis.

Reayalt himself opened the door, but he was clearly surprised to see me. "Oh . . . Imager Rhennthyl, it is Imager, isn't it? I was expecting Master Schorzat."

"I'm certain he'll be here shortly. I'm here on a different matter, and it shouldn't take very long." I paused. "By the way, I didn't thank you for sending the study I did to my parents. That was a most kind and thoughtful thing to do, and both they and I appreciated it."

"From what I know of imager training, it was not likely that you would have been able to recover the painting, and it is quite good. Oh . . . please come in. If you wouldn't mind, we could just talk in the foyer here."

"That would be fine." Without much preamble, I launched into my explanation of my task, but not mentioning Emanus, ending with the same question I'd used before. "Has anyone made any inquiries about me?"

"No. That is, no one outside the guild. Elphens did ask about you a few days ago, because he thought the workmen building his new dwelling and studio had seen you there. There had been an imager there, he said."

"I was there. I hadn't realized that Madame Caliostrus had left L'Excelsis, and I wanted to ask her much the same question as I just asked you."

"Ah . . . that explains much."

"There's another aspect to this that may involve the guild, if indirectly."

He stiffened ever so slightly.

"Emanus . . . or Grisarius . . ." I went on to offer my incomplete story about the old artist.

"I had not heard that," offered Reayalt. "It is regrettable, but perhaps understandable."

"Why might that be?"

"Emanus always did take too great an interest in matters political, and even some dealing with intrigue, but I thought he had learned his lesson."

"I'd heard that there was more to his removal as guildmaster than just selling a representational painting."

"Most definitely. That was just a convenient, if true, reason to cover up an indiscretion so that the guild would not be tarnished by untoward gossip."

"Do you think his death might be related to those . . . indiscretions?"

Master Reayalt shook his head. "I cannot say that it is not possible, but it would be highly unlikely. Most of those involved are now dead."

"The High Holder . . . ?"

He looked at me sharply. "It might no longer matter, but I still see no reason to go into that."

"You don't think it could involve his daughter, then?"

"Most certainly not. She may not . . . be all that her peers would like, but she is well above any reproach or scandal, unlike her mother. How . . ." He shook his head.

"If that is so, it puzzles me as to how Emanus might know about assassins, and why anyone now might wish to kill him," I offered.

"It doesn't puzzle me," replied the guildmaster. "Emanus was truly brilliant, as well as the finest portraiturist of his time. He watched everything, and could deduce what people might be doing or have done from the smallest of intimations. Yet for all that brilliance, he never truly understood how dangerous that knowledge was to himself, and to the guild."

"That was why he was removed?"

"Essentially."

I asked a few more questions, the replies to which offered nothing new, and inclined my head. "Thank you. You've been most kind. If you or others do hear of the kind of inquiries I've mentioned, I would appreciate knowing of them. The Collegium does not like to lose young imagers, especially when most have still been in training."

"I can see that, Imager Rhennthyl."

His glance toward the door reminded me that he was expecting company, and further inquiries would intrude on dinner. So I took my leave and made my way back to the coach, asking the driver to return to the Collegium, but by the lower part of the Boulevard D'Imagers.

Sitting in the coach, I considered what I'd learned. Someone had been looking for me well before I'd been shot. It was likely that the Ferran had hired the first assassin and both were working for someone else. Based on what Master Reayalt had let slip, I was convinced that Emanus's daughter's mother had indeed been a High Holder, and that the scandal had been hushed up. What that had to do with the killings of junior imagers I had no idea. I hadn't talked to Dolemis or Aurelean, but I'd never spent that much time with them, and Aurelean was so wrapped up in Aurelean that he wouldn't have been able to tell anyone very much about anyone else, and he wouldn't have remembered what he'd said—unless it bore on his future.

I studied the sidewalks as the coach neared the Bridge of

Hopes, but I didn't see anyone looking even vaguely like the Ferran. But then, if he were there, he wouldn't be looking as I'd seen him. Master Dichartyn wasn't in his study, and I hurried to the dining hall, arriving very late, when most were lingering over dessert. But I did sit with Dartazn and Menyard, and we discussed the state of the world, about which we'd heard nothing new. Since we hadn't, I supposed that war had not yet broken out.

Afterward, I again stopped by the administration building, but no one was there.

57

Numbers can mislead, but less so if one understands what lies behind them.

On Mardi morning, it was a struggle to get up in time to stagger off to Clovyl's exercise group, but I reached the exercise rooms just after the sun's first rays angled over the east side of the quadrangle and just before Master Dichartyn.

"Rhenn!" he called from behind me.

"Yes, sir?" I stopped and waited.

"Meet me in my study before you take the coach to the Chateau."

"Yes, sir."

That change in schedule required more rushing, and a very hurried shower and breakfast so that I could get to Master Dichartyn and still have time to make the duty coach. How he managed it, I didn't know, because he was waiting behind his writing desk, looking calm and unrushed, neither of which I felt.

"What did you discover, if anything, last night?"

"Someone was looking to find me as early as around the end of Avryl. There were two men. They matched the general description of the Ferran and the man who shot me . . ." I told him what I'd discovered, and my suspicions about Master Estafen and Grisarius. "Oh . . . I also talked to Guildmaster Reayalt. He said no one had asked about me . . . but he was expecting Master Schorzat for dinner."

"That's not surprising. They're cousins."

"I don't mean to be forward, sir, but Reayalt became guildmaster and had something to do with Emanus being forced to step down—"

"Master Schorzat is aware of that and has confirmed certain circumstances with his cousin. For the moment, that is all you need to know."

"Yes, sir." I was already getting a little more than tired with Master Dichartyn's secrecy. So far, it hadn't done all that much to protect me, and I certainly hadn't done anything to jeopardize the Collegium. "Should I make more inquiries or wait a few days?"

"Do you think that you'll learn that much more from the others you could easily talk to?"

"I don't think so, sir."

"Then I'd suggest you wait. We've traced Madame Caliostrus to Cleville—that's a small town near Rivages. We're waiting on a report." He paused, then said, "You'd better catch the duty coach."

"Yes, sir." I rose, inclined my head, and hurried off in my messenger/guard uniform.

The only interesting event of the morning was when a purported stonecutter on his way to see Councilor Alucion "tripped" and rolled down the grand staircase. The duty coach carted him back to the Collegium to recover. I didn't get to ask about that until lunch, when Baratyn sent Martyl and me down to the kitchen, where we sat in the small alcove with platters of creamed rice and fowl.

"How did you know he wasn't a stonecutter?" I took a mouthful of the rice and fowl, bland, but probably filling, trying to ignore how hot the kitchen area was.

"The little things. He tried not to say much, but he was too well spoken. His hands were too pale and too soft, and he wore soft-leather boots that were almost new."

"He tried something before you even reached the councilor?"

"He had a pistol hidden in his jacket. I waited until we were on the stairs and suggested that he shouldn't take it in to see the councilor. He tried to use it on me and lost his balance."

I didn't press on that. "Who do you think he was?"

"Jariolan, if I had to guess. The Ferrans usually don't attack councilors in the Chateau, and the Caenenans are usually darker. Besides, their new High Priest is sending an envoy to work out a trade agreement. That's what I overheard High Councilor Suyrien telling Glendyl."

"Their merchanters are all bottled up in Caena, and they've lost their High Priest, and we're talking about a trade agreement?"

Martyl laughed. "It's better than calling it a surrender agreement, isn't it? They'll probably have to lower tariffs on our goods and pay damages. The Council cares more about golds and results, not what they're called."

My mouth was full, and I nodded, then took a sip of the grisio that had come with the meal. The wine was the best part.

"Did you hear about Selastyr?" asked Martyl.

"Is he the tall blond third who works with Menyard?"

"Worked. He had a girl who lived with her older sister and her husband near the Sud Bridge. He went to see her last night. When he got out of the hack, someone shot him. He died right there."

"No shields . . . then."

Martyl shook his head. "Most of the imagers who do equipment work and design can do detail imaging, but they don't manage shields well. And . . . Reynol, he may be an expert with ledgers, but he wouldn't know a shield if he ran into it."

"Are field imagers and security imagers the only ones who can handle shields?"

"We're not the only ones, but we're most of the ones who can."

Although I'd suspected the answer before I'd asked the question, I was glad for the confirmation. "It seems to me that we've lost a lot of junior imagers this year."

Martyl nodded, then swallowed, and took a sip of wine before replying. "That's what Baratyn said. Usually, most of the ones who die get killed by their own mistakes, and that's maybe three or four in a whole year."

If I'd counted right, four had been shot since I'd been at the Collegium, five if I counted the attempts on me. But then, I wondered about those killed by "mistakes." I'd seen three of those in half a year, and those were the ones I knew about. The more I saw, the more I realized what I wasn't seeing. "We've had something like two or three attempted attacks here every week. Is that usual?"

"That's about right."

Two or three a week—and the Council was in session, on and off, for thirty weeks out of fifty. That was between sixty and ninety attempted assassinations of councilors a year. Was Solidar that hated?

"You'd think that they'd learn, but it keeps happening." Martyl shook his head. "Some of them are local, too. They think there are too many High Holders on the Council or too few guild representatives, or like that Madame D'Shendael, they think that there ought to be councilors elected directly by the people. Can you imagine where that would lead?"

I could.

When we finished eating we had to hurry back up to the main level to relieve Baratyn and Dartazn.

58

Do not concentrate on sums when nothing adds up.

For the rest of the week, little or nothing beyond the routine occurred at the Council Chateau. That did give me a chance to practice more in the way of observation skills. I did note that Baratyn flicked his eyes up for just a moment before he gave directions.

Nor did I hear anything from Master Dichartyn. In fact, at the morning exercise sessions, he scarcely even looked in my direction. In the running, he was just slightly slower than I was, but over three milles, it generally meant I finished a good fifty yards ahead of him.

Then, just before I left the Chateau on Vendrei, looking forward to a pleasant weekend, especially on Samedi, Baratyn handed me a message.

"It's from Master Dichartyn."

I opened the envelope and read the short message.

In my study at fifth glass.

Under the single line was a spare "D."

I had just enough time to get back to the Collegium and change into my grays and get across the quadrangle to the administration building before the bells in the anomen tower to the south began to strike.

Master Dichartyn was standing by the open window of his study and motioned for me to enter. I did close the door, but I didn't sit down because he didn't.

"We finally have that report on Madame Caliostrus." Master Dichartyn looked both stern and weary at the same time.

"She and her son Marcyl were killed back in early Avryl. She was staying with her sister. The sister and Caliostrus's daughters had gone to market, and the husband was at work on the river. The boy and his mother had their throats cut. There wasn't much of a struggle."

"Thelal?"

Master Dichartyn's smile could have been a shrug. "Most of the golds were missing from the strongbox."

"She didn't believe in banks. That was a sore point between her and Master Caliostrus."

"The other thing is that I talked to the Civic Patrol again." He shook his head. "Some of the wall stones around one of the windows in Caliostrus's studio were blown out."

"Paraffin and waxes won't do that."

"No, and that suggests some sort of explosive was involved. Thelal was an ironway laborer for a time. He was dismissed for small thefts."

All that made a sort of sense. If Thelal had planted—or even just hidden—the explosives in the studio, waiting for the right time, I'd inadvertently committed his murder for him. "But . . . why would he hide explosives in the studio?"

"Where else could he put them? Most nights, he didn't know where he'd be sleeping."

"Then you think that Thelal doesn't have anything to do with my shooting?"

Master Dichartyn frowned. "The patrollers don't think so, but I don't like coincidences. Every male in that household is either dead, or nearly so, in your case. The surviving daughters are more than a hundred milles away. Are you certain that you didn't see something?"

"Once or twice, I overheard Madame Caliostrus mention things like 'your worthless brother.' She didn't like him around at all, but I only saw him once or twice a year, I'd guess."

"He knew you were there, then."

"He had to. I was there more than ten years."

"Please think about it, if you will . . . and try to be more observant. If you had been when you were a portraiturist . . ." He shook his head.

I couldn't change the past. "Is there anything else, sir?"

"Should there be?"

I felt that there should be, but what, I couldn't have said. "Not that I know, sir."

"Rhennthyl . . . never mind. You can go." He paused. "I'll be gone for a few days."

I left. Master Dichartyn was clearly worried about more than who had been shooting at me, because the circles under his eyes were deep and dark, but he didn't want to say. Or didn't dare.

Was that part of what I had to look forward to as a counterspy imager? I couldn't say I was a counterspy yet. I was just a hidden security guard for the Council, but, if I ever wanted to be more, would I have to keep more and more secrets?

I decided to go look for Dartazn or Reynol. Martyl was going off Imagisle for a dinner with relatives, and Menyard had mentioned at breakfast that he was leaving for the weekend. He didn't have to deal with Clovyl's exercises and runs on Samedi morning.

59

When you finally think you understand things is most likely when you don't.

On Samedi morning, Clovyl's exercise group was markedly smaller. Out of the ten or so who appeared regularly, the only ones I knew personally—or even by name—were Martyl, Dartazn, Baratyn, and Master Dichartyn. The other six ranged in age from their late twenties to twenty years beyond that, but all were well-muscled and trim, and several of the older men ran faster than I did, although no one came close to

Dartazn. That morning, while I knew Master Dichartyn would not be there, neither was Baratyn, nor were two others. Given their absences, and the circles under Master Dichartyn's eyes, as I struggled to keep up close to Dartazn in the run that ended the morning workout, I couldn't help but wonder what they might be doing.

After recovering from the run on my walk back to the quarters, I took a cool but thorough shower and shaved. Then I dressed and headed across the quadrangle to the dining hall, where I met Martyl. Dartazn joined us as we sat down at the long table. I poured a full mug of tea and waited for the platters of sausage and fried flatcakes to reach us.

"Master Dichartyn and all the seniors were gone. Did he say anything to you yesterday?" asked Martyl.

Dartazn laughed. "He never tells anyone anything they don't have to know. Not me, not you, not Rhenn."

"He only told me he'd be gone for a few days, after pointedly reminding me that I should have been more observant back when I was a portraiturist and didn't know I needed to remember every conversation within ten yards." My words came out edged with vinegar.

They both laughed.

"It's one thing to tell me that about what I do now . . ." I stopped and just shook my head.

"He's done that to all of us," Martyl said.

"Something's afoot." Dartazn paused to take a healthy helping of sausages.

None of us spoke for a time, perhaps because we enjoyed the sweet berry syrup on the flatcakes and because we were hungry after having been up and active for several glasses.

"What do you think is happening?" I finally asked. "You two have been imagers longer than I have."

"Most other lands know that starting a war with Solidar isn't the best idea," said Dartazn slowly, "but their rulers often face pressures to do something. That can lead to attempts at assassinations, sabotage, that sort of thing."

"That sounds like Master Dichartyn has gotten wind of something."

"It could be . . . or it could be that they're all off meeting to go over what might happen."

We talked for a time, speculating to no real result, and before long, Martyl rose. "I'm to meet my uncle at the ironway station, and I'd better be there. He's never been to L'Excelsis."

We all walked out of the dining hall together, but then I had to hurry out to my studio to work on the portrait of Master Poincaryt—except he didn't come. Instead, Beleart arrived just after eighth glass had chimed.

"Master Poincaryt won't be able to make the sitting today, sir. He will be here next Samedi."

After Beleart departed, I headed back to my own quarters, Once there, I sat down at my desk and thought about the day ahead. Although I would be having dinner with Seliora and her family, I needed to talk to a few more people—perhaps even Elphens and Aurelean. It couldn't hurt to see if Father or Khethila had any ideas or suggestions, or if either had seen anything.

I decided to start with Father at the factorage and walked from my quarters over the Bridge of Desires to West River Road. That was actually closer to my quarters, but had I been taking a hack directly to my parents' house, it would have been more costly, not that I lacked coins. In fact, I had more funds than I'd had in years, and I'd actually used the tiny one-room branch of the Banque D'Excelsis in a nook off the dining hall—just an unmarked door behind which was a single teller cage—to open an account. Even with what I'd spent on hacks and food over the summer and early harvest, I had slightly more than five golds put by. Unlike poor Madame Caliostrus, I felt better not having to worry about a strongbox. I also had no doubts about the Banque; it wasn't about to short the Collegium.

As I stepped onto the bridge, I was holding full shields. That made a warm morning even warmer, but I could see clouds to the north and west. That could herald a cooler afternoon, or one just as hot—and steamy. Just off West River Road, I hailed a hack.

"Alusine Wool—south on West River, a half mille past the Sud Bridge, on the west side."

"Yes, sir. We can do that."

When I left the hack in front of the factorage, I took a moment to study it. The building was still the same old yellow-brick structure that stretched a good seventy yards along West River Road. The loading docks were out of sight in the rear, and the covered entry was centered on the middle of the building. As I climbed the three steps to the double oak doors, I noted that they had been sanded clean and then revarnished, and the dark green casement trim repainted.

Inside, it was darker, and cooler, and I took several steps farther into the open area before the racks that held the swathes of various wools. To one side was another set of racks with the lighter fabrics—muslin, cotton, linen. Despite the name of the factorage, Father had always carried a wide range of fabrics, colors, and patterns.

"Master Rhennthyl . . . we'd not expect you here." The balding man who stepped forward was Eilthyr, who was now in charge of the day-to-day work on the floor.

"I thought I'd drop by." My eyes flicked to the raised platform at the back, from where Father could sit at his desk and survey everything, not that he sat there much if there were potential customers.

Khethila was at the desk—looking at me. I had a very unsettled feeling about that.

"Yes, sir . . . your father . . ."

"Mistress Khethila can help me, I'm most certain. But . . . thank you."

"Yes, sir."

As I skirted the sample racks, I could hear the exchange between the warehouseman, who had appeared from somewhere, and Eilthyr.

"The imager . . . ?"

"That's the factor's eldest . . . used to be an artist."

". . . looks more like a commando . . . wouldn't want to cross him . . ."

". . . takes after the old man, that way . . ."

I had to smile at the thought of my taking after my father.

Khethila was standing by the time I walked up the low steps to the desk. "Rhenn . . . I didn't expect to see you here."

"I'd actually wanted to ask both you and Father about some things, but I have the feeling he's not anywhere around."

"Neither Mother nor Father is. Mother took the ironway to see Aunt Ilena, and Father went back to Kherseilles."

"Rousel made a mess of the accounting, didn't he?"

Khethila looked at me, her eyes too bright. "It's awful. He borrowed against his inventory, and when the shipments from the Abierto Isles took longer to arrive, the interest was higher, and he borrowed more . . ."

"Father won't lose everything, will he?" That was my greatest fear.

She shook her head. "No, but it could cost close to two hundred gold crowns."

"Two hundred?"

"That's if everything goes wrong. Father and I worked out a way to amortize the debt against the building there that will lower the interest on what Rousel owes."

"You're running things here, aren't you?"

"Mostly." She grinned. "Father's surprised. I do have to be very careful and always say that I've checked with him, and I do when he's here." After a pause, she asked, "What did you want to know?"

"I'd appreciate it if you didn't tell anyone outside the family, but people have been shooting at me, and I had to wonder if you've noticed anyone lurking around the house or coming in here and asking about me."

"You told me you'd been shot. I didn't tell Mother, you know?" She paused. "You said shooting. Has someone else . . . ?"

"Someone has been following me, and they did shoot at me again," I admitted. "I'm fine. They didn't come close to hitting me." In a way, that was deceptive, but I didn't feel I could explain. "Master Dichartyn thought I should ask everyone I knew, and my family, if they'd seen anything strange."

Khethila shook her head. "I haven't seen anything like

that, but I will keep an eye out, just in case." She glanced past me, toward an older man who had entered and was walking toward Eilthyr. "You're sure you're all right?"

"I'm fine." I glanced down at the book on the corner of the desk. It didn't look familiar. "What's that?"

She flushed. "It's my guide . . . sort of. Madame D'Shendael wrote a volume on the basics of commerce and finance for the wives of High Holders and factors. She said it was a treatise for women who lost their husbands through illness and accident, to help them understand matters so that they were not helpless."

"It's much more than that, isn't it?"

That brought a grin.

"How did you find it?"

"I finished her *Poetic Discourse* and her *Civic Virtue,* and I went to the bookshop near the square. The only book of hers I could find was this one." She held it up. The name on the spine was *A Widow's Guide.* "I almost put it down, but since there wasn't anything else there, I started to read. I almost burst out laughing, right in the bookshop, by the third page. There are things in there that Father never even thought of, but I didn't tell him where I got them."

"How many books has she written?"

"Not that many. There's one other one, and I ordered it, but I don't remember the title. It's about the role of women in fostering culture, I think."

"She's quite the writer."

"She is, and she writes well."

"I know. You've quoted her at me a few times."

"She's worth quoting."

I just smiled. "How long will you be in charge here?"

"Father hopes to be back by next weekend. I gave him a set of guidelines for Rousel. I told him to tell our dear brother that they came from an old treatise on commerce."

"But they came from that?" I gestured toward *A Widow's Guide.*

She nodded. "Can you join me for dinner?"

I shook my head. "I have an engagement."

"Who is she?"

"Someone . . ." I grinned.

"Rhenn!"

"If it turns into something really serious, you'll be the first to know. Come to think of it, you are the first to know that there is a someone."

"She's part Pharsi and dark-haired, isn't she?"

"Why do you say that?"

"You've never looked at any other kind."

"Yes . . . and that's all I'll say."

She grinned once more. "And she's as poor as . . . as a bookkeeping clerk?"

"I answer your questions, and you'll figure it out. Besides, I have to talk to a few other people, hopefully before they start shooting at me again."

Her grin vanished. "You will be careful? Promise?"

"I will."

She gave me an embrace, and I headed for the door.

Outside, I only had to wait a bit to hail a hack, and before long we were headed north on the West River Road, then over the Nord Bridge and east on the Boulevard D'Este.

When I finally reached Master Kocteault's studio and knocked on the door, Aurelean was the one to open it. His eyes widened. "Rhenn? You're an imager? I had heard something of that. I do suppose that is natural for one with artistic pretensions . . . I mean abilities."

"That's true. You always have been outstanding at determining pretensions . . . I mean abilities, Aurelean. But enough of the trivial. I'm here on imager business. Might I come in?"

"Oh, of course. Imager business, how droll." He stepped back and let me enter and close the door. "What can I do for you? Master Kocteault is not here."

Was he ever there? "You're the one I came to see, and it's rather simple. Has anyone asked you about me, or where I might be found? Or for that matter, have any strangers showed up at the hall who have asked questions . . . any time that you can recall since last spring?"

"That sounds more personal than imager."

"It's not. Several imagers have been shot at. I'm only one of them, and other imagers are tracking down the others, but the Collegium thought I might know best whom to talk to among the artists."

"Shooting at imagers," mused Aurelean, the superciliousness gone for a moment, "that's not good." He frowned. "I don't remember when it was, except it was a cold Samedi in spring, I think. I did see two people talking to one of the apprentices—it might have been the one who drowned last month, now that I think of it. I remembered it because one of them had the square-cut beard that all the poseurs who think they might be artists used to affect."

"That was the only time you saw anything like that?"

"Nameless, no. I'm sure there were other strange things. There are always strange occurrences if one only looks, but that is the sole occasion that I can recall."

I nodded. "Thank you. If you do see anything, or recall anything, you could drop me a note at the Collegium."

"I could, I suppose."

I smiled. "By the way, even if you did it to flatter Master Kocteault, it was a very good portrait of his daughter."

He actually flushed. "Why, thank you."

After I left Aurelean, I found another hack and had him drop me off at Elphens's new dwelling and studio. No one was there, although it was clear he had moved in. I wished that I'd had the hack wait, because I had to walk to the end of Bakers' Lane and wait more than a quarter glass to find another to take me down to the square. By then it was well past noon, and I was more than a little warm.

I slipped into Lapinina, but I didn't seen anyone I knew, not surprisingly, because most artists would not have been there that early. I took the smaller of the two vacant tables.

Staela approached. "Sir?"

I looked up at her. "Whether I'm an imager or not, Staela, I'm still Rhenn. What do you have that's cool to drink and light to eat?"

She was silent for just a moment. "There's a Kienyn white

we brought up from the cellar, and the chopped fowl salad is good."

"I'll have both."

"Yes, sir." She slipped away before I could say anything . . . or even sigh.

Within moments she returned with a tall fluted glass of a slightly bubbly amberish wine. "The Kienyn. That's three."

I put a silver on the table. "For the wine and the salad."

She scooped the coin up and left two coppers before nearly fleeing.

I sipped the Kienyn and listened. No one was talking. The only sound for that moment was the buzz of a fly that circled somewhere above my head. I continued to sip and wait. Still, no one said anything.

Only when Staela reappeared with the greens and chopped fowl and I began to eat did a few words began to flow around the small bistro.

". . . be hot like this for another two weeks . . ."

"More like three . . ."

". . . think this is hot . . . ought be in Caena . . ."

". . . their High Priest . . . changed his mind once the Navy blockaded his ports . . ."

". . . different High Priest . . ."

"They're all the same . . ."

". . . know the imager?"

". . . might be the one who was an artist . . ."

". . . too tall . . . too much muscle for an artist . . ."

As Staela tried to slip by, I motioned. "The Kienyn is good. Have you always had it?"

"No . . . just this summer. Would you like another?"

"In a moment." I gestured to the chair. "Please sit down. I do have a few questions to ask you, and they're on behalf of the Collegium. Imager business. Nothing secret."

She did seat herself, if with an air of resignation.

"I don't know if you've heard this, but someone has been shooting at imagers, often young ones, or those in training. I was one of them. What the Collegium would like to know is whether you ever noticed anyone who seemed to be following me, or who asked about me, or talked about imagers."

"Sir . . . I try not to pay attention to what people say. I don't know as I recall anything like that."

I nodded. "I can see that. Do you remember a man in a square beard—you know, the kind that you see in all the old paintings of artists, but the kind no artist has today?"

There was only a momentary frown before Staela replied. "There was one fellow. Some of the journeymen pointed him out when he left. They laughed and said he was a would-be artist. That's why I remember. He used to come here on Vendrei nights and Samedi afternoons, maybe for a month this spring. He didn't say much. He just listened to the others. He was here for a while, then never showed up again."

"Did anyone ever come with him?"

"There was another fellow once in a while. He wore a yellow vest one time. I only noticed because he paid for the other one's wine with golds. He didn't seem to have a silver to his name. Just golds." She looked at me directly for the first time. "That's all. Honest. That's all I remember."

"Thank you. I would like another Kienyn."

"Coming up."

Staela wasn't quite so stiff after that, but I could tell that she still wanted me to leave. While I didn't gulp down the second glass, I also didn't linger over every last drop, but I did leave her a half silver tip.

The only other place I'd ever visited even halfway frequently was Rozini's, on the far side of the square. I wandered over there, and asked several of the servers, but no one remembered me or anyone asking about me. After that, I still had time to kill, and I didn't really feel like going back to the Collegium. So when I saw the bookstore sign, I wandered inside.

A soft-looking young man with thick spectacles appeared almost immediately, emerging from behind a carrel of books. "Might I help you?"

"I was just looking."

"We don't see many imagers here, sir."

I smiled. "I'm sure you don't, but I'd wager you see my sister every so often."

"Your sister?" While polite, his tone suggested the impossibility of an imager having sisters.

"Khethila D'Chenkyr. Tallish young woman, husky voice, likes books by Madame D'Shendael."

"She's very well read." Again, the tone was condescending, suggesting that, whether we were related or not, no imager could possibly be well read.

"She is indeed, and I'm certain she got the habit from all that I read her when she was younger." I smiled politely and turned away.

Before long, I did find the shelf that carried Madame D'Shendael. There were copies of both *Poetic Discourse* and *Civic Virtue,* but neither *A Widow's Guide,* nor the other book were on the shelves. Because I'd heard enough of Khethila's quotes from the *Discourse,* I picked up *Civic Virtue.* Right behind the frontispiece was an etching of a woman, and the scripted typeface below read *Madame Juniae D'Shendael.* There was something about the etching, and I studied it, wondering whether it had been done by Estafen, but the signature in the corner was that of Teibyn, who was known to be better at etching portraits than at painting them.

I flipped the page and came across the dedication:

To my mother, for reasons more than enough.

I would have been disappointed, somehow, if it had been to her father or any man, perhaps because of all that Khethila had said.

Then I leafed back to the portrait etching. At that moment, I recognized her. The etching showed her as a mature woman, but she was the same woman as the girl in the miniature . . . and that realization left me more confused than ever. How could she be Emanus's daughter? High Holder status always ran through the male line—unless there were no male heirs—and then the eldest daughter, but only if she married within a High Holder family and her husband took the family name. In addition, High Holders were anything but forgiving. Or was the threatened disclosure of Juniae's parentage why Emanus had let himself be removed? But why would he have been killed years later over that?

It was still only just past second glass. So I took a hack back to the Bridge of Desires, walked across it in the hot afternoon sun, back to my quarters. In the end, I did take another shower, because I was so hot and sweaty, and changed once more.

My timing was more precise than during my call on Seliora the Solayi before, and I stepped out of the hack just before the single bell proclaiming half past four struck. Unsurprisingly, Bhenyt was there to open the door and escort me up to the main living level.

Seliora was waiting, as lovely as ever in a dress composed of a flowing filmy dark green skirt and a black short-sleeved top, not terribly low-cut, but certainly not excessively modest, either. She smiled, then took my hands.

We did embrace and kiss, if relatively chastely and quickly.

"We decided we'll need to eat on the terrace. It's just too hot down here in the main dining room. We can go up now."

I followed her up the steps and then out onto the terrace. She was right. It was definitely cooler there. I glanced to the northwest. Those same clouds I'd seen that morning still lurked in the sky, but they didn't seem to have moved at all.

"We have a choice of drinks." Seliora nodded toward a small cabinet-like table set just forward of the north wall, west of the double doors. A serving man in a white shirt and a dark green waistcoat stood behind it.

"Shall we see?" I smiled at her, enjoying being with her.

We walked to the portable sideboard where we agreed on white Cambrisio.

"The table on the east there is still in the shade," Seliora pointed out.

Not only was the table shaded, but at that corner I could feel a light but cooling breeze. As we sat, I realized we were the only ones on the terrace, except for the serving man.

"The others will be here shortly. I told them all five."

"You're a devious woman."

She laughed, musically. "You'll find I'm far more practical and less romantic than you think. Once everyone arrives, we won't have a moment to ourselves." She lowered her voice. "I like being with you, and I see them all every day."

"How did your week go?"

"About the same as most others, except that High Holder Unsaelt finally decided that he wanted a new dining set for his hunting lodge out near Tacqueville. He has to keep the same crest, but he wanted to know if we could make it a bit less tired and more vital . . ."

For a time, I just listened.

Abruptly, she looked at me. "You're very quiet. Is something bothering you? Have I upset you?"

"No." I didn't have to force the smile because my thoughts certainly weren't her fault. "I've talked to a number of people today, and what I found out wasn't exactly encouraging. First, I stopped by the factorage. Father's gone back to Kherseilles, and Khethila's the one holding things down. Rousel's made some very bad decisions . . ." I went on and explained that, and then what I'd found out from Aurelean and Staela. ". . . Someone was after me in Avryl, but even after that, it sounds like they killed an apprentice to keep it quiet."

"It had to be someone besides the first assassin," she pointed out. "He was dead when the drowning happened. Could it have been an accident?"

"It could have been, but that makes more coincidental accidents than I'm comfortable with. Did your mother find out anything?"

"She wants to tell you herself."

I wanted to know, but I could understand that. I heard steps and saw Shomyr walking toward the sideboard. "Have you ever read anything by Madame D'Shendael?"

Seliora shook her head. "I'm not that much of a reader, except books on looms and engines. They're work to read, though. Madame D'Shendael . . . she's the one who has the salon, and she had all those hard times."

"What hard times?"

"She miscarried, lost a child, and her mother was executed for killing her father when she was nineteen."

I almost froze at that. "Where did you hear that?"

"Oh, you hear things when you deal with High Holders, especially if you pretend you're not listening." She smiled. "It's amazing what people will say when they think you're well beneath them and say a lot of simpering 'sir's and 'madame's."

More of Seliora's family began to appear—Odelia, and then Aegina, followed by Betara, and Shelim . . . and then by a much older woman with steel-gray hair, who had to be Grandmama.

Betara and Shelim walked to the table where we were sitting. Each carried a goblet of either red Cambrisio or perhaps Dhuensa.

"You don't mind if we join you?" asked Betara. "Grandmama Diestra will be here in a moment."

Seliora and I just smiled, and Betara and Shelim settled into the chairs across the circular polished white oak table from us. "It is much cooler here than in the dining chamber. The dinner might be a bit cooler as well, since it has to travel two flights of steps to get here."

Shelim stood again and pulled up another chair for Diestra before I could.

No one spoke for several moments.

"You asked Seliora if we could find out anything about people trying to shoot you," Betara said casually. "We thought it might be better to dispense with that unpleasantness before dinner." She paused to sip her wine, Dhuensa, I realized. "Grandmama Diestra talked to a few . . . acquaintances." A wry tone entered her voice as she went on. "You must have offended someone a great deal. Late last spring a contract price was put out on a recently promoted imager tertius. They wouldn't give a name, but they might as well have. Ten golds—that's the price for a taudischef. Rumor has it that the morteprix was guaranteed by Artazt—he was a taudischef in the hellhole—because his brother was killed by the imager . . ." She paused and looked at me.

"Diazt was from the hellhole. He was the one who died when they tried to kill me."

"It gets interesting after that," Betara said with a smile.

I didn't like the way she said "interesting."

"The first assassin shot the imager, but was killed by him. That suggests that we're talking about you, Rhenn."

"I couldn't have guessed."

"Artazt wasn't happy, and he went to the assassin's family to demand back the golds he'd advanced, but when he left with the golds, he disappeared. His body was found garroted in a nearby alley, and a silver cord was knotted around the rope still twisted about his neck. Oh . . . and the golds were still in his wallet."

I'd heard about the silver knot. It was the traditional indication that a High Holder was displeased, and that, unhappily, strongly suggested that High Holder Ryel had something far worse in mind for me than a simple execution.

"You do seem to make powerful enemies, boy." That was Grandmama Diestra.

"It's hard not to when people are trying to kill you," I replied.

"If you weren't an imager, you'd long since have crossed the Bridge of Stones," offered Shelim.

"We all know that, Father," murmured Seliora.

"What about the Ferran?" I asked.

Betara shrugged. "He's local, but he's not. That is, he's been in L'Excelsis for years and years, but he wasn't born here, and he has no relatives here. He's an assassin, but no one has ever seen him when he's killed someone, and no one knows who hires him. But it's not someone that anyone in L'Excelsis seems to know."

All that seemed to say that three different people had wanted me dead—or worse, in the case of High Holder Ryel—for differing reasons. The good news was that one was dead, and the manner of his death meant that his friends were likely to forget coming after me. The bad news was that two others, who were clearly more dangerous, were still after me.

"That would say that the Ferran works for spies . . . or is he one?"

"Even spies need tools," Betara said. "The Ferran is a tool."

Whose tool? The other question was equally concerning. Just what was I getting into with Seliora? Anyone who had a family with contacts like theirs . . . I wanted to shake my head, but I just nodded.

"That's what we've been able to find out," Betara said.

"The best measure of a man is his enemies," offered Grandmama Diestra. "You're looking fairly tall for a young man."

I offered a laugh. "So long as I'm vertical and tall."

The three older family members laughed. Seliora only smiled, and I was glad for that.

"You're an imager who works at the Council Chateau," said Shelim. "Do you know what the Council is going to do about this coming war between Ferrum and Jariola?"

"No, sir."

"If you have to call me anything, Rhenn, just call me Shelim."

"I'll try . . ." I paused. "There's nothing that we've been told, but I thought that the Oligarch was the one who was pressing Ferrum."

Shelim shook his head. "The Ferrans need Jariolan coal for their ironworks, and they want it more cheaply than the Oligarchs want to sell it. They've got a modern standing army, and they're trying to get Khasis III and his council angry enough to declare war. That way, Ferrum can invade and claim self-defense and take the coal mines. They're close enough to the border that Ferrum could just annex that part of Jariola. . . ."

From there the discussion progressed on to the sorry state of the world.

"Is everyone ready for dinner?" That was Shomyr, who now stood in the space behind and between his mother and father. He grinned. "Cook is threatening to turn the tenderloins into jerky."

"You're just hungry," replied Shelim, "but we can continue the discussion at table." He rose.

We all moved to the long table set in the middle of the terrace. The sun was close to setting, low enough in the west that some of its light was already dimmed, and the breeze was a trace stronger. I was seated across from Seliora, if one place toward the doors. I could still look at her and easily hear what she said.

The first course was a cool duck and leek broth, something I'd never had before, but with the spices, it was refreshing and not too heavy. After that came fresh thin gourd strips, steamed, in pasta with a cream sauce, but, again, a light one. Then there were the venison tenderloins, marinated in some liquor diluted with what I thought might be Sanietra, and braised, served with boiled and fried dark rice with a naranje sauce.

Dessert was a Naclianan flan, with thin slices of fresh peaches on the side.

The whole time, everyone at the table discussed what was happening in the world—not trade, not furniture making.

Sometime after eighth glass had rung and Artiema had dropped behind the buildings flanking the river, while I had enjoyed the conversation and learned more than a few things, it was also more than clear that Seliora and I were not going to get any real time alone, and I was getting tired. It had been a long day. "I should be going before long," I murmured to Seliora.

"Before you go, Grandmama would like to see us alone— just over there at the small table on the east side, where we sat earlier."

I hadn't even noticed that her grandmother had left the main table.

We walked over.

"Just sit there, young man. You, too, Seliora." Her voice was firm, without the slightest trace of the age in her face and frame. Even if she hadn't been Seliora's grandmother, I would have obeyed.

She looked at me, except that it was more as though she

looked into me, through me, and beyond me—all at the same time. So, if with less intensity, did Seliora. Abruptly, the older woman shuddered, then took a long deep breath.

I looked to Seliora. She was pale.

Diestra looked to her granddaughter.

Seliora nodded.

"What is it?" I finally asked.

"It is better that we do not say much," Diestra spoke quietly, but firmly. "Has Seliora explained why?"

"Yes. If I understand correctly, I face danger, or dangers, and if you try to explain, the odds are much higher that I will face even greater dangers."

"That is so. The Collegium is not your enemy, but neither is it your friend."

"I think I already understand that. The Collegium acts on behalf of Solidar and of all imagers, not necessarily on my behalf."

The two nodded again.

"Make no enemies that you do not have to make, but make enemies rather than show weakness." Diestra smiled sadly. "That is the finest of lines to draw and the narrowest of paths to walk."

I understood that as well.

"Most important, always take care for your safety, no matter who or what presses you toward haste."

What that meant, I thought, was to hold shields anywhere outside a familiar dwelling or the Collegium.

There wasn't much to say after that, since neither Seliora nor her grandmama would have said more. So, after I offered my thanks to her parents, Seliora and I walked down the side staircase alone.

At the bottom, before stepping out into the main level foyer, she turned and threw her arms around me, holding me firmly and murmuring, "I do love you. Don't ever forget it. No matter what the temptations." Then, before I could question or protest, her lips found mine.

How long we clung to each other I wasn't certain, but I finally asked, "Next Samedi . . . for dinner? Without family?"

That brought a sad smile. "It might be best if we asked Odelia and Kolasyn to come with us. We could come back here later and talk on the east terrace."

"That's not a bad idea." Not ideal, but better than not seeing her.

"Odelia would like it, and Grandmama would approve."

After another long kiss, we left the landing and crossed the foyer to the front door.

"Good night." I paused. "Fifth glass on Samedi."

"Fifth glass." She walked down to the street level door with me, then unbolted it.

"You stay here."

She smiled and brushed my lips with hers, then stepped back and opened the door.

Of course, there was no hack nearby, and it took me almost a quarter glass, with Seliora watching, for me to hail one.

Just as he pulled up, almost at the same moment as I heard a single crack, a blow struck my shields, spinning me around and almost knocking me off my feet. As I straightened a second struck my shields, but braced as I was, I barely flinched.

I turned quickly, regaining my balance and glancing around. I thought I heard distant hurried steps fading away. In the darkness beyond the circles of light cast by the oil lamps of NordEste Design, I could see no sign of anyone. Neither moon was out, since Artiema had set earlier, and Erion had not risen. In that dimness, I didn't expect to discover the shooter, but felt I should look. I glanced back up the steps to where Seliora still held the door ajar.

"I'm all right," I called.

Then I walked to the hack. "I was a bit clumsy there. The Bridge of Hopes, if you will."

The driver's mouth opened, then shut. Finally, he said, "The Bridge of Hopes. Yes, sir."

At that, I climbed into the hack, still holding my shields and making certain that Seliora had closed the door.

Why had the assassin waited to shoot? And what had he used?

The only explanation I could come up with was that he wanted a witness of some sort. Either that or he'd had trouble with his weapon, and that didn't seem all that likely.

I didn't let down my shields until I was back in my quarters with the lock and bolt secured. I hoped I'd be able to sleep.

60

Acknowledging needs does not require disavowing them.

I woke up early on Solayi and immediately wrote a quick note to Seliora, reassuring her that I was unharmed and fine. Then I wrote a letter of thanks to her parents, even though I'd be able to post neither until Lundi. Almost none of the seconds and thirds were at breakfast, and I ate quickly and alone, then made my way to the library—in the building adjacent to the dining hall. I'd been there only a handful of times, basically to find out things for my essays for either Master Jhulian or Master Dichartyn.

The front foyer was dark, unlit, but the door was unlocked. That bothered me for a moment. Then I laughed. There wasn't any point in locking it, not in the middle of the Collegium. It would be difficult for an outsider to steal the volumes, and any insider who did risked so much that even the densest young imager would think twice.

In the dimness, it took me close to half a glass to find the D'Shendael book—*On Art and Society*. I could have lit the lamps, but since I didn't know where to look, and the library wasn't that dark, I would have spent even more time lighting than looking, and then I'd have had to snuff them all. I glanced at the title page and the dedication. It was merely to "The nameless artist who has made us who we are."

High Holder or not, I felt sorry for her.

I took the book with me, but I remembered to write it down on the check-out list before I carried it back to my quarters and began to read. I leafed through the pages, skipping over them. Still, I found myself caught by an occasional sentence or phrase.

Not only does the value of art to a society indicate that society's type and degree of civilization, but so also do the uses of art which are valued and those which are not, and the placement of each in the daily functions of that society . . .

The finest of lines separates the most inspiring and beautiful of art from that which is self-indulgent and decadent . . .

All art is political. Thus, an artist may support a society, oppose it, or stand outside it. Those who support are naïve or sycophantic; those who oppose are fools; and those who stand outside are hated by all . . .

After spending more time than I probably should have reading the book, I went to lunch, thinking that at least I could tell Khethila that I'd read a work of Madame D'Shendael.

The dining hall was even more deserted at lunch. I doubted that there were more than a score of imagers, and I thought I was the only third. After eating, I decided to risk matters. I returned to my quarters, slipped the letters into the inside pocket of my summer waistcoat, and set out. Remembering Seliora's cautions, especially after the night before, I raised full shields as I left the quadrangle. The day was far cooler with scattered clouds, some of them a dark gray that suggested a real possibility of rain later in the afternoon. Within less than a quarter glass I had walked over the Bridge of Desires, hailed a hack, and was on my way to NordEste Design, hopefully to see Seliora.

No one shot at me when I got out of the hack and walked

up the steps . . . and lifted and dropped the knocker—twice. I heard muffled footsteps, and, after several moments, Bhenyt and the twins opened the door.

"Master Rhennthyl, please come in," offered Bhenyt formally.

I didn't want to correct him. I just said, "Thank you."

"He's here, Aunt Seliora!" called Hanahra, or maybe it was Hestya. They were both smiling, as only girls who are almost women can smile a knowing smile that they feel but do not truly yet understand.

Seliora stood on the edge of the maroon Joharan carpet in the second-level entry foyer—alone except for Bhenyt and the twins. She was dressed less formally, in white linen trousers and a blouse, with a navy blue linen vest. She still looked lovely.

I stepped forward, stopping short of sweeping her into my arms.

"I thought you might come . . . after last night. I was certain you were hit by the bullets. I felt you weren't wounded, but I still worried."

I extracted the note from the inside pocket of the summer waistcoat. "I wrote a note, but I decided that delivering it personally was better. Even if you weren't here, someone would be able to let you know I was well."

She leaned forward and kissed my cheek.

Someone uttered a sound half between a giggle and a cough.

"Oh . . . since I'm here, would you give this to your parents." I handed her the other letter.

She took it and turned to the entourage. "You've all seen that he's here. Now you may go." Even though she smiled, there was cold iron behind the words.

"Yes, Aunt Seliora," the twins said, inclining their heads and not quite skipping toward the far end of the entry foyer. Bhenyt followed, then ducked into a doorway on the left.

"The twins called you 'aunt.' I thought they were Odelia's sisters."

"They are, but they always saw me as an aunt, and now it's

a habit, even for Bhenyt. Methyr thinks it's funny." Her face twisted into a wry smile. "He's like all younger brothers . . . difficult."

"I've never seen or heard . . . Aegina's husband." I wasn't quite certain how to phrase that.

"He was murdered five years ago."

I had to wonder how Grandmama Diestra took to having one of her daughters' husbands killed.

"Grandmama was not pleased. Neither were a few others, when she was finished."

"Ah . . . what happened?"

"Their dwellings caught fire. They died, but they were heroes because they died saving most of their families . . . except one older boy who was in the family . . . enterprises. He was also a hero. Grandmama paid for their funerals." She gestured toward the archway that led to the staircase. "We should go up to the east terrace. It will be empty, and since you've come so far, I'm sure you'd like to rest." She grinned. "I'd wager that it won't be a quarter glass before either Aunt Aegina, Odelia, or Mother arrives with some refreshments."

"Your chaperones are always so kind and thoughtful." I laughed as I accompanied her to the stairs.

We did enjoy a longer embrace on the landing halfway up.

The east terrace door was already propped open, and I had the sense that someone had left not too long before, a reminder that Seliora belonged to a family where there were few secrets among them, but where little went beyond the family. That realization concerned me, because I was being made almost part of the family.

I turned to her. "Is Kolasyn as warmly treated by the family?"

"He's a very nice person, kind and good," replied Seliora.

That was an answer. "Why me?"

"Because." That mischievous smile appeared for a moment.

I waited.

"We're linked . . . somehow . . . and we have to find out how."

"Pharsi far-seeing?"

"Grandmama, Mother, and I all sense it."

That was another answer, and a chilling one, in a way.

"And there's this." She wrapped her arms around me and kissed me.

I had no trouble responding. She had a very definite point there, and it went beyond that physical intensity. Not that I didn't very much enjoy the physical.

Once we were seated in the two chairs flanking the small circular table, Seliora turned to face me. "I had Bhenyt see if he could find the bullets this morning, as soon as it was light."

"Did he?"

She handed me a small felt bag across the table. "Grandmama says that they're from a sniper's rifle, but that the bullets are longer and heavier."

"Is there anything she doesn't know?" The bag felt heavier than I would have thought, and I untied it and eased the bullets out. Both were flattened, at an angle, and they were far longer and heavier than those that had been fired when I'd been attacked with the flower seller. After a moment, I replaced them in the bag and slipped it into my inside waistcoat pocket.

"Grandmama believes that you die when you stop learning. She has no wish to meet death any sooner than necessary."

"Do you follow her example?"

"I wouldn't dare not to." That mischievous smile reappeared momentarily.

"Do you know anything more about Madame D'Shendael?"

Seliora shook her head. "Why?"

"I have the feeling that somehow, she's involved in why people are targeting me, but I can't seem to discover any reason why." I went on to explain what I'd deduced. Master Dichartyn might not care for my revealing that to her, but I had the feeling that Seliora and her family were more than capable of holding secrets—and I needed all the help I could get, because I didn't see much of it coming from the Collegium at the moment.

"Grandmama could find out about her parents through Ailphens."

"Ailphens?"

"He's the advocate for NordEste. Since the mother was executed there will be a record somewhere."

Her matter-of-fact response underscored how little I knew about certain practical aspects of life.

"Rhenn . . ." Her voice was gentle.

"What?"

"We all have different talents. I never could have figured out that she was Grisarius's daughter. Our talents complement each other."

"You're also kind and diplomatic."

"Not to her family." Betara stood in the doorway to the terrace. "If she wants, she can peel varnish off finished wood—and hide—without ever raising her voice." She moved forward with the small tray that she carried, noiselessly.

"Mother . . ." Seliora was smiling.

"I did take the liberty of assuming you would still like Sanietra, along with the summer almond biscuits and the apple slices." The small platter with the dainties and fruit went in the middle of the front edge of the table, and a glass of Sanietra, with a napkin, beside each of us.

"That was a very good assumption," I replied with a smile.

"Grandmama was very pleased to meet you." Betara smiled, and I could see from where Seliora had gotten the mischievous expression. "I'll let Seliora fill you in. Enjoy yourselves. It is a beautiful afternoon." With a nod, she slipped away.

I lifted the tall narrow goblet. "To you and a beautiful afternoon."

She blushed, ever so slightly, as she lifted her own goblet. "To you."

I hadn't realized how dry my throat was until the Sanietra cooled and moistened it. "Very good . . . and timely. You and your mother do have a sense that way." As well as in other ways.

"I'm still learning."

"Your mother was offering a reminder."

"Mother can be very direct."

"And you'd prefer to be a little less so."

Seliora nodded. "But there's no help for it. It's as much about the family as about you. Grandmama feels everyone should either contribute to the family—or strike out on their own."

"She doesn't like the idea of the family supporting those who don't contribute at least their share."

"Or as much as they can, once they're grown." I had no idea where her words were leading.

"Contribution isn't just how one can add to the golds. We're not badly off that way."

I gestured to the building that surrounded us. "I can see. But you don't want men to know that. Wasn't that why you met me at the hall . . . and why Odelia does as well?"

She nodded. "Also, flaunting wealth is a form of Naming."

I could definitely see that.

"You must have guessed that Grandmama came out of the taudis. She's always said that she's done what she had to, but that she didn't have to like it . . . only do it well. To this day, she won't let anyone else talk to her oldest . . . acquaintances."

"That's all you have to say, I think."

Seliora raised her eyebrows. "I can finish it, but I'd be interested in how close you are."

"I'll try to put it in . . . general terms." I took another swallow of Sanietra. "Your grandmother wants the best for her family, and, frankly, I think you're her favorite. She also knows that it's very difficult to retain golds without various forms of power. One form is being able to provide a good or a service that is highly valued, and that is something that she and your mother and father have established with NordEste Design. I'd wager that your father is the best furniture crafter in L'Excelsis, and possibly was the very best without a guild patron or master. By emphasizing furniture with specialized textile upholstery, and with her taudis contacts, they created something unique."

Seliora nodded again. "Is that all?"

"Do you want me to go on?"

"No, but it's necessary. Just remember what I said to you last night . . . and that I asked you to dance before you became an imager."

Last night? I almost nodded somberly as I recalled her words.

"In a very general sense, power can come from two sources. One is the ability to apply force without using the established resources of a society. The other is the ability to use force sanctioned by society. Your grandmother retains the first ability. She's kept her children from that source, at least partly. But she's no longer young." I looked to Seliora, wondering if I'd said enough or too much.

Her face was a pleasant mask.

"Grandmama has been concerned for some time what will happen to the family, and her hope is that you—and whoever you choose—will save it." I laughed, ruefully. "That's quite a burden to put on you . . . or Odelia."

"You didn't mention Shomyr."

"He's too kind, I would judge, and Methyr's too young, and L'Excelsis still respects men in power, at least in officially sanctioned positions. There's only one high woman maitre in the Collegium, and look at the attacks Madame D'Shendael has undergone."

"You *knew* this?" Her voice was steady, but I could sense . . . something . . . behind it.

"Not until you said what you did about your grandmama. Then, all the pieces fit. I think I was feeling some of it, but I hadn't thought about it in that way before. I was just interested in you, even from that night last Fevier when you asked me to dance . . ."

I looked to Seliora, seeing the brightness of unshed tears. "To fall in love, and then to find that everyone looks to you . . . you're braver than I might be." I stood and eased around the table, drawing her to her feet and putting my arms around her.

For a long moment, she was as stiff as if she had been carved from ancient oak.

Then she clung to me, shuddering silently. Finally, she lifted her head and murmured softly, "I didn't want that. I wanted you. I want you."

"You and your grandmama are alike in one way," I said quietly, still holding her.

She looked up at me, questioningly, still holding me.

"You're both honest. She could have said nothing, just encouraged you, made things easy. You could have said nothing. Neither of you did. For that, I respect you both." I kissed Seliora gently.

What I didn't say was that her grandmama knew how to use honesty to the greatest effect . . . or that I might need Seliora and her family every bit as much as they needed me. But then, I doubted that I needed to say it. Seliora already understood that, whether she consciously knew it or not.

"You don't mind?"

"No. Not in the slightest." Perhaps strangely, I didn't. I'd already learned that having needs didn't make a person less—or more.

The kiss and embrace that followed my words made any words superfluous.

We had barely reseated ourselves and gained a measure of composure when I heard footsteps on the wooden floor of the short hallway from the main upper hall.

Seliora gave me a wry smile as she blotted her eyes. I only had to swallow several times.

Grandmama Diestra stepped out onto the porch, favoring one leg. She looked at Seliora, then at me. "I see you told him, girl."

"No, Grandmama. I offered him a few words, and he told me."

She looked at me. "Is that right?"

"Yes, madame."

She nodded. "You two are right for each other. That doesn't mean it will work out. Working it out means working it out. You're right for this family, Rhennthyl, and this family is right for you. Will that work out? I don't know. What I do know is that inside a family, or between a husband and a wife, secrets destroy trust. So does a failure to talk honestly and directly, but not hurtfully. Marriages and families are built on trust."

What could I say to that?

"What do you have to say about that, Rhennthyl?"

"Seeing what you want to see is another form of dishonesty. Are you seeing what you want or what really is?"

Diestra laughed. "That's a good question. Self-deception would destroy everything I've built, and I'm too old to bother with it. You've seen the dangers of self-deception in others. What about in yourself?"

"I'm too young to be expert in it, but it would be easy enough to fall into that habit."

"Fairly put." She nodded. "Whatever you two decide, decide it honestly." With that, she turned and left.

For a moment, Seliora and I just looked at each other.

"Is she always that direct?"

"When no one but family is present . . . always. With outsiders, sometimes. She was talking to you as family."

I took a long slow breath. "I've been avoiding it, but . . . you need to meet my family. It's not you; it's me. Mother has been after me to 'find the right girl' for years. But part of me worries that no one will be right so far as she's concerned because she's so into form and formality. Since I'm trying to be honest, there are two parts to that. The first part is that I don't want to face disapproval. The second part is that I don't want to put you through an examination and silent inquisition."

Seliora laughed.

"I didn't think it was funny."

The laugh turned into a gentle smile. "It's not. I worried horribly when you had to meet the family. I was laughing about your calling it the 'silent inquisition.' That is what mothers often do. So do sisters and cousins. I've done it to Odelia. Most men don't notice, or they pretend not to."

"Her previous escort?"

"He wasn't suitable."

"After what Grandmama Diestra just said, I'd hate to think

what she'd have said . . ." I shook my head. "She wouldn't have said anything, would she? I just wouldn't have ever been able to get in touch with you, except by literally kidnapping you, would I? And that would have been anything but wise."

"You understand more than you want to admit." After a pause, Seliora added, "When do you think the examination over dinner will take place?"

"I'd guess that Mother will want it on the twenty-eighth. Samedis are about the only truly free night I have right now, and I'd be surprised if Father will be back by this coming weekend. Mother is in Solis visiting Aunt Ilena. I'll have to write her about it, and she won't get a letter before Mardi, and it might not be until later in the week . . ."

Seliora nodded. "You'll let me know."

"I will indeed." The letter to my parents was one letter I wasn't looking forward to writing in the slightest.

Seliora turned and faced me, looking solemn. Then her grin appeared. "Since we've been ordered to be honest, tell me what you like best about me."

That was scarcely a trial. "I was stunned and bedazzled by the fact that you asked me to dance . . . and I still am. And what do you like about me?"

"That you could take the disappointment of leaving the guild and rebuild your life without self-pity . . ."

We spent more than a glass in that fashion, growing more serious as we talked, before I realized that I needed to go, a revelation hastened by several rolls of thunder from the approaching storm. Our parting was brief, if amorous, and I did manage to hail a hack and climb inside before raindrops began to splatter on the stone pavement of Nordroad.

I gave the hacker a three coppers extra, then hurried from the hack toward the bridge, with the rain pelting down around me. Along the way, I learned that even strong shields didn't stop rain . . . or not much, and I wondered why. I'd have to experiment with that—but not dressed as I was.

61

*Plaques held too close to the waistcoat can be so close
as not to be able to be played.*

Once I returned from services at the Imagisle anomen on
Solayi, I drafted and then re-drafted a letter to Mother. Then
I wrote it once more and set it aside. On Lundi morning, after
exercises and a run where I finished somewhat closer to
Dartazn, I struggled back to my quarters, showered, shaved,
and dressed. Then I read the letter a last time.

> *Dear Mother,*
> *For some time now, you have been suggesting that I needed
> to find a young lady who was intelligent, congenial, and
> suitable. In view of your wisdom in this matter, I have qui-
> etly been pursuing that objective and believe I have
> discovered such a young woman. Inasmuch as you have
> suggested that you would like to have me and a suitable
> young lady of my choosing to dinner, I would like to ask if
> that invitation remains open for me and Mistress Seliora
> D'Shelim.*
>
> *Rather than write too much about her, I will only say that
> she comes from a well-off and commercially successful
> family and is quite intelligent. She has a solid knowledge
> of the textile field and numerous manufacturers, and I be-
> lieve you will find her most charming.*

I signed, sealed, and addressed it, then tucked it into my
uniform—we were allowed to wear the Council uniforms to
breakfast—and headed to the dining hall. On the way in to

eat, I picked up one of the newssheets—*Veritum*—and scanned the lead story on the diplomatic communiqué sent from the High Priest of Caenen to the Council—and clearly leaked to the newssheet. Part of the quoted text read, ". . . we strive for a vision of Duality that is true to our faith but a vision that also encompasses peace and prosperity for all Terahnar . . ." The story also noted that the Caenenan forces near the border with Tiempre had "completed their training maneuvers" and were returning to their regular bases.

Another story near the bottom of the front side of the sheet reported on a series of explosions in near-abandoned dwellings in taudis in Nacliano near Estisle, Liantiago near Westisle, and a particularly large explosion in the "area known as the hellhole" near L'Excelsis. Civic patrollers found a number of bodies, as well as materials and weapons linked to a "certain foreign government." The exact causes of the explosions were unknown, but thought to be the "accidental" detonation of unstable explosives.

At that moment, Dartazn gestured, and I joined him, Martyl, and Nansyar, a third I knew only by name and face.

"I see you were reading about the strange and wondrous events in the world."

I nodded as I poured some tea. "The events in Caena were strange and wondrous, but not unexpected. I'd hope that the cost wasn't another name on a plaque."

"As do I," added Martyl, "but that's something we'll just have to wait out."

"What do you think about the taudis explosions?"

"Pure happenstance." Dartazn's words were edged with irony overlaid with gentle sarcasm. "What do you think?"

"About the same."

Nansyar glanced from Dartazn to me, and then to Martyl. "I hate it when you covert types do that."

"We all have our little secrets," said Martyl, with a laugh. "You don't tell us what goes on in the armory laboratories."

After that, we talked about how the communiqué might affect the situation between Ferrum and Jariola. About all we agreed upon was that the cooling down in Otelyrn would allow the Navy to move most of its warships to the waters off Jariola and Ferrum. Then we took the duty coach to the Council Chateau, where I did post the letter, but where nothing unusual or of import occurred on Lundi . . . or Mardi.

On Meredi morning, though, right after we arrived, Baratyn gathered us together. He smiled, not unkindly, as he glanced at the three of us. "We are approaching the end of Agostos, and I imagine some of you know what that means."

Dartazn nodded solemnly. Martyl showed no expression, and I just stood there, not having any idea what Baratyn meant.

"On the last Friday of Agostos, Vendrei, the thirty-fourth, is the annual Harvest Ball of the Council. You will be present, and in addition to keeping your eyes open and your abilities ready, you will be expected to dance, when necessary and if asked, or if you see a lady in an embarrassing situation and clearly needing a partner. This takes precedence over all other personal and professional engagements, unless directly mandated otherwise by Master Dichartyn. Is that clear? Good. Now for today. The Council will be debating the communiqué from Caenen, and the Executive Council has decreed that no visitors or petitioners will be received."

After Baratyn dismissed us to our assignments, I turned to Dartazn. "Why is this ball on a Vendrei?"

"I'm glad I wasn't the only one to ask that. I did, two years ago. Master Dichartyn was not kind." He smiled. "It was originally a function only for High Holders, and having it on Vendrei made the point that the common working and trade types could not have attended even if they so wished."

"Even when the Councils then had guild and factor councilors?"

He nodded. "The Executive Council was composed of High Holders for the first century. It was also a way of emphasizing their . . . superiority."

I'd forgotten the early makeup of the Executive Council. "Thank you."

Right after a very short break for a bite to eat just after noon, Baratyn walked over to where I was watching the upper west corridor.

"Master Dichartyn sent a message. You're to report to his study as soon as you return to the Collegium this afternoon."

"Yes, sir. Did he say why?"

Baratyn offered a wry smile. "He never does."

I hadn't seen Master Dichartyn since the previous Vendrei, but that was no surprise.

Once I got back to the Collegium, I didn't go straight to the administration building, but made a very slight detour through my quarters to pick up the felt bag Seliora had given me. Then I continued on to his study.

The door was closed, and I knocked.

"Come in, Rhennthyl, and close the door."

I did, and then took the seat before his desk.

"What have you been up to?" Master Dichartyn still looked tired. "What have you discovered?"

"Were all the explosions mentioned in *Veritum* what you used to deal with spies?" I asked in return.

"Rhennthyl . . ."

I ignored the stern tone and dropped the bag with the bullets in it on the writing desk. Even through the cloth, they made a satisfactory clunk. "These were fired at me on Samedi night."

"I'd appreciate it if you would provide a somewhat longer explanation, Rhenn."

I did, without details about exactly where I had been or with whom, just that I'd been hailing a hack on Nordroad at the time I'd been fired upon.

When I had finished, he took the bag, eased the bullets out of it, and examined them. Then he looked at me again. "What flattened them?"

"My shields. What else? The Ferran, if that's who it was, is a very good shot."

Master Dichartyn gave a low whistle. "If I'm not mistaken, those are from a Ferran sniper's rifle—but a midrange weapon, with a more massive bullet. It's designed to penetrate more than flesh—unarmored carriages, for example. It is a good thing you've been working on your shields."

At that point, I wanted to strangle him. I forced a smile.

"I understand your position, sir, and the idea that there are things I should not know because I have no need to know. I am very junior in your organization. There isn't anyone any more junior. But . . . if you will pardon me, I am getting very tired of being a target and not knowing why." I wanted to point out that I doubted many imagers could have survived those bullets, and that it might not be a bad idea to give me more information if he wanted to keep that talent around the Collegium. I didn't. I wanted to see what he'd say. Besides, it was clear that withholding information worked two ways, and not telling him that I knew what he wasn't saying might work to my advantage. The way things were going, silence couldn't work any more to my disadvantage than offering more than he asked for. For the sake of the Nameless, and with a quick silent prayer not to let me fall prey to the Namer, I hoped so.

"Rhennthyl . . ." That single word carried great exasperation.

I ignored it and replied politely, "Yes, sir?"

He looked at me, attempting intimidation.

I returned the look, not bothering to look away. I didn't feel antagonistic; I just didn't feel like being subservient. I also held full shields, if very close to me.

After a moment, he nodded, then spoke. "You know how few imagers we have, and even fewer have the capabilities you and those like you possess. How can we question everyone about everything? Even if we had enough imagers, or could use all the civic patrollers, do you think that the citizens of L'Excelsis would put up with it for long?"

"No, sir. They're wary of us as it is."

"Every action has a link to something, and if we can make our enemies act, then that proves their danger and also provides that link. One of our duties—mine and yours—is simply to be targets, to offer our enemies someone and something at which to strike, so that we can discover them and destroy them. Why do you think Maitre Dyana and I have spent so much time and effort on building your shields and your techniques with them?"

"So that I can be a target and survive, clearly."

"And so that others can as well," he said gently. "Every single time you, Martyl, Dartazn, or Baratyn, or the others, remove someone who is a danger, you reinforce the Collegium, and Solidar. Every time you survive an assassination attempt you do the same."

"Sir . . . won't people learning that make them even more afraid of us?"

"Think about it, Rhenn. How many people does an assassin dare tell? And what did that hack driver see? He saw you fall or get knocked down. You got up and took the hack. That's dangerous? The only one who's likely to feel fear is the assassin."

He did have a point there.

"Is that all you've discovered?"

"I've also learned a few other things, sir. Diazt's brother—he was a taudischef in the hellhole—took out a contract on me . . . for ten golds. After I killed the first assassin, he tried to recover the golds and was garroted. The garrote rope held a silver knot, but there have been two attempts on me since then, presumably not from Diazt's family or the source of the silver knot."

"Where did you find this out?"

"I promised I wouldn't tell anyone, sir. It was hard enough to find it out as it was, and I'd like to be able to ask again, if I need to."

"If that's the way it is, that's the way it is." He paused. "You didn't promise anything that might compromise—"

"No, sir. There's no crime or wrongdoing involved."

"How did you . . ." He shook his head. "All I can say, Rhennthyl, is that you had best keep improving your imaging abilities." He paused. "Unless you hear from me, you're to meet with Maitre Dyana tomorrow evening at seventh glass in the corridor outside the dining hall. You need to learn about poisons. A great deal, before it's too late." He stood, stifling a yawn.

"Oh . . . one other thing, sir. I did discover the name of the woman in the miniature. A later etching is in one of her books."

"You don't give up, do you?"

"Would you, sir?"

He gave me a wry smile. "I'd appreciate it if you'd keep that to yourself. The fewer who discover we know that, the better the chance we have to use that knowledge to find out who's shooting at you, and those other junior imagers who have not been fortunate enough to have your skills." He stifled another yawn. "Good evening, Rhennthyl."

There wasn't much else I cared to say. I nodded. "Good evening, sir."

Then I went back to my quarters and changed into my imager grays before going to dinner. When I got to the dining hall, I found Martyl with Menyard and Reynol, and we sat near the head of the table. I was more than a little surprised to see Master Dichartyn at the masters' table, because he almost never was there for dinner, not that I'd expected it, since he had a wife and children. With him was another man I'd never seen, perhaps ten years older than I was.

"Who's the master with Dichartyn?" I asked Martyl.

"He has to be another master, but I've never seen him. He might be from Estisle or one of the other Collegia."

"Or a regional," added Reynol.

"Regional?" I'd never heard of the term.

"Could be," mused Martyl. "They report periodically to Master Dichartyn."

"What's a regional?" I finally asked.

"A regional representative of the Collegium. All the cities that don't have Collegia have them, and some of the larger towns do. They're . . . well . . . let's say that they operate sort of like field types do, except inside Solidar."

For a moment, I just sat there, holding my wineglass. Then I took a sip. There was nothing in any of what I had read about regionals, but then there was nothing about silent guards or covert imagers, either. The more I learned, the more I realized how little I'd known . . . and perhaps still did.

62

*Well-chosen words create pain that lasts longer
than that from a flogging.*

When I returned from the Council Chateau on Jeudi, I found
a letter awaiting me in my letter box. It was addressed to me
in Mother's perfect script, and she must have dispatched it by
special messenger, rather than by regular post. After looking
at it several times, I broke the seal right there in the corridor,
opened it, and began to read.

> *Dear Rhennthyl,*
> *I was delighted to receive your letter, which arrived at the*
> *house in my absence, and I am most certain that your father*
> *will be equally pleased, especially if you have found a young*
> *woman of suitable background and intelligence. Knowing*
> *that you have found someone suitable in background and*
> *demeanor would bring great happiness to both of us.*
>
> *Of course, we would be more than delighted to meet her*
> *over dinner here at the house, and, if you have no objec-*
> *tions, we would suggest next Samedi, the twenty-eighth, at*
> *fifth glass.*
>
> *Khethila was pleased that you stopped by the factorage, as*
> *am I. It never hurts to have a male relative of such import*
> *appear. Upon reading your letter, which I did share with*
> *her, she mentioned that you had declined an invitation to*
> *dine with her, and that the reasons for that demurral were*
> *obvious in light of your letter. Like your father and me, she*
> *looks forward to meeting Mistress Seliora D'Shelim.*

The implications were clear enough. While I knew Seliora was certainly up to the not-so-silent inquisition, I wasn't certain that I would be.

The only other notable aspect of Jeudi was my meeting with Maitre Dyana. She was as composed, as direct, and as contemptuous of foolishness and thoughtless questions as ever, as when I offered a question as to why there was such sudden urgency in my learning about poisons.

"Why indeed? Dear boy, please think. You have shields as strong as any imager, and stronger than most. They could be far more effective if you would practice finesse as well, but you are young, and finesse is seldom appreciated by the young and strong, not until they have been defeated by old age and treachery, both of which are far more effective than thoughtless youth and strength."

She'd as much as admitted that, were I careful, my shields would protect me against direct attacks. "That suggests that I will be placed in situations where I will be vulnerable to such treachery."

"Brilliant. Positively brilliant. Now . . . might we continue?" Without waiting for a response, she pointed to the goblets lined up on the conference table of the chamber where she had instructed me before. "What you need to do is image the tiniest bit of the wine or whatever you suspect onto a test paper strip and watch. The paper strips are treated. If it's a cyanotic poison . . . the strip will turn green, if joraban, a maroon . . ."

I could see a problem there.

"Yes?"

"If there's joraba in red wine . . ."

"You don't need to worry about that. You can only put joraba in clear liquids. Its nature is such that it tends to change the colors of anything. But . . ." She shrugged. ". . . that does mean you need to be aware of the proper colors of various wines. That is one reason why High Holders are such experts on vintages. Those who are not often suffer strange and fatal maladies . . ."

I had no doubt that the coming sessions with Maitre Dyana would be even more painful.

63

*Rain, shadows, and sunlight all conceal and reveal,
just in different fashions.*

Vendrei was without incident, excepting for another long
evening session with Maitre Dyana. So was early Samedi
morning, except that we had to run through a heavy rain, and
my exercise clothes were sodden by the time I returned to my
quarters. Even so, I managed to get to breakfast, eat, and
arrive at my makeshift studio with enough time to get my
paints set up and even get in a little work on the background
of the portrait before Master Poincaryt arrived punctually at
the first bell of eighth glass.

Recalling his "homily" about observation, I watched as he
entered the studio, noting how, without seeming to, he sur-
veyed me and the entire space of the converted workroom
before taking his seat. I could see that might also be a good
habit to form.

As he sat down, he smiled. "Yes . . . I do. Most covert
imagers learn that early, if they survive."

"I'm still working on what you suggested, sir."

"You're still young enough that such intensity can be taken
for interest. As you get older, you will have to learn observation with circumspection, but by then, you should be able to
pick up on what you see and sense almost without thinking
about it." He laughed. "Among the High Holders, observation is played as a game, if one with very high stakes. The
one who can learn the most while revealing the least is usually the winner."

In that sense, I'd just lost . . . but I'd learned in doing so.
"If you would turn your head to the left, just a touch, sir?"

I painted for a solid glass, a little tentatively at first, because I hadn't been working with the brushes all that much, but I could feel the touch come back before long. I managed to get most of the area around his forehead and eyes, as well as finish the nose, and get the shape of the jaw set with the underlying base.

As the first of the nine bells rang, Master Poincaryt rose. "I hope you will pardon me, Rhennthyl, but I do have a meeting with High Councilor Suyrien and Councilor Rholyn."

"Yes, sir. I trust it will go well."

"One never has a meeting without knowing exactly how it will go and how to ensure that it does." He smiled warmly. "Otherwise, what is the point?"

After he left, I thought about his parting words. He'd as much as said that he would be controlling the meeting between Rholyn, the councilor who represented the Collegium on the Council, and High Councilor Suyrien, the High Holder who chaired the executive committee of the Council, and who, in effect, spoke for the Council and all of Solidar. That also suggested that such a meeting was necessary, and that, at the least, there was not total agreement between Suyrien and the Collegium. I had no doubts there would be agreement when the meeting ended.

I spent almost another full glass working on the portrait, because I felt I needed to do so, but as I cleaned up, I realized another aspect of the Collegium. Master Poincaryt had come from the covert branch now headed by Master Dichartyn, and that suggested to me that Master Dichartyn might well be being prepared to become Master Poincaryt's successor.

The Collegium was almost completely deserted by noon, and I ate with Reynol, who complained about having to deal with "great complexities" in the Collegium accounts, making things balance so that everything appeared in its proper place when the accounts were presented to the Council.

"To the Council?" I took a mouthful of saoras, thin strips of goose fried in spice oil, then covered with cheese and baked in a puff pastry.

"Absolutely. We provide services to the Council, for which

we are paid. The armory has contracts with the Navy, that sort of thing. Even the . . . well . . . let us just say that almost every part of the Collegium provides goods or services to someone, and we receive an annual payment from the Council for resolution."

"Does that mean resolution of the imager problem, by training them, and keeping them from being a problem, so to speak?"

"It's not spelled out anywhere, and it dates back centuries. That's all I know. Some things account clerks don't ask about." Reynol did smile.

I sipped the wine, a slightly bitter white plonk I couldn't identify. "Why do you think other lands don't have something like the Collegium?"

"Why would they want them? Half of them don't want imagers because their religion or faith or what have you says we're evil and unnatural. The others either tolerate them with restrictions or quietly force them out or kill them because they don't fit."

I had to think about that. "You mean because absolute rule, like in Caenen, can be turned upside down with imagers who can kill tyrants without ever being detected?"

"Right. But even outside influence worries those in power. In Jariola, there are really only forty-five members of the oligarchy. That's hereditary. What if an imager went around killing, over time, those members with a given view? That could change things, and they don't want change. In Ferrum, they believe in using machines and foreign contract workers to keep wages and costs low. That reduces the power of the guilds—they really don't have them the way we do—and increases the power of the factors. They don't even have anything like High Holders, only the wealthiest of merchants. A Collegium in Ferrum would certainly reduce the power of the merchanters."

"So, for different reasons, neither Ferrum nor Jariola cares for imagers. What about Tiempre?"

"They're crazy. They have this idea that any talent that only a few people have is the mark of Bius, the black demon, because Puryon, their oh-so-just god, bestows the potential for every true believer to have the same abilities as any other, if in differing levels, if they only believe. So all imagers are demons."

"How can they believe that? People are different."

Reynol just laughed. I had to as well.

After lunch, I found a shaded bench on the eastern side of Imagisle on the north end where there was a slight breeze off the water and sat down to try to think.

What had I discovered about those trying to kill me, and how had I discovered what I had? In the simplest sense, I had observed and talked to people. The problem now was that I had few enough people left with whom I could talk that I had not already contacted. But it could be that I'd been looking at the problem in the wrong way. A number of junior imagers had been killed over the past half year, and none of them had angered High Holder Ryel or taudischef Artazt. Some had been killed even before I'd entered the Collegium, and there were killings still happening, if intermittently. Why? Just because someone didn't like imagers?

For a time, I just sat there, looking at the river, but I didn't come up with any sort of answer. Yet . . . there was something. I just couldn't see what it was.

Because I had a very strong feeling that trying to run down Elphens or other portraiturists wasn't going to tell me any more, I finally returned to my quarters and read, mostly from *On Art and Society*. I didn't know that I agreed with much of what I read. Juniae D'Shendael's commentary did spark speculation, particularly her assertion that the reason there were virtually no women artists was because, historically, no one wanted to invest in training a woman when she had a fifty percent chance of dying in childbirth, and being surrounded by males, she would likely have a hundred percent chance of becoming pregnant. After having a child, she'd be able to devote less time to art and would require more food, especially if nursing.

I'd have to caution Khethila about not quoting too liberally from that volume.

At half past four, I was in a hack headed for Nordroad and Hagahl Lane. I had slipped a set of poison testing strips inside my waistcoat, not that I expected to be poisoned, but for practice. A very light drizzle had begun to fall, and I wished that I had an umbrella, not for me, but for Seliora.

I arrived almost a quarter glass early, but, seemingly as always, Bhenyt opened the door.

"Master Rhennthyl, please come in."

"Are you the permanent doorman?" I asked jokingly.

"I like to see who's coming, and, besides, Mother says it's a way to meet people." He smiled. "Aunt Seliora gives me things, too."

Bhenyt carefully slid the lock and the bolt in place, and then we walked up the steps, where he took his leave.

I waited for a time in the main-level entry hall, taking in the paintings set at intervals, as well as the hangings. I had a feeling about one of them, an elaborate geometric design of silver and dark gray on a rich green. It was far newer than the others. I didn't recognize any of the paintings, all of them landscapes or city scenes, although I thought one of the scenes looked like it might have been painted by Elphens or his former master—except it was signed by someone called Arhenyt, who from the style might have been Rhenius's father.

Although I heard no steps, I sensed someone and turned to see Seliora entering the main hall from the archway leading to the stairs. She wore a black dress with a brilliant filmy green vest, trimmed in silver, with a silvery scarf.

"Do you all move so quietly?" I grinned.

"No. Shomyr and Father shake the stairs and the floor." Seliora gave me a warm embrace and a gentle but quick kiss before stepping back. "Have your parents returned?"

"I received a reply from Mother late on Jeudi, and a letter to you wouldn't have gotten here much before I did."

Seliora raised her eyebrows. "And?"

"Because we're being honest, you can read her response." I handed her the envelope.

She extracted the letter, slowly reading it. Then she looked up and smiled, enigmatically.

I wasn't about to ask what lay behind the expression. I knew. I also knew that Mother was in for something she had never encountered, not even with Remaya, who was a house cat compared to Seliora's mountain cougar.

"You're smiling," Seliora said.

"I think I'll enjoy observing next weekend."

"You can be evil, Rhenn. I'll be as charming as I know how."

"And you say I'm evil?"

That got me another enigmatic sidelong glance. "Where might we be going to dine?"

"I'd thought that the Promenade might be good."

"Could we try Terraza?"

"It's better, I take it?" I'd never heard of it.

"It is. You also don't pay for what you don't get."

"Odelia and Kolasyn?"

"I thought we could meet them there."

I just offered a shrug and a grin.

As we headed down the steps to the door, Seliora gestured. "In the closet at the bottom of the stairs, there are several umbrellas."

After finding the closet, I took a large navy blue umbrella and then held it over Seliora as she used a brass key to lock the door behind us. We had to wait a bit to hail a hack, and for that I was glad for the umbrella, not so much for me as for Seliora.

If it had not been for the misting rain—and the exposure—Terraza would have been almost close enough to walk, only about a mille, just around the corner on a narrow lane off the Boulevard D'Este, not all that far from Master Kocteault's, I realized, when we got out of the coach-for-hire.

Not only that, but Odelia and Kolasyn already had a table, a circular one in the far corner, perhaps the best in the restaurant. The woman who guided us there only glanced at me perfunctorily, after admiring, if most covertly, what Seliora wore.

Terraza itself was a good three times the size of Lapinina, but only half that of Felters. The walls were a simple and clean white plaster, with brick pillars showing, and the floor was a clean dark gray tile. All the tables had white cloths, and the wall lamps were of antique brass, frequent enough so that it wasn't gloomy, but warm in feeling.

Odelia smiled as I seated Seliora, then murmured just loud enough for us to hear. "That was quite an entrance. Everyone kept looking at you two."

"They were looking at Seliora," I pointed out, "not me."

"Any time a beautiful woman appears, escorted by a tall, muscular, and impressive-looking imager, people will look," Kolasyn replied.

"That's no reason," I said with a laugh.

"For some people, it is," replied Odelia.

A serving girl appeared with two bottles of wine, one red and one white.

"I ordered their house wines," Odelia explained. "They're good."

I managed not to laugh. Odelia and Seliora were definitely better off not being High Holders, not from what I'd heard about the way High Holders treated their wives and daughters.

I decided on the red wine, although I couldn't have said why. It was light, like a Dhuensa, but had a stronger and fruitier taste, yet I liked it. I lifted the glass to Odelia. "You were right. This is good."

She smiled, and her eyes flicked to Seliora.

This time, I did laugh as I turned to my partner. "You told her what to order?"

"I just suggested." Her voice was low and demure, and I could see the mischievous grin struggling to appear.

"Have you ordered everyone's dinner as well?" My tone was light because I was actually enjoying the banter, and I could barely keep from laughing again.

"You're right," interjected Odelia. "He does have a sense of humor."

The serving girl appeared. "The special tonight is lamb tournedos, with mint yogurt, blue glacian potatoes, and spice-steamed summer beans. . . ." She went on to list more entrees than I could remember fully, which was fine, because I wanted the lamb.

Once she was finished, I nodded to Seliora.

"The greens and fowl with the Cambrisan reduction."

"The roast mushrooms and the duck confit," added Odelia.

"The same for me," said Kolasyn.

"Greens and the lamb special . . . pink, not red," I said.

After she left, there was a moment of silence. I looked to Kolasyn, perhaps because he had said so little and I so much. "You were talking about reasons why people do things. Do people really have reasons?" As I talked, I slipped out one of the testing strips, holding it well below the edge of the table, and concentrated on imaging the tiniest drop of wine from Seliora's narrow goblet.

He smiled, then shrugged. "I think so. With people, there's a reason for everything. The trick is to figure out the reason. Sometimes, they don't even know it themselves, but if you can discover it, then you have an advantage."

"Are you sure that everyone has a reason?" asked Seliora, her voice carrying genuine interest. "Besides just having to act?"

I imaged another drop of wine, this time from my goblet.

"If they didn't have some reason," Kolasyn replied, "no one would do anything. Maybe they're hungry, or tired . . . or just don't want to leave a decision to their wife . . ."

I did grin at that.

I also got a very gentle elbow in the ribs.

The testing strip showed nothing abnormal in either Seliora's wine or mine.

At that point the first course arrived.

Between the food and the conversation, light as it was, everyone seemed to enjoy the dinner. I also tested the wine and the sparkling water that Odelia had asked for.

Then, just as the server set the lemon tart that was my dessert before me, Seliora glanced toward the frosted-glass door of Terraza. That was the second time she'd done that, I realized. I leaned toward her and asked in a murmur, "Someone out there?"

"Rhenn . . ."

"If I know what's there," I replied in a low voice, "I'll be fine. I don't want anyone else around." I slipped from my chair. "If you all will excuse me for a moment . . . I need to stretch. Some of the exercises and running may be catching up with me. I should only be a moment."

Seliora's glance all but screamed "Take care!"

I was holding full shields as I stepped out into the continuing light drizzle, and I had them angled, in a way that even Maitre Dyana might have actually approved.

The first bullet barely shook me. I turned, looking through the misty evening, then saw the muzzle flash from beside the trunk of a tree less than twenty yards to my left, across the narrow lane. The jolt staggered me, but only for an instant.

I imaged oil across the stones of the sidewalk behind the tree, since I couldn't make out any figures. Rather I tried, because the oil just formed a momentary tent in midair before slipping to the ground as two men sprinted from the tree and up an alley. One of them had used an imager's shield. An imager's shield?

I started after them, then slowed as I heard hoofs on pavement, but I went far enough to see down the alley and make sure that they had indeed left and that the alley was empty. Then I walked back to the restaurant, realizing that the shield I had encountered hadn't really been so much strong as different, and that if I'd had a moment longer, I might have gotten through it. Had that been why the two had fled?

One had to be an imager, the other probably the Ferran. What chilled me as much as the presence of an unknown imager was the fact that someone knew where I'd be and when. The imager's presence also confirmed that Emanus's death was not accidental and had a part in matters, even if inadvertent, but it still made no sense to me, except that it did suggest that Emanus had known something that the imager believed I now knew. But what could that be?

Before reentering the restaurant, I glanced around again, but the street was empty, not surprisingly, given the rain.

"Do you feel better?" asked Seliora as I returned, after wending my way around several tables.

"The cooler air helped." I smiled, then sat down again, murmuring to her, "Everything's fine. They've gone."

Odelia raised an eyebrow, but I just smiled, before taking a bite of the lemon tart. It was every bit as good as the rest of the meal had been. Seliora had a thin slice of almond cake, drizzled with chocolate.

Surprisingly, at least to me, the total for all four of us was only a bit over six silvers, a healthy sum, but not what it could have been.

When we left Terraza, Odelia gave Kolasyn a hug and a kiss, and then joined us for the hack ride back to NordEste Design. I thought Kolasyn looked a bit dejected as he started to walk down the Boulevard D'Este.

Once we were back at Seliora's, Odelia vanished, and Seliora and I made our way up to the east terrace. Through the mist and the rain, we could barely see three blocks, and certainly not even a fraction of the distance to Martradon. In the darkness, the terrace was cool, but not uncomfortable, especially not after the long embrace that Seliora bestowed upon me as soon as we were clearly alone. We did move the chairs so that we sat side by side, with no table between us.

"I was worried when you went outside at Terraza. What happened?"

"There were two of them. One fired. I tried to image oil so that they'd slip, but I couldn't see them, and it didn't quite work. They had a coach or trap or something around the corner and were gone before I could get close."

"Someone with golds, then."

"Someone who knows imagers, too. They never let me get a moment's look at them." That was as much as I wanted to say about that, at least until I talked to Master Dichartyn.

"They're watching you, aren't they? What can you do?"

"Be careful, and try to learn more. I don't know what else I can do. Do you?"

Her fingers tightened around mine. "No. I wish I did."

"Has your solicitor found out anything about Madame D'Shendael? I still think there's a connection."

"I had to go through Grandmama on that. Yesterday, she said it was taking longer than Ailphens thought, but there might be something."

"Did she say what?"

Seliora shook her head.

"Since we can't solve any of those problems, not now anyway," I said, "tell me what your best memory is of when you were little."

"Little or really little?"

"Let's start with really little."

"That was the time that Grandmama and Mother took me to Extela one winter. I don't remember why they went, but they took me, and I got to play in the snow, real snow, and there was this fuzzy black puppy . . ."

We talked for more than a glass, before I thought I heard steps, quiet ones. I turned in the dimness to look directly at Seliora.

She smiled, and nodded, and we got up.

After a time, we stepped apart.

"I'd like to see you tomorrow . . ."

"I'd like to see you, but it is the twins' birthday, and it should be their special day. Also, perhaps you should see your parents. It might not hurt."

She was right about that, much as I hated to admit it.

In the hack on the way back to the Bridge of Hopes, something Kolasyn said came back to me. "With people, there's a reason for everything . . . the trick is to figure out the reason."

What were the simplest reasons to kill junior imagers? Because it was harder to kill senior imagers? Because if someone killed junior imagers . . .

I swallowed. Could it be that simple? That cold? And if so, why hadn't Master Dichartyn mentioned it? Or was I supposed to tell him—again?

64

❧

*To those who fail to understand, the most fantastic
in life remains disappointing.*

For all the excitement of Samedi, I did sleep soundly that
night, well enough that I did not wake until well after breakfast, possibly because the day was so dark and gray, although
the rain had stopped. Since Master Dichartyn didn't have the
duty, he wasn't around, and I had no way to reach him easily.
Besides, what could he have done to track down an unknown
imager on a Solayi? I'd certainly let him know on Lundi. So I
just took my time, still pondering over the strange shield used
by the Ferran's accomplice, and thinking about how I might
overcome it should I again come into contact with its wielder.

Menyard was the only third I knew well at lunch, and I
joined him and several others, but mostly, I just listened and
ate. After lunch, I crossed the Bridge of Hopes, holding full
shields, something that was no longer much of an effort, and
took a hack out to my parents' dwelling.

Mother actually was the one to open the door. "Rhenn!
What a pleasant surprise." Her smile was certainly welcoming. "Your father will be so pleased."

I followed her into the family parlor, closing the door
behind me. Khethila was lounging in Father's chair, reading
something, but it wasn't one of the D'Shendael books.

"Do have a seat, dear. I'll tell your father that you're here."

Khethila closed the book and moved to the settee. "I want
to hear all about her."

"In a moment," I replied, not that I was about to tell anyone anything more than the absolute minimum. "Have you
yet read *On Art and Society*?"

"The bookshop hasn't found a copy yet."

"I've read several chapters . . ." I grinned.

"You have it?"

"The Collegium library does. I was able to borrow it." I glanced toward the back hall leading to Father's private study. "Don't let Father see it. I'd suggest not quoting from it."

"I'll like it, then?"

"It might make even you think differently."

"How?"

"She says that financial pressures and childbirth are why there have been almost no women artists. Also that art can easily become a male pretension."

"She really wrote that?" Khethila frowned.

"You'll have to read it yourself." I looked down the hall. "Father's on his way."

She gave me a mock glare, which vanished as Culthyn hurried in and plopped himself on the settee next to her.

Once Father arrived in the family parlor and seated himself, Mother settled down in her chair and looked at me. I ignored the look and sat in the straight-backed chair that was at an angle to both the settee and Father.

"Tell us something about her, Rhenn," Mother pressed.

"Where should I start?" I smiled. "Let me see. Her eyes are stars on a moonless night, her hair darker than jet ebony, her lips redder than flame, her skin fairer than Artiema full at harvest . . ."

"That's poetry stuff," complained Culthyn. "You mean she's got really black hair and red lips? She can't have white eyes like the stars."

When Culthyn talked that way, he reminded me of Rousel at that age, and it wasn't a pleasant memory.

"You could be a little less poetic, dear," suggested Mother.

"She has black hair, not quite shoulder length when it's down. Her eyes are black, the irises, that is, and she's about a head shorter than I am."

"That still makes her tall for a woman," Father said.

"Not compared to her cousin. Odelia is almost as tall as I am."

"What else?" prompted Mother. "What about her family?"

"They're well off. That, I can assure you. She has a brother a bit younger than Culthyn, and another brother who's a bit older than I am, I think."

"You don't know?" asked Khethila.

"I didn't ask. I'm interested in her, not them."

Culthyn grinned.

"She's involved in the family business, and they make custom and quite costly furniture, usually for High Holders."

"Exactly what does she do?" pressed Father.

"Believe it or not, it's rather technical, and she can explain it far better than I can, and I'm certain she will be more than happy to do so next week. Oh, she's also a very good dancer, far better than I am, and she has a good sense of humor, and a nice smile."

"Is she fat?" asked Culthyn. "You didn't say she was pretty."

Both Mother and Khethila glared at him. Under the pressure of two sets of eyes, he shrank back into the sofa.

"No, she's not fat. You'll see."

"Your description about her suitability leaves a great deal of room, Rhenn," Mother said.

"I've discovered that sometimes it's best not to say too much. Seliora is very open, and I'm sure you can determine what you think next week after meeting her."

"Seliora . . . that sounds like . . ."

"She's Pharsi . . . but they've lived in L'Excelsis for at least three generations."

"Remaya is a lovely girl," Mother offered.

That was a concession it had taken her ten years to make, although I wasn't about to complain, since I hoped it would make matters easier for Seliora . . . and me.

"Remaya's a woman with a child, not a girl," Father said with a gruff laugh.

After a moment where no one spoke, Culthyn looked at me. "Rhenn, you promised you'd show me what imagers do. You promised."

I thought about that for a moment. It might keep the subject changed, and I was no longer forbidden to use imaging, but I had to use it appropriately, of course. "All right." I glanced to the bookshelf, then smiled. At one end of a line of books was a bookend, a marble L shape with a crystal globe anchored to both sides of the green marble. There was only one because, years before, Rousel had knocked the other off when he'd thrown a school book at me, and it had fallen and shattered. I stood and walked to the bookshelf, looking at the bookend. There had to be enough stone and sand nearby outside the house so that imaging wouldn't be that hard. I concentrated, visualizing a second bookend, identical to the first.

Then, there was one, sitting in the open space of the shelf beside the first.

I turned to Mother. "A bit late, but . . ."

Her mouth had opened, just a little. I had the feeling that she'd never been quite sure whether I was really an imager. Father's eyes had widened.

"Is that all?" Disappointment colored Culthyn's voice.

"Can you do that?" I countered.

"No." The response was sullen.

"Imaging is like anything else. It's work, and it has to be practical."

"You take all the fun out of things."

"Culthyn." Mother's voice was like ice in midwinter. "Apologize."

"I'm sorry, Rhenn."

"If you don't want to go to your sleeping chamber, you will be civil to your brother," Father added. "From what I've heard, there aren't many who can do what he just did."

"Yes, sir."

Before anyone else could speak, I did. "Father, I'd be interested in learning what you've heard about trade and shipping, especially between Solidar and Ferrum or Jariola." I did want to know, and I didn't want the conversation headed back to more questions about Seliora.

"Well . . ." He rubbed his thumbs against the sides of his forefingers, the way he sometimes did when he was thinking.

"I heard from Peliagryn that there was a skirmish or something between some Ferran ships and ours in the north ocean, and most of their vessels got sunk. After that, the factors in the isles sent word to Rousel that traders in Ferrial are refusing to accept Solidaran wools. They're afraid of confiscation if matters get any worse . . . things aren't quite so bad with Jariola. At the same time, I really have trouble with the Oligarch. Those types don't really understand commerce at all . . ."

I listened carefully, and not just out of politeness.

Later, we had tea and cakes before I left, and Mother didn't press me again on Seliora, but she did mention three times how much she was looking forward to meeting her.

That evening at services, Chorister Isola offered a phrase in her homily that, once more, stuck with me as I walked back to my quarters, perhaps because of what Culthyn had said about my imaging not seeming to be so much.

". . . Exalting one's name is a vanity of vanities, for a name is merely an ephemeral label that will vanish and be forgotten soon after we have turned to ashes and dust. Even those whose names are remembered are forgotten, because all that is remembered is a label. To seek to do great deeds for ethical or practical reasons is a mark of courage or ambition, if not both; to do so to make one's name famous is a vanity of the Namer."

I could see that was another example of the narrowest of paths, as Grandmama Diestra had put it. But I had the feeling that all the paths before me were narrow.

65

Perfection can lead to great imperfection.

While I tried to run down Master Dichartyn on Lundi, he didn't show up at the Collegium before I had to leave for the Council Chateau. Then, as it often seemed at the beginning of the week, little happened, and we were back at the Collegium well before fifth glass. I actually found Master Dichartyn in his study and able to see me.

"What do you have to report?"

"On Samedi night, someone followed me and took another set of shots . . ." I explained the details of what had happened, as well as my failures with the oil and the strange shield.

"The oil was a good idea," he said with a nod, "but the way you tried to apply it shows a lack of experience. Think of it this way. A shield will deflect things thrown at it, but what about those things already there or placed before it?"

I could have hit my head with my palm. So obvious! All I'd had to do would have been to image the oil on the stones beyond the shield so that it was in place when he ran over it.

"That's how you learn. By making and surviving mistakes."

"What about the other imager's shield?"

"That just confirms that he's a foreign imager. He's more than likely the one who hired the Ferran. That's almost a certainty."

"But why are they still after me?"

"They think you know something. Do you?" The corners of his mouth turned up, but his eyes weren't smiling.

"I don't think so, but I thought of something else. You've

probably already figured this out. This year the number of young or junior imagers who've been killed is much higher than ever, and almost all have been shot. But why would anyone kill young imagers? The only answer I could come up with was because they can't kill older ones, but that means someone has decided to keep killing the younger ones so that in time there won't be any older ones."

"You're right. That's the most likely conclusion. We don't have any proof, but the same thing was happening to young imagers in Liantiago and Nacliano. Unlike here, there they did kill several assassins and the killings have stopped for now. One assassin was caught, and he confessed that he'd been paid five golds for every killing, but he couldn't identify who paid him."

"It has to be someone from someplace like Caenen or Jariola or Ferrum, or maybe even Tiempre," I said.

"Possibly, but those aren't the only lands that don't like imagers, and assassinations, even five golds—or ten—a head are far cheaper than war."

What surprised me was that Master Dichartyn didn't seem all that upset. Was that because such attacks had been more common over the years than I knew? And why hadn't they caught the assassins in L'Excelsis when they had in Westisle and Estisle?

"It seems odd—"

"That we still have assassins at large?" He shook his head. "You killed one. I've killed one. So has another imager. Three were killed in Westisle and two in Estisle, and there have been no more killings there for over two months. What that proves is that whoever is in charge of the operation is here, and that there is probably only one person from whatever land is involved, certainly no more than two. Is there anything else?"

Not about that, because he wasn't about to say. "The ranks of the Collegium don't show a Maitre D'Image, sir. Have there been many?"

"The Collegium—and Solidar—is fortunate to have one every few generations. More often would not necessarily be good for either. After the great imager of Rex Regis razed the walls of L'Excelsis and destroyed a third of the Bovarian population, and then created, or re-created, the Council Chateau, there was a certain amount of fear of imagers. Supposedly, that was why the first Hall of Imagers was created, as much to identify where imagers were as anything. That hall was actually right about where we are now . . ."

I'd known that the first Hall had been the start of the Collegium, but it was strange, in a way, to be sitting where it had been.

". . . the fear died down over time, but never abated, although it was helped when Cyran destroyed Rex Defou and put his son on the throne. Knowing there are so few great imagers—those whom we would term Maitres D'Image today—the Council will defer to one, knowing that they are infrequent, not that they have much choice, but it is another form of balance. Other lands know that one could rise, and they do not wish to provoke Solidar. In times when the Collegium does not have one, Solidar will not press other lands too hard. Nor will the Council even when one does head the Collegium at the height of his powers, because to do so would invite retaliation after his death . . ."

"Is that why there are four Collegia?"

"We use the term as if there were four. There is really only one, split into four different locations, but such a separation renders the Collegium less vulnerable, especially in times when its powers are less, or less apparent."

"What about the regionals? Do they report to you or to Master Poincaryt?"

"You are assuming that I have some sort of position, Rhennthyl."

"No, sir. From observation, I know you have some sort of position, even though it appears nowhere. I also suspect that Master Poincaryt was your predecessor in that position."

He chuckled. "And you, Rhennthyl, with your brashness, will either be dead in ten years, or my successor. The odds, unfortunately, heavily favor the former unless you can learn greater skills in forbearance and dissembling." He paused, then added, "Dissembling is not inherently dishonest. It is the skill of disguising what you feel and know until you can act with the highest chance of success. Live dissemblers are far more useful than dead heroes. How are your latest studies with Maitre Dyana going?"

"As you would expect, sir. I'm learning, but not so well or with as much finesse as she would prefer."

He did laugh at that, heartily. Then he said, "You must realize that Maitre Dyana comes from a background where the slightest misstep can cause great pain, if not death. Demand for perfection of skills in all areas comes naturally to her."

"Sir . . . you've suggested that many High Holders are not among the brightest . . ."

"That does not mean they are not highly skilled, and the harnessing of a wide range of finely honed skills to a lack of intelligence can be deadly to those nearby."

I hadn't thought of it in that way.

"You do have certain strengths, Rhenn. I don't mean as an imager, but beyond that. I'd like you to think about what they are, and what they imply for the way you should act. Unless something comes up that is urgent, I will meet you here after you leave the Chateau on Jeudi, and we will discuss what you think those strengths might be." He stood.

So did I. "Yes, sir."

With half a glass remaining before dinner, and rain once more threatening, I hurried back to my quarters and thought about what Master Dichartyn had said. Besides strong shields, and the ability to paint, what were my strengths? In the end, I could come up with only one, and that was my ability to combine what I knew with what I felt to come to a conclusion that was usually right—often long before I could have proved the correctness of that conclusion.

The other thing I realized, again, was that I was being used as a target and a lure for whoever was trying to attack the Collegium. I was not being given any advanced training in attacking, or ways to attack, but only in defense, and after a time, if one cannot attack, one usually loses.

After dinner, and then after my exercises with Maitre Dyana, I felt totally exhausted. She was instructing me in the use of imaging to detect poisons in food, and that reinforced my sense of being trained as a lure. Tired as I felt, I still forced myself to write a letter to Seliora thanking her for a wonderful Samedi and telling her that my visit with my parents had gone as expected and that they looked forward very much to meeting her.

The only problem was that, once I dropped into sleep, I had nightmares about having dinners with High Holders and trying to determine what was poisoned and how, especially after I discovered a tiny silver knot set by my cutlery at a formal dinner in an ornate dining hall I did not recognize.

66

Observing an observer is often boring, but vital.

On Mardi, the only thing that happened of note was that a petitioner tried to get to Councilor Suyrien. Dartazn had to kill him, and Baratyn and the civic patrollers discovered that the assassin had killed the factor who had the appointment and taken his place.

That evening, Maitre Dyana, in the midst of attempting to instill more finesse in my poison diagnostics, suggested that half of diagnostics was observation before the fact, and that I still tended to rush before I had all the information.

"Patience, dear boy. Observation in detail with patience."

If she were still alive twenty years from now, I thought, she'd still be calling me "dear boy," which I suspected was a more pleasant way of saying, "Think before you act, idiot."

On Meredi, I received from the Collegium tailor a formal white and gray uniform jacket to be worn to the Council's

Harvest Ball the following week. I tried it on, and, unsurprisingly, it fit perfectly. I had to admit that it looked far better than the standard gray waistcoat.

Of course, right after arriving back at the Collegium on Jeudi afternoon, I marched myself to Master Dichartyn's studio.

As soon as I sat down, he asked, "Why do you think an assassin tried to kill Councilor Suyrien?"

That certainly wasn't the first question I expected. "Because he's the head of the executive committee, and effectively runs the Council."

"That is a statement of fact that is meaningless. What has he done to cause someone to want to kill him?"

"I don't know, sir. From what I have heard, he is opposed to changing anything."

"That is true. What does that tell you about the assassin—or whoever paid him, if it turns out he was hired?"

"He feels he has been hurt by the present system or strongly wants change or both."

"Many people feel that way. They don't try to kill a councilor."

"Either blood or golds or both are involved."

"Better. Think about this. You've read the newssheets, have you not, with the stories about more hostilities between Ferrum and Jariola—and the skirmish between one of our flotillas that was positioned to keep Ferran warships from attacking Jariolan merchanters?"

"Yes, sir."

"There is the possibility of war between Ferrum and Jariola. Which land is less popular in Solidar?"

"Jariola, I'd say. The Oligarch makes people think of an overbearing rex."

"What about among the factors and merchanters?"

I thought about my father's reactions. "They're probably even more in favor of Ferrum, and they're not happy that the Council's attempt at evenhandedness is costing them."

"Now, while it has not been made that public," Master Dichartyn went on, "Councilor Suyrien has suggested that Solidar may have to support Jariola, given the belligerent stance of Ferrum. He has also stated that he fears the dangers of a nation whose policy is ruled only by profits. Can you see a possible link to the assassin, at least in terms of views?"

"Yes, sir."

"Now . . . have you considered what I asked of you on Lundi?"

"Yes, sir."

"Then summarize your conclusions." He sat back and waited.

"Well, sir . . . I've thought about this for a long time, but the only significant strengths I seem to have are very strong shields for someone of my level and the ability to combine what I know with what I feel to come to a conclusion that usually seems to be right—often long before I could have actually proved the correctness of that conclusion. The implication behind that is probably what Maitre Dyana keeps saying, and that's that I need to be more patient. At least, in most cases." I couldn't help adding, "I don't think I'm the single-handed hero type who can charge into the taudis and capture scores."

"What about your portraiture ability?"

"That's a strength, and it probably added to my imaging ability, but, outside of providing portraits for the Collegium . . ."

He nodded. "Those probably are among your strongest points, and the implications are correct so far as you have carried them. We also don't train, as you put it, single-handed heroes. We often act alone, but it's far more effective, and far safer, to act from the shadows . . . or in direct sunlight with everyone watching in a fashion where no one realizes what you've done, and even when they do, where no one connects it to you or the Collegium." He smiled. "Next week, at the Council's Harvest Ball, above all, observe. Observe and try to correlate what you see with what you know and what you feel. It may surprise you."

"Yes, sir."

"What are you doing this weekend?"

"Taking the young lady who saved my life to meet my parents."

He fingered his chin, then nodded. "For all of our sakes, use your shields and be careful . . . and observant."

After I left, I had, more than ever, the feeling that I was the lure for a much larger predator than I'd first imagined.

67

Professional interrogators should study mothers.

Fortunately, Samedi morning was clear, cool, and with a light breeze that made the long run that followed Clovyl's exercises and the session in physical self-defense seem almost pleasant. I finished somewhat closer to Dartazn, but not much. I hurried through cleaning up and eating, so that I could get to the studio and get some work done on some of the details of the portrait that didn't require Master Poincaryt before he arrived.

He was as punctual as always, settling into the chair. "Good day, Rhennthyl." He settled into the chair. "I apologize for my absence last week. There were some matters to deal with."

"Beyond the infiltrators in the taudis, sir?"

A smile crossed his face. "You know, Rhennthyl, I find these sessions most useful. They provide a time when I am awake, relatively rested, and without people and details clamoring for actions and solutions." He turned his head. "This way?"

"A touch away from me, just a little." I paused. "Good."

I had to admire the way he'd handled my question. Just a smile, and warm words on another subject, hinting that he wasn't about to deal with my query. Before I lifted my brush,

I just studied him again, looking from the canvas and back to him. Then I caught it. The way I'd painted his left temple was as though in a different light setting than the cheekbone below. I concentrated, trying to visualize it just so . . . and then it was just that way on the canvas. I had to smile. In a way, it was ironic.

I worked steadily for a good quarter glass before he spoke again.

"Master Dichartyn has briefed me on the situation in which you find yourself. How would you describe it? Honestly, but as dispassionately as possible."

"The Collegium has been good to me, sir. That I cannot deny, and I've learned a great deal. At the moment, though, I do feel more like the lure for a large and unknown predator lurking somewhere out beyond the Collegium."

"That's a fair description of the situation. I would point out, however, as I am certain Master Dichartyn has already told you, that all imagers are in a sense lures. Our duty and responsibility is to draw such predators in order that they do not prey on Solidar itself."

"He has said that, sir."

"Good. I felt sure he had. You'll be at the Council's Harvest Ball next Vendrei, I trust?"

"Yes, sir. Won't you?"

"No. On such social occasions, my presence would have, shall we say, a dampening effect on the atmosphere. The chief maitre of the Collegium must take care never to put himself in a position where he might be seen to challenge or dim the authority of the Council."

I realized I'd already understood that without actually having thought it through. I just hadn't applied it to the Ball.

"The Ball is one of those occasions when you have a chance to observe and learn without being observed that much yourself. If someone is observing you, of course, it is significant, and something to consider." He paused. "How long before I might see the portrait?"

"You can look at it anytime, sir. I have your face mostly done, and the garments."

"After we're done today. I dislike surprises, especially those I can prevent."

He said nothing more for the rest of the session, clearly lost in his own thoughts and concerns. When the first bell of ninth glass struck, he looked to me.

"Yes, sir. I have more than enough to work on before the next session."

Master Poincaryt stood, stretched, and then walked toward the easel, circling it and then studying the unfinished work. After a moment, he nodded. "They were right. You're as good as many of the master portraiturists." A wry smile followed. "It's accurate, and lifelike, but you're an imager, and it's not as flattering as those of Master Estafen. More accurate, but not so flattering."

"Master Dichartyn has always stressed accuracy, sir."

The chief maitre laughed. "Master Dichartyn also informed me that you have a certain . . . shall we say . . . way of reducing egos. I would suggest you not employ it at the Ball." He stepped back from the unfinished portrait, looked at it once more, then turned. "Next week?"

"Yes, sir."

He was almost at the door before he stopped and half-turned. "Rhennthyl?"

"Yes, sir?"

"Being a lure does not mean one is defenseless. Nor does it preclude action. Just make certain that such action is in your best interests and those of the Collegium." With that, he smiled and left the studio.

I ended up painting for almost another glass, leaving just enough time to clean up and walk to the dining hall. With good fortune, I'd be able to finish the portrait in one or, at the most, two more sessions. It was a good work—perhaps not my very best, but better than that of many masters.

After lunch with Menyard, I stepped out into the foyer and walked to the main entrance. I glanced up at the plaques . . . and froze. Another name had been added: Claustyn, Maitre D'Aspect, 727–755 A.L.

Had he been the one to remove the old High Priest of Caenen . . . or had he just been killed as part of the operation?

Menyard stopped. "You didn't know?"

"No. I don't usually come this way, and I'm never here for
lunch, except on Samedi and Solayi."

We just stood there for a moment. I couldn't say that
Claustyn had been a close friend, but he'd been warm and
welcoming when I'd first become a third and changed quarters, after the confrontation with Johanyr. He'd introduced
me to other thirds with grace at a time when I'd needed and
appreciated that kindness. It made me think. Had I been that
way? No . . . but there hadn't been any new thirds in the last
few months, not near my quarters.

Still . . . that was something I needed to remember.

Menyard and I left the dining hall silently, and I walked
along the west side of the quadrangle back to my quarters.

For a time, I just thought. Then I decided to go to the library to see what there might be on High Holder Ryel. Lures
could learn, I supposed.

Once I reached the library and began to search the stacks,
I began to realize how little written information there was.
Oh, there was a listing of all the High Holder houses, but it
was more than a century out of date. There was also a book
on the limits of High Holder low justice, but after skimming
that, I realized that it was just a simplification of what Master
Jhulian had pounded into me—or forced me into pounding
into myself. In the end, I spent almost two glasses learning
that I wasn't going to find that information in a book.

After that, I returned to my quarters, read a bit more of *On
Art and Society,* then washed up once more, and headed out
to pick up Seliora for our silent inquisition.

I took the Bridge of Desires and hailed a hack there—it
couldn't hurt to vary which bridges I used. Then, after we
reached NordEste Design, I paid him to wait while I went
inside to get Seliora. I supposed that he could have left, but I
had the feeling that no hacker really wanted to stiff an imager.

The twins were the ones who opened the door, and this time it was Hestya who yelled up the stairs. "He's here, Aunt Seliora!"

Hanahra just grinned.

"How was your birthday?"

"Good." They both smiled shyly, looking away, then followed me up the stairs.

I only waited a moment, after the twins hurried away, before Seliora stepped through the archway from the staircase, wearing another dress I had never seen, this one with a black skirt emphasized by narrow panels of a brilliant but dark green silk. The bodice was also black, but the sleeves were of a filmy silk that matched the panels in the skirt, and her scarf was silver, trimmed in the same green. She also wore a jade-ite pendant on a silver rope necklace with matching earrings.

"You look stunning!" And she did, more than stunning, in fact.

"I thought I had better." She smiled. "Pharsi girls try harder."

I winced at the out-of-context quote.

She bent forward and brushed my cheek with her lips. "I'm sorry. I know you don't feel that way, but . . . let's just say that it was a difficult week."

"Some High Holder trying to be too familiar?"

"His son . . ."

"Do I know the name?"

"I don't know." She smiled, mischievously, and somehow sadly, all at once. "Alhyral D'Haestyr."

"His father is on the Council."

"Young Alhyral made that point . . . several times. I finally told him that his choice was between his father having no furniture and him not having me or his father having furniture and him not having me. Then he asked how I could possibly turn down the heir of a High Holder, especially one so supportive of merchants, crafters, and factors. I said that was the only option, because I was not raised to deal with High Holders, and he was not raised to deal with Pharsi women. He persisted, until I pointed out that Pharsi women don't believe in sex without a binding commitment to marry, and that we also don't believe in divorce, and that there are no unhappy Pharsi husbands. Some dead husbands and unfaithful fiancés, but no unhappy ones."

I whistled softly. "And that was the polite version."

"I didn't have to use the pistol." She laughed, softly, warmly, then wrapped her arms around me. "I'm so glad you're here."

I kissed her, and she returned the favor with ardor—but only for a few moments. "I don't think I'd better be too disheveled when I meet your family."

She had a very good point, and I escorted her out to the waiting hack.

The driver smiled, as if to say that now he understood why I'd paid him to wait.

Once we were in the coach, I asked, "Have you heard about Madame D'Shendael?"

"Grandmama said that she had one last source to go with what she got from Ailphens yesterday."

I didn't press on that, because, if Seliora had known more, she would have told me.

We arrived just before fifth glass, and Khethila was the one to open the door. Her eyes widened, but she didn't gape.

"Khethila, this is Seliora. Seliora, my sister Khethila."

"I'm so pleased to meet to you," Khethila said.

"And I, you," replied Seliora warmly.

"Please do come in. The formal parlor is to the right." Khethila stepped back to the left.

I let Seliora step through the open door first, then followed.

"She's gorgeous, Rhenn," Khethila leaned forward and murmured in my ear as I turned to escort Seliora into the formal parlor. "I'll tell Mother and Father that you're here," she added in a louder voice.

Seliora and I barely stood in the parlor long enough for her to glance around the room before Mother and Father arrived, trailed by Khethila.

"Seliora, these are my parents. Father, Mother, this is Seliora."

Seliora inclined her head demurely. "I'm honored to meet you both. Rhenn has said so much about you."

"Not too much, I trust," replied Father.

"Enough to know that you're both exceptional. Anyone who has the understanding to let their son pursue art shows great perception." Her words could have been artificial or glib, but Seliora offered them in full honesty and directness, in a way that could not be denied.

"Please, do sit down," Mother said, her eyes barely leaving Seliora for a moment. "Would you like Dhuensa, or red or white Cambrisio?"

I glanced to Seliora.

"The Dhuensa, if you please."

"For me, too," I added.

"I'd like the white Cambrisio, and your father would like the Dhuensa." Mother looked to Khethila, and I understood that unspoken command. Mother wasn't about to miss anything.

"I'll be right back," Khethila said. "Don't say anything too exciting."

I understood that as well, but I didn't say a word until Seliora and I were seated on the formal loveseat. "Where's Culthyn?"

"Oh, he's over at a friend's for the evening," Mother replied. "We didn't want to inflict him on Seliora for her first dinner here."

That wording was either accepting or encouraging. The latter, I hoped.

"He hasn't gotten into too much trouble this week, has he?"

"No more than normal." Father's words were dry. "He is learning how to handle accounts and seems to like it."

"That's because Khethila's the one teaching him, dear." Mother smiled. "Seliora. That's a beautiful name. Is it a family name?"

"I was named after my grandmother's grandmother. I'm told that was because she had black hair and black eyes, also. It means 'daughter of the moon' in old Pharsi."

"Do you have any brothers or sisters?"

"Two brothers, one older, one younger."

At that moment, Khethila returned with a tray, quickly offering the goblets to each of us, and then taking the corner straight-backed chair.

"Rhenn hasn't said much about your family or what they do," Father injected.

Seliora glanced at me. "Rhenn can be very protective, I've already discovered. It's an endearing quality. There's no secret about what we do. My grandmother was the one who created the family business, and we're all involved in it in some way or another. It's NordEste Design."

For the most fleeting of moments, there was a deep silence.

"*The* NordEste Design, on Nordroad?" Father asked.

Seliora nodded.

"Dear . . . I'm afraid I don't know as much about this as the men. What is it exactly that you do?" Mother ventured.

Seliora tilted her head, as if at a loss to describe her work. "I'm the one who picks the fabrics for all the upholstered pieces, and I sometimes negotiate with the mills. For custom fabrics, we have several powered looms, and I'm the one who oversees them. I also maintain and repair them. And I do the custom embroidery and fabric designs, and work them out and punch the jacquard cards."

"You don't actually embroider?" asked Khethila.

"No. We handle too many pieces to do it by hand. Well . . . there are some individual pieces we might have to have repaired by hand, when it wouldn't make sense to set up the looms for such a small section of fabric. Then I'd hire that out to one of the seamstresses we can trust."

Khethila was working hard to conceal a broad smile.

"How did you come to meet?"

Seliora flashed a smile. "We have individual guild memberships, because of the way we're set up. I met Rhenn at one of the Samedi dances, and one thing led to another. There were interruptions. He couldn't leave Imagisle for a time, and I was gone for a month this past summer. We had to visit a number of textile manufactories."

"You must tell us a little about your family. . . ."

"It is a rather large family. . . ." Seliora continued, gently, sometimes humorously, beginning with Grandmama Diestra and continuing down toward the youngest. ". . . and the twins, they're Odelia's younger sisters. Because I seemed so much older, they decided that I had to be their aunt, not their cousin . . ."

The bell rang, signifying dinner was ready.

"This is most interesting, but we should repair to table." Mother rose, moving to make sure she was the one guiding Seliora to the dining chamber, through the direct door from the formal parlor, the one that was so seldom used. "This way, dear."

Father followed, and Khethila lagged. So did I, knowing she had something to say.

She did, although her words were barely a whisper. "Pharsi . . . and from a *very* wealthy family. Father won't be able to say a word. How did you ever find her?"

"I didn't. She found me. Pharsi foresight, the same way Remaya found Rousel."

For a moment, that stopped her. "She really has it?"

I nodded, adding in a lower voice, "Far more than Remaya or anyone I've heard of."

As soon as we had gathered around the table with Seliora at Father's left and me at his right, and Mother on Seliora's right, Mother spoke up.

"Would you like to offer the blessing, Seliora, or would you prefer to have Rhenn do it?"

"If you wouldn't mind one from my family."

"That would be lovely."

We all bowed our heads.

"For the grace that we all owe each other, for the bounty of the earth of which we are about to partake, for good faith among all, and mercies great and small. For all these we offer thanks and gratitude, both now and ever more, in the spirit of that which cannot be named or imaged . . ."

"In peace and harmony," we replied.

"That was lovely. Thank you," Mother said. "I thought a

cool soup might be best for harvest, although it is rather late in the season."

The cool soup was limed vichyssoise, and served as a backdrop while Seliora finished the Shelim family history, although in the Pharsi tradition, I knew, it really should have been called the Mama Diestra family history.

After the vichyssoise, Nellica appeared with serving dishes . . . and more serving dishes, as well as two bread trays, but the main course was a veal regis, where the veal filets were split, filled with thin spicy ham and a pungent cheese, then quick-fried, slow-heated, and covered with a naranje cream sauce. Rich as it was, I knew I couldn't eat that much of it.

Seliora had small helpings of everything. I took only what appealed to me.

"Rhenn, you didn't try the glazed rice fritters . . . or the twice-baked yellow squash."

"That's because I don't have an interior large enough for everything here," I protested.

Mother turned to Seliora. "What do you think of the veal?"

"It's excellent. It's your recipe?"

"My mother's, actually . . ."

I listened, mostly.

After we had finished eating the main course, Khethila rose from the table and nodded to Seliora. "Might I ask your assistance, Seliora?"

Seliora smiled and eased from her chair. "I'd be pleased."

Once the two had left, Mother looked to me. "She is beautiful, Rhenn, truly beautiful in that way that only Pharsi women can be."

"She is." I almost replied that she had saved my life, but decided that was information better left for later. "She's also very modest, and very careful. I knew her for months before she ever revealed who she was."

"How did she manage that?" Father demanded.

"Very simply. Because of the nature of what NordEste Design does, as she pointed out, they have to have guild members. Seliora is a member of the Woodworkers' Guild, although she is actually a textile engineer and designer. Officially, on the guild rolls, she is an upholsterer. She came to the Guild Hall on Samedis, always with her older cousin. Odelia is most formidable." I laughed. "In six months, I've had one dinner with her alone, and that was in a public place. Otherwise, there's always been a member of her family within ten yards . . ."

"As there should have been," Mother replied. "I do approve of that, and of parents who care so for such a beautiful daughter." She paused, as if to ask a question, then smiled. "You are fortunate."

"That she and her family would accept an imager calling on her? I am." I wasn't about to explain the reasons. It was far better to let her think what she did.

Shortly, Seliora and Khethila returned, and dessert arrived.

Small talk dominated dessert, apple tartlets, with a lemon glaze, followed by tea. After we finished, and a silence persisted for just a few moments, the kind of silence that everyone should recognize as a signal for farewells, and that too many do not, Mother cleared her throat, gently.

"You must let Charlsyn take you two back to NordEste . . . or . . ." Mother stopped.

"Everything is at NordEste," Seliora replied. "The manufactory is on the street and lower level, and our family quarters are on the second and third levels."

"We'd be pleased to accept that offer." I would have been stupid not to, for many reasons, including the fact that Mother and Father had to have paid Charlsyn extra to stay to take us, and not doing so would have merely wasted their coin and cost me.

Once we were in the family coach and on the way back to NordEste, I turned to Seliora. "You were magnificent."

She smiled ruefully. "I'm glad you think so. With all that food, I won't be able to fit into anything I own. How did you manage growing up?"

"You saw. I just didn't eat everything. But I did miss it when I was with Master Caliostrus." I didn't say more, thinking of both of them . . . dead, even if it now appeared as though much of it wasn't totally my fault. Instead, I asked, "What did Khethila want to know?"

"Girl things." Seliora smiled, mischievously. "She wanted to know if you were good to me. She also said that she'd never seen you so protective of anyone."

I let it drop at that. Seliora would have said more if I'd needed to know, and I didn't want to waste my few moments alone with her.

The embraces were in the coach . . . because even I realized that discretion was the better part of valor—at least so long as I was being forced to act as a lure for who knew what. But I did walk her to the door, and I extended my full shields to cover us both. I also obtained her permission to call on her on Solayi.

After that, I had Charlsyn take me to Imagisle the long way, to the Bridge of Desires. I didn't see anyone strange, and no one shot at me, but when I reached my quarters, I wasn't sure whether not being shot at or having weathered the family inquisition was the greater relief.

68

The fashion of speech tells its truth, spells its falsehoods.

The only thing that mattered much to me on Solayi was seeing Seliora, but I was again most careful with my shields and kept an eye on who and what might be around. The only thing at all odd was a covered wagon, similar to a tinker's wagon, drawn up to a hitching post a block off the Bridge of Desires. I didn't see anyone around it as the hack I'd hailed carried me past, but they couldn't have been far, because the old gelding hitched to the wagon wasn't that heavily tied. The wagon didn't follow me, though, and there was no one nearby when I left the hack in front of Seliora's.

She answered the door, wearing trousers and a simple cream shirt. She still looked beautiful, and I told her so.

"You just see what you want to see."

"Not so. Master Poincaryt told me that I was the most accurate and unflatteringly honest portraiturist he'd ever encountered and that I had the nasty habit of deflating egos."

"They're not women."

I wasn't going to win that argument. "They're not you." I put my arms around her.

For a moment, she reciprocated. "I already have some Sanietra and fruit and biscuits set by on the east terrace."

So we climbed the steps. When we reached the terrace, I was happy to see that the chairs and table had been arranged so that we sat side by side, with smaller side tables flanking us. There were two glasses of Sanietra and thin breads with fruit slices on a small platter.

I also got a far warmer welcome than I had in the main hall.

After that, when we were properly seated, I asked, "The day after, what did you think of last night?"

"Your parents are sweet. They don't understand you, and they worry about you."

"They worry about the wrong things," I pointed out, "and they'd worry themselves to death if they knew half of what's happened to me." Not to mention what hadn't happened and might yet.

She smiled. "I'm glad you don't protect me that way."

That brought me up short. Why didn't I? Because I knew Seliora was stronger? "I trust you to understand. Also . . . your family . . . your background . . . you all do understand the undercurrents. My father knows they're there, and he does his best to avoid them, without overtly even acknowledging their existence."

She poured Sanietra for us, then said, "Grandmama found out some of what you asked about Madame D'Shendael."

I waited.

"She was the only child of High Holder Shendael and his wife Helenia. According to Ailphens, everyone was surprised that there was even one child, given all of Shendael's young male friends . . ."

I kept my nod to myself.

". . . the estate was really Helenia's, but of course she had to marry to keep her status. Right after the daughter—that's Madame D'Shendael—reached eighteen, Shendael was shot. Helenia was charged with the murder. Ailphens said that sections of the public records are missing, except for those dealing directly with Helenia's execution." Seliora looked to me.

"What did Grandmama add?"

She shook her head ruefully. "Shendael's only male relative died on a hunting trip when his rifle exploded. That was actually right after the trial."

"How do you think Emanus managed it?" I asked.

"Do you think he had anything to do with the senior Shendael's murder?"

"No, but I'd wager that he had that male relative killed so that no one could contest his daughter's holding." I'd also have wagered that Helenia hadn't been the one to fire the shot that killed her husband, but that she'd accepted the blame to save her daughter, not that I'd ever find any proof of any of that.

"That doesn't explain why Emanus was killed," Seliora pointed out. "If Madame D'Shendael were worried about her father . . ."

"He gave up everything to protect her. It can't be that."

"It has to be connected to her in some way."

We talked a bit more, agreeing on that, but we couldn't think of how, at least not based on what we knew. Finally, Seliora lifted her glass and sipped, then asked, "What are you doing next week?"

"Did I tell you that I have to stand duty, so to speak, at the Council's Harvest Ball?"

"When is that?"

"Vendrei night. I'm also supposed to watch closely for trouble and be ready to dance with any woman in distress or who appears to have been deserted on the dance floor, so to speak."

"What women?"

I shrugged. "I don't know. I've never been to anything like it. I've been told it's for councilors and their guests, and that a great many who attend are High Holders."

"You'd better be even more careful about any young High Holder women."

"Even more?"

"Rhenn . . . isn't it obvious? What kind of man is the only kind that a woman who wants to escape that gilded prison could marry? Especially a younger daughter of many in an important family, or one from a declining family."

I hadn't even thought of that. My face must have showed it.

She offered her soft and warm laugh. "You're handsome, intelligent, and muscular, and to be at the Ball, even as a sort of guard, means that you're a more promising imager. Also, you're one of the few that they can meet."

"But . . . no one has ever said that we're imagers, and we're not allowed to admit it."

She laughed. "Don't the councilors know? And you think that some of them wouldn't tell their families?"

Once more, she had a point. "I don't even know if there will be any women of that age and inclination."

"If there's a fancy ball and men . . . there will be. Not the type you'd prefer, but you may well be the type that they prefer. Don't let them." The last words were as warm as those that preceded them, but I could sense claws within them.

"Yes, mistress."

She mock-slapped me, her hand stopping just short of my cheek, then tapping it lightly.

"Beyond the Ball, nothing is happening, except you. I'd hoped we could do something next Samedi."

"Would you mind attending a wedding with me—on Samedi?"

"A wedding? Is someone in the family getting married?"

I hoped she wasn't asking me. Much as I liked, even loved Seliora, I wasn't certain I was ready to be married.

"No, I'm not even hinting. You aren't ready." She kissed my cheek. "It's Father's niece Yaena. If you could meet us here at a little before noon?"

"I can do that, but I don't have wedding garb." I did, from Rousel's wedding, but as an imager, I couldn't wear it, and I wasn't certain it even fit any longer.

"Your grays are suitable anywhere." I got another kiss.

In the end, we didn't talk so much as just sit in the afternoon and be with each other.

69

Everyone has rules; but yours are always wrong.

On Lundi evening, Maitre Dyana dismissed me after lessons saying that she'd taught me what I could learn about poisons and imaging at the stage of life experience I had, an interesting way of putting it, I thought. On Mardi, Master Dichartyn said that he'd be too occupied to see me, except in a dire emergency, for at least a week. I also received a short letter from Mother.

> *Dear Rhenn,*
> *We all enjoyed meeting your young lady ever so much. She is charming, cultured, intelligent, and beautiful. I can understand your caution, but, as Culthyn said, "Rhenn should be ashamed of himself for making everyone worry so much."*

I strongly doubted Culthyn said any such thing, but it was a convenient fiction through which Mother could chide me for making her worry about my not finding a suitable young lady.

> We all hope it will not be too long before we see both of you again. We are considering having a larger dinner for some of our friends near the end of Erntyn, and trust you will be able to join us then. I will send you the formal invitation when we receive them next week . . .

Now that I had found a suitable young lady, Mother couldn't wait to display her to everyone. But I suppose that was minor compared to what else was happening in the world.

According to the newssheets, particularly *Veritum,* the situation between Jariola and Ferrum was continuing to worsen. On Meredi morning, the lead story featured a statement by the Ferran minister of state that described Jariola as "a land governed by reactionary landholders who understand nothing of commerce and less of government." He went on to claim that oligarchs like Khasis III and certain High Holders in other lands were mere parasites on a country's productive capability, as were worker drones who wanted employers to pay for everything while working less and less. From that alone, even had I not been forced to study Ferrum in more depth by Master Dichartyn, I wouldn't have had much trouble in determining that Ferrum was what I would have called a mercantile empire.

Other than those events, not much of interest occurred during the week, and, while I was interested in seeing what happened at the Council's Harvest Ball, and learning what I could from observing, I was far more interested in seeing Seliora on Samedi, even if it happened to be a family wedding.

On Vendrei morning, as soon as we arrived at the Council Chateau, Baratyn gave us a final briefing on the Council's Harvest Ball.

"As I told you, not everyone will be a councilor or a family member. Each councilor has five invitations, and each invitation is good for two people, usually a couple, but it could be for daughters or sons. In addition, there are invitations to the justices of the High Court of Solidar and a number of other functionaries, including the more important envoys from other lands. You will doubtless see other faces you have seen at the Collegium. Do not speak to them unless they address you. Your function is twofold, to watch for anything untoward and to stop it without anyone noticing"—his eyes flicked to me, momentarily—"and to serve as dance partners for ladies in need, with discretion, or if asked. You will, of course, wear the formal white and gray jackets. You all have one, do you not?"

After dismissing us, he beckoned to me and drew me aside. "One other thing, Rhenn . . . for purposes of the Ball, when guests are announced, in the case of unmarried women you may hear something like Mistress Mearjyn D'Something-Alte. The suffix 'Alte' is added so that all know she is the daughter of a High Holder. You should note that whenever possible."

"Yes, sir."

"It's not just a formality. It has been known that some of such daughters have asked those who have served as you are serving to dance, and it is well that you know their status. Oh . . . the suffix is also used for unmarried sons as well, but that shouldn't prove a problem. They won't be asking you to dance."

In short, treat them with great respect and charm, I translated, unless you want to be on the bad side of their sire, which is something that the Collegium would prefer not to occur. But then, how could I be on much worse footing with High Holders than I was? I caught myself on that. Being on the bad side of two High Holders would be far worse than having only one wanting to do worse to me than killing me.

We left the Collegium early that afternoon, because the Council had adjourned at noon so that they could prepare and dress properly. From the duty coach, on the other side of the ring avenue circling Council Hill, I noticed the same high-sided and roofed wagon I had seen on Solayi evening. It was the kind that had several small porthole windows. The single horse was the same old gelding, and the teamster was apparently trying to adjust something with the traces, although I couldn't be sure, but I caught myself wondering what that sort of wagon was doing there, especially twice in a week. If it happened to be there when we returned, I'd let Baratyn know.

70

The difference between an imager and a councilor is that the first understands the limits of the world, while the second only understands the limits of government.

The duty coach brought us back to the Council Chateau just before seventh glass, and I didn't see any sign of the old wagon or of anything else out of the ordinary.

The Council's Harvest Ball began officially at half past seventh glass, but as we had been warned by Baratyn, no one even began to arrive until a quarter before eight. Moments after the first carriage arrived, others pulled up in the drive below the main entry steps, a drive that was normally restricted to councilors alone. Then people began to walk up the outside stone steps and in through the grand foyer past the ceremonial guards and finally up the grand staircase. They took their time on the grand staircase.

"Councilor Hemwyt D'Artisan and Madame D'Hemwyt!" The deep voice announcing the first arrival boomed from a small balding man standing at the left side of the center archway into the great receiving hall.

While people entered and were greeted by the three councilors on the Executive Council, Baratyn and I stood against the west wall just inside the Hall, which was on the south end of the Chateau and effectively occupied the space above the grand foyer. Dartazn and Martyl were stationed along the east wall.

"Councilor Etyenn D'Factorius and Madame D'Etyenn!"

"The Honorable Symmal D'Juris and Madame D'Symmal!"

In less than a quint glass I had begun to lose track of all the names, and in another quint, I was sure I had no idea of all those who were at the Ball.

"In a few moments, when most of the councilors and their guests are here," Baratyn said quietly, after edging toward me, "I want you to move until you're along the wall about even with the middle of the dance floor."

"Yes, sir." I nodded, then almost froze at the names I heard being announced.

"Dulyk D'Ryel-Alte and Mistress Iryela D'Ryel-Alte . . ."

The names sounded like they were Johanyr's brother and sister, something I didn't care for at all, and I moved slightly to the left to get a better look at the couple as they stepped through the central archway into the hall. She was blond, almost white-blond, and petite, if shapely, and wore a gown of silver and shimmering blue, with a glittering silver scarf, trimmed in black. Her brother was a younger and leaner version of Johanyr. Although he was of slightly larger than average height and moved gracefully, there was also a sense of smallness and pettiness surrounding him, although I could not have explained why I felt that.

They vanished into one of the groups of younger people on the east side of the hall, near the sideboards that held various vintages, with uniformed servers behind each.

"Shendael D'Alte and Madame D'Shendael."

That name caught my attention as well. Madame Juniae D'Shendael could not have been said to be unduly attractive, but rather handsome, with a strong chin and nose, and mahogany hair cut as short as any woman I'd seen in L'Excelsis. Her husband was wiry, shorter, and blond.

"The Honorable Klauzvol Vhillar, envoy of Ferrum, and Mistress Cyana D'Guerdyn-Alte."

The Ferran envoy coming right behind Madame D'Shendael? Was that just coincidence? And escorting a High Holder's daughter, when supposedly the Ferrans weren't exactly fond of the High Holders as a class?

"The Honorable Dharios Harnen, envoy of the Abierto Isles, and Mistress Dhenica Harnen."

He'd brought his daughter, who looked younger than Khethila and slightly ill at ease.

"The Honorable Herrys Charkovy, envoy of Jariola, and Madame Charkovy . . ."

Apparently, the envoys had arrived at the same time, just after Madame D'Shendael. Given her criticisms of the Council, I wondered who had invited her, and I looked toward Baratyn. "Madame D'Shendael?"

He grinned. "Councilor Caartyl always invites her. It irritates Councilor Suyrien no end."

Caartyl . . . there was something there, but I couldn't grasp it for a moment. Then it hit me. Caartyl was the guild member on the Executive Council, and he was the one that the strange factor Alhazyr had visited—a visit that had disturbed Master Dichartyn.

In the background, the orchestra, set on a temporary dais at the south end of the hall, opposite the entry archways, began to play. Baratyn nodded to me, and I began to edge toward my designated station.

A good half glass passed as I watched the dancers, and those moving to and from the sideboards, or standing and talking, holding wineglasses. Dartazn danced past several times with an older woman I did not recognize, perhaps a relation of some sort.

As the orchestra paused between dances, I couldn't help but notice a slender woman in blue and silver walking in my direction, casually half-twirling the end of a long black and silver scarf. As she drew closer, I realized that she was Iryela D'Ryel. I also had the feeling that I had seen her sometime before, but I couldn't place where it might have been. How could I have seen her? I kept a pleasant smile on my face and waited for her to pass.

She didn't. Instead, she stopped and looked at me, closely. "You're Rhennthyl, aren't you?"

"Yes, mistress."

"Please . . ." She offered a smile that was half wry and half tired. "I'm Iryela, and you're an imager tertius, at least." Her voice was pleasant enough, if slightly higher than I would have preferred. "You're also the one who put my brother in his place."

I eased full shields into play, if so close to my skin that no one could have detected them, without punching or slapping me. "I beg your pardon?" I also scanned the area around me, but no one seemed to be paying much attention to us. That didn't mean someone wasn't—or wouldn't.

"Johanyr . . . you must remember him?" A tinge of amusement colored her soprano voice.

"Yes, I encountered him several times." That admitted nothing.

"Encountered—a fair way of putting it, perhaps better than he deserved." She smiled. "Would you dance with me?"

I couldn't say no. "I would be honored."

A faint, delicate, and pervasive floral fragrance came with her as she slipped into my arms when the orchestra began to play and we eased out among the other dancers. Her eyes were a gray-blue that her gown and scarf intensified.

"You're in great danger, you know?" Her voice was lower, conversational, and as matter-of-fact as if she'd told me that it would rain on the morrow.

"I have the feeling, Mistress Iryela, that I may always be in great danger. Pleasant as it is, dancing with you could also present a danger."

"Oh, I doubt that. Certainly no more danger than already exists. I won't ask you to kiss me, nor to marry me. At least, not for a time, and please call me Iryela."

"I'm not of High Holder background," I said with a laugh. "Nor do I have the dancing experience to go with it." She wouldn't ask for a kiss, or more, for a time? Did that suggest Maitre Dyana was correct, that her father would take his time in dealing with me? Or was it just a part of a more elaborate plan or charade?

"You're more than adequate, and better than most of your peers, and far more handsome."

"And you are far more beautiful than yours, as you must know, and possibly more deadly." But she wasn't nearly the dancer that Seliora was.

"That's a compliment I have not heard before. My father would be pleased, but it would be a pity to tell him. I almost might, except that would please Johanyr and Dulyk, and that would not please me."

Iryela was playing a deeper game than I could discern, but it was clear that she had a purpose, one that I wasn't even certain I wanted to consider. "Brothers often view matters in a different light."

"Do you have a sister?"

"I have one. I'm quite fond of her, as I'm certain you know."

She smiled. "You do me much credit."

"I suspect I give you less than your due, since you were so easily able to find me."

"You assume that I was looking for you. Is that not rather presumptuous?"

"I think not, not if I assume that it was not for my appearance or my station or my nonexistent wealth."

"More and more interesting."

More and more dangerous. "No . . . you are the one of interest, for so seldom does one of great beauty, position, and charm ever appear in my world."

"More flattery yet." She laughed.

"Flattery, yet truth, as you well know."

"I see no others coming to take me from you, Rhennthyl."

"That only says that none dare cross your will."

"Were that it were so." There was just the tiniest edge behind the laughing words.

When the orchestra paused, I released her and inclined my head.

She returned the gesture. "If you would not mind escorting me back to my younger brother."

"My pleasure, mistress."

"Iryela."

"My pleasure, Iryela."

Her brother was in a small group with another younger man and a woman slightly younger than Khethila. "Iryela . . . we are honored at your return."

"As pleased and honored as I am, dearest Dulyk." She smiled, sweetly, then inclined her head to me. "Thank you for the dance, Rhennthyl. I did enjoy it."

"My pleasure, Iryela." I took a step back, inclined my head to her, and eased away, but slowly enough to try to overhear what might be said.

". . . most politely done, dear sister, if rather direct . . ."

". . . do believe in courtesy, Dulyk . . . and always will . . ."

"You are so refreshing, sister dearest . . ."

I concealed a wince as I moved back toward my station. Iryela lived in a family that made even Caliostrus's ménage seem warm and welcoming.

In less than half a glass, the orchestra would stop, and Councilor Suyrien would offer a toast to all the guests of the Council, but before that, I needed to return to my post.

"Do you know who asked you to dance?" asked a figure in formal black—Master Dichartyn. He'd caught me by surprise, because I'd still expected him to be in gray or gray and white.

"Mistress Iryela D'Ryel-Alte, and she used me as some sort of insult to her younger brother, who is her escort tonight—and possibly even to her father."

Master Dichartyn nodded. "There is always infighting for survival in High Holder families."

"You're suggesting I might use that?"

"I would suggest nothing at the moment. Any conflict between you and High Holder Ryel has not yet begun, and the longer before he announces his intent, the better for you."

"In what fashion will he announce it?"

"Let us just say that you will know without any doubt."

Another of his infuriatingly vague statements! I hoped he

would say more, but when he did not, I knew I would get nothing further, and I asked, "Do you have any instructions?"

"No. You can move around more. Just observe what you can." He slipped away before I could reply.

Ahead, I saw a girl—tall enough to be a woman, but too young—watching the dancers. She was alone. Well . . . that was one of my duties, and perhaps if we stayed to the outside of the swirl of dancers I might see or learn something.

"Mistress, might I have the honor of a dance?"

Her eyes widened just slightly as she turned to me, but she recovered quickly. "You might." Her smile was practiced, but with a stiffness that was slightly awkward and charming.

I took her into my arms and out among the dancers. Young she might have been, but she was a far better dancer than I.

"You dance exceedingly well, mistress."

"Alynkya, Alynkya D'Ramsael."

I liked the fact that she didn't add the "Alte" to her name. "Your father is the councilor from Kephria, then."

"He is. My mother was indisposed, and she asked him to bring me."

She was even younger than she looked, perhaps because she was so tall, but I should have guessed because the councilor was the tallest member of the Council, by a good half head, if not more.

"How do you like the Ball?"

"I don't know many people here."

"Do you live here in L'Excelsis or in Kephria?"

"Kephria, most of the time."

I danced with Alynkya for two dances, and then her father arrived and danced with her. He only smiled at me, patronizingly. I'd have to remember that, not as a grudge, but as a fact. I'd also have to remember Alynkya and wish she retained some of that youthful charm and directness. Probably not, given her father, but one could hope.

Near one of the sideboards, I caught sight of Madame D'Shendael. She was talking to someone—the Ferran envoy.

I eased closer as the two talked, then took a position where I could ostensibly watch the dance floor, but from where I could overhear most of their conversation, or glance in their direction.

"You have often suggested that Solidar has little music, Klauzvol. What do you think now?"

"This is a nice little orchestra, madame, but it is a pity that there are not others like it. For the capital of a great nation . . ."

"One cannot have everything, as you have said before. Our artists are superb . . ."

"Ah . . . that is indeed true, but so are those of Ferrum, particularly in Ferrial . . ."

I wanted the opportunity to speak to Madame D'Shendael, as well as to get a closer look at the envoy, but I certainly couldn't speak directly to her, or stare. So I looked at her for a moment, then looked away. Several moments later I did the same, while trying to project a clueless curiosity.

After three of my attempts, she turned and glided toward me, trailed by the Honorable Klauzvol Vhillar.

"Young man?"

"Yes, madame?" I did turn to her, smiling pleasantly. "Might I be of some assistance?"

"You seemed, shall we say, less than fully interested in your duties, whatever they might be."

"Madame, that is doubtless true. I was attempting to see, without being too obvious, if you looked like the etched portrait in the front of *On Art and Society*. My sister has all of your books. I don't know whether she's finished that one, because she just got it. Even though she's never been married, she found *A Widow's Guide* invaluable . . . I beg your pardon."

She had laughed, a sound somehow harshly melodic, but not mocking. "So I still have readers."

"Yes, madame." I needed to get Vhillar closer. "You haven't changed that much since Emanus painted that miniature . . ."

I could sense her stiffen . . . ever so slightly.

"That's less than common knowledge. How would a young man such as yourself know such a distinguished portraiturist?"

Vhillar kept a pleasant smile on his face, but edged closer.

"I was a journeyman portraiturist before I came here. Emanus liked a chess study I did, and offered several comments about it. We talked several times." At that point, I extended the faintest image-probe, and immediately sensed a shield reaction—of the same sort of shield that I had sensed outside Terraza. There couldn't be another foreign shield like that—not unless there were far more imager agents in L'Excelsis than Master Dichartyn knew, and that was doubtful, but still a disturbing possibility.

His eyes widened, if only fractionally, and I could sense a strengthening of his shields, but I concealed my surprise, both at his shields and his reaction, although I had half-expected to find him an imager, for reasons I could not have explained.

"You are rather young for this kind of approach, are you not?" offered Vhillar without any hesitation. "And such familiarity with a lady you do not know might not be considered . . . seemly . . . by your superiors." His smile was pleasant and polished, as was his voice.

"I confess brashness, madame . . . and sir, but only because of my admiration and that of my sister for Madame D'Shendael for her writings and all she has endured . . . to bring those words to life so that others can read them. Admiration and the wish to hear the words of one so distinguished is certainly not undue familiarity."

"Such artistry in flattery," Vhillar offered. "Such charm beyond your years and experience."

I only smiled, looking at Juniae D'Shendael and inclining my head politely. "My thanks for your words, madame."

"He means well, I believe, Klauzvol," replied Madame D'Shendael. "Presumptuously, but with honest brashness. Shall we dance?"

"My honor, madame." Vhillar glanced at me quickly as he swirled her onto the dance floor, but the look was one that committed my face to memory.

I'd have to be more than careful. I'd revealed to Vhillar that I knew what he was, and I doubted he wanted anyone to know that, but how else could I have discovered it? Then, it could be that Master Dichartyn already knew, and that was a reason why he was here.

I scanned the great receiving hall, slowly, trying to do so casually, but I didn't see Master Dichartyn or Baratyn. Besides, Baratyn wouldn't understand, nor was I going to have the time to explain the complexity of the situation. If he'd been the one with the Ferran outside Terraza—and I was almost certain he was—he'd already killed, or arranged the killing of close to ten imagers, not to mention at least four attempts on me. In addition, he was friendly with an influential High Holder with ties to those on the Council—and that High Holder's father had most likely been killed because of his conversation with me. And from that last look at me, it was clear that Vhillar knew exactly who I happened to be— and that I knew who and what he was.

I still couldn't see Master Dichartyn, but I didn't want to chase him down, not at the moment, with the formal toast about to occur. Since Vhillar was an imager, that would be a perfect opportunity to create havoc. He might not, but . . . I was supposed to prevent that sort of thing—if I could.

I moved toward the table where the formal toast would take place, trying to use the deft but purposeful moves of an assistant who needed to be somewhere but did not wish to offend. I also tried to project that feeling, and some must have picked up on it because people moved aside just slightly. Before long I had stationed myself behind and to the left of the small table behind which Councilor Suyrien would make the toast. With my back to the wall, I looked out at the dancers.

Among those closer who were waiting to watch the toast was the Honorable Klauzvol Vhillar, with Mistress Cyana D'Guerdyn-Alte now at his side. He did not look in my direction, and they were positioned so that the equivalent of two lines of people were between them and the open space separating those gathering to watch from the small toasting table. I didn't see Madame D'Shendael.

As the last bells of ninth glass died away, Councilor

Suyrien emerged from a group of High Holders and their wives or daughters or mistresses and stepped toward the table. The sounds of the orchestra faded away, followed by a drum roll and then a quick trumpet call I did not recognize.

A uniformed server brought three bottles to the table, still corked and sealed. The councilor said something, and the server quickly removed the foil and cork from one of the bottles, then set a goblet down and poured the sparkling white into it.

I watched the goblet, hoping I'd guessed correctly.

The wine settled—then trembled—and I knew, not that I'd ever be able to prove it.

I concentrated, trying to image what was in the toasting goblet away, and replacing it with wine from the second unopened bottle.

This time the trembling was more pronounced, but no one seemed to notice. Certainly, Suyrien D'Alte did not as he picked up the goblet, raised it, and declaimed, "For Solidar, for the Council, and in thanks for a fruitful harvest!"

Then he lowered the goblet and put it to his lips. At that moment, I extended a shield on one side of the glass—the side between Vhillar and the councilor.

Something, a tiny something, hit the invisible shield and rebounded, unseen by most, except for the older woman in front, over whose shoulder a fine mist sprayed. She merely frowned, then used her scarf to brush away the misty drops.

"For Solidar, for the Council, and in thanks for a fruitful harvest!" came a low echo from the bystanders.

Not terribly enthusiastic, I thought, but I had the feeling that High Holders were not given to much in the way of public enthusiasms.

I could feel eyes on me, but I continued to survey the crowd. As my eyes passed those of Vhillar, I could see his eyes narrow. Abruptly, he looked away, then guided Mistress D'Guerdyn-Alte out onto the dance floor as the orchestra resumed playing.

Councilor Suyrien had left the toasting table, as if glad to be done with that task, and resumed his conversation. To one side, perhaps five yards, I could see Councilor Haestyr murmur something to Councilor Caartyl. They talked for a moment or two, then nodded to each other and returned to those they had escorted.

I began to move away from the toasting table, trying to convey the sense that I'd finished another task and still trying to locate Master Dichartyn, when a voice called to me. "Young man."

I turned. The summons came from Madame D'Shendael. What exactly did she want? I smiled and moved to her. "Yes, madame. Might I be of assistance?"

"You may. I find I need a partner."

She was a good dancer, better than Iryela, but still not quite so good as Seliora, and she said nothing until we had gone halfway around the floor.

"Was what you said about your sister total nonsense or truth used to a purpose?"

Obviously, she didn't believe in High Holder circumlocution. "It was quite truthful, madame. My sister found a number of the financial advisements of great use in the family business. She was also first captivated by your *Poetic Discourse* and later by *Civic Virtue*."

"I don't believe you answered my question."

"I believe I answered it as well as I can, madame."

She smiled. "That is an answer, of another kind. What is your name?"

"Rhennthyl."

"Rhennthyl D'Imager, I would imagine. No . . . I know you cannot comment. A rather silly fiction, if you ask me. What about Emanus? Was that true as well?"

"Yes, madame."

"It is rumored that he was killed by an imager, and that you visited him shortly before he died."

Rumored? Most likely, Vhillar had told her it was a rumor, possibly as a way to discredit the Collegium. "I had heard something to that effect, but he was well when I left him, and, frankly, madame, I was looking forward to talking to him again. I was shocked to learn of his death, and I did not know of it until several days later."

That surprised her, and her surprise and her choice of words confirmed what I already knew, even if I could not prove it.

"I am truly sorry for you, madame." That was a risk, but someone should have expressed some sympathy for her father's death, especially after all he had suffered for her.

Her lips tightened, as if she were about to retort. Then she nodded. "It is sad when a great artist dies and is not able to be recognized."

"I have studied the works of all the current masters, and none exhibits his excellence. I suppose that was one reason why I was so pleased when he praised my chess study." That wasn't quite true, because I hadn't realized how great an artist he was until later, when I'd seen the miniature, but the spirit of my words was true.

She was silent for a time as we circled the floor. As we made one turn, I caught sight of Martyl dancing with Alynkya, and the young woman looked happy. I couldn't help but contrast her to both Iryela and Madame D'Shendael, both surrounded by intrigue and plotting.

Then the music ended.

"Thank you, madame."

She smiled. I think there was pain behind the smile, but I don't know that anyone else would have seen it, except Seliora, had she been there. "Thank you, Master Rhennthyl. Take care." There was the slightest emphasis on the last two words. I escorted her back to her husband, who did not even turn as she rejoined whatever conversation was in progress.

After that, I moved around the dance floor, always watching, but no one else seemed to need rescuing, and no one else asked me to dance. Master Dichartyn was still nowhere to be seen, and although I glimpsed Baratyn across the dance floor, he was headed toward the grand staircase. Should I follow him?

It was nearing tenth glass, midnight, when the Ball would end.

Suddenly, a jolt of something shivered my shields, and my entire body began to tremble, until I managed to erect a second set within the first. Still shaking inside, I turned slowly.

From a good ten yards away, the Honorable Klauzvol Vhillar gave the faintest of nods, and a knowing smile, before turning away, High Holder Guerdyn's daughter on his arm.

I understood what was behind that. Vhillar clearly wanted to lure me into trouble, or something to precipitate a scandal. Or worse, he would just leave so that he could strike later, and he was letting me know that. I couldn't let him do that. Yet, what could I do? Master Dichartyn was nowhere to be seen, and I was getting tired of being a target and a lure. A lure? What had Master Poincaryt said? A lure didn't have to be defenseless, and I could act in the best interests of the Collegium. The Collegium certainly didn't need a hostile and renegade imager loose in L'Excelsis—envoy or not—and if I waited to discuss such matters with Master Dichartyn I wouldn't have the chance to stop being a lure and a target.

No matter what both Maitre Poincaryt and Maitre Dichartyn said about my value to the Collegium as a lure . . . they weren't the one being attacked time after time. I slipped away with the purposeful stride of a man headed for the jakes, except once I neared there, I turned to the steps.

"Sir?" asked the obdurate guard.

"I need to get something for Baratyn." I tried to project urgency.

"Ah . . ."

"I won't be long." I was past him and headed down the steps, quickly, but not at a run. Once on the lower level, I took the west-side service door and eased along the narrow maintenance walk next to the foot of the wall, using a cloak of shadows. Someone might well see someone in the shadows, but not more than a dim figure at best. I found the ornamental topiary that I recalled, the one offering the most concealment close to the outside stone steps, and sat down behind it, where I could view all the steps down to the drive where the coaches and carriages were beginning to queue up.

I waited a good half glass out there, watching as guests

departed and worrying about whether Baratyn or Master Dichartyn would come looking for me. That was the last thing I wanted. I was Nameless-tired of being the target, and no one seemed that interested in solving the problem, only in using me to flush out the guilty. Well, I'd flushed him out, and I'd figured a way to deal with him as well—if it worked, I reminded myself.

Vhillar was among the later guests to leave, and he moved casually, yet deliberately, his eyes scanning the area on each side of the outside stone steps. Was he expecting me to act? I had the feeling he was concerned. He should be.

He paused after descending several steps, then spoke a few words to Mistress D'Guerdyn-Alte. After a moment, he escorted her down another few steps, before stopping to exchange a few words with another couple. He glanced toward the outer open carriage gate, and then back toward the east side of the Chateau. That worried me. What besides me was he seeking? Or was something else planned?

I shook my head. For the moment, I needed to concentrate on Vhillar—before he was too far away for my imaging to reach him.

First, I imaged colorless oil across the steps, three deep, directly below him, and well beyond his shields, and used a partial shield—something Maitre Dyana had taught me—to block any reflections from the lamps flanking the stone steps.

Vhillar took one step down, then another, then a third, before his boots slipped, one, then the other. His arms flailed as he let go of Mistress D'Guerdyn-Alte. She just stared, because I'd been accurate enough that she hadn't stepped in the oil.

In that moment when Vhillar lost his concentration, and his shields faltered for a moment, I drove through them and imaged air, lots of it, into the major vessels in his brain, then imaged a blast of air at the back of his head—enough to drive him headfirst into the stone farther down the steps, angled so that his temple would hit first.

Mistress D'Guerdyn-Alte had frozen, watching as he fell, but then she screamed.

I imaged all the oil away.

At that point, I was more than a little dizzy, and all I could do was sit in the shadows as two guards came running down the steps. Others began to gather.

After several moments, when the dizziness passed, I slowly eased back along the wall and well out of sight.

I was almost to the west-side door when I saw a figure in the shadows outside the Chateau's lower wall, moving to the west. I decided to keep moving around the Chateau past the west service door and toward the east-side door we used as imager messengers. Why I wasn't certain, but it felt as though I should. I slipped through the north gardens and then struggled over the wall, once more using a slight shadow shield in addition to full shields, but I still lost sight of whoever it was who had been in the shadows.

At that moment, across the ring road from the Chateau, I saw the same ancient wagon I'd seen twice before, with the same old gelding, and the same porthole windows. The wagon was tied up almost directly across from where the duty coach had stopped and stood waiting, but at a slight angle to the duty coach. It was also located in the direction in which Vhillar had been looking. My stomach tightened.

I kept moving along the wall, toward where the duty coach waited, wishing that I'd made a greater effort to find Master Dichartyn, but there was no help for that now. Finally, I stopped, a good twenty yards away, and began to study the wagon. There was something about it and the way the sagging wagon body was angled slightly toward the duty coach. Sagging wagon body? What was in that wagon?

At that moment, a shadowy figure appeared, if indistinctly, in the shadows at the near end of the wagon. Was it the same man whom I had followed around the Chateau? What was it about him? Could it be the Ferran?

He had what looked to be a large tripod, on which was mounted something long and thick, far larger than a rifle, and he moved closer to the end of the weapon, so that its shape and his merged.

Behind me and to my right, there was a click and a glow of light as the east main level door from the Chateau opened.

As three figures emerged into the night air, I heard voices.
"Where in the Nameless is he?"

". . . guards said he went down the inside stairs . . . in a
hurry . . ."

"Hurry or not . . . Dichartyn's going to hang him out . . ."

The last and loudest voice was Baratyn's.

My eyes flicked back to the old wagon, and the entire
wagon rocked ever so slightly. One of the porthole windows
opened inward, and the shadow figure leaned slightly forward.

I knew I had to act. I imaged fire and flame into the wagon,
and whatever the weapon beside it might be, praying to the
Nameless that I didn't believe in that I would be in time before something worse happened.

I tried to strengthen my shields, but . . . everything exploded.

Shields and all, I felt myself being lifted and flung. . . .

71

*If deductions require absolute proof, then they are
rendered worthless.*

When I woke, I was looking up at a gray ceiling. I was back
in the infirmary, and Master Dichartyn and Master Draffyd
were both standing over me. My head ached, and various
pains were shooting through my chest and back.

"How bad is it?" I managed to ask.

"For what you've been through," replied Master Draffyd,
"not all that bad. You'll live, although it may not feel like it
when you try to move or breathe deeply. You might have a

cracked rib, and you're bruised all over. In fact, you'll be on your feet—very carefully—once we put you in a rib corset."

He was right. As he and Master Dichartyn gently maneuvered me into the grayish corset, I felt like my entire chest and rib cage were pressing in on my lungs. It was far more painful than the gunshot wounds I'd taken from the assassin, but the very worst of it subsided once Master Draffyd had laced the corset up tightly. It was more like a cross between a flexible brace and a corset.

"How's that?" asked Master Draffyd.

"It's better . . . painful, but not nearly so bad."

"You'll stay here tonight, just to make sure, but I'll let you go in the morning."

"I'm supposed to attend a wedding tomorrow," I offered.

"Not your own, I hope."

"No, sir."

"If you take a coach and don't walk too much—and stay out of any explosions—you should be all right. But don't take off the wound corset without help. You'll have to come here to wash up."

"Yes, sir."

"Not a word about this, Draffyd." Master Dichartyn said. "I'd appreciate a word or two with him alone."

The younger master nodded and left the room, closing the door behind him. I knew that Master Dichartyn had more than a word or two in mind.

Master Dichartyn looked at me and shook his head. "You did wrap up everything in a neat way that didn't implicate the Collegium, albeit with rather messy consequences. From the evidence remaining, it's fairly certain that the explosion you triggered took out three assassins, and the one body whole enough to be recovered from that explosion was that of the Ferran. But why did you kill Vhillar?"

"Besides the fact that he was the one hiring the assassins, you mean?" I wanted to shake my head. "You didn't know, sir?"

"He was an agent of Ferrum and a spy. All their envoys

are, but that's to be expected. Even hiring assassins is to be expected. That's not a reason for killing him. For expelling him, yes, but killing envoys leads to repercussions. The Council may have to recall our envoy to Ferrial before something similar happens to him. Maitre Poincaryt will want an explanation, and so do I. A good explanation."

I just looked at him for a long moment before asking, "Who was the body?" Then I realized he'd already told me, but I'd almost forgotten that in the surprise of learning he didn't know that Vhillar was an imager.

"The body was that of the Ferran. The others were shredded."

I winced. "What about the duty coach driver?"

Dichartyn shook his head. "That happens. But why Vhillar?"

"He was the imager."

For the first time, his mouth opened. "Vhillar, an imager?"

"Most certainly," I replied.

"Oh . . . and how did you know that?"

"I tested his shields, and he tried an image attack on me during the Ball. He was the one who hired the Ferran, and he tried to poison Suyrien during the toast. I imaged the poisoned wine out of his glass and replaced it with some from a closed bottle. There's probably a vacuum there, and they won't be able to uncork it."

"So . . . that was why Constanza D'Amerlen had that burn on her shoulder."

"Ah . . . not exactly. That was Vhillar's second attempt, and it hit an invisible shield in the air. The spray flew back."

His face hardened. "Rhennthyl . . . why didn't you explain this or find me?"

"I never could find you, and there wasn't time to explain that the wine was poisoned. You see, the wine was in the glass and unmoving except for the tiny bubbles. The goblet was on the table, and then the wine trembled, but not the goblet or the table. And after I blocked both attempts, Vhillar looked at me, but he didn't do anything until just before he left when he tried to kill me. I tried to find you, but I didn't want to leave the hall because I wouldn't have been able to watch Vhillar . . ." I tried to explain, but so much of it rested on what I'd felt about how things went together. ". . . and there was also some link between Juniae D'Shendael and Vhillar. Not an affair, but something else. I'd wager it's linked somehow to Emanus, and that's why he was killed, but that's only a guess."

"Your 'guesses' have been rather accurate in the past. I have the feeling this one may be as well." His tone was dryly ironic. He fingered his chin before speaking again. "If Vhillar had succeeded in poisoning Suyrien, the blame would fall on the Collegium, either for doing it or failing to prevent it, and Ferrum's greatest opponent on the Council would be dead, probably to be replaced by Councilor Haestyr, who is far more favorably inclined toward them."

"Councilor Haestyr said something to Councilor Caartyl after the toast. Caartyl looked most unhappy for a moment."

Master Dichartyn was the one to look displeased at that. "You realize that there is absolutely no proof linking the assassins to Vhillar, nothing except what you saw and felt."

I hurt, and I was getting tired of the cross-examination. "Then talk to Madame D'Shendael, and ask her who told her that an imager killed her father . . . pardon me, who told her about the rumor that an imager killed her father."

"How did you know that?"

"She asked me to dance . . ." I backtracked and told him about both encounters with Juniae D'Shendael. ". . . and how else would she have known?"

"You are not making matters much easier, Rhennthyl."

"Maitre Poincaryt told me that lures don't have to be defenseless, and too many junior imagers have already died."

"He said that to you?"

"Yes, sir—about the lures, that is."

"Even so, you're asking me to take a great deal on faith."

I just looked at him, again, for a long moment, before replying, "If I might say so, sir, far, far less than you have asked me to take on faith and without full knowledge. If I had known more, I might have been able to act in a . . . less messy fashion. Besides, Envoy Vhillar tripped on the steps and split his skull. Most regrettable, but accidents do happen, and there was no poison involved . . ." I was so tired I wanted to yawn, but I was afraid of just how much that might hurt.

"Then what would you suggest the Council do with regard to Ferrum to explain the death of their envoy?"

"Send a very polite sealed communiqué to the head of their government"—I was so dizzy I couldn't remember the official title—"telling them that the Council deeply regrets the accident, and that for the sake of everyone involved, it should remain that way, unless, of course, Ferrum would like it known that their envoy was an imager, which would raise the question of how many others might be."

"You have a very nasty mind. They could still deny it."

"Send a letter from Master Poincaryt saying that one of the functions of the Collegium is to keep renegade imagers out of Solidar, and that who else would better know who was an imager. Besides, even the charge would create problems for them. People half-expect it from Solidar, I'm sure. So any countercharge shouldn't affect us much." I looked at him. "You should have thought of all that. Or did you?"

"I did, mostly, but I wanted to see if you were really as devious as Master Poincaryt thinks."

"Am I?" That bothered me.

"No. You're worse, because you have the ability to incorporate more of the truth in what you do."

I closed my eyes, then opened them.

"Rhennthyl . . . after this, you can't stay at the Chateau."

"Why not?" I was tired, bone-tired, but I was irritated. I'd done my job, better than Master Dichartyn had done his, and he was telling me that I couldn't keep doing something I'd done well? Maybe I'd been messy, but I'd gotten it done.

"The first reason is because you aren't ready to supervise people, but you have more imaging skills than Baratyn, possibly more than he will ever have. You also jump to conclusions. Most of the time, so far, you've been right, but the higher you get in the Collegium the more convoluted and complex matters you will have to deal with can get, and that will increase the possibility that you'll be wrong. Masters can't afford to be wrong often, especially in dealing with the Council and High Holders. The second reason is that you still have trouble distinguishing when to be patient and when not to be."

"So you're going to send me off to the armory or something?" I almost didn't care—except I did.

"No. I have an idea, but I'll have to talk to Maitre Poincaryt about it. I'll have to brief him tonight anyway after the mess you made. He shouldn't find it out from anyone else."

I almost snapped back that, if he'd told me more, we wouldn't have had such a mess. If I'd known about Vhillar . . .

Then again, that was hindsight. Besides, expressing my anger at him wouldn't help me any, and he already warned me about impatience once.

"Now . . . get some rest. I'll talk to you in the morning."

After he left, I did close my eyes, then.

72

Trust does not demand details.

When I woke the next morning, every muscle in my body, or so it seemed, felt stiff and sore. Getting out of bed was torture, but I staggered to the jakes and back to the room, where I sat on the single straight-backed chair. I didn't even want to think about climbing up into the bed. One of the obdurates brought me tea, and then Master Dichartyn arrived, still in his exercise clothes.

"You'd do anything to avoid exercises, wouldn't you?" But he did grin. "How do you feel?"

"Achy-sore, dull pain everywhere, except when I move, and then it's not so dull."

"You're young. You'll recover."

Since he still hadn't told me what lay ahead of me, and he wasn't volunteering, I had to speak, before he left. "Last night you said I couldn't return to the Chateau and that you'd have to consider something else."

"Oh, that."

He was baiting me, but I managed to say, "Yes, that. At my age, knowing one's future does matter somewhat."

"Not so much as you think," he answered wryly. "Matters seldom turn out as planned, as you should know. Still . . . I did talk to Master Poincaryt, and he agreed. It's an assignment that has been necessary now and again. You'll be assigned to the civic patrollers as Collegium liaison. That will allow you to become a Maitre D'Aspect, but you already have those skills. So that won't be a problem. You'll also be in a visible position, which may work to your advantage in other matters. Then again, it may not. That will depend on you in large part."

I didn't care for the implications of his words about visibility. They referred to whatever attack High Holder Ryel was certain to initiate against me, and I could only hope that I would be prepared, because I had a strong feeling that whatever Ryel did would bypass the Collegium. I'd already seen enough of High Holders to understand that. But there was no point in saying so. I only asked, "Is this a hidden rank, or can I tell people?"

"You can tell anyone you want to—even the young lady—because we and the Civic Patrol want it known that their liaison is a master imager."

"Why a liaison to the Civic Patrol? Or is that a way of shuttling me aside? Why couldn't I just be a field operative?"

He shook his head. "That would be a waste of your talents. Besides, the liaison position is a far better choice for you."

I hated having to drag things out of him, but he was also demonstrating that I needed to be patient, I supposed. "Begging your pardon, sir, but could you explain that?"

"That's why I'm here. First, you have the basic and even more than basic imaging skills to handle it, and it will give you a chance to observe a side of life that will give you the necessary experience."

This time, when he paused, I just waited.

"You'll be appointed, effective Lundi morning, but you won't report for at least another two weeks. That will give you time to heal some. Also, the patrol commander can make sure that everyone knows what you did outside the Chateau. Patrollers are impressed by imagers who risk their lives to save their comrades. They'll be glad to have someone like you. The other aspect of the position is that, while they cannot command you, the same is true of you. You cannot give patrollers orders. Do you see why this is ideal for you?"

I wasn't sure that I did. Going from working in the Council Chateau to effectively being an assistant to the patrollers—that was ideal? I tried to gather my thoughts together, and Master Dichartyn smiled faintly, but let me.

Finally, I replied. "I'll be able to use imaging to help them, and perhaps protect a patroller now and then. I'll have to figure out things before I can say anything because I can't order anyone to do anything. That means I'll have to be logical and precise enough that they'll do what I suggest."

He nodded. "It's not a demotion of any sort. It's a different path, and it is frankly a harder one, but there are some consolations. As I mentioned before, the first is rank. To be a liaison, you have to be at least a Maitre D'Aspect. That's because, without master status, no one above the street patrollers will pay much attention. The second is that you'll learn a great deal more about L'Excelsis and the way things truly operate."

"I'm ready to be a Maitre D'Aspect?" Attractive as the idea was, I didn't want a rank that I couldn't carry out.

"You have all the imaging talents already, and the basic knowledge of the Council and the Collegium, as well as great knowledge of the factoring and trade and artisan classes. What you lack is the knowledge of a wider range of human experience. Without that, the combination of your instinctive abilities and your imaging capabilities will get you into greater and greater difficulties. I won't gloss this over. If you are not careful, you could still get into great danger in this position, but Master Poincaryt and I both feel that this is by far the most practical way to get you the experience you need."

I still wasn't totally convinced of that, but I was fully convinced that it was the only true opportunity open to me after the night before—and experience or not, I still didn't see what else I could have done.

"What do you think you should tell the others about last night?" he asked.

Again, I had to think a moment. "I should tell them that you discovered something, and I was working with you. I'd just finished when I saw the wagon, and I realized that they were going to open fire on the others, and I just did what I could."

"You don't think you should say anything about Vhillar?"

"No. It should remain an unfortunate accident, and people will lay it at your feet or Baratyn's, but they won't know for certain, and that's how it should be."

"What will you tell them we were working on?"

"The assassins, if they ask."

Master Dichartyn nodded. "You realize that it must always be that way? In other events as well?"

"Yes."

"Why?"

"Because the less anyone knows, the more protection offered to imagers and the Collegium. There's no reason to hide the explosion. That was too open, and that's why it should be my fault."

"Your fault?" The question was bland, and that concealed and revealed at the same time.

"Yes, sir. If I'd been more observant and more careful, I wouldn't have had to use fire to blow up the wagon, and that wouldn't have injured me and killed the driver."

"That's not true, you know?"

"Yes, sir, but it's better said that way, because it implies that senior imagers could have handled it better. It also sends a message that junior imagers, when attacked, can overre-act."

Master Dichartyn laughed. "I hadn't thought of the last point. Except for you, and perhaps Martyl, it's probably not very accurate, but it will help in these times." He paused. "I heard something about a wedding?"

"Yes, sir."

"What time will you be leaving?"

"Half before noon, I'd thought."

"I'll have one of the spare coaches stand by to take you."

"Won't the drivers be upset . . . because of what I did?"

"I've already spread the word that you put yourself in front of everything when you didn't have to. I also told them that you'd survived five assassination attempts, and that you were the one who killed four of the five assassins here in L'Excelsis. The drivers understand that an imager can only do so much."

I hoped so.

"That's all for now. I'll see you in my study at seventh glass on Lundi."

"What about the Chateau? They'll be shorthanded . . ."

"They'll manage. They did for a year before you arrived." He offered a parting smile.

After Master Dichartyn left, Master Draffyd came in and examined me, then said I could go. I carried the soiled white and gray formal coat back to my quarters, then dressed for breakfast. I'd wash up, as I could, later.

The summer gray waistcoat was a tight fit over my shirt and the rib corset, but I managed it, even if it took me a while to button it.

Then I went—or walked very slowly and stiffly—to break-fast.

I barely got into the dining hall when Martyl hurried over to me. "We were all worried. Are you all right?"

"Mostly. I just got out of the infirmary, and I'll have to wear a brace for a while to protect my ribs."

"Come over and sit with us. The word is that you won't be at the seconds and thirds table for long. Is it true?"

"I'd really like to sit down with you all." And I did. I was hungry, and the flatcakes and syrup and sausage looked and smelled wonderful.

As I ate, there were more than a few questions.

"Did Johanyr's sister really ask you to dance?"

"Was that Madame D'Shendael you danced with?"

"Who was the other High Holder's daughter?"

"What happened out there with the wagon?"

I answered as many as I could truthfully, and the others along the lines Master Dichartyn and I had discussed.

"You won't be coming back to the Chateau?" asked Dartazn.

I shook my head gingerly. "Master Dichartyn thinks I need to do something different. I'm going to be the Collegium liaison to the civic patrollers."

"You're going up to Master D'Aspect, aren't you? I knew it!" said Martyl. "You're going to be one of the youngest masters ever."

"That's because they don't know what else to do with me." My voice came out wry.

"It's also because they can't make anyone a liaison," Dartazn said, "who doesn't have shields that will take bullets. Otherwise, they'd be dead in a month."

Master Dichartyn hadn't mentioned that, but it didn't surprise me, although it did send a chill down my back.

After breakfast, I made my way back to my quarters. It took me a good glass to wash up and shave, because lifting my arms even to shoulder level was painful, and then I had to dress again. What with one thing and another, I did make it to the duty-coach stop before half past nine. There were two coaches waiting.

The driver of the first raised an arm and beckoned. "Master Rhennthyl?"

"For better or worse, that's me."

"Thank you for trying the other night, sir." He smiled. "Where to?"

"NordEste Design." Getting into the coach was more than a little painful. My face probably showed it, because when we got to NordEste, the driver vaulted down to tie the horses to the bronze hitching post, then came back to give me a hand.

"Thank you."

"Should you be here, sir?"

"I promised I would be."

He nodded knowingly.

I managed to get up the steps without wincing too much. Shomyr was the one who opened the door. "Rhenn . . . we're glad you could be here." He paused. "Are you all right?"

"I'd have to say that I'm walking wounded, but I'll recover." The inside steps were worse than those outside, or it could have been that climbing another set was harder.

When I stepped into the second-level entry foyer, I could see Seliora arranging what looked to be gifts on a side table. Should I have brought one? I hadn't even thought about it, and I didn't know the bride or the groom.

Suddenly, as if she had sensed me, Seliora turned, then hurried toward me. "Rhenn! I'm so glad to see you." As she neared, her face filled with concern. "What happened to you?"

"Do you want to hear what's good or not so good?"

"Since you're here, I'd rather you started with the bad. But first . . ." She leaned forward and kissed me gently.

I did enjoy that for an all-too-brief moment before she stepped back.

"I'm bruised all over, and I might have a cracked rib."

"You'd better sit down. Then you can tell me what happened."

I took one of the straight-backed chairs next to a settee farther back along the west side of that overlarge entry hall. "What about the wedding?"

"It's here, up on the north terrace. We have time. Now tell me what happened." Seliora sat at the edge of the settee, looking at me, waiting.

"I told you about the Council's Harvest Ball last night, remember?"

"You didn't get bruises and a cracked rib from a lady High Holder."

"No. I got them from an explosion that I set off to keep all of us more junior imagers from getting killed. The Ferran had set up a wagon . . ." I went through the "official" explanation quickly, mentioning only my concerns about Vhillar and that he'd had a fatal accident just before I dealt with the explosion. ". . . and I woke up in the infirmary. Three assassins are dead, and one was the Ferran."

She looked into my eyes. "There's more."

"There is," I said, "but I have to leave it at that. It's better that way, especially for you and me. And you can tell everyone that I did get the Ferran."

She reached out and squeezed my right hand, gently but firmly. "I'm glad you trust me enough not to lie." She held up a hand. "I know you can't tell me everything, and, most times, you shouldn't, but please don't lie to me. Just tell me that there's more, the way you just did, but that we'll have to let it go."

"I can do that." As I said it, I realized something else. Unlike my parents, or Master Dichartyn, or anyone else, except maybe Khethila, Seliora trusted me, trusted me implicitly. For a moment, my eyes burned. I had to swallow before I could say more. "Thank you."

Her smile warmed me all the way down.

We sat there, with Seliora leaning forward slightly, holding hands, just holding hands.

After a time, she said, "Grandmama said that you would get the Ferran. I was afraid you'd be hurt even worse. I saw an explosion sweeping over you."

"That's a good way of describing it."

"You said that you had some good news?"

"I'm being advanced to master imager—the most junior master. Maitre D'Aspect—and I'll have a new position."

"With the civic patrollers?"

"How did you know?"

"I didn't, but I did have a vision of you in the middle of a group of patrollers, and I couldn't figure out why that would be." She paused. "That's not a normal position, is it?"

"No. It's used to season talented and difficult junior master imagers. Master Dichartyn hopes it will give me enough experience so that I can make better decisions based on that experience."

Seliora nodded. "Grandmama will be so pleased—a master imager."

"And your parents?"

"They were pleased from the moment they met you, but Odelia helped with that. She really would like to marry Kolasyn."

I understood that as well.

"What about the wedding? The one with your cousin, I mean." I flushed as I realized the double implication of my last words.

Seliora laughed, warmly and kindly. "We have time."

And so we did.

TOR

Voted

#1 Science Fiction Publisher
20 Years in a Row

by the *Locus* Readers' Poll

Please join us at the website below
for more information about this
author and other science fiction,
fantasy, and horror selections, and to
sign up for our monthly newsletter!

www.tor-forge.com